D1139626

The Confessions of
Catherine de Medici

C. W. GORTNER

The Confessions of Catherine de Medici

Hodder & Stoughton Ltd
A division of Hodder Headline
338 Euston Road
London NW1 3BH

HODDER

First published in Great Britain in 2010 by Hodder & Stoughton
An Hachette Livre UK company

First published in paperback in 2011

1

The Confessions of Catherine de Medici is a work of historical fiction. Apart from
the well known actual people, events, and locales that figure in the narrative, all
names, characters, places, and incidents are the products of the author's
imagination or are used fictitiously. Any resemblance to current events
or locales, or to living persons, is entirely coincidental.

A CIP catalogue record for this title is available from the British Library

B format paperback ISBN 978-0-340-96297 -8
A format paperback ISBN 978-0-340-99586-0

Typeset in Plantin Light by Hewer Text UK Ltd, Edinburgh
Printed and bound in the UK by CPI Mackays, Chatham ME5 8TD

Hodder Headline's policy is to use papers that are natural, renewable and
recyclable products and made from wood grown in sustainable forests.
The logging and manufacturing processes are expected to conform to the
environmental regulations of the country of origin.

FT
Pbk

www.hodder.co.uk

*For Erik, who always reminds me there is more to life;
and for Jennifer, who always makes me laugh*

Bottle! Whose mysterious deep
does ten thousand secrets keep,
With attentive ear I wait;
Ease my mind and speak my fate.
— RABELAIS

The Valois

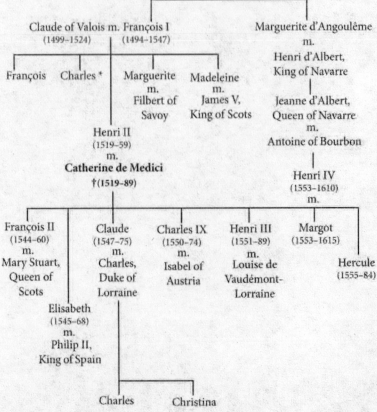

Claude of Valois m. François I
(1499–1524) (1494–1547)

Marguerite d'Angoulême
m.
Henri d'Albert,
King of Navarre

François   Charles *

Marguerite
m.
Filbert of
Savoy

Madeleine
m.
James V,
King of Scots

Jeanne d'Albert,
Queen of Navarre
m.
Antoine of Bourbon

Henri II
(1519–59)
m.
Catherine de Medici
†(1519–89)

Henri IV
(1553–1610)
m.

François II
(1544–60)
m.
Mary Stuart,
Queen of
Scots

Claude
(1547–75)
m.
Charles,
Duke of
Lorraine

Charles IX
(1550–74)
m.
Isabel of
Austria

Henri III
(1551–89)
m.
Louise de
Vaudémont-
Lorraine

Margot
(1553–1615)

Hercule
(1555–84)

Elisabeth
(1545–68)
m.
Philip II,
King of Spain

Charles   Christina

* not mentioned in novel

† only surviving children listed

BLOIS, 1589

I am not a sentimental woman. Even during my youth I wasn't given to melancholia or remorse. I rarely looked back, rarely paused to mark the passage of time. Some would say I do not know the meaning of regret. Indeed, if my enemies are to be believed, my unblinking eyes stare always forward, focused on the future, on the next war to fight, the next son to exalt, the next enemy to vanquish.

How little they know me. How little anyone knows me. Perhaps it was ever my fate to dwell alone in the myth of my own life, to bear witness to the legend that has sprung around me like some venomous bloom. I have been called murderess and opportunist, savior and victim. And along the way, become far more than was ever expected of me, even if loneliness was always present, like a faithful hound at my heels.

The truth is, not one of us is innocent.

We all have sins to confess.

PART I
1527–1532
The Tender Leaf

I

I was ten years old when I discovered I might be a witch. I sat sewing with my aunt Clarice, as sunlight spread across the gallery floor. Outside the window I could hear the splashing of the courtyard fountain, the cries of the vendors in the Via Larga and staccato of horse hooves on the cobblestone streets, and I thought for the hundredth time that I couldn't stay inside another minute.

'Caterina Romelo de' Medici, can it be you've finished already?'

I looked up. My late father's sister Clarice de' Medici y Strozzi regarded me from her chair. I wiped my brow with my sleeve. 'It's so hot in here,' I said. 'Can't I go outside?'

She arched her eyebrow. Even before she said anything, I could have recited her words, so often had she drummed them into my head: 'You are the Duchess of Urbino, daughter of Lorenzo de' Medici and his wife, Madeleine de la Tour, who was of noble French blood. How many times must I tell you, you must restrain your impulses in order to prepare for your future?'

I didn't care about the future. I cared that it was summer and here I was cooped up in the family palazzo forced to study and sew all day, as if I might melt in the sun.

I clapped my embroidery hoop aside. 'I'm bored. I want to go home.'

'Florence is your home; it is your birth city,' she replied. 'I took you from Rome because you were sick with fever. You're fortunate you can sit here and argue with me at all.'

'I'm not sick anymore,' I retorted. I hated it when she used my poor health as an excuse. 'At least in Rome, Papa Clement let me have my own servants and a pony to ride.'

She regarded me without a hint of the ire that the mention of my papal uncle always roused in her. 'That may be but you are here now, in my care, and you will abide by my rules. It's midafternoon. I'll not hear of you going outside in this heat.'

'I'll wear a cap and stay in the shade. Please, Zia Clarice. You can come with me.'

I saw her trying to repress her unwilling smile as she stood. 'If your work is satisfactory, we can take a stroll on the loggia before supper.' She came to me, a thin woman in a simple gray gown, her oval face distinguished by her large liquid-black eyes – the Medici eyes, which I had inherited, along with our family's curly auburn hair and long-fingered hands.

She swiped up my embroidery. Her lips pursed when she heard me giggle. 'I suppose you think it's funny to make the Holy Mother's face green? Honestly, Caterina; such sacrilege.' She thrust the hoop at me. 'Fix it at once. Embroidery is an art, one you must master as well as your other studies. I'll not have it said that Caterina de' Medici sews like a peasant.'

I thought it best not to laugh and began picking out the offensive color, while my aunt returned to her seat. She stared off into the distance. I wondered what new trials she planned for me. I did love her but she was forever dwelling on how our family prestige had fallen since the death of my great-grandfather, Lorenzo Il Magnifico; of how Florence had been a center of learning renowned for our Medici patronage, and now we were but illustrious guests in the city we had helped build. It was my responsibility, she said, to restore our family's glory, as I was the last legitimate descendant of Il Magnifico's bloodline.

I wondered how she expected me to accomplish such an important task. I'd been orphaned shortly after my birth; I had no sisters or brothers and depended on my papal uncle's goodwill. When I once mentioned this, my aunt snapped: 'Clement VII was born a bastard. He bribed his way to the Holy See, to our great shame. He's not a true Medici. He has no honor.'

Given his prestige, if he couldn't restore our family name I didn't know how she expected *me* to. Yet she seemed convinced of my destiny, and every month had me dress in my uncomfortable ducal finery and pose for a new portrait, which was then copied into miniatures and dispatched to all the foreign princes who wanted to marry me. I was still too young for wedlock, but she left me no doubt she'd already selected the cathedral, the number of ladies who would attend me –

All of a sudden, my stomach clenched. I dropped my hands to my belly, feeling an unexpected pain. My surroundings distorted, as if the palazzo had plunged underwater. Nausea turned my mouth sour. I came to my feet blindly, hearing my chair crash over. A terrifying darkness overcame me. I felt my mouth open in a soundless scream as the darkness widened like a vast ink stain, swallowing everything around me. I was no longer in the gallery arguing with my aunt; instead, I stood in a desolate place, powerless against a force that seemed to well up from deep inside me . . .

I stand unseen, alone among strangers. They are weeping. I see tears slip down their faces, though I can't hear their laments. Before me is a curtained bed, draped in black. I know at once something horrible lies upon it, something I should not see. I try to stay back but my feet move me toward it with the slow certainty of a nightmare, compelling me to reach out a spotted, bloated hand I do not recognize as my own, part the curtains, and reveal

'*Dio Mio,* no!' My cry wrenched from me. I felt my aunt holding me, the frantic caress of her hand on my brow. I had a terrible stomachache and lay sprawled on the floor, my embroidery and tangled yarns strewn beside me.

'Caterina, my child,' my aunt said. 'Please, not the fever again . . .'

As the strange sensation of having left my own body began to fade, I forced myself to sit up. 'I don't think it's the fever,' I said. 'I saw something: a man, lying dead on a bed. He was so real, Zia . . . it scared me.'

She stared at me. Then she whispered, '*Una visione,*' as if it was something she'd long feared. She gave me a fragile smile, reaching out to help me to my feet. 'Come, that's enough for today. Let us go take that walk, *sì*? Tomorrow we'll visit the Maestro. He'll know what to do.'

2

My maid awoke me before dawn. After a quick breakfast of cheese and bread, which I devoured, she dressed me in a simple gown, tied back my thick auburn curls with ribbon, and fixed a hooded cloak about my shoulders. She then hustled me into the courtyard, where Aunt Clarice and the towering manservant who accompanied her on errands waited.

I was excited to be going out into the city at long last, but I still expected us to ride in a closed litter. Instead my aunt pulled up her own hood, clasped my hand, and led me out the gates into the Via Larga on foot, her manservant close behind.

'Why are we walking?' I asked her, even as I thought it would be much more fun to see the city this way, instead of peering out from behind the litter's curtains.

'We're walking because I don't want anyone to know who we are,' replied my aunt. 'We are Medici and people will talk. I don't want everyone in Florence saying Madama Strozzi brought her niece to visit a seer.' Her hand tightened on mine. 'Do you understand? Ruggieri might be much sought after for his talents, but he's still a converted Jew.'

I nodded uncertainly. I knew my aunt often sent for the Maestro to concoct herbal drafts; he had even helped heal me of my fever, but now that I thought of it I realized I'd never seen him in person. Did being Jewish mean he couldn't visit us?

We progressed down the Via Larga. Since my arrival in Florence three years ago, I'd left the palazzo exactly four times, all for formal outings to the *duomo*. Each time a retinue protected my person and impeded my view, as if any intermingling with the populace would endanger my health. Now as my aunt guided me into the city, I felt as if I'd been released from captivity.

The rising sun bathed the city in saffron and rose. In the residential districts about the palazzo, the air still reeked from the night's carousing. We wound through narrow lanes, avoiding pools of waste. I longed to stop and admire the looming statues poised in niches along the way, to gape at the engraved copper heralds of the baptistery and the *duomo*'s brick facade, yet my aunt propelled me forward, skirting the bustle of the marketplace for the back streets, where old houses leaned like decrepit trees, shutting out the light.

I saw the manservant slip his hand to the sheathed knife at his waist. It was much darker here, the air thick with the smell of ordure. I stayed close to my aunt as I glimpsed scrawny children scampering down side streets, emaciated dogs at their heels. A few old gnarled women in tattered shawls huddled on the stoops of their houses and watched us pass. After several bewildering turns, we came before a rickety timber-framed house that seemed about to collapse at any moment. Here, my aunt paused; her servant banged on the lopsided door.

It opened to reveal a slim boy with tousled hair and sleepy brown eyes. When he saw us, he bowed low. 'Duchessina, I am Carlo Ruggieri. My father has been expecting you.'

My aunt pressed a small cloth pouch into my hand. Startled, I glanced at her. 'Go,' she said. 'You must see the Maestro alone. Pay him when he's done.' She pushed me forward when I hesitated. 'Do not tarry. We haven't all day.'

I assumed this Carlo must be the eldest of the Maestro's sons; I could see another smaller boy peering at me from behind him. I offered a tentative smile and the little boy sidled up to me, a small grubby hand reaching for my skirts.

'This is my brother, Cosimo,' said Carlo. 'He's four years old and likes sweets.'

'I like sweets too,' I told Cosimo. 'But I don't have any today.' He seemed to like the sound of my voice and clung to my hand while Carlo led me into the house's shadowy interior, filled with a strange sharp smell. I glanced at a yellowed skull on a stack of musty parchments before he took me up a creaking staircase. The smells grew stronger: I detected camphor, herbs, and a bittersweet odor that reminded me of autumn, when pigs were slaughtered.

I heard Carlo cry out, 'Papa! The Medici is here!' and I reached the landing as he pulled open a narrow door. 'He wants to see you alone,' he added, and he said to his little brother, 'You must let her go now, Cosimo.'

With a pout, Cosimo released my hand. I straightened my shoulders, moving into the Maestro's study. The first thing I noticed was the light. It streamed in columns through an open louver set high in the exposed ceiling, illuminating a room not much larger than my bedchamber in the palazzo. Shelves lined the walls, stacked with books and glass jars with murky objects in fluid. In one corner a mound of pillows were arranged about a brass-topped table. A large marble slab on a trestle dominated the room. I was startled to see a body on it, half-covered by a sheet.

Bare feet poked up from under the sheet. I paused. A voice that seemed to come from nowhere said, 'Ah, my child, there you are!' and then the Maestro shuffled into my view, his sunken features framed by a silver beard. He wore a stained apron over his black robe. He motioned. 'Would you like to see?'

I moved to the slab. I had to stand on tiptoes to see over the edge. The body belonged to a woman, her head shaved, her torso split open from neck to pelvis. There was no blood or bad smell, other than that of herbs. I expected to be disgusted, scared. Instead, I found myself fascinated by the withered blue lungs and shrunken heart nestled within in a cage of broken ribs.

'What are you doing?' I said softly, as if she might hear.

He sighed. 'Searching for her soul.'

I frowned. 'Can you see a soul?'

His smile cracked the crevices of his face. 'Do you always need to see something in order to believe in it?' He took me by the hand and brought me to the recessed corner and pile of cushions. 'Now, sit. Tell me why you have come.'

I still wasn't sure what I was supposed to say, but the gentle way he looked at me made me want to tell him the truth. 'I . . . I saw something yesterday. It frightened me.'

'Was it a dream?'

'No, I was awake.' I paused, thinking about it. 'But it was like a dream.'

'Tell me what you saw.'

I did. As I spoke, I felt again that horrible sense of helplessness and heard my voice tremble. When I finished, the Maestro folded his hands. 'Was someone you knew on that bed?' He smiled when I shook my head. 'I see. That is why you were scared. You expected to find a loved one and saw a stranger instead. He was a young man, yes, with the mark of violence on him?'

A chill crept up my spine. 'How do you know?'

'I see it in you. Oh, you mustn't be afraid, my child. There's no reason for fear, providing you understand that few would accept what you've just told me.' He shifted closer. 'What you experienced yesterday is called a presentiment. It may foretell the future or be an echo from the past. The ancients believed it is a gift from the gods; they revered those who mastered it. But in these dark days, it is often seen as the sign of a witch.'

I stared. 'My aunt said it was a vision. Is this why I'm here? Am I cursed by evil?'

His laughter rang out. 'I've seen many mysteries but I've yet to uncover proof of any curses.' He chucked my chin with his knobby finger. 'Do you believe you are evil?'

'No. I hear mass every day and I venerate our saints. But sometimes I have bad thoughts.'

'As we all do. I assure you, there is no curse. I cast your horoscope when you still were a babe and I found no evil there.'

He had cast my horoscope? My aunt had never mentioned it.

'Why did I have this . . . this vision?' I asked him.

'Only God knows the answer, though I warn you, it might not be your last. For some, such visions are common. For others, they appear in times of peril. And the gift runs in your family. It was said your great-grandfather Il Magnifico could sometimes see the future.'

I didn't like this at all. 'What if I don't want it?' I said. 'Will it go away?'

His eyebrows arched. 'The Sight cannot be denied. You've no idea of how many would forfeit their souls for something you'd deny so freely.'

'Do you have it?' I asked, enticed by the idea that I possessed something so coveted.

He sighed, lifted his eyes to gaze about the room. 'If I did, would I need all this? No, Duchessina. I've just the skill to chart the stars and interpret in their course a path for men. But the heavens are not always forthright. *"Quod de futuris non est determinata omnino veritas"*: No truth can be determined for certain that concerns the future.'

I reflected for a long moment before I said, 'You can have my gift if you want it.'

He chuckled, patting my hand. 'My child, even if you could give it to me I couldn't possibly learn to master it in the short time I have left.' He paused. 'But you can.'

His voice lowered. 'I've lived long and suffered much. I foresaw at your birth that you would live even longer. Thus, you too shall suffer. But you'll never endure what I have. You'll not feel the pain of searching your entire life for something that eludes you. You will fulfill your destiny. It may not be the destiny you want, Caterina de' Medici, but fulfill it you will.'

He reached out to caress my face. I wrapped my arms about his bony frame. For a moment, he seemed as small as me. Then he pulled away. 'You honor me with your love, Duchessina. In return, I want to give you this.'

He reached into his pocket, opened my hand, and set in it a vial with a fine silver chain dangling from its cap – a deceptive sliver, filled with amber, which fit across my palm.

'Therein is a potent liquid. You must never use it unless you have no other recourse. If employed the wrong way, at the wrong time, it can be deadly to you – and to others.'

'What is it?' I thought it impossible that anything so small could be so powerful.

'Some would call it deliverance; others would say it is poison.'

I was startled. 'Why would I need poison?'

'Let us hope never. Nevertheless, it is my gift to you.' He went silent, his head cocked. 'Now, hide the vial and keep it safe. Your aunt grows impatient. You must go.'

I had been taught it was rude to refuse a gift and so I slipped the vial about my neck, tucking it under my chemise. 'I hope we can visit again soon, Maestro,' I said. Then I remembered the pouch and removed it from my cloak pocket. 'This is for you.'

He took it from me as though it were of no account. 'Go with God, Duchessina.'

I was moving to the door when he said suddenly, 'One more thing.' I paused, looked over my shoulder to where he stood in the shadows. 'Tell Madama Strozzi that she must be ready to see you safe,' he intoned. 'Tell her Rome will fall.'

I nodded uneasily and stepped outside, where Carlo waited. Glancing back one last time, I saw the light had shifted. The Maestro now sat in darkness yet somehow I knew he was smiling.

Carlo took me back out, where I thanked him and started to say goodbye. Cosimo burst into tears. 'Don't leave us!' Carlo had to hold him back as he tried to throw himself at me.

I smiled at Cosimo. 'But I must go. I have to get back home. I promise to return soon.'

'You can't,' he said, and tears slipped down his grimy cheeks. 'Everyone will be dead.'

'Dead?' I looked at Carlo. 'What does he mean?'

Carlo rolled his eyes. 'He always says strange things. Cosimo, stop it. You're scaring her.'

Cosimo gazed at me with a desolate expression. I felt a sudden emptiness as I leaned to kiss his cheek. 'I'll see you soon,' I said, and I forced out a smile. 'Be good and mind your brother.'

My aunt was waiting for me in the exact place where I'd left her. As the manservant came forth from his vigil by the house, she said: 'Did he answer your questions?'

'I suppose so,' I said, and I remembered the Maestro's warning:

Few would accept what you've just told me. I added, 'He says I'm studying too much and had a fainting spell.'

I don't know where the words came from, but they were obviously the right ones because my aunt's entire face brightened with unmistakable relief from within her hood. '*Bene,*' she said. She took my hand in hers and paused. 'Did he tell you anything else?'

I repeated the Maestro's last puzzling words. 'Do you know what he means?' I asked.

She shrugged. 'Half the time, I wonder if he himself knows what he means.' Without another word, she took me by the hand and we returned to the palazzo.

As we walked, my other hand strayed to my bodice, where I felt the vial close to my heart.

3

'Caterina, my child, wake up!' I opened my eyes to find my maid-servant bent over me, a candle in her hand, its wavering flame throwing enormous shadows against the walls. 'Madama Strozzi wants you in the hall,' she said. 'You must dress quickly.'

I nodded, slipping out of bed and letting my maid take off my nightdress and lace me into a gown. As she hastily plaited my hair, I wondered what my aunt wanted. There had been a palpable tension in the palazzo lately, especially after I told my aunt what the Maestro had said about Rome falling. I'd also begun to change. Since the discovery of my mysterious gift, I secretly questioned everything. Though I didn't realize it at the time, I can see now that I had ceased to be a credulous child. I tried to invoke my gift, in hope of seeing my future, but I had no visions, no presentiments. I had no idea of how much my life was about to change.

My maid moved about my chamber, shoving my silver-handled brushes, my shawls and shoes into a cloth bag. 'Are we going somewhere?' I asked.

She shook her head. 'Madama instructed me to pack your things. That's all I know. Her manservant is waiting for you outside.'

'See that you get my casket, then,' I said, pointing to my coffer. The small silver and ivory box was the only thing I had from my mother. She had brought it with her from France as part of her dowry and the red velvet lining still smelled faintly of her lavender perfume. I had hidden the vial Ruggieri gave me inside its secret compartment.

The palazzo was dark, quiet. I could hear the rustle of my soft-soled shoes on the marble floor followed by the thud of the manservant's boots as he led me to the hall. I found my aunt waiting, surrounded by a haphazard collection of valises and chests. The high walls were stripped of tapestries and paintings, the gilded furniture half-piled in the corners.

I could feel my heart beating fast in my chest. My aunt grabbed hold of me, held me so tight that my bodice dug into my ribs. 'You must be brave,' she whispered. 'Braver than you've ever been. The time has come to show the world that you are a true Medici, born and bred.'

I stood petrified. What had happened? Why was she saying this to me?

'You cannot understand,' she went on, her voice wavering, choked by rare tears. 'But I have no other choice. They've ordered it. The Signoria of Florence has banished us.'

I knew the Signoria were the ruling body of Florence, elected by its citizens. Unlike other city states in Italy, Florence was a republic and extremely proud of it. The Signoria had always been kind to us. They often dined at the palazzo with my aunt and her husband, a large group of older gentlemen who drank too much wine and ate too much, and told me how pretty I was.

My aunt went on in a fervent voice, as if she'd forgotten I was there. 'The shame of it! Forced out of our own city like thieves in the night. I always said Clement would be our undoing. He brought this upon himself. I don't care what happens to him – but you, my child, my Caterina; you mustn't be made to pay for his crimes.'

'Crimes?' I echoed. 'But what has Papa Clement done?'

'No! Never call him that! Everyone hates him because he'll do anything to save his own skin. Don't you see? He fled his own See even as Rome was sacked by Charles V. You mustn't let anyone think you care for that coward who dares call himself pope.'

I stared at her. Was she mad? Charles V was of the Hapsburg family, the emperor of Germany, Austria, Spain, and Low Countries. He was an avowed defender of the faith, though I remembered my uncle saying once that he was also parsimonious and ruthless, eager for conquest and always quarreling with either the canny French or heretic English. Still, he wore the crown of holy emperor, blessed by papal favor, and I didn't believe he'd dare invade Rome.

My aunt went on, her voice cracking: 'Clement should have heeded the emperor's demands and offered up the money to pay the Imperial troops. Instead, he insisted on standing on his idiot pride and supporting the French, though the soldiers were knocking on his door.' She brandished her fists. 'Now the Holy City is in flames and Florence rebels against us. He has doomed us all!'

She turned back to me. The sudden stillness that overcame her was worse than anything I'd heard so far. 'You warned me,' she whispered. 'You told me the Maestro had foretold this. He said, "Rome will fall." But, like Clement, I was too headstrong to listen.'

I wanted to flee back up the stairs and shut myself in my rooms, but my aunt's stare froze me where I stood. 'The Signoria has promised you'll not be harmed. But you must obey them, Caterina. You must do everything they say.'

A wave of cold black fear overcame me. I did not hear him move toward me until her manservant set his huge hand on my shoulder. All of a sudden, I knew. It couldn't be happening. My aunt had witnessed my birth and the death of both my parents. She'd relinquished me to Rome because she had no other choice, but she came back for me, to bring me to Florence and raise me herself. As much as I'd resented her iron rule, I never doubted her love. She couldn't do this. She couldn't forsake me.

My voice erupted in a high-pitched scream. The manservant clamped his hand over my mouth; I smelled his rough skin as he swept me off my feet. I tried to bite him, fueled by sudden rage. I kicked and flailed even as his arms girdled me with iron strength. My aunt wept. 'Please, my child, it's for your own good. We must keep you safe!'

The despair in her voice made me resist with all of my strength, landing a kick to the manservant's side as he hoisted me over his shoulder. He began walking purposefully toward the courtyard. My stomach heaved. I beat my fists against his granite back as we entered the dark courtyard with its lovely fountain in the middle, adorned by the preening bronze *David* with his silly hat. He kept walking, to the palazzo's main gates.

Outside in the street I heard howling, as if demons leapt from the cobblestones. A man in a hooded cloak stepped from the shadows by the gates and said, 'Give her to me.' I writhed and yelled as I was handed over. The stranger smelled of soot and musk; as he hoisted me up onto a chestnut horse, I looked into his dark eyes. He was young, handsome. He whispered: 'I am Aldobrindi, secretary of the Signoria. Be still, Duchessina, for both our sakes.'

I heard the gates open and pictured the demons waiting, pitchforks in hand. He mounted in back of me, draped something dark and heavy over my head: a cloak to hide my presence.

He led us out into the street. Though I couldn't see the crowd filling the Via Larga, I heard their deafening chant: 'Death to the Medici! Death to the tyrants!'

A whip cracked; the horse pranced in agitation. Aldobrindi growled, 'Out of my way, rabble. I am a member of the Signoria!' There was a moment of terrifying quiet. I crouched further against him, trying to make myself as small as possible, fearing I'd be discovered, yanked from the saddle and torn apart.

Then we started to move again, the horse seeming to tiptoe through the city, where screams and smoke smothered the air. Peering through a hole in the cloak, I espied the oily flicker of torches smearing past my vision, held high by running figures; there were cries, shouting. I tried to stay calm. But the farther we rode, the more frightened I became. I had no idea of where he was taking me or what would happen to me when we got there.

By the time we came to a halt before a high gate set in an imposing brick wall, I swayed with exhaustion. The stranger took me off the horse. I couldn't feel my own legs as Aldobrindi led me through the gate into a stark cloister. A single torch burned, casting an eerie light over the rough stone pilasters and a dilapidated well in the cloister's center.

A black-robed figure came forth. 'Welcome to the Convent of Santa Lucia.'

I gasped, looking up in horror at Aldobrindi. This was the house of the sisters of Savonarola, devotees of that mad prophet who'd preached against the Medici and was burned at the stake by my great-grandfather.

The Convent of Santa Lucia was the most impoverished in Florence; that it still stood bore testament to the nuns' persistent hatred of my family, as they would never profit from our largesse. My aunt could not have known I was being brought to this place; she would have fought against it till her last breath.

'You cannot leave me here,' I said, and my voice seemed to split apart. But he bowed to me and retreated, leaving the nun to seize me by the arm.

'The end has come,' she hissed. 'Your uncle, the pope, cowers in his citadel in Orvieto while the emperor lets loose his wolves in Rome. This is what your family's pride has brought us: the wrath of God. But this time, there will be no escape. Here, you will atone for the Medicis' sins.'

I gazed at her anonymous face, seamed by loathing, her colorless stare starved of pity, and I knew she didn't see *me* at all. Tears burned in my eyes as she dragged me past the spectral row of nuns watching motionless from the portico, and down a musty corridor into a windowless cell, where another nun waited.

The door banged shut behind me. With cold efficiency, the nun stripped me of my clothing and left me naked, shivering. She removed something from her robe pocket; I cringed at the glint of scissors in her hand. 'If you resist, it'll go worse for you,' she said.

My tears broke free as she grasped my braid and cut. With the pink ribbon still twined around it, my auburn hair dropped at my feet. A wail clawed my throat. I bit down on it, shuddering as though I stood in snow, refusing to show my humiliation as the nun cropped my hair to its roots.

When she was done, she threw a coarse wool robe over my goose-pimpled skin and thrust a ragged broom at me. 'Clean it up,' she ordered, and she watched as I swept the lustrous coils into a pile. When I was done, she met my eyes. Her look was like a field in winter, barren of life.

Without a word she locked the door and left me alone in the dark, with the smell of mildew and rustle of rats in the walls, stray remnants of hair on my feet.

That night, I cried myself to sleep.

Every day for weeks, I was marched to their frigid chapel and forced to kneel for hours on stone until my knees bled. I had to observe every nuance of their rigid order; I was not allowed to talk and I had one watery meal a day, followed by interminable prayer dictated by the clang of a hollow bell. I was never alone except at night, when I sat in my cell and heard the distant blast of cannons. I didn't know what was happening beyond these walls, but lamentations echoed from the streets and ash fell from the smoke-filled sky to bury the convent's meager vegetable patch.

One night a sister pressed her lips to my door and said in malignant glee: 'The plague has come, along with the French. Your uncle hired diseased foreigners to bring Florence to its knees but he'll not prevail. We will die before we let the Medici rule our city again.'

The nuns doubled their quota of prayers, in vain. Four of the older sisters fell ill and perished, choking on their vomit and riddled with buboes. I lost all semblance of dignity, imploring them to let me go, into the streets if necessary, like a stray dog. But they only regarded me as if I were an animal they prepared for slaughter.

I envisioned my death. For what seemed an eternity, I prepared for it. No matter how it came, I told myself I must be brave. I must never show my fear, for I was a Medici.

Then, after nine long months of assault, with the city's magnificent fortifications reduced to rubble and the people dying of starvation, the Signoria had no other choice but surrender.

The army financed by my uncle marched in.

The nuns panicked. They moved me into a large room, brought me cheese and dried meats from the cellar, where they'd hidden their best supplies. They told me they only followed the Signoria's orders, that they never meant to hurt me. I regarded them dully, my scalp crawling with lice, my gums bleeding, and my body thin as a twig. I was so tired of waiting for death that I didn't even have the strength to hate them anymore.

Within days, Aldobrindi arrived. I'd eaten enough to receive him without fainting, clad in the same gown I was wearing when he took me from my palazzo. His shocked expression betrayed him. I must have looked like a skeleton in a child's damask and he fell to his knees to beg my forgiveness. His plaintive excuses drifted past me; when he was done assuring me that I would be released and sent to Rome, I asked quietly, 'Where is my aunt?'

There was a laden pause before he replied. 'Madama Strozzi had to leave the city but even from exile she never stopped fighting for you. She caught a fever and' – he reached into his doublet, set a sealed envelope in my hands – 'she left you this.'

I did not look at her letter. I closed my fingers over it and felt through the paper the invisible presence of the woman who'd been such an enormous part of my world it was impossible to imagine her gone. I did not cry. I could not. My grief ran too deep.

That same day I left Santa Lucia for Rome. I did not know what lay ahead for me.

All I knew was that I was eleven years old, my aunt was dead, and my life was not my own.

4

The city I left was in shambles; the city I returned to was unrecognizable. I had been warned by my escort that Rome had suffered great calamity during the Imperial siege but as we rode over the hills into the Tiber Valley, I could not believe my eyes. I had fleeting memories of the brief time I'd spent among the damp marsh airs and magnificent palazzos of the Eternal City; it was enough to make me wish I didn't remember anything at all.

A smoking pile rose against the desolate landscape; as we entered the city, I saw empty-eyed men and a few ravaged women sitting with their heads bowed amid burned-out husks that were once homes, surrounded by a wreckage of looted heirlooms and trampled relics. I caught sight of a group of children, their clothing in tatters; they stood silent, still, as if uncertain of where they belonged. My stomach sank as I realized they were now orphans, like me, only they had no place to go. Save for the mules used to haul away debris I saw no animal, not even the usually ubiquitous cats. I looked away from the bloated corpses piled like kindling in the streets, from pools of congealed blood swallowing the reflection of the bruised sky, and stared straight ahead as I was led to the Lateran Palace, where, I was told, I would be lodged.

Apartments had been readied overlooking the trampled gardens, as well as a household of noblewomen waiting to attend me. Among them was Lucrezia Calvacanti, a fair-haired girl with luminous blue eyes and willowy elegance, who informed me that His Holiness my uncle had not yet returned from Orvieto but had left word I was to have every luxury.

She smiled. 'Not that we've much to offer. The papal apartments were ransacked, everything of value stolen. But we've

enough food and should count ourselves fortunate. We'll do our
utmost for you, Duchessina, but I'm afraid silk sheets are out of
the question at this time.'

She was fifteen years old and addressed me like an adult who
didn't need protection from the realities of the world. I appreciated it. I did not want to be coddled or lied to anymore.

In my bedchamber I sat on the bed and watched the sun sink
below Rome's pine-tipped hills. Then I took out my aunt's letter.
It was a few lines, written in a dying woman's scrawl.

*My child, I fear I will not see you again in this life. But I will never
stop loving you and I know that God in his Mercy will watch over
you. Remember always that you are a Medici and are destined for
greatness. You are my hope, Caterina. Never forget it.*

I pressed the letter to my chest, curled up on the bed, and slept
for eleven hours. When I awoke I found Lucrezia seated on a
stool at my side. 'You've suffered much,' she said matter-of-factly.
'But now you must be like the beast, which lives only for the day.'

'How can I?' I asked quietly. 'Unlike the beast, I know what
tomorrow can bring.'

'Then you must learn. Whether we like it or not, my lady, today
is what we have.' She reached over, took the crumpled letter from
me. 'Let me store this,' she said, then she marshaled the other
women in, surrounding me with industrious solicitude. Only steps
away Rome was steeped in blood, but within those four walls, for
the first time in a long time, I felt safe.

And so I had recovered when Papa Clement arrived.

The flames of a scarred candelabrum shed muted light as I
approached the papal throne and sank to my knees. Papa Clement
motioned me to my feet. As I stood and observed him, I tried to
recall what he had looked like before, so I might mark some
change in him. He had fled Rome, forced to watch from afar as
the Imperial troops desecrated his city, but to me he looked as if
he had just returned from a respite in the country, his angular
cheeks high with color, his full lips cradled by a silver-threaded
beard. He wore ivory-white robes without a stain on their

luxuriant folds; when I glanced at his feet, I saw gold-embroidered velvet slippers. Only when I met his eyes did I see the effects of his exile: luminous blue-green in color, they were sharp, appraising, and narrowed. I realized I did not know him at all. He must have felt the same. He regarded me as though I was a stranger, his embrace weak, as if he didn't mean it.

'They will pay,' he muttered. 'All of them – the nuns of Santa Lucia, the Florentine rebels, that traitor Charles V: they will pay for what they've done.'

I knew he wasn't speaking to me; and as I curtsied again and backed from his presence, I saw the cardinals of his Curia arrayed in the corners, watching me like hawks.

I felt a chill. Whatever they planned, I was sure it wouldn't be nice.

Papa Clement didn't summon or visit me for months; he left me in the care of my women. It took several weeks before I was able to sleep through the night without jolting awake from nightmares of the grim months locked away in Santa Lucia. I was gratified to learn the sisters of Savonarola had been levied with a crushing fine and an order to disband; I was less pleased to discover that Papa Clement had refused to restore Florence's republican rights, setting one of his overlords over the city instead. Lucrezia did not mince her words around me: 'He will keep Florence under his heel and see to it that the emperor Charles V is served an equally bitter dish.'

I knew she was right. But I was still young and content to keep my distance, to walk the gardens, to read and be fitted for new gowns, and eat and sleep as much as I liked.

Lucrezia kept me informed of the goings-on at the papal court, which surged back to life even before the soot and grime of the desecration had been cleansed from the walls. Shortly before my thirteenth birthday, she told me the French king François I had dispatched a new envoy to Rome and Papa Clement had requested that I entertain him.

I stared at her. 'What am I supposed to do? Serve his wine?'

She gave a hearty laugh. 'Of course not! You'll amuse him with a French bass dance; His Holiness has hired an instructor for you. We mustn't forget to prepare for tomorrow and your feminine skills have been sorely neglected. The time has come to make a court lady out of you.'

'I thought you said I should be like the beast,' I grumbled. I didn't like the sound of this at all, but I had no other choice and so for the next weeks I was drilled mercilessly by a dapper, over-perfumed man who barked and prodded me with his white wand, declaring that a mare had more grace in her hindquarters than I did in my entire body. I hated dancing. The countless silly curtsies, fluttering hands, and coy glances annoyed me in the extreme.

Still, I learned it well enough to perform for the French. While my uncle lolled in his throne, flushed with wine, the ambassador regarded me with an enigmatic smile, eyeing me up and down as though I were on auction.

Days later, I bled for the first time. As I cramped and gasped, Lucrezia declared it a sure sign that I'd bear many healthy sons. Despite the discomfort, I observed in fascination the subtle changes taking place in my body, the new heft and silkiness in my breasts, the supple widening of my hips and bloom in my skin – all of which seemed to occur overnight.

'Will I be pretty?' I asked Lucrezia as she brushed my hair, which had grown out even curlier and fuller than before and which she liked to adorn with pearl caps and braided ribbons.

She leaned over my shoulder, gazing at me in the mirror. 'You *are* pretty,' she said. 'Those big black eyes of yours would captivate any man, and your lips are full enough to rouse a bishop's lust – not that it's that difficult with a bishop,' she added, with a wicked wink.

I giggled. Though she was my chief attendant, appointed to oversee my household and guide me, in truth she was like a sister and I was grateful every day for her presence. With Lucrezia's help, the scars of my trials had faded and I realized that I'd once again begun to look forward to whatever my future might hold.

My answer arrived soon enough. One afternoon Lucrezia came

to tell me I'd been summoned by Papa Clement. She did not know why, only that he wished to see me in private, and together we made our way to his apartments, through corridors hung with tarps and bustling with artisans laboring to restore frescoes damaged by the occupation.

As we approached my uncle's gilded doors, I was overcome by a stirring of my gift. It wasn't that helpless plunge into a netherworld I'd experienced in Florence but rather a quiet, almost imperceptible sense of warning that made me turn nervously to Lucrezia. She smiled in encouragement. 'Remember, whatever he says, you're more important to him than he is to you.'

I entered the spacious gilded room and knelt; my uncle sat at his massive desk, peeling oranges, their sweet tang filling the room and soaking up the scent of old perfume and smoky beeswax. He motioned. I went to kiss his hand, adorned with the seal of St. Peter. He was dressed in his white robes; around his neck hung a crucifix studded with emeralds and rubies.

'I'm told you are a woman now.' He sighed. 'How time passes.' His leather blotter was littered with rinds; he sucked a slice, gesturing to a nearby stool. 'Sit. It's been too long since we spent time together.'

'I was here only last month for the French envoy's visit,' I said, and I paused. 'I would rather stand, if Your Holiness doesn't mind. The gown is new and uncomfortable.'

'Ah, but you must get used to such things. Proper attire is of the utmost importance. In the court of France such matters are considered de rigueur.'

He retrieved a jeweled knife and sectioned the fruit. The aroma it released was like sunlight, making my mouth water. 'You should know these things. After all, your mother was French.'

It was on the tip of my tongue to remind him that I'd never known my mother. Instead, I murmured, 'She was, Your Holiness, to my great honor.'

'Indeed. And what might you say if I told you that France has asked for you?'

His voice was mild, reminding me of the days when I'd been

a little girl and he my devoted uncle. But I wasn't deceived; he had called me here for a purpose.

'Well?' he said sharply. 'Have you nothing to say?'

'I would say,' I replied, 'that again I am honored.'

He guffawed. 'Spoken like a Medici.' It was as if he had bared fangs. My knees weakened under my gown. Clement's gaze slid to me. 'You've learned the value of a neutral answer. It is an asset that will make your marriage all the less discomfiting.'

My blood turned cold in my veins. I thought I must have heard wrong.

'It is time you took your place in the world,' he went on, chewing his orange and spilling pale juice on his sleeve. 'In fact, the arrangements are almost complete. As part of your dowry, I'll offer the duchy of Milan, once the wedding takes place.' He glanced up. 'Who knows? One day you might be queen of France.'

A roar filled my ears. Here was his revenge, at long last. Here was his dagger thrust at Charles V: an alliance with the emperor's rival, François I, with me as his pawn. Wedding me to France would thwart Charles V's quest to dominate Italy and would give François his claim on the long-contested duchy of Milan, which was currently under Imperial rule.

'But King François is already married,' I managed to say, 'to the emperor's own sister.'

'Indeed. But his second son, Henri d'Orléans, is not and could one day inherit the throne. After all, I have it on good authority that François's eldest son, the dauphin, is quite sickly.'

He began peeling another orange, his spidery fingers digging into it. 'I trust your silence doesn't signify displeasure,' he added. 'I've gone to considerable expense and effort to see you to this state. The last thing I need is an unwilling bride on my hands.'

What could I say? He had the right to send me wherever he liked. Nothing I did short of killing myself could possibly free me and the cold finality of this fact hardened my voice.

'If it is your wish,' I said, 'then I am most pleased. May I ask a favor in return? I'd like to return to Florence. It is my home and I –' My voice caught. 'I want to say good-bye.'

His eyes turned cold. 'Very well,' he said. 'If you no longer find Rome agreeable, I'll appoint an escort.' He extended his ringed hand. As I kissed it, I heard him mutter: 'Love is a treacherous emotion. You'll fare better without it. We Medici always have.'

I backed toward the door as he peeled another orange, his lips curled in a complacent smile.

I returned to Florence in the fragrant heat of summer, accompanied by an entourage of guards and my women, including Lucrezia and a new companion, my dwarf, Anna-Maria – a fourteen-year-old miniature girl whose foreshortened limbs did not detract from her glorious mane of ash-gold hair, piquant face, and lively smile. I liked her from the moment I met her; Papa Clement had scoured Italy in search of her, as he insisted I must have my own fool in France, but I decided I'd not demean her by dressing her in bells. Instead, she would carry out the special task of seeing to my linens and hold a coveted position in my private rooms.

I found that in the family palazzo, little had changed. Florence still bore wounds that would take years to repair, yet our home remained untouched, silent as an elaborate tomb. I settled in my beloved late aunt's rooms, where the sheets still carried her scent and her alabaster-inlaid desk was set with her writing utensils, as though she might walk in at any moment.

And there I discovered my silver and ivory casket, in a drawer under unfinished letters. I took it out as if it might vanish, traced the chipped lid with my fingertips. My aunt had hidden it here, among her things. She had known I would want it and had anticipated I would return.

I opened it with a click; within a section of the velvet lining that peeled back, I located the secret compartment and Ruggieri's vial, coiled like a snake. I clasped it about my neck, held the box in my hands, and let myself grieve.

My betrothal was signed in the spring. Papa Clement assembled an impressive trousseau to exhibit my wealth as a Medici bride, not hesitating to pilfer his treasury for jewels, including seven gray pearls reputed to have belonged to a Byzantine empress and now adorning my ducal crown. He also had my portrait sent to France.

In return, François I sent his son's portrait to me. It came wrapped in an exquisite satin-lined box; and as Lucrezia removed the miniature from it I beheld my future husband for the first time – a taciturn face, with hooded eyes, a pursed mouth, and the long Valois nose. It didn't awaken anything in me, and I wondered in that moment if he felt the same about me. What kind of marriage could two strangers with nothing in common possibly have?

'He's handsome,' Lucrezia said, with relief. She glanced to where I sat like stone on my chair. 'He doesn't appear to have suffered any ill effects from his three years in Spain.'

Anna-Maria frowned. 'Why was he in Spain?'

'Because he and his brother, the dauphin, were sent to the emperor Charles V as hostages when King François lost the war over Milan,' I replied. 'The king also had to wed Charles's sister, Eleanor.' To my dismay, I had the childish urge to stomp my feet and fling the picture across the room, to throw a tantrum that would put on display my utter helplessness. Biting back my tears, I flicked my hand. 'Put the picture away and leave me.'

That night, I sat awake and gazed out into the sultry Florentine night. I let myself mourn everything I had lost before I decided my course. My life in Italy was over. It might not be what I wanted but it was my fate. Now I must look to the future and prepare.

After all, I was a Medici.

PART II
1532–1547
Naked as a Babe

5

After two weeks at sea, my ship dropped anchor in the Bay of Marseilles. It had been a terrifying storm-laden voyage that made me vow to never leave land again. If I'd had any inclination to ruminate on the vagaries of fate, which had led me to a foreign country and husband, my overwhelming relief to see something other than churning sea obliterated it.

Lucrezia and Anna-Maria removed one of my new gowns from the leather chests, smoothed its crumpled folds, and corseted me into it – a brocade concoction so encrusted with gems I thought I'd scarcely be able to totter up on deck, much less ride through Marseilles to the palace where the French court waited. I also donned my formal ducal coronet for the first time, inset with the seven pearls. Trussed in this finery, I waited until my new household treasurer, René Birago, came to inform me that Constable Montmorency's barge had arrived to bring me ashore.

I nodded. 'Then I must go greet him.'

Birago gave me a smile. He was Florentine, in his mid-twenties, and chosen by Papa Clement to supervise my finances. Despite a slight limp, which he blamed on periodic gout, he had an ageless grace that denoted a lifetime spent at the papal court, his lean figure clad in a scarlet doublet cut in the close-fitting Italian style, his fine light brown hair combed back from an angular forehead that emphasized his hooked nose and shrewd dark eyes.

'*Madama*,' he said, in a voice made for whispering in ears, 'I suggest you remain here. Montmorency may be the constable and His Majesty's chief officer, but you are the Duchess of Urbino and soon-to-be duchesse d'Orléans. Let France pay its respects to Italy, for a change.'

It was a clever remark from a clever man, guaranteed to make me smile. At least I had a little bit of Italy to keep me safe, I thought, and I lifted a hand to my chest; beneath my bodice, I felt another piece of Italy – Ruggieri's vial.

My women gathered about me as the French boarded the galleon. They were all magnificently appareled, jewels winking in the sunlight on caps and doublets. Without looking away, I whispered to Lucrezia, 'Which one is the constable?'

'There,' she said, 'by Birago: that must be him. He's like a barbarian, so big and dressed in that funereal black.'

She was right. Montmorency did seem like a titan, his shoulders blocking the sun, his starched ruff a mere ruffle around his bullish neck. Birago had told me he was in his late thirties, a champion warrior who had fought ferociously during François's war over Milan. I was prepared for someone with little tolerance for anything Italian, considering he'd wet his sword in the blood of countless of my countrymen. Yet when he bowed over my hand, I saw that despite his leathery skin and severe gray-blue eyes, his expression wasn't unkind.

'It is my honor to welcome Your Highness in the name of His Majesty François I,' he declared in a monotone. I inclined my head and said in French: 'My lord constable, to be greeted by you makes me feel as if His Majesty himself were here and this realm my home.'

The crevices at his eyes deepened. Though he didn't speak again as he led me to the barge, his firm hand on my sleeve assured me I had made my first French friend.

My ride through Marseilles was a blur. Upon reaching the palace, I had only a moment to compose myself before I set my hand again on the constable's arm and was brought into the hall, where hundreds of nobles lined an aisle leading to a dais bunted in crimson.

A clap of hands plunged everyone into silence. '*Eh, bon!* The bride is here!'

From the dais, a man descended with feline grace, dressed head to toe in silver tissue, his auburn hair sweeping to his shoulders, a trim beard emphasizing his secretive lips and large aquiline nose. I went still. I had never seen a face like his before. It was as if the full spectrum of life had carved itself upon his flesh with unrepentant arrogance, every gully and rivulet the mark of a soul that held nothing back. He was far past his much-vaunted youth; but François I of France was still a sight to behold, a king for whom power had become an accoutrement, who had savored everything life could offer save self-denial.

We stared at each other. His hooded green eyes shone mischievously. Mortified, I realized I'd forgotten my obeisance. As I started to curtsy, he waved a jeweled hand.

'*Mais non, ma fille,*' and he embraced me, rousing spontaneous applause. '*Bienvenue en France, petite Catherine,*' King François I breathed in my ear.

He brought me to his family. I kissed the hand of Queen Eleanor, the emperor's sister, a rigid Spanish princess fenced in by women. I then greeted the king's eldest son born of his first marriage to the late queen Claude. François, called the dauphin in honor of his being heir to the throne, was a tall youth with gentle brown eyes and the pallor of a chronic invalid. I almost bumped heads with his daughters, the princesses Marguerite and Madeleine, who were so nervous they curtsied at the same time as me. As we giggled in unison, I saw they were close to me in age, and I thought perhaps we might become friends.

I turned to the king. He gave me a small twist of a smile. I understood. 'Is His Highness Prince Henri not here?' I asked.

François's face darkened. 'He's a boor,' he muttered. 'He doesn't know the meaning of propriety. Nor, it seems, does he own a timepiece. But do not worry. The wedding takes place tomorrow, and by God he *will* be here.'

It sounded far more like a threat than a reassurance. I lifted my chin. 'How could he not?' I said in a voice loud enough for all to hear. 'It's not every day France has occasion to wed Italy.'

François went still. He lowered his gaze and his hand slipped into mine. 'Spoken like a true princess,' he murmured, and raising our clasped hands he cried, 'Let the feast begin!'

He swept me into a banqueting chamber, where I sat on the dais beside him. The court swarmed the tables arrayed below us; as servitors entered bearing platters of honeyed heron and roast swans, the king craned his head to me and whispered, 'My son may be reluctant to show pleasure with his bride, but I, petite Catherine, I am enchanted.'

Without hesitation I replied, 'Then perhaps it is Your Majesty whom I should wed.'

He laughed. 'And you've got courage to match those pretty black eyes.' He paused, searching my face. 'I wonder if my son will appreciate you, Catherine de Medici.'

I forced out a smile, even as his words sent a chill through me. Had I come all this way to be the wife of a prince who wanted nothing to do with me?

As platter after platter was set before me, and François drank goblet after goblet of spiced wine, I began to feel invisible until he touched my hand and said, 'Montmorency's nephews wish to greet you, my dear. Smile. They are his pride and joy, born of his beloved late sister.'

I started to attention. Standing before me were the constable and three young men.

They made an immediate impression with their tawny good looks, highlighted by their unadorned white doublets, and their sense of quiet familial unity.

Montmorency said, 'May I present my eldest nephew, Gaspard de Coligny, seigneur of Châtillon?'

I leaned forward. Gaspard de Coligny had thick, dark gold–colored hair and lucent pale blue eyes, his angular face imbued with melancholy. He might have been Milanese, attractive yet remote, as the nobles of that city are apt to be. I thought him in his early twenties. In fact, he had just turned sixteen.

'I am honored,' he said in a low voice. 'I hope Your Highness will find happiness here.'

I gave him a tremulous smile. 'Thank you, my lord.'

He paused, his eyes searching mine. I thought he would say something else, but he bowed once more and returned with his brothers to their table, leaving me to stare after him, as if he'd revealed something precious I might never find again.

François sighed. 'His father died recently. It is why he wears white, the color of mourning here. Madame de Coligny passed away years ago; with his father gone, Gaspard is now head of his family. The constable dotes on him.' He slid his eyes to me. 'You could do worse when it comes to friends. Montmorency is one of my most loyal men and his family lineage is ancient. His nephew shares these traits, and at court, *ma petite,* lineage is everything.'

So, Gaspard de Coligny was an orphan, like me. Was this why I felt such kinship with him?

A host of other nobles followed, tripping over themselves in their haste to ensure the king saw that they too respected his new daughterin-law. By the twentieth course, and after twice as many greetings, I despaired of remembering everyone's names and titles. I was grateful when the king rose to declare that I must be tired. He led me from the dais to the one opposite ours, where Queen Eleanor had sat out the evening in ironclad silence.

I felt pity for her. Like me, Eleanor had been used on the royal market and apparently refused to adapt. I'd heard the Spanish were thus, zealous of their identity, and I knew her example was one I'd be wise not to emulate. Come what may, I must blend in, become one with this court, which for better or worse was my new home. As I passed the constable, I glanced at his nephew. Gaspard inclined his head; I looked in vain for a glimpse of his eyes.

Pages dressed in the Valois colors of blue and white opened the door. François left me to the attentions of my women; I didn't speak with them as they relieved me of my costume, meeting Lucrezia's knowing eyes as I lay down in the unfamiliar bed.

Alone, I lay awake and thought that my aunt Clarice had been wrong.

I might be not so important after all.

6

I awoke the next morning to find my ladies clustered about me. Not having slept well in over a week, I buried my head under the pillows. Lucrezia dared to shake my shoulder. 'My lady, His Majesty and the court await you. The ceremony, it is scheduled for today.'

I groaned. Then I went still. I peered from under the pillow. I could smell the heated lavender in the copper tub my ladies had hauled in and filled with hot water, see the frothing folds of my wedding costume arranged on the table. 'Is he here?' I asked.

Anna-Maria gave a sad shake of her head. I felt a wave of humiliation. 'Well,' I snapped, 'if he's not here, who exactly am I supposed to marry today?'

Lucrezia replied, 'His Majesty says that if need be he'll see you wed by proxy.'

At this, Anna-Maria burst into tears. In between her sobs, I gathered that she deemed me the unhappiest princess in Christendom.

'I don't know about that,' I said, trying to make the best of an awful situation. 'But there must be happier ones.' I submitted to their ministrations, emerging two hours later weighted in my cerulean velvet, with diamond arabesque sleeve cuffs like shards at my wrists.

Despite the suffocating heat, a crowd milled in the courtyard. I paused. God help me, I didn't want this. I didn't want to marry some boy who didn't have the decency to show his face. Then François emerged from among his gentlemen. He bowed, raised my hand to his lips. His smile was sardonic. 'You said perhaps you ought to wed me instead. Well, now is your chance.'

I had to smile. An aging satyr, he was still unlike any man I'd ever met.

More of the same awaited me at the cathedral, only now the sea of courtiers, nobles, and petty officials had become an ocean. Once more, all eyes – glittering like birds of prey's above powdered cheeks – fixed on me as I descended from the carriage and resisted the urge to yank the sweat-sodden folds of my gown from between my buttocks. François guided me to the altar as if I were a galleon in my overblown costume. As I approached I saw no sign of my groom.

The king stood beside me. The bishop looked as if he wished the earth would swallow him. François barked: 'Well? What are we waiting for? The bride is here and I will stand as proxy. On, man, on!'

I wondered if his wedding to Queen Eleanor had been like this. How could it be otherwise? Political marriage, by its very nature, wasn't designed to inspire sonnets. But even in the most politic of alliances, the actual couple was present to recite their vows.

The bishop fidgeted with his missal, seeking the appropriate passage, though he must have had ample time to prepare. I wanted to giggle. The entire occasion struck me as ridiculous, a farce of a marriage founded on a lie.

In that moment, the clanking of spurs on marble flagstone shattered the quiet. In a fluid movement, everyone swiveled about. I saw a tall youth striding toward us, yanking off leather gauntlets and shoving them into his belt. Behind him surged a coterie of disheveled men. François stiffened. No one needed to tell me the bridegroom had made his appearance.

As I beheld Henri d'Orléans for the first time, I felt some relief. At least he was not ugly. At fourteen, he held his broad frame with the discipline of a born equestrian – one who, given the choice, would rather live in the saddle and thought little of that which did not yield to bridle or crop. He had the Valois aquiline nose, narrow eyes, and raven-wing hair, but his expression was morose, as if all joy had curdled inside him. He hadn't changed his clothes, coming before us in his hunting gear with flecks of crusted blood on his jerkin, no doubt from some creature he'd slaughtered. Behind him, I glimpsed a tall rapier of a man of perhaps twenty years of age;

he had a sharp thin face and he looked at me as if I were something unpleasant he'd stepped in. His lips pursed. He was Francis de Guise, I'd later discover, Henri's closest friend and eldest son of the realm's most ambitious and rabidly Catholic family, which had been ennobled with a dukedom by François and now owned vast tracts of land in northeastern France.

I lifted my chin. My husband-to-be did not utter a word.

François hissed, 'Ingrate!' I went cold as Henri didn't bother to glance in his father's direction. My wedding was becoming a catastrophe; I had to intervene. I was a Medici, niece to the pope. More important, I was my aunt's child, in every way that mattered.

I turned to the bishop. 'If you would . . . ?' And François stepped aside for Henri to take his place. He smelled worse than he looked, and I stared straight ahead as I repeated the words that made me Henri d'Orléans's wife.

After the wedding, we were subjected to another banquet.

This time, Henri sat at my side on the dais, and while we didn't look at each other I was certain the hour at hand loomed in both our minds. So much, in fact, that I couldn't eat anything of the fifty-seven courses set before us in dizzying succession nor feign my delight in the gifts that the nobles piled at our feet.

At the stroke of midnight, the hundreds of courtiers crammed into the palace corridors to cheer us on to our nuptial suite. I surrendered my wedding gown for a white lawn nightdress and was led into the adjoining room. Henri stood by a vast bed hung with garlands, talking to his friend with the hawk's stare. My husband wore a translucent linen shift that clung to his muscular body like wet skin. Most women, and some men, would have been overjoyed to have such a man in their bed. Maybe in some part of me, I was too, for my heart thumped like a drum. I also felt queasy as I avoided his friend Francis de Guise's leering smile and allowed Lucrezia to tuck me under the covers. The bishop blessed the bed; the courtiers drank a final salute to our happiness, and the tapers were doused. Everyone left to resume their revels.

Silence descended. I lay utterly still.

I wasn't ignorant of what people did on their wedding night. Lucrezia had given me a brief explanation and I had seen dogs mating; still, the thought was not appealing.

He rose from the bed. My breath hissed through my teeth. He wouldn't dare leave me alone! Then a flame flared, and he stepped from the shadows with a candle. He set the candle at the bedside, sat on the mattress, and cleared his throat.

'I wish to apologize for any offense I may have caused you.'

At the sound of these, his first words to me, I shifted up on my pillows.

'I failed to greet you when we first met,' he added. 'My behavior was inexcusable.'

His apology sounded stilted and I suspected the king had reprimanded him.

'It was,' I said. 'Surely I did nothing to merit such offense.'

He glanced away. The candle flame cast a wavering shadow across his chin. Thus would he look someday, I thought, when he grew a beard. He was very handsome, even if he still smelled like a goatherd, but that didn't mean I should care for him. In fact, I sensed it would go far better for me if I did not.

'No, you did nothing,' he said at length. 'Though there are those who say . . .' He raised his eyes back to me. His look was cool, impersonal. 'Some say this marriage isn't worthy of me.'

I was taken aback. 'Not worthy? How so?'

Now it was his turn to look discomfited. He hadn't expected me to question him. What, did wives not have tongues in France?

'I should think it's obvious,' he said, with a stiff lift of his chin. 'I am a prince of France, while you . . . you are the daughter of wool merchants.'

I remained quite still against my pillows. I'd never heard anyone describe me thus and for a moment I almost laughed aloud, it was so absurd. My amusement died when I realized he was serious. He believed I was beneath him.

'My family may come from modest origins,' I said, 'but we now count among us two popes and several lords. In Italy, families like mine are considered noble, as we've –'

'I know about your family,' he interrupted. He'd not expected my candor, either, it seemed; tears and maidenly pleas, yes, but never candor. Every moment that passed deepened my contempt. He was like any boy forced to do something against his will, eager to maim the object of his discomfort without a thought for the consequences.

'Still, you are fortunate to have a prince in your bed,' he went on, and I knew these weren't his words. He might believe them now that he'd been apprised, but someone else had put this malicious notion in his head, someone he trusted. Who?

I wasn't about to defend myself to him, though a part of me wanted to remind him that my origins sufficed for his father, who'd hankered after my country for years and taken my dowry money and my uncle the pope's promise of future duchies, quick as you please. Instead I said, 'Indeed. It's a great honor.'

He stood silent, chest and jaw thrust out like a fighting cock's. 'Of course, I don't fault you for your lack of lineage. I'm sure you would have preferred to remain in Italy with your people.'

I was silent. I would never admit aloud how little I had left to mourn in my native land.

'And I'm told this needn't be disagreeable,' he said, interpreting my silence for agreement. 'If we do as required, in time we can live as husband and wife.'

It was a night of truth. I wasn't yet fifteen, a novice in matters of the heart, but even I knew a successful marriage did not depend on personal preference. Women like me often wed strangers. If they had survived the disappointment, so could I.

I nodded. Satisfied, he blew out the candle and slid back under the covers. 'Good night,' he said, and he turned over. Within seconds, his breathing deepened, punctuated by a guttural snore. He slept like a man well exercised, which, in a manner of speaking, he was.

I stayed awake for hours, staring up at the dark emptiness of the bed canopy.

7

From Marseilles we traveled to the valley of the Loire in the heart of France.

Surrounded by laughing men in fitted velvets and bold ladies with painted faces, along with hundreds of carts bearing precarious loads of furniture, utensils, carpets, and tapestries – everything the court might need – I was in awe. Nothing I'd seen in Italy could compare to this court's extravagance, snaking along the roads like a multicolored ribbon frayed at its edges by a cacophonous multitude of servants and barking hounds, the king always at its center, surrounded by his men. I often glimpsed a striking red-haired lady at his side, clad in jade satin, her long throat glistening with jewels, her hand touching François with familiar intimacy. She was not presented to me, but I guessed she must be his mistress and I thought of his staid Spanish queen, who'd bid me a stiff good-bye in Marseilles and gone another direction with her entourage.

And the land we traversed was astonishing – so immense it made Italy seem like a calcified spine. I beheld well-fed vales under luminous skies that arched overhead like azure-painted vaults; majestic forests that spread as far as the horizon and fertile fields cradling spacious townships, where livestock grazed in wide paddocks and rivers sloped in sinuous curves under stone bridges. At my side Lucrezia rode as wide-eyed and open-mouthed as me; and Anna-Maria, who'd weathered our travels with admirable nonchalance, whispered, 'It's like something out of a storybook. It doesn't seem real.'

I couldn't have said it better. France *was* an enchanted realm, and I thought I could be happy here in ways I had not foreseen:

free to create myself anew without the weight of the past. Anything seemed possible in such a beautiful country; and when the king caught my eye he winked, as if he could sense my thoughts, and he leaned to my ear to whisper, 'Wait until you see my Château of Fontainebleau. You will discover that I've spared no expense in creating a palace worthy to hold its own even among the Medici.'

He was right. Fontainebleau emerged from the alabaster mists of the Loire Valley like a fantastical dream, the first place in France I would call home. From stucco nymphs that seemed to writhe on the wainscoting of its gilded great gallery to lavish corridors festooned with the king's prized collection of paintings, including Leonardo da Vinci's superb *Madonna of the Rocks* and his odd little *Giaconda*, I recognized François's passion for everything Italian. He had sought to re-create a vision of my land that I no longer held, one of supreme artistry and extroverted exuberance, and he was so delighted in my interest he even took me on a personal tour of his château, pointing out the oleander-dusted grottoes that echoed courtyards of Tuscany and bathing chambers that boasted heated floors and mosaics like those of ancient Rome.

I soon discovered that Henri and I weren't expected to share a household. Indeed, royal couples don't coexist as other married people do. Queen Eleanor was never at court, preferring to reside in houses designated for her personal use, and I took this tactic model as my cue. I let Birago oversee my affairs and plunged into my new life, which included lessons with the princesses Madeleine and Marguerite.

As I had hoped, we became fast friends.

Thirteen-year-old Madeleine was a delicate creature, fashioned of porcelain skin and weak lungs. She adored poetry, which she read even in periods of illness, and many afternoons I spent at her bedside, reciting aloud. In contrast, ten-year-old Marguerite was tall and robust like her father, a freckled redhead with a spirit that exceeded any boundaries imposed on us. At first she was content to test my mettle with my knowledge of Cicero and Plato; once the classroom grew too confining, she took me on outings to explore Fontainebleau's less apparent wonders. We were never alone at first; our ladies shadowed and chided us, until with a boisterous laugh, Marguerite grabbed my hand and yanked me, running and breathless, away from our dismayed companions, who squawked in distress, unable to keep up with us in their court gowns.

'Look at them.' Marguerite chuckled when we reached our destination and I doubled over to catch my breath. 'Like hens with nothing better to do than flap their wings. I'll never be like that when I'm old enough to decide my own life. I will never be a useless woman.'

'Of course not,' I said, in unabashed admiration. She seemed quite grown up in my eyes, and everything I longed to be. 'You are a princess. You can do whatever you like.'

'True.' Her green eyes met mine. 'I am a princess. But even princesses can't do as they please, without the will to fight. Look at you: weren't you married off without as much as a by-your-leave to my brother?'

She didn't mean to offend. She stated the matter as she saw it. But the mention of Henri stung all the same. I remembered what he had said about me and suspected that, like him, others in this court regarded me as an upstart foreigner with little to commend her.

'I don't lack will,' I retorted. 'Many princes vied for my hand. Your father made the best offer, but Henri means nothing to me.'

Her eyes sparkled. 'Naturally. He 's your husband. You can always take a lover once you bear him sons. Look at Papa: he had to wed Charles V's sister but that hasn't stopped him from seeking his pleasure. He has his Petite Bande of ladies to entertain him. One day, so shall we.'

I thought of the red-haired woman I'd seen with the king and ignored the mention of childbearing, unlikely at this stage in my marriage. I said slyly, 'Ladies?' and Marguerite giggled. 'Well, there are women who prefer it. But I'll have a dozen gentlemen instead. My father's sister, my aunt Marguerite, was like that before she wed the king of Navarre. She had men hanging on her every word, reciting her poems aloud, and professing their undying love.'

Oh, she was bold. I couldn't resist her uninhibited spirit. Marguerite showed me more of the world than I'd ever seen. She purloined books from the king's private library, which illustrated astonishing acts of fornication, and dragged me off to the pavilion by Fontainebleau's artificial lake where lovers often had their trysts.

Hunched down in the gooseberry, we spied through the branches as the pictures we'd gaped over turned to flesh before our eyes. I knew that the act those ladies with their splayed thighs and gentlemen with their pumping hips enjoyed was what should have happened to me on my wedding night and consoled myself that one day I would indeed, as Marguerite professed, take a lover so I might experience for myself those mysterious desires of the heart.

Not all was fun and games. Though I delighted in the independence that let me wander at will, at liberty to indulge my newfound interest in art and books, I realized being a princess of France was much like being a Medici; the king's daughters dwelled always under the expectations of their rank. One day, they too would wed, leave for distant courts, where they would be strangers representing their nation. And the classroom was their training ground. Here, we spent six hours every day, adhering to a regimen of mathematics, history, languages, and music, as Madeleine showed me upon opening her notebook one morning. 'We had a mythology lesson yesterday.'

'Taught by old Snigger-Puss,' Marguerite interjected. 'But today I told him we felt a touch of ague. You know how he fears sickness – almost as much as he does soap and water.'

'Sinigiar-Puss,' I repeated, the French name eluding me. Marguerite enunciated: '*Snigger-Puss*. We call him that because he wears dusty robes and snuffles like an old cat.'

Madeleine piped in. 'But he's very kind. He always gives us high marks.'

'He can't do otherwise,' Marguerite reminded her, laughing. 'Papa brought him from Flanders to teach us. He's a Humanist; all our tutors are Humanists. Papa says they're the best instructors because they liberate the mind without subjugating the spirit.'

'What about your brothers?' I asked. 'Do they also study with you?' I'd not seen Henri in weeks and had begun to wonder if we were expected to be estranged like the king and his queen. The forbidden trips to watch the lovers by the lake had reawakened the private worry that my marriage was not as it should be.

'Oh, no!' said Marguerite. 'Our brother François has his own household and obligations as dauphin. But he visits sometimes.'

I couldn't ask about Henri. They'd assume I knew about his life, when in fact all I'd managed to glean thus far was that he stayed close to his friend Francis de Guise and liked to hunt a lot. Still, it might not be too revealing if I asked if he attended lessons here . . .

The classroom door burst open. With exuberant cries the princesses rushed to greet their father, who swept them up in his arms. Not for the first time, I felt a pang of emptiness; while I had been received at François's court as though I were one of his children, I now understood what it was like to have a father. I had never felt like an orphan until I saw the king with his daughters, and I stood apart awkwardly, feeling I didn't belong.

François put an arm about Marguerite's waist and pinched Madeleine's cheek. He cast a smile in my direction. 'What?' he declared in mock severity. 'No lessons today?'

Marguerite said, 'We sent Snigger-Puss away. We wanted to spend time with Catherine.'

'Snigger-Puss, eh? And do you think that a suitable name to teach your new sister?'

'She might as well learn it now,' said Marguerite. 'Then she can devote herself to her Aristotle and Plutarch without wondering why her teacher smells like mold.'

François roared laughter. 'Did you hear that, Anne, my love?

She says her teachers smell! *Mon Dieu*, what a mouth she has. A sword cuts less.'

'Indeed,' replied a cultured voice. 'It seems Her Highness is cut from the same cloth as her father,' and the red-haired lady in green stepped from among a group of women who had slipped in, trailing skirt-tails and perfume. Marguerite had told me who she was: Anne d'Heilly, duchesse d'Étampes, François's mistress and more of a queen at court than his wife would ever be. With her wide feline eyes and abundant coppery hair entwined with pearls, she moved to François, nodding at the princesses before directing the full power of her regard on me. 'And how fares our *petite italianne*? Is she growing accustomed to our ways?'

I glanced at the king. He lifted his brow as if to encourage me. Swallowing the knot in my throat, I returned my gaze to his mistress. 'Madame, I've felt at home from the moment I arrived. I love France.'

'Is that so?' Her carmine mouth parted in a cold smile. 'How charming. It's not every day that France has the opportunity to win over a piece of Italy, is it?'

I didn't know what to say to this and hastened to my stool as the king sat between his daughters. The duchess wafted past me to her women, her skirts brushing my legs. I sensed icy restraint as she perched on the upholstered window seat. The women arranged themselves about her, a bevy of privileged airs and overdone faces. Her eyes seemed indolent. Even as I felt them fix on me, I didn't dare meet her gaze. Then suddenly François exclaimed: 'Did you hear that, Anne? Madeleine says Catherine has already mastered Plutarch.'

'Has she?' drawled the duchess. Her habit of turning everything she said into a question gnawed at my nerves. 'She must be quite advanced. I hope she won't find her time here wasted.'

'Oh, I won't,' I cried, startling everyone. 'I won't at all, madame!' Maybe I thought she'd deny me these hours in the classroom with the princesses or maybe she'd unnerved me with her unblinking stare. Whichever the case, I trembled from head to foot as she took a long, appraising look at me and rose with daunting resolve.

'Your Majesty, I believe it is time for the duchesse d'Orléans and me to become better acquainted. Perhaps Their Highnesses would enjoy a stroll in the garden?'

Duchesse d'Orléans; she wanted to speak with one of her women. I rose quickly, to flee. 'My dear,' she drawled, 'where are you going? You are the duchess, *n'est-ce pas?*'

I froze. Everyone filed out, leaving me alone with the royal mistress.

She motioned me to the window seat and I obeyed. Dear God, what had I done? How had I offended? 'Their Highnesses are quite taken with you,' she said. 'You excel at making friends, it seems.'

'Their Highnesses, they . . . they are kind. I . . . I enjoy their company.'

'As you should. Yet being the married one, you must also set an example.' She draped her arm across her chair, exposing a dazzling emerald bracelet. 'Do you understand?'

My mouth went dry. 'No, madame. Have I displeased His Majesty in some way?'

Her laughter was brief, a seductive vibrato. 'On the contrary. He too is quite taken with you. Enchanted, in fact. I, on the other hand . . .' She left her chair to step before me. Her nail caught me under my chin. 'I do not like rivals, little one.'

I stared at her. 'But I . . . I am no rival. How could I be?'

She flicked her hand. 'You're almost fifteen. At your age, I was considered quite a force.'

'But I am not like you. I could never challenge you.'

She hesitated. A spontaneous smile warmed her face. 'You don't understand, do you?'

I went limp. 'I fear not.'

She perched beside me, so close I smelled ambergris on her throat. 'I don't see how you've avoided the rumors; it's the talk of the court. They say as your husband pays you no mind, you'd lure François to your bed to prove he wasn't a fool to bring you here.'

I gasped. 'He's my father-in-law! I love him, yes, but not like that. It . . . it would be incest.'

'Only if you're related by blood,' she purred, and a remarkable transformation overcame her. One moment she'd been a fearsome personage; now, with her hair about her face like a halo and laughter on her lips, she became a mischievous girl. I could see why François adored her.

She regarded me with open curiosity. 'I do believe you are indeed what everyone says you cannot be: an innocent. And I, it seems, have been deceived. I believed you sought to take him from me. Mind you, you wouldn't be the first.'

I couldn't move. The court mocked me. They deemed me a neglected, conniving wife. They talked about me behind my back.

The duchess said softly, 'What are you thinking?'

I averted my eyes. My voice failed me. I felt like a simpleton before such polished sophistication, even as I longed to spill out my misgivings to her.

She sighed. 'I see. Not everything the court says is false.'

She spoke with such assurance, as if the secret were branded on my face, that I had no will to pretend otherwise. 'Yes,' I whispered. 'Henri . . . he doesn't care for me.'

'Oh, my dear, does his indifference hurt you so much? You want him to love you and you resent that he's so devoted to his friend Guise and that horrid mistress of his.'

A pit opened inside me. 'He . . . he has a mistress?'

'Why, yes.' She waved a hand. 'Everyone knows. Or at least we think we do. No one is quite sure who she is to him, exactly. She was his governess for a time, brought to court to train him in proper etiquette after he returned from Spain. Oh, the abuse he poured on his father was terrible! He blamed François for sending him away and still does, which infuriates François. So, he appointed her to ensure Henri learned to behave as a prince should. But her charge ended on Henri's thirteenth birthday and she returned to her château in Anet. It's believed he visits her there. He says he's hunting, but how much can any man hunt?'

My skin crawled. Henri had a mistress. He played me for a

fool. *In time,* he'd said in Marseilles. In time, we would learn to
live as husband and wife. Was this what he meant? That I should
be complacent while he consorted with his ex-governess? That
I'd become the object of lurid speculation because he had made
a mockery of our marriage?

The duchess added, 'I thought you knew. It's not uncommon
for men of Henri's age to become infatuated with older women,
but in time the interest fades. Indeed, once you get with child by
him, he'll forget about her.' Her voice edged with a hint of spite.
'She'll be a crone by then, in any event.'

I stiffened. 'How many years older is she?'

'Oh, she's at least forty-three. She hides her age well, I'll grant
her that, but she's still a widow with two grown daughters. Some
say she's attractive; I can't for the life of me understand the appeal.
Always dressed in that dreadful black and ugly coif – cold, she
is, cold and hard. François says she has coins for eyes. He doesn't
approve of her hold on Henri.'

'What is her name?' I whispered, afraid to know, as if hearing
it would make her materialize before me.

'Diane de Poitiers, widow of the seneschal of Normandy. We
call her la Sénéchale.' She arched her brow. 'I gather you also
don't approve.'

'Approve?' I spat before I could stop myself. 'He has no right!
How can I get with child if he spends all his time in his mistress's
bed?' As soon as I spoke, I wished I could snatch back my words.
I had offended her. After all, she too was a royal mistress.

The duchess contemplated me for a long moment. Then she
said with clipped precision, 'Men will dally; and as women, we
must endure. But no man should place dalliance above duty.
Unlike our Sénéchale, I have always known my place. The king
has had his children and wants no more; his marriage to his
second queen, Eleanor, is one of strictly political convenience.
But your marriage is a different matter. As Francois's second
heir, Henri is expected to sire sons. This cannot continue. I'm
afraid we must speak with His Majesty.'

'Oh, no! Please.' I was overcome by panic. I felt my entire future hinged on keeping my virginity a secret. 'I don't want anyone else to know . . . It . . . it is humiliating.'

'I don't see why. No one thinks you're to blame.'

I struggled to control myself. I had the feeling that the duchess had her own reasons for disliking the Sénéchale; perhaps she too saw a future already before her, a time when she would be too old for the king to care about her. No matter the case, it wouldn't serve me to play the helpless virgin, not when I might find the assistance I needed through her influence.

'Couldn't you help me some other way?' I ventured. 'I'm certain that if Henri and I could spend some time together, he'd come to see the error of his ways.'

She paused, eyeing me. 'Yes, perhaps he would,' she said. 'And as women, we must stick together, yes?' She smiled. 'We'll start with a new set of gowns. Your Italian dress is very distinctive, but you must look entirely French now. I'll also have you ride the hunt with us, as an honorary member of our Petite Bande. You do ride, don't you?'

'I do,' I said quickly. 'I like riding.' In truth, I had never ridden a hunt, but I had brought a splendid gold and leather saddle from Florence with me and I thought it would stand out.

'Good. Riding _la chasse_ with us is sure to bring you notice.'

'And that's good?' I asked, for I wasn't sure if it was the kind of notice I should aspire to.

She tossed her head, laughing. 'Nothing could be better! You have Madame d'Étampes on your side, my dear, and if there's one thing I excel at, it's how to win a man.'

I was thus initiated into the king's intimate circle. It took several weeks to get my new gowns fitted, and in the meantime I began practicing my riding every day on a docile mare, using my Florentine saddle, which had a higher ridge and shorter stirrup length than customary in France and thus, Madame d'Étampes informed me, allowed me the extra advantage of being able to hike up my skirts to show off my ankles. 'You do have lovely legs, my dear,' she remarked. 'And the gentlemen always appreciate a hint of thigh.' She trilled laughter; I think she enjoyed grooming me, seeing me as some special project she undertook for the king.

Finally I was taken with the Petite Bande to the hunt.

I didn't like it. The hounds barked incessantly, the men drank too much too early, and the women vied with each other for attention. I also learned to stay far from the actual killing, for the celebrated *chasse* was just an organized massacre, with grooms setting up nets in a circle while wranglers beat the bushes with rods to scare up quail, pheasant, rabbit, and other creatures and send them bounding into the nets, where, defenseless, they fell to the gleeful thrust of spears and arrows shot by the ladies on their mares. The animals' agonized cries and their blood soaking the ground nauseated me; I didn't understand how otherwise sophisticated people could delight in such savagery. I would have preferred to ride with the king in honest pursuit of hart or boar, but women weren't allowed, though in my saddle I could ride as hard and fast as any man. Disregarding the calluses on my hands and on my buttocks (for these hunts consumed hours) I spent the time perfecting my horsemanship skills while the women sated their bloodlust, until one morning I set heels to my mare and spurred after the king.

I was rewarded by his astonishment, and his men's staring disapproval, when I came to his side. 'Let me ride with you today,' I said, and he looked at me before he nodded. 'You'd best know how to use that bow,' he said, and he spurred his stallion forth, his hounds baying as they caught scent of prey. I followed, reveling in the sensation of the forest rushing past me, laughing aloud when a low branch snagged my riding cap and tore it from my head. Leaning in my saddle against my mare's powerful neck, I urged her on, determined to keep pace. And there, on the edge of a clearing, I saw the hounds corner a young doe, her ears flattened against her exquisite head, her expressive eyes distended in fear as she bucked at the circling dogs with her hooves.

François beckoned me. His men were about him, yanking at their lathered steeds and watching me with disdain. 'She's yours,' said the king. 'Do her proud.'

I met his eyes. I didn't want to kill that valiant beast fighting for her life; my heart resisted even as I took up my bow and fitted the arrow. I waited until the doe rose on her hindquarters to evade a lunging dog. I closed my eyes, let the arrow fly. I heard the men gasp. The taut silence was broken by the houndsmen shouting at the dogs to stay put; when I opened my eyes I saw the doe dead on the ground, my arrow protruding from her chest.

I turned to François, who gestured for me to dismount. Cutting off the doe's right ear, he took its bleeding edge and drew it down my cheek, the blood still hot. He handed me the ear. 'Though you pitied her,' he said, 'you did not hesitate. That is the way of life, *ma petite*. Sometimes we must strike first, before we are struck in turn.'

He turned to his men with an ebullient laugh. 'My daughter-in-law has brought me pride this day! She hunts as well as any man, and better, I think, than many of you.'

As the men returned his laughter with halfhearted enthusiasm, I glowed. That day, I rode back to the château with the king at my side, the doe's blood dry on my face and her ear weighting my belt pouch. By the time I arrived, the court had gathered in the courtyard. I smiled when I glimpsed the disbelief on the ladies' faces as they saw me riding beside François with dried blood on my face; now they actually had something to talk about, though I wasn't so naïve as to believe I was any safer. While I could now ride the hunt with the king, I was still a barren wife; and after the dauphin, Henri was next in the line of succession.

I had to bear sons to secure the Valois line. If I failed, like the doe whose life I had taken today, I too could be brought down.

I therefore contrived to be seen as often as I could, hoping to gain further notice and perhaps entice one of the ever-present gossips to send word to Henri that his wife, the duchess, was becoming quite the presence at court. I cajoled Marguerite to the galleries, the halls, and the gardens, where we sat with our women arranged about us in all their decorative profusion.

After weeks without a sign of him, I felt like a fool, dressed to the teeth and looking all the more desperate for it. I'd have killed a thousand does rather than endure the ladies who paused to greet me with predatory smiles and the gentlemen with their exaggerated bows, all of whom no doubt went on to whisper behind their hands that la Medici was trying especially hard these days to appear as though she hadn't just stepped off the boat. Honorary member of the Petite Bande or not, in their eyes I was still the foreigner who'd had the luck to snare a prince – though how long I'd keep him was debatable, considering he preferred the company of his mistress.

It was then that my hatred for Diane de Poitiers took root in my heart. I had not even seen her, but if I could have I'd have poured the vial of poison Ruggieri had given me into her goblet. She had tainted my new life, turned it into something fearful, and there was nothing I could do to thwart her. One afternoon as I sat ensconced in my uncomfortable finery, a book sent to me from Florence in my hands, enduring the courtiers' barbed regards even as I feigned to be immersed in the pages, I realized I could bear no more. I came abruptly to my feet.

Marguerite turned to me. 'Catherine, are you well?' she said, even as she looked toward an approaching group of courtiers, the type she liked to engage in banter to prove her intellectual superiority.

'I'm restless, is all. I think I'll walk awhile.'

She moved to accompany me; I stopped her. 'You mustn't disappoint your friends. They'll cry to heaven if you don't stay and humiliate them with your knowledge.'

She smiled. 'Are you sure you'll –'

'Naturally,' I said before she could say anything else, and I went down the gallery to the far doors, moving as fast as I could in my stiff brocade.

As soon as I was out of sight, I ripped the crescent hood laden with seed pearls from my head, tore off my starched ruff, and threw them aside, not caring that they'd cost a good sum. I undid the silver-tipped laces at my collar and shook out my hair from its confining net, letting it tumble over my shoulders. Tucking my book into my pocket, I made for the terrace.

Peace. Peace and quiet was all I wanted right now, my uncertain future be damned.

Skirting the artificial lake, I moved into the unkempt part of the palace grounds, where the manicured knot gardens faded into a dishevelment of chestnuts, willows, and ferns. There were meandering paths here, dappled with sunlight. I heard birdsong, the rustle of leaves; I saw the fiery dart of a startled fox. I'd almost forgotten how beautiful France was outside the glittering artificiality of the court.

I'd explored this area once before with Marguerite and now sought a clearing we'd found, where the grass grew thick. I thought I'd lie there awhile and read. But I must have taken a wrong turn somewhere, because I found myself in a copse of silver beech. Fontainebleau wasn't surrounded by walls; I could get lost in the woodlands, and so I paused.

It was then I espied a figure moving ahead of me among the trees.

He wore a cream-colored doublet and leather breeches, with riding boots that reached to his thighs. His head was uncovered, his thick tawny hair ruffled as he moved with his chin down, hands clasped behind his back. He seemed so engrossed in thought that I started to step back, lest I disturb him. A twig cracked underfoot, unnaturally loud in the silence.

The man froze. He turned. We stared for a long moment at each other before he bowed. My heart gave a pleasant start. It was the constable's eldest nephew, Gaspard de Coligny.

We walked toward each other. Though I hadn't seen him since my nuptials, I remembered him well and it crossed my mind that our chance encounter might be misinterpreted if witnessed by others, given the court's licentiousness. I shrugged. Who would see us here? And if they did, perhaps it would reach Henri's ears and rouse his pride, as even he, for all his neglect of me, wouldn't want the court saying his wife had taken to walking alone with other men.

'Forgive me if I startled Your Highness,' he said. His voice was deep but low, his simple apparel and faint growth of beard a refreshing lack of vanity rarely seen at court.

'Oh, not at all,' I replied, and to my ears I sounded a little breathless.

'I'm glad of you. I thought I was lost.' As I met his piercing pale blue eyes, I was aware of my loose hair, the open chemise at my throat. I felt heat rise in my cheeks. 'I was beginning to think I might end up lost in the forest,' I added, with a laugh. 'I fear I've turned myself quite around.'

His smile was gentle. 'You're a few steps away from the formal gardens. There's little forest left on this side of the château. Most of it was destroyed to build His Majesty's great gallery.'

'Where his Italian paintings hang? Oh, that's a pity – though it is a beautiful gallery.'

'It is,' he said, but I sensed he did not share the king's passion for art. The silence that settled between us was not awkward. Rather, I found his presence comforting, as if we'd known each other a long time and didn't require meaningless chatter. At length, he said, 'Whenever I come to court, I try to come here, to think. I've just arrived and already I find the noise and crowds of people distracting. I'm not used to it.'

It was true that I hadn't seen him at court at all. 'Do you not come often?'

He shook his head. 'Since my father died, I've too many obligations at my estate in Châtillon. But my uncle, the constable, would like nothing better if I took up residence here, of course, to further the family name, as sons of noblemen should.'

'I was sorry to hear of your father's passing,' I said.

He inclined his head. 'Thank you. He was a good father. I still miss him.'

'You're lucky to have known him,' I said. 'My parents died within a week of my birth. I never had a chance to feel their love for me.'

In the resulting quiet, I looked away. What had possessed me to say something so intimate to someone I scarcely knew, for all his kindness?

He said softly, 'I've heard of your trials in Italy. You are brave indeed to have gone through so much at so young an age. It cannot have been easy to then leave everything you've known behind for a foreign land.'

I turned back to him. 'Am I that obvious?'

'To those who care to look.' He smiled again. 'Your Highness needn't worry. It seems to me that very few at this court notice much beyond their own self-interests.'

'Catherine,' I said. 'Please, call me Catherine.'

'I'm honored.' He held out his arm. 'Would you let me accompany you to the gardens?'

I set my hand on his arm. I felt taut muscles under his sleeve, and a soothing gratitude came over me as he led us toward the château. Our heels rustled dying leaves on the loam; he pointed out a vivid red cardinal and I saw in his intent gaze that he was a man who revered nature. I wanted to share something with him and withdrew the book from my pocket.

'I received it from Florence last week,' I told him. 'Isn't the binding exquisite? No one binds books as they do in my native city. This is a special edition, made for my family.'

He took the slim red calfskin and gilt-folio volume. The careful way he opened the cover suggested his intellect. I was surprised, however, when he said, 'I know this book. It was written for your great-grandfather, Lorenzo the Magnificent.'

'It was! Machiavelli dedicated it to him. This version was bound and then sent by the merchant guild as a gift. How did you know?'

'*The Prince* is famous even here in France. I've read it several times.' He met my eyes. '"From this arises an argument: whether it is better to be loved than feared. I reply that one should like to be both one and the other; but since it is difficult to join them together, it is much safer to be feared than loved when one of the two must be lacking."'

'You quote from memory,' I marveled.

'Machiavelli's treatise is considered one of the most elucidating on how men in power ought to behave.' He handed me the book. 'Do you understand what he says?'

I nodded. 'I think so. His Majesty recently said something similar. He told me, "It is the way of life. Sometimes we must strike first, before we are struck in turn." But I think it's always better to find compromise or, as Machiavelli would say, to be loved.'

'Indeed.' His voice turned somber. 'That is wisdom. I wish His Majesty thought the same of those in his realm who most merit his regard.'

The air took on a chill. Around us, the trees began to thin, giving way to manicured paths and decorative herb patches. 'I fear I don't quite know what you mean,' I said, unsure I should be discussing the king, my father-in-law, in this manner with him.

He frowned. 'Have you heard of the protests in Paris?'

'No. The court hasn't been to Paris yet. I've heard the king doesn't like to go.'

'Yes, he would. You see, his Huguenot subjects are demanding the right to be heard before his Council because the authorities have been arresting them for importing forbidden books.'

'Huguenots?' I echoed. I had heard only a brief mention of them in passing at court.

'Yes. Protestants, followers of Jean Calvin. Up till now His Majesty has chosen to ignore their existence. But I fear a time fast approaches when he'll have to take them into account.'

I paused, my fingers tightening about my book. 'You speak of heretics.' A ripple of disquiet went through me. I had not expected our conversation to take such a turn. Until now, the most controversial subject I'd faced was my husband's attachment to his mistress, and I suddenly felt as though I'd dwelled in perfumed oblivion to the dark currents running beneath my feet.

'Not everyone in France considers them as such,' he said. He paused, with a wry laugh. 'If my uncle heard me say that, he'd flay me alive.'

'Are you . . . ?' I wondered what I'd do if he said he was. I'd never met a heretic before. All I'd heard about them was that they were ravening madmen who spat on our statues and desecrated our churches, and caused no end of trouble for Rome. I'd been a Catholic all my life, but I wasn't sure I should hate these so-called heretics as much as I'd been told. I'd had better occasion than most to know that the Church of Rome was not clean of sin.

'I am not,' he said, his voice infused with a genuine fervor that marked him even more apart than his appearance. 'But we are each created in God's image and must be allowed to seek our path to Him in our own way.'

'The church says we have only one way to God,' I said. 'Would you argue with Rome itself?'

'Rome does not understand the world anymore; it clings to customs that are dying.' He looked intently at me. 'Do you think these people lack souls? Do you think we have the right to persecute them because they choose another way to worship?'

His words stirred something in me. In truth, I hadn't given any of this much thought. 'The church claims animals do not have souls,' I said carefully. 'The same is said for heretics.'

'Then you've not seen a man burn. If you did, you would not doubt he has a soul.' He paused. 'I trust I haven't offended. I felt that as you asked, I should speak the truth.'

'No, no. I am grateful. It's been an elucidating talk.'

He smiled. 'And, I hope, one of many to come. Though I suggest we keep it between us. Most people at court would not understand what we've discussed.'

'Of course.' I took his arm again, enjoying the fact that we had a secret. We moved into the formal gardens, where the flash of jewels and vibrant colors by the fountains alerted me that the court had spilled outdoors for their evening promenade. From amid the gallants and ladies, Marguerite caught sight of me and moved quickly to us. 'Catherine, where have you been? I was worried. You said you were going for a walk.'

Coligny bowed. 'Her Highness and I happened upon each other and she asked that I accompany her. I apologize if we caused any concern.'

Marguerite gave him a sharp glance. 'We owe you our gratitude, then.'

I saw she was perturbed, a rarity for her, and held out my hand to Coligny. 'Thank you, my lord. I hope we'll have occasion to meet again soon.'

Coligny raised my hand to his lips. His kiss was cool, his slight beard prickling my skin.

Marguerite led me away. 'You were with him for over an hour! I'd been looking for you everywhere! There's a banquet tonight. Come, we mustn't be late.'

For the first time, I barely listened to her. Coligny had made me forget my troubles, awoken my mind to wider concerns. I wanted to speak with him more, to lose myself in his profundity, and I glanced over my shoulder. He stood still, a solitary figure among the courtiers. I felt an abrupt emptiness, almost like a loss, and wondered if I would ever see him again.

That night as we devoured platter after platter, I watched François brooding on his throne. The courtiers frolicked, dancing and drinking and sharing petty gossip, all dressed in their glittering finery, all oblivious to anything but their immediate pleasure.

Usually François would be among them, exchanging quips and flirting, the duchess at his side, but tonight he didn't seem to see them, and Coligny's words went through my mind. Wondering if the situation in Paris had worsened, I scoured the court as if I might somehow spy one of the Huguenots among them. What did they look like? Could I mark them by their bearing, their dress? I imagined them all in black, brandishing their forbidden books as they confronted the king. If they were so prevalent in Paris, surely there must be some among us. I was fascinated by the thought, eager to lay eyes on these unseen people whose existence had alerted me to the fact that not all was wealth and indolence in this realm I called home.

Then I saw my husband, clad in a mud-stained doublet and boots, walking toward the dais where the king sat nearby. I heard him say, 'Your Majesty wanted to see me?'

François's face twisted. 'How dare you come into my presence stinking of horse sweat?' he yelled. 'Go! Wash yourself and see to your wife. By God, see to her this very night or I'll not be responsible for my actions.'

All thoughts of heretics fled my head. I felt as if the very eaves crashed down around me as Henri shot me an accusatory look and marched away. The duchess clucked her tongue. I caught her eye; she gave an apologetic shrug. The courtiers began to whisper; I heard a ribald mocking laugh ring out, sensed all eyes upon me. At the first opportunity, I begged leave to retire.

That night, for the first time since Marseilles, Henri came to my rooms. It was the hour I'd worked so hard to achieve, yet when he walked in, wearing a white robe that emphasized his pallor, his black hair falling in a stiff wave to his collar, I could barely say a word.

He stared at me. 'Did you tell him?'

I shook my head. 'No. But His Majesty, he –'

'He can go to the devil. Lie down. It's time we put an end to this insulting affair.'

I turned to the bed and lay down. I was terrified. Here he was at long last, to do what our marriage required of him. It was the moment I'd longed for, the reason I had changed my entire appearance, and still I had to fight the urge to look away as he unfastened his robe, exposing his erect organ. 'Lift it up,' he said, pointing to my nightdress, and I did, feeling my stomach tighten with cold and fear. He knelt between my legs, thrust them apart. Without a word he pushed himself inside me. I clamped my lips against a sudden searing pain. I opened my legs wider, trying to envision the lovers by the lake, to seek some kind of pleasure in this forced sterile act, in the feel of his hard body grinding against mine.

The pain was almost unbearable. I couldn't believe anyone would willingly subject themselves to it as he pumped harder, faster, before he gasped and went still. Even as I lay spread-eagled and stunned, feeling something warm and sticky seeping out of me, he fastened his robe and walked out, banging the door shut behind him.

Sitting up, I forced myself to look. His whitish seed intermingled with my blood. I felt disgusting, used. I never wanted anything like this to happen to me again.

But as I staggered to my feet and walked, aching, to the wash basin, I knew I had no choice. His seed must stay inside me; Lucrezia had told me so. If it didn't, I'd never bear a child.

Despite all my efforts and pain, I had succeeded in surrendering my virginity.

Nothing more.

8

In autumn, we departed for the Palace of St. Germain on the outskirts of Paris. Built in red brick, with the king's emblem of the salamander in flames adorning its exterior in stone escutcheons, it was smaller and more fortified than Fontainebleau and I understood why François found it less to his taste than his airy Loire château. I looked forward to visiting the city. I'd heard much of Paris and its marvels, famed for the luxuries that merchants brought from all over the world. Hoping to find a sword of Toledo steel to give François for Christmas, I voiced to the princesses my idea of venturing out to the marketplace.

Madeleine sighed. 'Papa has forbidden us to leave the palace. He says Paris isn't safe.'

'Bah,' scoffed Marguerite. 'Papa is just angry because he has to meet with his Council all day, instead of going hunting or building something. I think it's a splendid idea. We can disguise ourselves and be back here before anyone knows it.'

'Why not ask the merchants to visit us, instead?' said Madeleine. 'They'll bring their best wares and we won't have to trudge through mud and muck like charwomen.'

Marguerite rolled her eyes. 'Because they'll triple their prices. Not to mention everyone at court will know Catherine bought a sword for Papa before she's even paid for it.'

Madeleine seemed to shrink into herself. 'Well, I couldn't. Anything might happen.'

'Then stay here. But don't you dare think of telling on us!'

I made my plans with Marguerite, and on the appointed morning we attended our lessons as usual. Afterward, during the hour when we played music or board games, we would sneak off.

I couldn't concentrate as the tutor droned on, Marguerite watching me over her book, hard-pressed to stifle her giggles. We'd stashed cloaks, walking shoes, and a purse of coins in the window seat. Everything was ready for our adventure.

The door opened and the duchesse d'Étampes swept in. The tutor yelped. As the princesses and I came to our feet, the duchess said, 'His Majesty has ordered everyone to retire to their rooms. The palace is under guard. No one is to enter or leave until further notice.'

Though her voice seemed calm enough, I'd never seen her so pale. We gathered our belongings and made to leave; at the door, she detained me. 'Not you, Catherine,' she said. 'The king would see you at once in his apartments.'

Madeleine and Marguerite shot fearful glances at me; it was then that I started to feel afraid. What had happened, that the king would close up his palace and ask for me?

As Madame d'Étampes and I walked down the corridors toward the royal chambers, we passed whispering courtiers huddled in the alcoves. None met my eyes. My fear spiraled.

'Madame,' I quavered, 'have I done something wrong?' I wondered if this had something to do with my marriage, if François had wearied of Henri's disdain and decided to set me aside. I had lived with the fear of being sent away for months now and I couldn't breathe as she reached into her gown and removed a crumpled paper that reeked of cheap ink.

On it, I read: *The Abuses of the Papal Mass, devised contrary to the Supper of Jesus Christ: The Church of Rome and its priests are idolatrous vermin, who renounce Our Savior's doctrines. Burn your pagan idols and not those who revere the truth of our Lord.*

I looked up at her. She grimaced. 'That is a Huguenot tract. They dared to set these pamphlets about the palace last night, while everyone slept. They must have bribed servants who share their heresy; François found them even in his private rooms. He is furious. Last week, he had to order twenty-four of these Huguenots arrested after they were caught printing copies of Jean Calvin's *Institutes*. It's why we came to this pesthole of a city:

François has to set an example that heresy will not be tolerated in France.'

So, it was as Coligny had said: François had been forced to acknowledge what he'd tried for so long to ignore. Obviously there were Huguenots in court; I had thought to mark them by their appearance, but they must blend in as well as anyone else, secretive and plentiful enough to have seen these pamphlets distributed. I still didn't know what to feel about them, but I was sure that I didn't want them upsetting the king or turning the realm upside down with their credo.

'They've forced his hand,' the duchess went on. 'Poor man, he's always preferred to act as if this realm is beholden in its entirety to Rome and Protestants don't exist.' She sighed. 'It's so unpleasant. I don't see what they think they'll achieve by this defiance. It's not as if their Lutheran counterparts in the Low Countries fare any better. From the Netherlands to Germany, the Hapsburg domains are riddled with chaos – and all over this so-called New Religion.'

'But this is just a pamphlet,' I found myself saying. 'It's paper and ink. His Majesty must know it can do no harm –'

She leaned to me, cutting off my words. 'Catherine, you must not think to interfere. François needs time for his temper to cool. And you've more important matters to consider.' She paused, searching my eyes. 'Word has come that His Holiness your uncle has died.'

I heard the news in silence. So, Papa Clement was dead. I realized I should have felt sad, as he had been the sole remaining link with my past, but all I felt was relief. I was free now. I would never again have to endure his intrigues or influence over me. At last I could be a Frenchwoman, embrace with all my heart and soul the identity I had forged for myself.

Then I heard her say, 'My dear, I know how wretched you must feel. Your uncle is gone and you've been left a pauper, without your dowry.'

'My dowry,' I echoed, startled. 'But wasn't it granted to the king upon my marriage?'

'No, your uncle promised much but he never actually signed the document giving François the superior claim to Milan.' She sighed. 'I wish I could help you, but I'm afraid this is something you must do on your own. Only you can save yourself now.'

I raised my eyes to her. The hour I had dreaded was upon me and I must face it. I thought of the siege in Florence, of how I'd fought to stay alive even after I was torn from my aunt and how I had survived. I could survive this too. Yet, though I told myself this, I trembled as the duchess led me in silence down the corridors to the double oak doors of François's private apartments.

I entered his study. The curtains were drawn, giving the room a murky feel; but I could tell even in the shadows where he stood that he was haggard, the toll of the last weeks etched on his face. He motioned to a chair. 'Sit, my child.' Before I knew what I was doing, I said quietly, 'I know my uncle has played Your Majesty false. I can offer no excuse for his behavior nor atone for the grievous damage he has done. I beg your forgiveness that my family's treachery has tainted the great trust you have given me.'

He stood quiet, looking at me. Then he came across the room and took my chin in his hand. He lifted my face to his, staring into my eyes. 'Many at court say I took you naked as a babe, that in exchange for the promises of a Medici liar I have saddled my son with a barren mare.'

His words were uttered without rancor, a mere statement of fact, and yet they plunged through me like nails. I did not flinch. I met his gaze and said, 'They are wrong. While you may have indeed taken me in naked as the day I was born, the love I bear for you is worth a thousand treasures. I would die before I would ever see you or France harmed.'

He did not move for a long moment. Then a chuckle sounded low in his throat. 'Yes, I know that were it up to you, you'd have handed all of Italy to me on a plate.'

'Yes,' I replied. 'I would. But as I cannot, I swear to you I will not prove your belief in me wrong. Come what may, I *will* bear you grandsons.'

A slow smile spread over his pale lips. He reached out to caress

my cheek and there was something in the way he moved closer
to me, in the way his fingers grazed my skin and his eyes turned
heavy and moist, that went right through me like a tiny bolt of
flame.

'Ah, my child,' he murmured. 'We could have enjoyed each
other once. How cruel a trickster is fate that we should be brought
together now, when I find myself in the winter of my decline and
you are still budding into your first spring.'

I didn't avert my eyes. I looked at his fallen skin, at the coarse
white hair threading his beard, and then I too reached up and
laid my hand on his cheek. 'Trickster or not,' I said gently, 'not
even fate could keep us apart. I am here now, my king. And here
is where I wish to stay.'

He enfolded me in his arms. 'Ah, my Catherine, your uncle
used us both cruelly, but you are right: at least he brought us
together. I'd not exchange you for anything, no, not even for
Milan.' He chuckled again under his breath. 'God spare me such
a choice.' He drew back. 'You needn't fear. As long as I am alive,
you will always have a place here.'

I melted against his chest. 'I will not forget my promise,' I said,
and he replied, 'I know. There are many ways to obtain our
desires, *ma petite*. Remember that, for it will serve you well.'

Shortly before Lent, I was overjoyed by the arrival of the Ruggieri
brothers, who had sent me a letter begging my help to escape
from Florence. I'd sent them money for their passage and a safe
conduct, and I greeted them in my apartments with open arms,
surrounded by my Italians. Our mutual cries and embraces, tears,
and eager questions revealed my household's homesickness, the
arrival of fellow countrymen always cause for celebration.

Eighteen-year-old Carlo had become a robust youth, tough-
ened by his trials. He appeared far healthier than Cosimo, now
thirteen but appearing much younger, and so weakened by the
voyage that after he drank a cup of broth, he curled on my bed
in my chamber and fell asleep.

My ladies made a supper from the Tuscan cheese, Sienna

olives, and wine the Ruggieris had brought as gifts. As we ate, I asked Carlo about Florence.

'Madama, the Florentines speak highly of you. They say you have redeemed the Medici name by your dignity and your position here in France.'

His words warmed my heart. Though I had nothing left there, I relished the thought that Italy still remembered me. Then I saw Carlo lower his eyes and I said softly, 'You're not telling me something. What is it? You can confide in me.'

'It's Cosimo. He has suffered greatly. He was grief-stricken when Papa fell ill during the siege and died. I thought he'd never recover.'

I nodded sadly, remembering the last time I'd seen the old Maestro in his attic study, surrounded by the paraphernalia of his calling. His death severed another link with my past, and my hand lifted to my chest, where, under my chemise, hung the little vial he'd given me.

Carlo went on: 'The authorities came and confiscated our house; they took everything. We were forced to beg in the streets until one of the convents took pity on us. The sisters let us tend their gardens and helped us send our letter to you.' He sighed. 'We've the clothing on our backs and Papa's scrolls. Cosimo carried them everywhere. Papa told him he had a gift. I never paid much attention to such things. What I want is to sail the seas, not be another Jew peddling trinkets. But Cosimo wants to learn. Still, he can't serve you in any real capacity –'

'Carlo!'

We looked up. Cosimo hovered in the doorway wrapped in one of my robes, his brown hair spiked about his face. He glared. 'I can serve her. I know enough to earn my keep.'

'Cosimo, she's a French princess now. She has herbalists and physics by the dozens.'

'Wait.' I beckoned Cosimo. He dragged his feet on the carpet, pouting, like the dirty child he'd been when I'd last seen him. I poured wine, served him a plate. He sat on the floor and ate with the greed of one who would never forget hunger. When he finished, I said, 'Tell me your plan.'

'I can serve you as a physic,' he said, with another scowl at
Carlo. 'I can make perfumes and lotions and medicinal drafts. I
know about herbs, and what I don't know I can learn.'

'Indeed?' I was amused by his earnestness. 'It so happens that
I lack a skilled physic, but there is no one at court I can apprentice
you to.'

Cosimo rose without a word and went back into the bedchamber. When he came out, he carried a bundle of bleached leather
tied at both ends. He pushed my platter aside and set the bundle
before me, untying it to reveal reams of parchment covered in
strange writing and symbols.

His eyes met mine. 'These were Papa's. I've been studying
them for months, every spare hour I could find. There are mysteries inscribed here, knowledge of the occult and divine. I can learn
everything I need. I don't need anything else.'

The chamber was plunged into a quiet so intense, I heard
nothing except the quickening of my heart. I recalled the Maestro's
words: *You will fulfill your destiny. It may not be the destiny you
want, but fulfill it you will.* Carlo arched his brow at me, oblivious.
When I looked at Cosimo, I saw that he knew. His power enveloped us in a way no one else could feel.

'I can help you,' I heard him say, though his lips didn't move.
'I can make your husband fall in love with you.'

The intimacy dissipated. I repressed the urge to rub my arms,
my skin goose-pimpling with a stir of my own gift. Cosimo had
it, as well. But whereas I'd neglected it, he'd set his entire being
to mastering it. What might I accomplish with him at my side?
If we worked together, how easy might it be to lure Henri to my
bed again so I could conceive a child? I wasn't looking forward
to enduring that humiliating act again but I must bear children,
lest the court deem me barren.

Cosimo turned away, an emaciated adolescent without a single
mark that set him apart. As he gathered the parchments, Carlo
said, 'Did he do it? Did he try to cloud my lady's mind?'

'Yes,' I said, surprised that he had in fact noticed. 'How did
you know?'

'He does it all the time. He should be an actor, not an herbalist.'

'He's exceptional. I'll make him my personal astrologer and buy him a house in Paris where he can devote himself to learning.' I looked at Cosimo. He returned my stare, his features smudged with grime. Then I said to Carlo, 'And you, my friend, will serve in the navy under His Majesty's banner. I myself ' – I lifted my voice as Carlo seized my hand to bathe it in kisses – 'will speak to the king tomorrow and ask him to grant you a post.'

After that, I went to bed for a nap. Yet even from behind the walls and locked doors, I sensed Cosimo reaching for me. The sensation was feral, dangerous, and oh so beguiling.

I secured Carlo a post in the king's navy and had Birago discreetly purchase a house by the Seine with a private quay for Cosimo.

I was seventeen years old. I had survived my first crisis in France. No one save Birago and Lucrezia knew that I stole away to visit Cosimo. I applied the perfumes and lotions he assured me would attract my husband and read books on herb lore, so I could teach myself how to crush leaves and petals into fragrant paste, which I then cooked in scented oil over a brazier.

Marguerite volunteered to be my assistant. We spent hours testing lumpy lotions and foul perfumes, the windows flung open to release the smoke from the brazier, our eyes tearing as we hunched over the pot. We scalded, exfoliated, and chaffed our faces and throats more times than I care to count, Marguerite lathering my mixtures on me until they started to burn and she raced about wetting cloths, trying to remove the offending substance before I burst into flame. She didn't know that each time we failed to discover the aphrodisiac I sought, I almost screamed in frustration. She held my hands while my skin blistered and I muttered that I'd have to wear another high-necked gown for the rest of the week. Then she'd say, 'Let's try again, only this time add more lavender,' and we'd hunch over the pot once more.

How could I have known no amount of tincture of rose would conjure the love I craved?

After weeks of wasted experiments, I sat out the evening banquet in morose silence, a ruffled collar covering my most recent rash. The court cavorted, their ribald laughter ringing in my ears; I envied their conceits, their foolish rivalries and vanities, for at that moment all I could envision was a future devoid of all comfort. I wanted the feast to end so I could retire to my rooms and shout at the walls.

Then the hall fell silent. Heads inclined to heads; a single gasp issued and died. I froze.

Henri appeared at the head of the staircase leading into the hall, clad in a dramatic black and silver costume. I stared at the garters encircling his muscular thighs, looked up past his codpiece to his chest, where he wore a jeweled brooch of a crescent moon, entwined with a bow.

The king and the duchess were making their rounds. François paused when he saw his son, his face registering surprise that for once Henri dressed as befitted the occasion. My heart started to pound; I sensed disaster looming, like a mass of darkness gathering at the back of my eyes. I fumbled for my goblet and tipped it over. I leapt up, yanking my skirts from the dripping mess.

At that moment, a woman stepped from the shadows behind Henri. Together, they walked down the stairs into the hall, not touching, yet so in tune they seemed to move as one.

She glided as if her feet didn't touch the ground, her silver-ash hair swept from her narrow brow, her slim figure set off to perfection by a dramatic gown of black and white that echoed Henri's ensemble. She wore no jewels save for the same crescent symbol on her breast, drawing every courtier's stare as she came to stand beside my husband.

I stared at her, horrified. She was like a marble statue come to life, a mature woman at the height of her powers, all too aware of her impact on others. I'd imagined a plump, affectionate governess; a wanton with smeared lips and dyed hair; and as if she could hear my thoughts she raised her eyes to me. A smile curved her mouth. It was a smile unlike any I'd seen, mocking and triumphant, exposing that dark place in my soul where fear and envy reigned.

Clutching my skirts, I fled from the hall. I didn't stop running until I crashed into my apartments, causing my ladies to yelp and start from their stools.

Lucrezia came to me. 'My lady, what is it? You look as though you've seen a ghost.'

'That . . . that woman. Diane de Poitiers. She is here, in the hall.' And as I uttered her name, I thought the vile taste of it would stay with me forever. '*Dio Mio,* she's not old. She's not ugly.' I pressed my hands on my dressing table, saw my long fingers with their painted nails, laden with rings. Looking up into the polished glass, the face staring back at me was like a stranger's – an overblown Italian in a Frenchwoman's paint, who lived on royal sufferance.

'Go,' I whispered. 'All of you. Leave me.'

Little Anna-Maria hastened out. Lucrezia stayed put. 'You mustn't let her do this to you. You are Catherine de Medici, duchesse d'Orléans. Who is she but your husband's whore?'

I drew a shuddering breath, willing myself to take hold of my fury. 'Yes,' I heard myself say in a voice that didn't sound like my own. 'Who is she, eh? A nobody! The widow of a court functionary, an exgoverness. My great-grandfather was Lorenzo de Medici, overlord of Florence; my family has sat on the throne of St. Peter.'

I turned to Lucrezia. 'And yet she dares show her face at this court; she dares walk into the hall with my husband at her side and look upon me as if I were her servant.'

'Perhaps she is afraid. Perhaps she realizes now how much she could lose.'

'Afraid?' I let out a burst of acid laughter. 'Of what? *Me?* '

'Yes. You are his wife; one day you will bear him sons. She has nothing to offer him save her body and she knows that cannot last forever. She may look young but she isn't, and she depends on his fidelity. A woman like her can be easily discarded. It happens every day.'

I paused. I hadn't seen it like that before. The woman I'd seen must be already in her forties; after all she had borne children, been widowed. She also must know I held the king's affection; that despite my lack of issue François refused to send me away. Was this why she'd come out in the open, dressed in matching colors with Henri like some knight and lady of lore? Had she finally realized that if she did not concede something, she could lose everything?

'That's it,' I breathed. 'The king summoned Henri and she came with him. She knows Henri cannot evade his duty anymore, not even for her. She had no other choice.' I waved my hand. 'Quick, help me change. He'll be here soon.'

Lucrezia divested me of my gown and helped me into my nightdress. While she sat vigil in the adjoining room, I pushed a brush through my coiffure until my hair tumbled loose, thick with curls, and long enough to sit on. Opening my robe, I cupped my breasts, gauging their heft, teasing my cinnamon-colored nipples erect. I surveyed my body as I might a commodity, marking the fine length of my legs, my calves toned from riding, my ankles strong but not too thick, my thighs wide and well shaped.

I smiled at my reflection. I might not be statuesque like her, made of marble and satin; but I was hardy and young. She clung to her youth, while mine stretched before me like a fertile field.

A tap came at the door. I tied the tassels of my robe and summoned an expectant smile when Henri stepped in. He paused, as though he wasn't sure he would be welcomed.

'Husband, this is an unexpected pleasure.' I slowly walked to my sideboard and the decanter of wine. He accepted the goblet I gave him with an awkwardness that made me want to chuckle.

He cleared his throat. 'We must speak,' he began, and I nodded, sitting in my chair. He regarded me for a long moment before he blurted, 'My father sent word to me. He demands we have a child. He says it is imperative, given my brother the dauphin's health.'

I did not betray my surprise. Though he was here as I'd hoped,

I hadn't known about the dauphin, who suffered from weak lungs like Madeleine. He was so invisible at court, keeping to his own household and pastimes, I sometimes forgot he even existed.

Henri paced my chamber, his hand clutching the goblet. 'My father's physicians do not think my brother will live much longer, so you and I must ensure the succession.' He took a long gulp of his goblet, turned to the decanter to refill it. I saw his hand was trembling.

I sat still, hiding my shock. If the dauphin died, Henri would become the king's heir. One day, *we* would be king and queen. It made my mind reel. I'd never looked that far ahead. Forever mired in safeguarding my present, I'd never stopped to consider the reasons behind François's stalwart protection of me. Did he see *me* as France's future queen?

I had just moved out of my insular existence into a vast unknown.

I heard Henri speak and pulled myself to attention to find him before me. 'I promise to be gentler this time,' he said, and I met his eyes. He tried to smile, and I realized he was ashamed. He had treated me cruelly the last time on purpose, as a punishment.

I rose and went into my bedchamber. Even if it hurt, I told myself, it would not last long. And this time I would get with child and prove myself worthy. Still, as I pulled back my sheets I felt fear and knew it had nothing to do with what he might do. What if it wasn't his fault? What if everything the court said behind my back turned out to be true?

What if I was barren?

Lucrezia had slipped in through the side door at some point to prepare the room. A candle burned by the bed; the curtains were drawn back. Shadows played over the ceiling. As I heard the rustle of clothing being discarded behind me, my hands shook and I fumbled at my robe.

'Catherine.' His mouth was at my ear. He took me by the shoulders, turned me to face him. He towered over me, his broad chest covered with dark hair, his arms and legs heavy with muscle. He wore only his braies. I could see his erection under the thin linen.

Without warning heat flared in me. I tried to suppress it. I didn't want to desire a man who saw me only as a vessel for his seed; I didn't want to love him. I tried to rekindle the fury and hatred I'd felt when I saw him with his whore, to shore up the contempt that protected me from the hurts he 'd inflicted. But none of it mattered as he leaned me back onto the bed and I watched, tremulous, as he drew my nightdress past my breasts, gradually revealing my nakedness. 'You are beautiful,' he murmured, as if he hadn't expected it, and he met my eyes. For the first time in our marriage, I felt he saw me as I was, not as the wife he never wanted, and his hands dropped quickly to the lacings of his braies, as if he was impatient to free himself.

He seemed impossibly large. Yet he entered me with a care that filled my eyes with tears and made me grateful for the flickering light that half hid my face.

This time, I almost cried out at the simultaneous pain and pleasure of it, his organ filling me until my entire existence became the sensation of him moving inside me, gathering momentum, his breath coming fast and low in my face as I arched my hips to meet his thrusts and my hands caressed his chest, tangling in the coarse hair.

A shudder went through him. I felt him enlarge even more and I whispered his name. He went still, his entire body taut as if he fought to keep something back, and then he gasped and plunged deeper, spearing me with a heat that spiraled into a thousand dancing circles, until I too was crying out, kneading him with my hands, my legs clasped tight about his waist.

He fell to my side, panting. I clenched my muscles, willing his seed to take root. As I turned to him, my entire body throbbing, he rose from the bed. I heard him gather his clothes and pull on his hose and doublet with a haste that filled me with shame.

I whispered, 'Stay with me tonight.'

And he replied quietly, 'I cannot.'

I reared up. 'Why? Was I not pleasing to you?'

He averted his eyes. 'You . . . you were. You are. But I am expected elsewhere.'

I couldn't stop the anger from tainting my voice. 'It's that woman, isn't it? You're leaving me for her. Does she mean so much that you'd humiliate me before the entire court?'

'She means everything.' He met my stare, his expression drawn, almost sad. 'I don't mean to hurt you. But you must accept what I can and cannot give. Once you have a child, you will not care so much anymore. You will have our son to love instead.'

I dropped my hands to my belly, feeling the pain of his words as if he'd struck me. I wanted to bellow that I would always care. I was the one who deserved his love, not that statue who held him in her thrall. But I did not, for I now realized what I'd kept even from myself, the delusion that had spurred me and kept me believing I had the power to change his heart.

If it hadn't been her, there would be another. But not me. Never me.

I turned from him. 'Go, then. Go to her.'

Without a word he left, closing the door softly behind him.

I awoke three months later to cramps. Crawling from bed, I staggered toward my privy pail, despairing that my menses had returned. My appetite had been ravenous of late, and I'd secretly begun to hope I might be with child, as my previous menses had been sporadic, not nearly as strong as before. But as Lucrezia rushed in to assist me, I felt my belly twist in a vicious knot and a viscous gush of blood splattered under my gown. I froze, gazing in horror at the clotted mess at my feet. Then my legs gave way and, with a stifled gasp, I crumpled to my knees.

Lucrezia replaced my bloodied nightdress with my robe and guided me to my chair. I moaned, hugging my midriff, rocking back and forth. 'No. Please God, no.'

I watched, aghast, as Lucrezia sopped up the blood and set the soiled cloths in the hearth. Only then did I whisper, 'No one can know. It would be the end of me.'

She nodded. 'I'll burn everything, including the dress. You rest now.'

'How can I rest?' My entire body started to tremble. 'I'll never be able to rest again. I've lost his child. What will I do now? How can I survive?'

'You will.' She fixed me with her stare. 'You are young. Many women lose their first one. He came to you before and he will again. He needs a son as much as you do.'

My eyes filled with tears as she stoked the embers, adding extra wood to build a fire that would turn the evidence of my womb's failure into ashes.

Two days later, the dauphin died.

9

At court, we donned white. Seated with the princesses in the royal crypt of the Basilica of St. Denis, I watched as the dauphin's narrow coffin was lowered into the vault. Though the king's eldest son had never been well, he'd not yet reached his twentieth year and François was devastated by his loss, haggard and pale as he knelt to kiss the engraved marble that would mark his eldest son's tomb before he moved down the aisle, followed by Henri. I saw in my husband's brief hooded glance in my direction that he was overwhelmed by his elevation as his father's heir, and I felt faint at the thought that now, more than ever, the entire court would be watching me for signs of the son I must bear.

The princesses stood. I started to step aside for Madeleine, when she murmured, 'No, you must go first. You're the wife of our dauphin now.'

I looked at Marguerite; she gave a sad nod. I bowed my head and stepped forth.

As I moved down the aisle, I heard the courtiers start to whisper.

The forty days of mourning was prolonged. Deprived of entertainments with the king in seclusion, all my fears returned, so that at night I barely slept, haunted by visions of my exile. Henri did not come to my bed owing to the mourning for his brother; and we sat stiff as effigies together during our first official appearance following mourning, when King James V of Scotland came to visit France to cement the two countries' alliance by seeking a bride.

No one could have foreseen that from among the multitude of ladies proffered to him, it would be shy Madeleine who captured James's heart. It was, of course, the perfect match, and I wondered if even in his grief François had planned it, fully aware that bellicose Henry VIII of England would be enraged that his Scottish neighbor had a new French queen in his bed.

Only weeks after James's arrival we stood in Madeleine's chambers, ladies rushing about applying last-minute touches to her bridal costume. Arranging the flowing veil of her coronet, I turned her to the mirror. She peered. 'Catherine, I look so pale. Maybe I should use some of that rouge you made for me?'

'Not today,' I said. 'Brides are supposed to look pale.'

She clutched my hands. 'Isn't it strange how life can change? Look at us: Only yesterday we were in the schoolroom together. Now you're dauphine and I'm to be queen of Scotland.' She glanced again at her reflection. 'I do hope I'll make a good wife to him. My doctors say I'm better.' As she spoke, she rubbed her sleeve. I'd seen the contusions on her arm, the result of a week of bleedings prescribed by her physicians. 'But I hear winters in Scotland are harsh on the lungs,' she added, 'and mine have always been weak.'

'James has plenty of castles to keep you warm.' I pried her fingers from her forearm. 'Now, stop fretting. It's your wedding day.'

The women shrieked as François strode in, ablaze in gold brocade. 'Bad Papa,' chided Marguerite. 'It's bad luck for a man to see the bride before she enters the cathedral.'

'Bah! Bad luck for the husband, perhaps, but never for the father.' He went to Madeleine. 'Your groom waits. Are you ready, *ma chère*?'

As she hooked her arm in his, he gave me a worried glance. The death of his eldest son still showed in his face and I knew he was anxious. Scotland was infamous for its unforgiving climate and nobility; how would our sweet Madeleine fare so far from the comforts of France?

I said, 'Her Highness was just telling us how happy she is. Surely, this is one of France's most joyous occasions, Your Majesty.'

'Indeed,' he murmured, 'as joyous as your own arrival, *ma petite*.' He turned a brilliant smile to Madeleine. 'To Notre Dame!'

After weeks of festivities, we accompanied the newlyweds to Calais for their departure for Scotland. We then returned to Fontainebleau, where François collapsed without warning.

His illness created immediate consternation. The courtiers whispered that the period of celebration had taxed the king, reopening a sore on his genitals that impeded his ability to pass water. For weeks he was sequestered behind closed doors, submitting to an onslaught of panaceas that left him disoriented and frail.

I held vigil with the Petite Bande. We were refused admittance to his rooms, leaving Madame d'Étampes to pace the corridors, helpless to assist the man on whom her entire life depended. When it was announced that His Majesty was on the mend, she donned her most opulent silk and jewels and awaited his summons.

To her surprise, and mine, François called for me.

From his bed he opened fever-glazed eyes. '*Ma petite,* you've changed your scent.'

'I made it myself.' I raised my wrist to him. 'Essence of jasmine, ambergris, and rose.'

He smiled faintly. 'It's very French. When you set yourself to something, you never give up. I admire your persistence. Perhaps you'll soon succeed in giving me a grandson as well, eh?'

'Yes,' I whispered. I didn't show my fear, though I knew that with those words he had issued his warning. One day he would die and I would be left alone in a hostile court. I had to secure the Valois succession and prove myself worthy to be queen.

I held his hand as he drifted into sleep. I should have been devastated by the knowledge that this glorious wreck of a man, who'd sheltered me against all odds, approached the end of his life.

But all I could think of was the insurmountable task awaiting me.

★ ★ ★

By midsummer, François had recovered and war with the Hapsburg emperor Charles V broke out over the disputed duchy of Milan. This time, the constable, his nephew Coligny, and my husband led our offensive, while the court lodged in St. Germain, near the safety of Paris.

The first moment I found, I slipped out alone to visit Cosimo. He was overjoyed to see me and led me into his upper-story room, which he'd filled with shelves of vials, jars, and books, much as his father's study had been in Florence; from the rafters hung cages of live birds.

'My lady,' he said, bowing with exaggerated subservience, 'you honor me with your visit.'

I eyed him. 'Cosimo, you look as if you haven't eaten or seen the sun in weeks. I trust you're not shutting yourself up in here all day. You can't live by magic alone.'

As he murmured excuses, his gaunt face glowing with eagerness to please me, I wondered if I did the right thing by coming to him. He was, after all, a servant whose bills I paid. How could he understand the torments I endured? Ever since that horrible morning when I'd miscarried, despite Lucrezia's insistence that women often lost their first babe, I lived in constant fear, tormented by the thought of banishment from France for failing to give my husband an heir.

Cosimo regarded me as if he could read my thoughts. 'My lady is troubled,' he said. 'You came to me because you are afraid. You can confide in me. I would die before I betrayed you.'

I started, meeting his penetrating stare and remembering the gush of blood and tissue, the cloths and nightdress curling to cinders in my hearth. A fist closed about my heart.

'I . . . I cannot fail,' I finally whispered. 'I must have a child.'

He gave a solemn assent. 'We shall examine the portents together.' He removed a dove from one of the cages overhead and with an expert twist of his fingers snapped its neck. Setting the twitching white-feathered body on the table, he took up a dagger and disemboweled it. I winced at the smell of its intestines spilling out, at the sight of its dark blood staining his hands as he peered at its organs. After a thorough examination, he looked up at me with a smile and proclaimed, 'I see no impediment to your ability to bear children.'

Overwhelming relief weakened my knees. I sighed, leaning my hands on the table. Then I heard him add, 'The loss of one doesn't mean there will not be others.'

I went still. I lifted my gaze to his. 'You . . . you know? You saw it?'

He shrugged. 'It is my gift. I see what others cannot. And I also must tell you to be patient, my lady, for your time has not yet come.'

I let out a raw laugh. 'How much more patient can I be? I've been in France seven years and I've nothing to show for it. That woman is to blame; she knows how much I suffer and she revels in it. By all rights, she should die.' I yanked the vial on its chain from under my collar. 'I have the means in this vial your father gave me years ago. I just need the opportunity.'

He arched his brow. 'You must not. Everyone would suspect.'

'I don't care. Henri would grieve for a time and then resign himself. There'd be an end to it.'

'Or he'd heed the rumors and never touch you again. The French already think every Italian is a poisoner at heart. And whatever is in that vial might leave a trace. No, my lady. Much as you long for her death, that is not the way.'

I wanted to shout at him in frustration, not because I thought I'd ever actually poison Diane but because he had dared to point out the consequences of an act I needed to believe I could commit. In my distress over the child I'd lost, whose existence I could never reveal, I blamed her. I believed she deliberately kept Henri from my bed; in my darkest hours I almost believed she'd made an unholy pact to expel that malformed being from my womb and thus leave me beholden to her for my very survival.

'Fine,' I grumbled. 'Find another way. But do it fast. I don't have all afternoon.'

Cosimo had already moved to his shelves and was reaching for a small wooden chest. 'She is of no consequence,' he said, opening the chest. 'I'll give you six protective amulets to wear under your clothes to deflect her evil and a skin lotion to attract him. When he next comes to see you, I will send you an elixir: half for you, half for him. Above all else, do not lose hope.'

'If hope were seed,' I said, taking the items from him, 'I'd be mother to an entire nation.'

He smiled. 'One day, that is exactly who you will be.'

I applied the lotion, affixed the metal amulets to my petticoats. I straightened my hair with hot irons and ordered new gowns by the dozens, anticipating word of Henri's return from the front and plying the duchess with questions about the war's progress. It all sounded much the same as any war, with the Imperial army entrenched and our officers blasting them with cannon, and it made me impatient, for I needed Henri back at court if I was to try the elixir on him.

Then fate struck again.

Gentle Madeleine died, a victim of Scotland's harsh climate and her own tender lungs. François locked himself in his rooms and refused to see anyone. I spent my days with Marguerite, comforting her as best I could. We were in mourning again, but François had no alternative but to heed James V's request for another bride. The Scottish alliance was crucial and the Guises wasted no time in proffering their daughter, Marie. That she too could lose her life in Scotland meant nothing; here was a chance to advance familial interests. The marriage took place by proxy, and soon after, weary of a war neither could win, Charles V and François signed a treaty.

Henri was recalled home.

At Fontainebleau, I prepared to receive him. I'd been drinking my drafts on schedule and organizing my rooms for weeks. I now paced, clad in crimson and rubies, attuned to the door. I'd sent Anna-Maria out to discover his whereabouts, electing to remain out of sight during the welcoming celebrations. The last thing I wanted was to look the frantic wife, the first to throw her arms about her husband as he entered the courtyard.

Feeling my ladies watching me, as they always did when they sensed my disquiet, I slid my hand to my pocket. When I felt the tiny bottle Cosimo had sent, I smiled. He'd promised its potent blend would make Henri think only of me. I'd drunk my half this morning. All I had to do now was slip the remaining half into his wine. Prodded into action, nature would do the rest.

My women sewed. I'd been less than even-tempered since learning of Henri's return and was about to apologize when the clatter of heels reached me. I straightened in my seat.

Anna-Maria burst in. 'His Highness is coming! But I overheard in the gallery that –'

I ignored her. 'I'll hear the gossip later. Sit down. Henri must think we didn't expect him.'

'But Your Highness must –'

'Later.' I pointed to her stool. With a desperate glance at the others, she sat.

Anxiety roiled inside me. It had been eight long months since we'd last seen each other. How would he find me? Would the elixir work? Would I conceive again?

Boisterous laughter preceded a group of men. I espied Henri's close friend and companion-in-arms Francis de Guise among them. He was still too thin and tall, but now his angular features – which would have been handsome had he not carried himself with such rigidity – were marred by a raw scar that cut down his cheek and puckered the left side of his mouth into a perpetual sneer.

'My lords,' I said warmly, 'how delightful to see you at long last. Welcome home.'

As the men bowed low, Henri stepped from their midst. I almost didn't recognize him. He wore a plain brown doublet, his gaunt features half-covered by a thick beard, his eyes nested in deep shadow. In his somber regard, I found a maturity instilled by months of watching his fellow soldiers die for France. My husband had gone to war and returned forever marked by it.

'Would you care for some wine?' I asked as he gave me a brief kiss on my cheek.

'I no longer drink wine,' he replied.

I faltered. If he no longer drank wine, how would I give him the elixir? Its taste was bitter; he'd notice it in water. I searched for some reason to insist he take a goblet when I saw him lock eyes for an instant with Guise. My stomach sank as Henri returned his inscrutable gaze to me.

I reached for his hand. 'I'm so happy you're back,' I said. 'I missed you. If you like, we can sup together tonight. I've so much to tell you.'

'I'm afraid that's impossible.' He withdrew his hand. As he moved to his men, I thought he hadn't said no, hadn't said he would not come later. The elixir wouldn't spoil. I could wait.

It wasn't until they left that I remembered Anna-Maria. 'What is this news you couldn't wait to tell me?' I asked, trudging to my chair.

'It's but a rumor,' Lucrezia interposed, indicating Anna-Maria had at some point told her.

I paused. I looked at my women. I waved all of them save Lucrezia out.

'It's Henri, isn't it?' I asked her. 'Out with it. What has he done this time?' I steeled myself for the recounting of some venality with Diane. Instead, Lucrezia said, 'It seems that while at war His Highness . . . well, he committed an indiscretion. The long hours on the front . . . like any man he sought some comfort. They say she was a young peasant girl, whom he visited only a few times. It would have ended there, only now she is with child. She claims it is his.'

My hands clutched my dress; I felt a dull crunch, something wet against my thigh. The bottle of elixir in my pocket: crushed. 'Does he . . . does he acknowledge her claim?' I asked haltingly.

'Yes.' Lucrezia paused. 'I fear there's more.' She met my eyes. 'La Sénéchale has requested that if the child is a boy, it be brought to her after its birth so she can raise it.'

I thought I wouldn't be able to contain the sick feeling inside me. I waved Lucrezia out and then doubled over on my chair, my stomach heaving. Nothing came out. I tasted foulness, but it was as if my horror and disbelief had become a part of me.

I knew that now I must sacrifice everything if I was to survive.

In August 1538 the peasant woman bore a girl. She was given a stipend and allowed to keep the child, as Diane had no interest in raising a female. But while my husband's mistress may have failed to get her hands on a child of his, I was not relieved. The very fact that Henri had sired a bastard invigorated the whispers at court of my continued barrenness, as there could be no doubt now as to who was to blame for our failure.

Every day that passed pushed me closer to the inevitable. Henri did not visit my bed or even see me for days on end, and I began to suspect that Diane actively campaigned against me, to destroy the little bit of pleasure Henri and I might find in our marriage. My sole comfort and protection was the king, whose professed love for me had not changed.

In the year of my twenty-third birthday and eighth anniversary of my arrival in France, François moved to the Château of Amboise. Perched on a promontory overlooking the Loire, Amboise boasted spacious gardens and elaborate wrought-iron railings; a favored residence, François had spent years embellishing it, and here he announced a new plan he 'd hatched to wrest Milan from Charles V.

'The constable thinks I should offer my twelve-year-old niece Jeanne d'Albret, daughter of the king of Navarre and my sister Marguerite, to Charles V's heir, Philip of Spain,' he told me as we strolled in the gardens. From the far end came muted roars and the musty odor of three lions he kept caged there, a gift from the Turkish sultan that he 'd not quite known what to do with.

'In exchange,' he went on, 'Charles can deed Milan to me and Jeanne will deed Navarre to Philip, once she inherits. Charles will leap at the chance; he believes his family, the Hapsburgs, hold the superior claim to the realm, while the current rulers, the d'Albrets, are usurpers. My sister Marguerite is the king of Navarre's widow; she'll be less than pleased at the prospect of handing over her daughter to Spain, but I don't intend to actually let Charles *keep* Navarre. I just want him to think I do, so I can get Milan.' He nudged me. 'What do you say, *ma petite*? Can we hoodwink that Hapsburg serpent?'

'I don't see why not,' I said. 'It's an excellent plan and I'm sure your sister will understand.'

He sighed. 'You don't know Marguerite. We used to be close, but after she wed and moved to Navarre, she changed. Her late husband, the king of Navarre, was a Huguenot sympathizer and she's become involved with their so-called cause.' His mouth twisted; it was the first time he'd mentioned aloud the troublesome Protestant cult to me. 'She patronized that antichrist Calvin for a time; rumor has it, she's even raised her daughter as a Huguenot, God help us.' He paused. 'You can be of assistance, *ma petite*. I've asked that Jeanne visit us; perhaps you could persuade her to embrace our Catholic faith. It's not as if a girl of twelve will know any difference.'

'I'd be honored,' I replied, thinking it would also help me to be of some actual political use.

Jeanne arrived a month later. Small in stature and thin, with the elongated Valois nose and narrow almond-green eyes, only her shock of red hair and spattering of freckles denoted her paternal blood. She stood on my threshold with her sharp chin lifted, dressed head to toe in unbecoming black.

I went to her. 'My dearest child, come in. We're so happy to see you.'

Jeanne stared at my prie-dieu. 'I cannot,' she said, in a high nasal tone. She stabbed with her finger at the statue on my small altar. 'That is idolatry.'

I chuckled. 'I am of the Roman Catholic faith; it is how we worship.'

'Well, I am of the Reformed faith and we are forbidden to look upon graven images.'

'She is not a graven image,' I said as I saw my sister-in-law Marguerite stiffen. 'She's the Madonna of Assisi, venerated for her kindness to cripples and sufferers of other deformities.'

'She's a statue. Calvin says that the cult of saints and

veneration of statues must be abolished, for that is not what our Savior preached.'

God save us, the child was an avowed heretic. I chuckled again to disguise my consternation, not so much with her words, which sounded much as I imagined, but rather with her conviction. What in heaven had Queen Marguerite been teaching her daughter? And how was I to counter it?

'Christ's mother was a woman of flesh like any other,' Jeanne continued. 'The worship of her cult derives from old pagan customs.'

Marguerite lunged to her feet. 'How dare you utter such vileness!'

Jeanne stuck out her lower lip. I let out an uneasy laugh. 'She recites what she's been told, much as we might recite Brantôme. She doesn't understand the half of it.'

'I do.' Jeanne narrowed her eyes. 'I also know why I'm here. They want me to wed a papist Spaniard, but I'll die first. I'm a child of God and you are fools who kneel before a cross.'

As my women gasped in unison, I gripped her thin shoulder. 'Enough. No more talk of religion, yes?' I propelled her forth toward an empty chair near me. My ladies flinched as if she might impart her contagion. With a searing glare at her, Marguerite marched out.

I hadn't expected such piety from my sister-in-law. But Marguerite had no intention of indulging a Calvinist nor would she ever. I was less dismayed because I could see how the child reveled in her effect on others; nevertheless, as I labored to mold Jeanne to conformity, I gained valuable insight into the new religion that most Catholics detested and feared.

To my surprise, once I grasped its doctrinal digressions, I found that the Huguenot credo was not all that different from my own. But Jeanne clung fervently to her faith and I made no progress in my attempts to convert her. Not that it mattered; upon hearing his ambassador's account of her, Charles V refused to even consider Jeanne as a bride for his son.

Enraged, François sent Jeanne packing back to Navarre and

plunged into a foul mood, intolerant of everything and everyone. I felt my own trap closing in. Given his present state, how long would it be before some conniving courtier suggested to the king that maybe the way to Milan could be bought through a new wife for Henri?

My stay of execution was at an end. I had to seal my pact with my own private devil.

I arranged for the meeting to take place at night in my rooms. I'd feared Diane might refuse or make an elaborate show of her arrival, but she came without fanfare. One minute I was pacing, rehearsing lines that tasted like soot; the next, the door opened and she stood on the threshold in a hooded cloak. Reaching up a white hand, she swept back her hood to reveal that sphinxlike face. She wore a dark blue gown, a rope of rare black pearls entwined about her alabaster throat.

Her voice was cultured, the voice of a courtier. 'I was surprised by your summons.'

My smile felt sharp on my lips. 'Oh? It's not as if you've lived unaware of me, madame.'

She inclined her head. 'Indeed. Your candor is refreshing.'

'Good. Then let me be even more candid: I believe it is time we became better acquainted, seeing as you're so close to my husband.'

Her eyes flickered. For a second, I glimpsed something dark, soulless. Face-to-face with that unblemished skin, staring into those cold blue eyes, I wondered how such a reptilian being could keep my husband enthralled. 'I fear you are mistaken,' she said carefully. 'While I am privileged to call His Highness my friend, I assure you I do not share his every intimacy.'

A satisfied thrill went through me. Regardless of what they did in private, she clearly didn't want any public impropriety. I'd overestimated her. She wasn't as confident as she appeared. Like me, she was treading water. She knew that once Henri became king she must consign herself to the shadows or come out in the open as my rival.

I drew out the moment before I decided to ignore her evasion and cut straight to the mark. 'I've summoned you because I think you'll understand my concern. You see, I believe His Majesty may soon have no other alternative than to annul my marriage.'

A vein in her temple twitched. 'Are you certain? I've heard the king bears you much love.'

'*His* love is not in question,' I replied, more sharply than I intended. 'However, no amount of it can cure me of this bane that so many believe I carry.' I paused, thinking of the secret charred in the hearth, only a few paces from where we sat. 'I refer to my lack of a child, madame,' I added. 'While His Majesty does love me, not even he can defend me forever. After all, I am expected to bear a son. If I cannot, then it would be best for all concerned if I did retire to a convent, where a woman of my unfortunate predicament ought to be.'

Her eyes narrowed. I had struck a nerve, perhaps the only one she had. She couldn't evade her encroaching age; she had limited time to fulfill her ambitions and she depended on me, the complacent wife. Another might not be so willing to stand aside and let her have her way.

'I regret this matter has so perturbed you,' she said, and she rose gracefully to waft to the window alcove, where she patted the cushions as though I were a pet. I perched beside her; she had no discernible scent, as if she were made of marble.

'I assure you, such situations are not uncommon,' she said. 'I wed my late husband in my adolescence and didn't bear our first child until my twenties. Some women need time to mature.'

My hands coiled in my lap.

'Nonetheless,' she went on, 'this being such a delicate matter, perhaps you would allow me the privilege of putting your concerns to rest?'

I wanted to wrap my hands about her alabaster throat, but at least she'd spared me the worst. She had relieved me of the need to further abase myself.

'I would be indebted to you,' I managed to utter.

She patted my hand, stood, and glided to the door, where

she paused to look over her shoulder. 'I've heard it said you rely on amulets, potions, and the like. You'll find you have no further need. Providing you leave the details to me, I promise you will soon give Henri a child. It will be a glorious day for all of us, I think.'

She sailed out, leaving me full of rage and loathing but also an unsettling sense of relief.

'Madame la Dauphine is with child!' Word raced through Fontaine bleau, causing matrons and widows to rise with an agility they'd not displayed in years, whispering the news to daughters and daughters-inlaw, who rushed into the gardens to inform husbands and lovers.

'Madame la Dauphine is pregnant! La Medici has finally conceived!'

From my window I watched them. The court had gloated for weeks over Henri's nightly passage to my rooms; what they did not know was that Diane had orchestrated everything. She ordered special drafts to strengthen my blood and his vigor and provided us with a chart detailing the best positions for conception. I'd straddled Henri and ridden him to climax; lain on my back with my legs in the air as he slid inside me. He 'd taken me on my side and on my knees; we enacted everything I'd once seen in that forbidden book Marguerite purloined from the king's collection and I stole every bit of pleasure I could in the process, acting the bawd for my husband and his mistress, for she'd told us that only the heat of our ardor would ripen my womb.

And every time, as Henri plunged and I cried out, I tried to avoid looking toward the shadows just beyond the bed, where she stood with her eyes fixed on us, directing our movements with precise, scythelike lifts of her fingers . . .

When I suspected our efforts had yielded fruit, I waited for the first nausea and weeks of malaise to pass before I sent word. She dispatched a midwife to examine me, who poked and prod-ded before proclaiming me both pregnant and fit.

Now the king came to me asking breathlessly, 'Is it true, *ma fille*?' and I smiled, hiding deep within my revulsion at what I had done to accomplish this moment. 'Yes, it is. I am with child.'

'I knew you wouldn't disappoint me! You'll lack for nothing. Ask and you shall have it.'

The moment he left, Henri entered with Diane. I stared at her as he kissed me awkwardly and let her step forth. She smiled. An enormous new diamond hung on her bodice.

'We are overjoyed,' she said, and she draped something cool about my neck.

I reached up: it was her rope of black pearls.

10

The grounds outside Fontainebleau congealed under January ice and snow; inside, my chamber was an inferno, hearths and braziers lit to a feverish pitch.

I'd felt the first pangs in the early afternoon, and my birthing room, draped in heavy arras, had become a world apart, dominated by women. Crouched on the stool with its wide hole, I writhed, pummeled by pain, oblivious to the smell of my own blood and urine.

'Push, Your Highness,' Diane hissed in my ear. 'Push!'

I tried to speak, to order her out, but the pain came at me with such force I felt I might crack in two. I howled. All of a sudden, a vast emptiness filled me. I felt a viscous gush of fluids and the rim of a basin shoved between my thighs to catch the afterbirth.

Through a haze of my own sweat, I gazed at Diane. She conferred with the midwives. Taut silence descended. I struggled to stand, my body throbbing. 'Is it . . . is my child . . . ?'

Diane turned around. She held the wailing babe swathed in white velvet. 'A boy,' she purred and she swept out with my newborn son, Henri's heir, pressed to her breast.

I collapsed against my pillows. I was safe. At long last, I had delivered my savior.

The next two years were fraught with trials. We fought a war that couldn't be won, depleting the treasury and enraging the people. Riots greeted each new tax imposed to outfit our armies and everywhere François turned he found reports that Lutheran preachers infiltrated the realm from the Low Countries to incite his people to seek solace in the Protestant faith. Destitute and in precarious health, he signed his final treaty with Charles V.

At court, I awaited the outcome of my second pregnancy. Since the birth of my son, christened François in honor of his grandfather, Henri had been visiting my rooms at regular intervals, prompted by Diane. Our carnal union remained passionless, but as though a sluice had opened, the time we spent was enough to conceive our next child.

Though I knew I'd struck a devil's pact, I had safeguarded my future.

In April 1545, after a mere three hours of labor, I gave birth to my daughter Elisabeth. She proved disappointing to those hoping for another son, but I was overjoyed and insisted on assuming full charge of her during her first months of life.

She was perfect, with her smooth Valois complexion and liquid-black eyes. I spent hours crooning over her, promising her everything I'd never known: safety, comfort, parents who would always care for her; with her dreams in my hands I found solace from the tumult of the world outside.

Unseasonal blizzards had dumped enough snow to bury entire villages and the abscess that had plagued François since Madeleine's wedding erupted anew. While he took to his bed, I fashioned a cocoon in my apartments, where I brought my young children to be with me.

It was the first time I'd had my two-year-old son to myself. Little François suffered from terrible ear infections, screaming for days until our doctors dosed him with opiates. Diane had used the excuse of his ill health to dominate his care, but she always retired to Anet for the winter, loath to expose her skin to wind or frost, and I hoped to bind my son to me while she was away. My initial joy in his auburn curls and faunlike grace was undermined, however, by the realization that he didn't know who I was. He regarded me as if I were some mistake, flinching when I took his chin in my hand and said, 'Mama. I am Mama.' I pointed to Elisabeth, cradled in Lucrezia's arms. 'That is your sister, Elisabeth.'

He screwed up his mouth. 'Deeane! I want Deeane!'

I closed my ears to his wails, enduring his tantrums because he was my child, my son.

One frigid evening as I sat with Elisabeth and watched him mutilate one of my lutes, word came that the king wished to see me. I went to François's apartments to find the fire in his great hearth ebbing, platters of food and goblets piled on the sideboard. Something was wrong. He never suffered laxness in his servants.

Then I smelled the odor.

He sat by the window, his black velvets accentuating his gauntness. The seals of a parchment he held rattled as he looked at me. 'Henry Tudor is dead.' He dropped the parchment to the floor. 'He succumbed three days ago, eaten alive by that ulcer on his leg. He'd grown big as an elephant, striking at ministers and disposing of intimates easy as you please. His last wife, the sixth one – she's lucky to survive him.' A bitter smile crossed his lips. 'His ten-year-old son has been crowned Edward VI. Hard times ahead: I hear Edward's maternal uncles already fight over the right to rule as regent in his name.'

I genuflected in respect for the passing of a sovereign, though I thought the world would be a better place without Henry VIII in it, his sordid life having repelled us for over a decade.

'He was fifty-five,' François went on. 'Three years older than me. I remember when we first met years ago. He was tall, golden, and rich as Croesus; he could have charmed devils from the pit.' He chuckled. 'That old snake Charles is the wise one. He refuses to go as we do, rotting on our thrones. He says he'll enter a monastery when he grows too ill to rule and divide his empire between his brother Ferdinand and his son Philip: Austria and the German duchies for Ferdinand; Spain, the New World, and the Low Countries for Philip. A pretty picture, calculated to cause me as much misery as possible – though he must have heard that I too cannot live much longer.'

I stepped to him. 'Don't say that. You just need to rest and recover your strength.'

He held up his hand. 'You've never lied to me before. Why

start now? I am dying. I know it and so do you. You have a sense for such things.'

I averted my eyes. The smell was stronger the closer I came to him, a terrible reminder I couldn't bear to face. How could I live in a world where he no longer existed?

He said softly, '*Ma fille*, why do you look away?'

'Because . . . I cannot bear to hear you speak like this.' My voice caught. 'You will not die.'

'Oh, I will, and sooner rather than later.' He clucked his tongue. 'Now cease your tears. I've something to say to you.'

I wiped my eyes, sitting beside him.

'Henri will be king,' he began, 'and you, queen. It's the cycle of life: the sun sets, the moon rises. Only such a moon I leave France! To think that of my sons, the one least like me, the one I've never understood, is the one who'll inherit my crown – it's almost too much to believe.'

'I'm certain that Henri loves you,' I said. 'You are his father. How can he not?'

He sighed. 'Loyal Catherine, will you defend him forever? It is your duty, eh, your obligation as his wife. But I needn't feign something I do not feel.' He paused. 'Yet perhaps Henri can learn to be a good king with you at his side. I've watched you these past years and you never concede defeat. You have the heart of a ruler, Catherine de Medici, and it shames me to think there was a time when I almost heeded my Council's advice to set you aside.'

'Your Majesty did as you thought best,' I murmured, thinking of how close I'd come to that disaster and what I had done to protect myself from it. 'I would not have protested.'

'I know. And I also know now that my son doesn't deserve your devotion. I hope one day he 'll prove worthy of it.' François fixed his gaze on me. 'But do not let devotion blind you. Beware that woman of his, that Sénéchale. She'll take everything if you let her. She'll force you to act the brood mare while she rules Henri and the court.'

It was the first time he 'd spoken of Diane. Her name sounded obscene on his lips.

'And his friends the Guises,' he added. 'You must watch them, as well. They'll seek to wield power through Henri. They aim high; I wouldn't be surprised if one day they sought to rule France itself.' He turned to his desk, took a scroll, and set it in my hands. 'This is for you.'

I unrolled the paper. I looked up at him in disbelief.

'I confiscated it years ago from a creditor,' he said. 'I don't recall the wretch's name. I never got around to restoring it, though it's a lovely place. The château sits by the river Cher, next to gardens and an old vineyard. It's called Chenonceau. It is yours now, to do with as you please.'

My own château, deeded to me by the man I had grown to love as a father. It all became horribly real. He was dying. Soon he would be gone and I would never see him again. I would never laugh with him; never ride the hunt at his side, never share his delight for painting, music, and architecture. He would be dead and I would be alone, without his protection.

The pain was visceral, squeezing off my breath. 'I am unworthy,' I whispered.

He reached out to cradle my face in his thin hands. 'You are worthy. Never forget that. Remember me, Catherine, always. As long as I live in your memory, I'll never die.'

There was no disguising his decline, his feverish eyes and emaciated frame. Word was sent to Henri, who'd gone hunting. I suspected I was pregnant again, but I had no chance to tell him, for no sooner did he arrive than we went together to François's apartments.

The skeletal man on that crimson-hung bed was unrecognizable, bones showing through his skin. Dr. Ambrose Paré, our royal physician, motioned to Henri. I stayed by the alcove, holding Marguerite's hand.

François reached out; Henri faltered. Gazing at his father, his face unraveled. They spoke in hushed voices before Henri staggered out. As he passed me, I saw for the first time the terrible burden he carried, the years of hatred for his father, for which he could now never atone.

François smiled at Marguerite. *'Ma fille.'*

Choking back tears, Marguerite kissed his brow, holding his hand before she left the room as if buffeted by an invisible wind. I alone remained. He murmured, *'Ma petite,* sit beside me.' I perched on the bed, took his cold hand in mine. His eyes closed. 'Ah, *c'est bon …'*

At midnight, he drifted into unconsciousness and Dr. Paré and the king's gentleman took my place. I tarried in the antechamber; at two in the morning, the sound of their weeping roused me from my shallow slumber.

I drifted into the deserted gallery. A figure materialized from the shadows, disheveled coppery hair framing her desolate face. Behind her trailed two pale women clad in black, the last remaining members of the Petite Bande.

'Is he … ?' said Madame d'Étampes. I nodded. She pressed her hands to her temples with a heartrending cry. The women started to lead her away when she turned to me, gripping my hand with ice-cold fingers. 'It's your turn now. Remember everything you've learned; remember that while men may fight each other in the open, we must engage in more private combat. Your battles are just beginning but you are the queen. Without you, she is nothing.'

I watched her walk away for the last time. Her glittering career was over; she had dominated the court, usurped the king's affections so that even his wife, Queen Eleanor, wouldn't set foot near him; she'd been adored, reviled, feared. Now she faced life alone, at the mercy of the woman who'd soon step into her role. And I feared for her. I feared what Diane might do to her.

I returned to my apartments, where I closed the curtains over the windows and sat on my bed. I waited for a tide of inconsolable grief. I had loved François as I had loved no other man, loved him for his excesses and his foibles, for his grandeur and his weakness; but most of all, I had loved him because he had loved me.

But I did not cry, not a single tear. I now had a purpose, nebulous as it might be: I would be queen. I could almost hear

François laughing, his spirit alive, full of mirth at what we'd contrived to achieve. I knew then that he would never truly die; it was his final gift, one that he had ensured I would carry for the rest of my days.

In me, he had bequeathed his immortal love of France.

PART III

1547–1559
Light and Serenity

11

After forty days of mourning, Henri and I made our first appearance as king and queen.

I still found it difficult to believe my father-in-law was dead, that the entire world had changed and now I was queen. I donned the white gown, barb, and veil of mourning and – as often happens in times of grief – fretted over the inconsequential, fearing the white would make me look sallow. My pregnancy showed and I felt the entire court's eyes upon me, gauging my suitability to share the throne with a Valois king.

Unlike me, Henri was serene. White suited him to perfection, highlighting dormant amber in his eyes and dark hair. The wisps of silver in his beard added dignity to his thirty years, and he showed patient grace as eager courtiers queued up to greet us. I too had to say a few words to each one and my neck ached from nodding in appreciation of their hollow well-wishes. I was about to sigh in relief as the last one bowed before us when I happened to look up at the hall entranceway and felt my blood surge.

Headed by Francis, duc de Guise since his father's death and known as le Balafré, the Scarred One, because of the injury he'd sustained on his face, the Guise clan cut a swath through court. The instant he saw them, Henri stood and left our dais. I stared in disbelief at the sight of my husband, our new king, welcoming that brood as if they were his equals. After he pounded le Balafré's back in camaraderie, he turned to kiss the hand of the duc's brother, the cardinal of Guise, whom I had always disliked.

Though still in his mid-twenties, Monsignor was already a seasoned diplomat who'd represented French ecclesiastical interests in Rome. Like his brothers, he stood to inherit vast wealth and he behaved as one who had never known anything else. With his swishing red silk robes and skullcap, his soft calf eyes, thick lips, and delicate hands, Monsignor reminded me of my late papal uncle. Bred to a life of luxury, behind his elegant facade lurked insatiable ambition, and I almost preferred his scowling brother, Balafré, who didn't even try to conceal his contempt of anyone who wasn't French, noble, and Catholic.

'Look at them,' I said under my breath to my sister-in-law Marguerite. 'They act as if they own him.'

Marguerite whispered back indignantly, 'My brother is blind when it comes to that family and they know exactly how to play him. You're wise to mistrust them. The Guises would have all of France bow to them, though they only have a dukedom because my father gave it to them.'

Her words carried an uncanny echo of my late father-in-law's warning. I lifted my chin higher, hiding my disquiet as Henri faced the court with the Guises at his side.

'My father, François I, is gone,' he declared. 'Though I mourn his passing, I must now reign in my own right. I shall be a king for a new age, restoring France's fallen glory so we can live in peace, protected from our enemies and in the grace of the one true faith.'

Fervent applause rose. I didn't understand why I felt such apprehension until he added, 'You see before you a sovereign confident of his place yet unversed in the ways of governance. Thus, I shall reconfigure my Council, starting' – he extended a hand to the cardinal – 'with Monsignor as head councilor and his brother, Francis le Balafré, duc de Guise, as my chief adviser.'

This time, a stunned hush greeted his words.

'And Constable Montmorency,' Henri went on, 'who served my father so loyally, shall assume an honorary seat on the Council, while his nephew Gaspard de Coligny will be named an admiral and assume charge of the defense of our ports.'

I found some reassurance in the mention of Coligny and his uncle, the constable. I hadn't seen Coligny in years, as he rarely came to court; but I had always considered him a friend, one I might need, while the constable was famous for his hatred of Diane and the Guises. Perhaps Montmorency would be an obstacle, I thought, until I saw the subtle smile on the cardinal's full lips. The constable's assignment had been his idea, of course, as it was wiser to have a potential foe at court, under his eye, rather than stirring up trouble elsewhere.

Henri had acceded to the Guises' every demand.

And now she appeared as if on cue, refulgent in ermine sleeves and mauve brocade. On her bodice glittered an enormous sapphire jewel. A jolt went through me; the last person to wear that jewel was the duchesse d'Étampes. It formed part of the queen's treasury, which Queen Eleanor, already on her way home to Austria, had never enjoyed. By wearing it today, Diane was making a statement that no one, especially me, could ignore.

She glided past the whispering courtiers to the dais as if her indifference might asphyxiate them. As she dropped into a curtsy before me, she lifted her eyes and I knew in that instant that she was delivering her warning. A terrible revenge had been exacted on Madame d'Étampes, and unlike her predecessor, Diane had no intention of recognizing her proper place.

'Madame de Poitiers,' announced Henri, 'sénéschale of Normandy. I hereby grant her the title of duchesse de Valentinois, in recognition of her tireless service to my wife, the queen.'

I remembered the nights when she'd stood by our bed, directing our copulation as if we were her creatures; she no longer participated now that my womb had been breached, but I thought it would be preferable to this public humiliation. I would have risen and marched out, protocol be damned, had I not felt Marguerite's hand on my shoulder. And as anger clouded my reason and I tasted iron in my mouth, I heard Papa Clement lilt: *Love is a treacherous emotion. You'll fare better without it. We Medici always have.*

Though I was the queen, I dwelled in a world ruled by Diane. As I'd feared, she had indeed wreaked her vengeance on the duchesse d'Étampes, appropriating her estates and casting her into ruin.

From her splendid new suite of apartments, Diane also took over my son François's household, calling herself his official governess and appointing his staff of attendants.

She had my husband's permission, so no one thought twice about how I felt. No one believed I'd amount to anything other than royal brood mare. Like many queens before me, I was expected to deliver a child every year and endure my husband's infidelity without reproach.

In short, there was nothing I could do to vanquish her, short of murder.

This possibility gnawed at me like vice, abetted by my pregnancy, which made me tired, ill humored, and relegated to a supporting role. Every time I heard of a feast she and Henri had organized or a hunting trip they undertook, my anger was such that it required all my self-control not to uncap my poison vial and be rid of her, consequences be damned. Less than a year after François's death, I couldn't venture outside my apartments without encountering her and Henri's entwined initials everywhere, sprouting on tapestries and eaves like mushrooms after a rain. God forbid Diane ever desired something of mine, for hard-pressed would I be to defend it.

Nothing made this more apparent than the matter of Chenonceau.

It happened a few months after Henri's coronation, in the autumn. The season was mild, the fields luxuriant and trees aflame in gold and russet. François had always said the Loire was at its most breathtaking in autumn and I decided to visit my château before winter set in. Unfortunately, I aired my intentions one evening during supper, and like clockwork, Diane floated into my apartments the next morning, refulgent in black damask and mink, her marbled hair arranged in a Grecian coiffure that reflected her decision to cast herself in a classical mode.

If she was fleet Diana, then I was earthbound Juno, seven months pregnant, my feet and hands swollen, my back aching, and my eyes not at all pleased to see her at this early hour. She dipped her head, her concession to obeisance. 'I understand Your

Grace wishes to travel to the Loire. His Majesty has asked that I accompany you, as any mishap could occur.'

'That's not necessary,' I said. 'I've asked the architect Philibert de L'Orme to accompany me and help me with the refurbishments, and I've more than enough attendants to ensure my safety.'

'Ah, but none so devoted as myself.' Her gaze lowered pointedly to my pregnant stomach. I could have slapped her. It was decided. Off we went to the Loire.

Chenonceau's beauty shone through its neglect. The gardens were devastated by wildlife and the vineyards left untended, but the château boasted peaked turrets and balconies overlooking the span of the Cher – a house fashioned of pearl and mist, made for a woman's sensibilities.

I fell in love with it the moment I saw it. So did Diane. She wafted through the vacant chambers with that cretin L'Orme (who knew very well which of us was better equipped to make his reputation) scampering behind her, jotting down her airy suggestions in his notebook. I was left in a chair in the hall, glowering at the charming lopsided vaults.

A few nights after our return, Henri came to me. When he told me Diane desired my château, I stared at him as if he'd asked me to run naked through court to amuse her.

'But the deed is mine,' I said. 'Your father gave it to me as a gift.'

He tapped his feet. Dressed in black brocade, her crescent moon embroidered in silver on his sleeves, he embodied the image of a king. His beard was full and soft, just as I'd thought it would be on our wedding night. We no longer needed Diane to prod us to our duty and I could imagine the feel of his hands on me even as I sat there. I thrust the thought aside, despising my weakness and desire for an act we enjoyed only for the sake of breeding children.

'She'll give you Chaumont,' he said. 'It is a fair exchange.'

'You might as well compare a hovel to the pyramids. Is not her palace at Anet enough?'

It was the wrong thing to say. Anet was their refuge from court and from me; and his voice hardened. 'Anet belongs to her. She can do with it as she pleases.'

'Indeed, providing she allows me the same.' I gave him a steady look that forewarned I was prepared to do battle if need be. 'Tell her I won't part with it for the Louvre itself.'

His jaw clenched. 'There is doubt whether my father acquired the château legally.'

'What of it? To confiscate property in lieu of a debt is a time-honored royal custom.'

'Nonetheless,' he said, to my astonishment, 'I shall appoint a tribunal to debate the matter.' He stalked out, his sole concession to his thwarted rage the slamming of my door.

The verdict was that François had acted illegally. Chenonceau was put up for auction, which precluded my participation as queen. There was one offer: for the paltry sum of fifty thousand livres, Diane bought my château lock, moat, and key.

To compensate my loss, she deeded Chaumont to me 'as a gift.' Mortified that I had let myself become embroiled, I insisted on paying for Chaumont so no one could say I'd taken anything from her for free. Then I stormed off to visit my new château.

Lacking any modern renovations and surrounded by a dense pine forest that rendered its stone walls perpetually damp, Chaumont's sole redeeming quality was its sweeping view of the Loire. I wept when I beheld it, ordering that I be taken back to court at once, where I barged into my rooms and threw objects at the wall.

I vowed never to return to Chaumont. But I did return, after the birth of my third child, my daughter Claude. This time, I brought Cosimo Ruggieri. He wandered the château in a daze, so enthused by its potential as an observatory that I handed him the keys. He closed up his house in Paris and moved in. As for me, I refused to have anything more to do with it.

Pride was one luxury I still thought I could afford.

12

Besides assuming charge of my son, Diane appointed herself overseer of the royal nurseries, where she basically had control of my children's upbringing. Still, I diluted her impact by appointing Madame and Monsieur d'Humeries, a noble couple with much experience, as my children's official governors, so I too could have some say in how they were raised.

In her typical hypocritical fashion Diane insisted on us feigning cooperation and instituted morning appointments with me to discuss the children's needs. A few months after she stole Chenonceau, she arrived to inform me she had a matter of great importance to impart.

'Monsignor the Cardinal and I were discussing His Highness's marriage,' she announced, trailing her hands over my tables as if to assess their cleanliness.

'Oh?' I looked up from my embroidery, wishing the floor would open up and swallow her whole. 'Aren't such discussions rather premature? François isn't even six years old.'

'He's our dauphin, heir to the throne. It is never too early to consider who shall bear him sons. The cardinal believes, and I think Your Majesty will agree, there is no princess better suited to wed His Highness than Mary Stuart, queen of Scots.'

I chuckled. 'But she's just a child herself, a girl-queen overseen by her widowed mother . . .' My voice trailed off. Scotland's regent since James V's death was Marie de Guise; Mary herself was half Guise. The vultures already planned ahead, ensuring that when my son became king, one of theirs would sit in my place. I'd have been flattered they viewed me as such a threat had I not been outraged by the way they'd use my son to further their ambitions.

Diane added, 'It would be a betrothal, to be ratified once they both are of age.'

'I see,' I said. And I did. 'Let me give the matter some thought.' I watched her turn to the door before I added, 'I assume His Majesty my husband has been apprised?'

She went still for a moment before carefully responding, 'His Majesty is occupied with Monsignor's upcoming embassy to Rome.' Her voice edged. 'But I'm certain he'll approve. The Scottish alliance is essential to our defense.'

'Indeed. Nonetheless, he must be consulted, yes? Perhaps tomorrow, after Council . . . ?'

Diane marched from my room in a huff.

Leaning back in my chair, I let out a gusty laugh. This time, I vowed, she would not win.

The next day Henri and I listened as the cardinal extolled the Scottish betrothal. Resplendent in ivory velvet, Diane sat nearby on an upholstered stool. I had also donned regalia, but compared with her swanlike grace I felt like a duckling in my pearl-studded azure gown, my stomacher pinching me like a vise.

'Your Majesties,' said Monsignor in his melodious voice, his expressive hands describing patterns in the air, 'by betrothing the queen of Scots to His Highness, we'll preserve the Scottish alliance; support my sister Marie's regency, and warn her Protestant lords we'll not tolerate further dissension, but most important, we'll gain a superior claim to the English throne.'

As I saw Diane nod, I piped, 'How so? I believe there is a king already on said throne.'

Monsignor paused in unpleasant surprise. He evidently hadn't expected me to have, much less express, an opinion. 'Indeed, Your Grace, but Edward Tudor is a Protestant heretic and not in the best of health.'

'That may be true,' I said, enjoying this chance to ruffle his composure, 'but he has two sisters and I believe the eldest one, Mary, is an avowed Catholic.'

He let out the impatient sigh of a tutor obliged to humor an inept pupil. 'She is, but the annulment of her mother's marriage cast doubts on her legitimacy. As for the other sister, Elizabeth, she was born of the witch Anne Boleyn, whom Henry VIII beheaded for adultery. Many claim that Elizabeth isn't the king's daughter. Thus, neither sister is suited to rule.'

Henri had sat quiet; when he spoke, his voice betrayed impatience. 'Her Grace and I are well aware of Henry Tudor's marital problems. We also know your niece Mary Stuart bears a claim to England through her paternal grandmother, Henry VIII's sister. Still, I share my wife's doubts as to the appropriateness of this proposed marriage for my son.'

Diane stood. 'Your Majesty, may I speak?' He nodded. 'The queen of Scots is two years older than His Highness. The death of her father has left her and her realm prey to the English. Monsignor and I therefore suggest she be brought here as a companion to His Highness, so they may develop the mutual affection born of a childhood spent together.'

'Oh?' Henri's expression warmed, to my dismay. 'And what says the queen of Scots' mother? Surely she doesn't wish to be parted from her only child.'

The cardinal intervened. 'My sister fears for her daughter's safety. She too begs Your Majesty's leave to send Mary here, where she can live under your protection.'

Nothing could have been more calculated. My husband was enamored of old-fashioned notions of chivalry; rescuing the helpless Scots queen from the English couldn't fail to incite him, as Diane and the cardinal knew.

Henri turned to me. 'Catherine, what say you?'

I wanted to say I'd prefer that my son wed Jezebel herself rather than take a Guise bride to his bed, but the truth was I had no logical reason for protest save that I mistrusted the Guises and Mary Stuart shared their blood. Otherwise, it was, in fact, the ideal union, one that would bind Scotland and France in an unbreakable alliance and fortify our standing in Europe.

I had been outmaneuvered by masters and I smiled with as

much dignity as I could master. 'What else can I say? It appears we must welcome little Mary Stuart with open arms.'

'Good, then it's settled.' Henri tugged at his doublet, eager to go change for his afternoon sport. 'Have an escort of galleons sent to fetch the queen of Scots,' he instructed the cardinal, 'and assure your sister that her daughter will receive honor here, by my word.'

The cardinal bowed. Henri said to Diane, 'Would you care to join me for a round of tennis?'

She smiled. 'I fear I cannot play, but it would give me pleasure to watch.' Inclining her head to me, she swept out with my husband, leaving me alone.

In early August Henri and I repaired to Lyons, where we were scheduled to make our royal entrance. It would not have been appropriate for Diane to be present, so she reluctantly remained behind with the children, leaving me to bask in the chance to show myself as Henri's wife and queen.

For ten blessed days, he and I dwelled under the same roof without her, receiving petitioners, strolling in the gardens, and dining in the hall with the local nobility. We even played cards at night. Henri seemed to turn softer, more tranquil: he smiled and was attentive of me as a person. I began to realize that removed from the wiles of his mistress he was at heart a simple man who relished peace of mind, and I had a glimpse of what our life might be when one evening a messenger arrived with an urgent missive.

Henri rolled his eyes as he cracked the seal. 'I wonder if my lord cardinal ever sleeps or if he spends his every hour with quill in hand.'

I chuckled, shuffling the deck of cards as he read. Suddenly he slammed his fist on the table. 'God's teeth, I won't abide that heretic rabble defying me!'

I set the cards aside. As I saw his jaw clench under his beard, I said, 'May I see it?'

He frowned. I never interfered in matters of state, much less where the cardinal was concerned. But Monsignor had won one round with the Mary Stuart betrothal and I wasn't prepared to cede to him again. I added, 'Perhaps I can be of some assistance.'

He extended the letter. It was quite simple: the Huguenots were demanding equal rights of worship and were distributing propaganda in Paris to this effect, much as they had during my father-in-law's reign, only this time Monsignor wanted them arrested and burned at the stake.

I looked up. 'Other than Monsignor's opinion, I see no evidence here that the Huguenots defy you. In his zeal, I fear our lord cardinal has taken to seeing traitors in every corner.'

Henri did not speak for a long moment, his fingers drumming on the table. Then he muttered, 'Perhaps. He did insist that I grant him leave to establish the Inquisition here.' He regarded me with narrowed eyes. 'You've never mentioned that you knew about the Huguenots.'

I resisted the urge to sigh. There was so much he didn't know about me. 'I hear the court talk,' I said. 'I do try to stay informed on any matters that might affect you, as a wife should.'

I watched the suspicion in his eyes fade; he was a stolid Catholic, too stolid in my opinion, but then to my surprise he laughed. 'And so you'd advise me based on gallery gossip?'

'I wouldn't presume. However, Machiavelli says the foundations of every state are good laws. I don't believe the establishment of the Inquisition in France is good law. Misguided as they are, the Huguenots are still your subjects. Persecution would only increase their defiance.'

'Machiavelli, is it?' He gave me a pensive look. 'Interesting . . . Still, these Huguenot gatherings must be curtailed somehow. Calvin does not rule here.'

'Then do it gently. Calvin does not rule here, and neither should the cardinal.'

As soon as I spoke, I paused, thinking I'd gone too far. Henri reached for his goblet, eyeing me over its rim. 'It appears I misjudged you,' he said. He reached over to pat my hand. 'Thank you, wife: common sense is a rare commodity. Now, deal those cards. I've a mind to win back all the money I lost to you over dice last night.'

We played until late. I basked in the newfound respect of his regard and the fact that he didn't pay the cardinal's letter any more mind.

When he kissed me good night, I was content to let him go alone to his bed. I didn't dare hope our rapport would bring us closer; but I recalled what my father-in-law had said before he died and I thought that with me to counsel him my husband could learn to rule in his own right.

13

Upon our return to Paris, I went straight to St. Germain, where my children were lodged. Word had come of Mary Stuart's arrival while we were in Lyons and I opted to meet my future daughter-in-law without ceremony. I didn't want the Guises to appear with Diane and Henri, obliging me to sit for hours on a hard-backed chair while the children played the lute and Madame and Monsieur d'Humeries hovered in the background like hawks.

So I went alone to the children's wing. As I reached the nursery door, I heard dispute.

'François can be the knight and I'll be the princess,' declared a strident voice in accented French. 'You'll be the evil queen.'

'But why? You're a queen already,' protested my daughter.

'Yes, but your coloring is darker. Therefore, you must play the queen.'

I edged closer, peering inside. Mary Stuart stood with her back to me, seven years old and more than a head taller than my François, who gazed at her in awe. Clad head to toe in white satin, her hair an ash-gold mane that fell to her stripling waist, she had one hand on her hip while she wagged the other at Elisabeth. My four-year-old daughter looked at her

as if she were an apparition, one Elisabeth wasn't certain she liked.

'I don't want to be the queen,' Elisabeth said again.

'Well, if you don't play her, who will?' retorted Mary, and I stepped in. 'I'll do it.'

The children froze. Or rather, my children froze. Mary spun about. 'And who are you?'

She did make an impression. She had exquisite bone structure, near-translucent skin, and almond-shaped eyes. Her nose was long, a Guise nose; her mouth showed perfect little teeth. Robust health was evident in her slim body, which had gone stiff at my appearance.

I chuckled. 'The question should be, my dear: Who are you?'

She passed her gaze over me. 'I am the queen of Scotland and the Isles, of course.'

'Is that so? And what if I told you, queen of Scotland and the Isles, that I too am royal?'

She scoffed. 'You can't be. I've already met His Majesty and Her Grace.'

My smile vanished. Diane. She thought Diane was queen.

My children watched as I stepped closer to Mary. 'So you've met the king and queen. Tell me, my dear, what do you think of them?'

'They're beautiful, as a king and queen should be.'

'Indeed.' I looked at my son. 'Do you find the queen of France beautiful, my prince?'

He cringed. 'Mary,' he whispered, 'this lady, she . . . she is –'

At that moment a disheveled young woman rushed in. She brought with her the smell of fresh-cut grass and roses, her fiery red hair tossed about a flushed face, her voluptuous figure squeezed into a far too ornate azure gown. She came to a halt, gasped, and dropped into a curtsy.

Mary went still.

'Please, rise,' I said. 'You must be Janet Fleming, our queen of Scots' governess.'

Janet Fleming stood. 'I am, Your Grace,' she murmured, 'to serve you, Your Grace.'

Mary lifted her stunned eyes to me. 'You . . . you are . . . ?'

I nodded and embraced her. 'Now,' I said in her ear, 'now you've met the queen.'

She shuddered in my arms. I drew back. 'Go on,' I said. 'Continue with your games.' I moved to the door and then I paused. 'You didn't answer my question, my dear.'

'Question, Your Grace?' She had recovered her poise with remarkable alacrity.

'Yes. Do you find me beautiful, as a queen should be?'

She replied without hesitation. 'Of course. All queens are beautiful.'

It was a devious answer. But it gratified me all the same.

The following year, I bore my fourth child and second son, Charles. A month overdue, he was a small babe, unusually quiet. Still, he bore a strong resemblance even in his infancy to his father; and my husband, who held himself aloof from the nurseries, took an immediate fancy to him, charmed by Charles's delighted gurgles whenever he showed up. Henri's fondness for our new son also meant Diane swooped in to take charge of Charles's household arrangements, insisting he needed two nursemaids because of his size, as well as extra attendants. Once more I was ignored, though I'd just given birth, and my hatred of Diane almost choked me.

But like me, she was about to discover the price she must pay.

I'd retired early from the evening banquet and sat before my dressing table, where Lucrezia brushed out my hair. Anna-Maria came to my door. 'Your Majesty, Madame de Valentinois is here,' and without leave, Diane pushed past her.

'Leave us,' I told my women, and I turned to her. 'Madame, I was just about to retire.'

Her mouth twitched. 'I had to see Your Grace. It's horrible. Horrible!'

I rose at once. 'What is it? What has happened to my children?'

She shook her head. 'They're fine. I've just come from their apartments and they sleep like angels. I'm not here about them. I'm here about that harlot who watches over them.'

I paused. This was an unexpected turn of events. 'Whom do you refer to: Madame d'Humeries or Lady Fleming?'

'Lady Fleming, of course. I've discovered she and the constable are lovers.'

I couldn't contain my burst of laughter. 'Handful the Fleming is, no doubt, but not even she would bed a man old enough to be her grandfather.'

My pointed barb regarding age went unnoticed; I refrained from adding that I rather liked Janet Fleming and the children adored her, for she was never averse to hiking up her skirts and joining them in a game of hide-and-seek or getting down on her knees to hunt for a lost toy.

'It is true,' Diane spat. 'Janet Fleming consorts with him. Friends of mine, trusted friends, have seen her sneaking in and out of his apartments. It cannot continue. Think of the scandal should her harlotry become public.'

Much as I hated to admit it, she wasn't being hysterical. Sexual indiscretions had a way of mutating at court. Anyone with a grudge against the Guises (and there were plenty) might use the indiscretion to cast calumny upon Mary, who would one day wed my son. I had no doubt Diane knew what she was talking about where Janet Fleming was concerned; after all, she had her spies and I'd experienced for myself how much she liked to watch in the bedroom, but I doubted Montmorency was involved.

I kept my thoughts to myself, however, enjoying the sight of her in a frenzy over another woman's immorality. 'It must be stopped! And Montmorency must be banished.'

'He does what is in most men's nature, madame.' I consulted my fingernails. 'Surely you don't suggest that I should reprimand him for indiscretion in his private affairs?'

She waved her hand. 'No, no. Monsignor will shoulder that task. Only he and his brother le Balafré require His Majesty's consent to send Montmorency away and . . .'

I looked up. 'Yes?'

'Well, His Majesty must first be persuaded of the gravity of the matter.'

'And you want me to inform him? If so, I should remind you that I could not do so unless I'd seen this indiscretion for myself – which of course is out of the question.'

She leaned to me, teeth bared. 'It's not as out of the question as you might think. They meet tonight in Montmorency's chamber. I know how to catch them in the act.'

I felt as if she'd spewed acid on me. I considered ordering her out. I did not because if Lady Fleming was engaged in a carnal affair, I needed to know. Nothing must blemish my son's bride. Besides, if I was right and Montmorency wasn't the culprit it would give me the perfect opportunity to prove Diane wrong. She'd be in my debt for a change, and I'd make certain to exact a hefty price.

'Very well,' I said. 'Allow me a moment to change, yes?'

We slipped down the corridors like errant schoolgirls. Should we be espied creeping through the palace, the entire court would be abuzz by morning, and I giggled at the thought. Diane still harbored a loathing of any public attention, promulgating her role as chaste adviser to the king and loyal attendant to me even as the court dubbed her the king's whore behind her back.

She unlatched the door to a deserted chamber that smelled of smoke and dust. Gliding to the alcove, she knelt, her face white in the moonlight. She pulled the carpet back, exposing a hole drilled in the floorboard. Light flickered in the room below. As muffled laughter reached us, she waved me forward. I heard a man's voice. Overcome by curiosity, I got down on my hands and knees and pressed my eye to the hole.

A woman slipped past my view. I assumed she was Lady Fleming, which she confirmed when she neared the candle by the bed and shook out that wealth of fiery Scottish hair. She began undoing her stays with languid seduction. A disembodied hand reached out, yanking the bodice from her. I felt a tingle in my own loins at the brusque impatience of that gesture, watching mesmerized as her plump breasts were revealed.

Warmth rose in me as I saw Janet Fleming put a finger in her mouth, moisten it, and begin toying with her nipples. This was lust. This was what I'd never share with Henri, what I had never experienced. At that moment I wanted to be her, oblivious to everything but my pleasure.

'Come here,' I heard the man say, his voice thick with desire.

'Can you see them?' Diane hissed in my ear.

I shook my head. Janet had shifted out of my view. I heard clothing drop, groaning as skin slid against skin. Then Janet fell upon the bed, her legs arching. The man stood before her, taut buttocks flexing. That well-toned flesh didn't belong to Montmorency, who was in his fifties, I thought; and as the man yanked Janet to him by the ankles, I suddenly recognized him.

With a stifled gasp, I flung myself back.

Diane scowled and thrust her eye to the hole. Her shock erupted from her in a drawn-out wail. I doubt they heard her, pounding and thrashing as they were. When she looked up to meet my eyes, her face resembled a pared skull.

The errant lover was none other than our own Henri.

Within days, Birago brought me the gossip flying through court. I stayed out of the fray and delighted in Birago's accounts of how everyone spoke of nothing else, speculating that Montmorency – upon noticing Henri's wandering eye whenever he visited the nurseries to see Charles – had sought to destroy Diane's influence over the king by facilitating the encounters with Janet Fleming. Diane had been through a similar debacle with the Piedmontese and shown discretion. This time, however, she was five years older; the veneer of a chaste friendship between her and Henri was long tarnished, and she set her spies to uncovering every sordid detail, thus making the event glaringly public. She compounded it by insisting on Janet's return to Scotland. Chastened and embarrassed, Henri agreed. This left Diane free to vent her wrath on Montmorency, who stormed from court declaring he'd not be ordered about by a 'strumpet.'

I laughed until my sides ached, even as I felt a pinch of jealousy over Henri's infatuation with the blowsy Scottish governess. Though I didn't relish his infidelity, the fact that Diane appreciated it even less was cause enough for rejoicing.

Then Henri himself came one night to see me. To my surprise, he didn't try to pretend nothing was amiss but rather grumbled outright that he didn't appreciate being made to look a fool. 'It isn't as if I gave her a title! It was but a romp. God knows, my father did worse in his time and no one reproached him for it.' He paused, looking at me. 'Were you upset?'

I sat straighter in my chair; it was the first time he 'd ever thought to ask me about my feelings. I didn't want to think of his reaction should he discover my part in this fiasco, until I realized he never would, because Diane – hypocrite that she was – would never tell him. The last thing she'd ever admit was that she'd gone so far as to spy on him through a hole in the floor.

'No,' I said at length, 'but the children are another matter. They loved Janet Fleming.'

He sighed. 'Yes, I didn't consider them.' He paused again. 'It really didn't upset you?'

I had accepted that he would never understand the complexity of my heart, the futile envy and hurt born of the knowledge that he would never grab *me* by the ankles.

So I made myself shrug with deliberate indifference.

He set aside his goblet. He had removed his doublet; under the lacings of his chemise I could see the dark hair of his chest. I looked down at my embroidery as I heard him say, 'Catherine, I wish others were as understanding as you.'

His hand cupped my chin. He leaned over, set his bearded lips to mine. He had never kissed me like this before: a firm union of our mouths that speared fire straight to my feet. I found myself drawing stifled breaths as his tongue probed mine and his hands wandered to my breasts, undoing my robe and peeling it back from my shoulders. I gasped as he gathered me in his arms and brought me to the bed, where he set me on the mattress, gentle as the evening light.

He removed his clothes until he stood naked before me. I had never looked upon him in his entirety before, not as I did then, and I never would again. But for that one time he was all I ever wanted to see – proud and tall, the taut musculature of his youth softened by the years.

He whispered, 'Tonight I want to make love to my wife.'

That night, I discovered passion as it is meant to be. There was
no obligation hovering over us, no watchful mistress, none of the
unfamiliarity of strangers committing the most intimate of acts.
There was just us; and it was the one time our desire met, collided,
and became one. For the most intoxicating of hours, I reveled as
Janet Fleming had – a woman in every sense of the word. He
stayed with me that night; his arms wrapped about me as I slept
with my head on his chest, lulled by the strong beat of his heart.

It was mid-December. Together, we conceived my most
beloved child.

14

After a few short hours of labor at our cherished palace of Fontainebleau, I held for the first time my third son, my Henri-Alexander, titled duc d'Anjou.

I adored him from the moment he was put in my arms. It wasn't just that he resembled the Medici, with his long-lashed black eyes and olive skin. There was something else, a palpable bond not severed by his release from my womb. I cradled him for hours; to my women's dismay, I even let him suckle my breast, though he had a nursemaid. Lucrezia thought it was unseemly that I should be seen giving my child teat like a peasant, but I did not care.

I wanted only to be with him.

The following year was one of the happiest I could recall, though 1552 was a year of war, with the outbreak of serious hostilities over Milan once again setting us to raise troops in Italy's defense against the Hapsburg emperor Charles V. This time, however, before Henri left for the front, in the hall in the presence of our entire court he took me by the hand and declared, 'In my absence, I entrust the queen, my wife, with the affairs of this realm. She is to rule over you, her decisions as respected and adhered to as if they were my own.'

Tears filled my eyes as he turned to me and murmured, 'You've earned this, wife.' It was an honor few queens of France had ever enjoyed, and as I gazed past him to the court, I caught sight of Diane rigid at her table, her face leached of color. Beside her, Monsignor glared. Now they knew I was not someone they could insult anymore, and this unexpected triumph made up for the years of ignominy I had been forced to endure.

That evening in my rooms, Henri spoke to me of my duties.

'Rely on the Council to guide you but remember you are the regent, not the other way around. Be firm, Catherine,' he added with a smile, 'as you so often are with me.'

Then he took me to bed and made love to me with the familiarity of an old friend.

I took my regency seriously. I met with the Council, held audience with ambassadors, and set our idle ladies to packing supplies for the front. At night, I wrote to Henri, detailing everything, even as the war that had begun with such high hopes turned against us. The Milanese, who had begged for our help, resisted our incursion, and together with his son, Philip of Spain, Charles V dispatched an impressive counterforce that soon drenched the soil of Milan with French blood.

Three months after he'd departed at the head of a vast army to wrest Milan from the Imperial yoke, Henri returned to France haggard and gaunt. More than half of the men who had gone were either wounded or dead, and we had emptied our treasury.

'I must sue for peace,' he told me. 'If we don't, Charles and Philip will crush us. I've failed. Milan will never be ours again.'

I sat at his side. 'You must do what is best for France.'

He nodded wearily and dispatched our envoys to the Hapsburg court. While terms were debated, word came that Charles V, beset by gout, had decided to abdicate, bequeathing Austria, Flanders, and the German provinces to his younger brother, while Spain, Netherlands, and the New World went to his son, Philip II, who wed the late English king's sister, Mary Tudor.

I bore my final children in the next two years. In May 1553, my daughter Margot was born; followed a year later by my fourth and last son, Hercule. Both came into the world under Taurus, a sign capable of equal ardor and treachery.

When I was thirty-six, I met Michel de Nostradamus.

Famine and poor weather beset the south along with a virulent outbreak of plague, which created a mass influx of peasants from the countryside into our cities. I read chilling reports from our lord mayors that entire cities were garrisoned to stop the plague from entering, the citizens trapped within and reduced to foraging for food as best as they could, while mass graves were dug.

Like everyone else, the thought of plague turned my blood cold; while we had not had a case at court since I'd come to France, all it took was one. Entire dynasties had been wiped out and so I instituted strict hygienic measures in my children's apartments, insisting that every floor be covered with carpets, not lousy rushes, and that linens be laundered three times a week. I suspected the plague was spread by filth; rats in particular horrified me, and I paid outrageous sums to stock our kitchens, the stables, and other outbuildings with cats.

When word came to me of a doctor who traveled the plague-stricken areas treating the sick with pills he concocted from rose petals, I was immediately interested. Michel de Nostradamus, I was told, was a converted Jew who had published a discourse on treating the plague. He'd lost his wife and now made his home in Provence; to my surprise, he was also considered a gifted seer.

I went to talk to Henri. 'I'd like to invite him to court.'

He reclined on a couch as our court physician, Ambrose Paré, dressed his thigh. He'd suffered a flesh wound during sword practice, and while not grave, the injury was inflamed. My husband clenched his teeth as Paré applied a poultice and started wrapping the wound in a fresh bandage.

'Michel de Nostradamus is a doctor,' I said. 'He can assist Dr. Paré with your leg.'

Paré glanced at me in weary gratitude. Henri was not an ideal patient. He hated being inactive and had already reopened the wound twice by insisting on riding.

My husband scowled. 'If he can help, summon him. I'm tired of bandages and poultices.'

'Thank you.' I kissed his brow and went to dispatch my summons.

Weeks passed without a reply. In the fall, we made our habitual move to the red-brick and stone Château Blois in the Loire Valley, where I had refurbished my apartments with new wainscoting and tapestries. Here, I spent hours overseeing my household affairs.

One afternoon without warning, Michel de Nostradamus walked in.

I looked up and went still. He was tall but otherwise unremarkable at first glance. Clad in a physician's black robe and peaked cap, his cragged face half-covered by a graying beard, he seemed like a tired merchant as he bowed before me. As his eyes rose to mine, I saw they were brown, piercing, and sad – eyes that conveyed infinite knowledge and weary tenderness.

'Your Grace,' he intoned, his voice somber, 'I've come from Fontainebleau. I was told you were here.' Though he didn't indicate his displeasure in any way, it was clear he implied that I'd made him travel at a cost he could ill afford.

I offered him a warm smile, sensing he'd not be placated by falsity. 'I regret the inconvenience, but you never answered my letter. How could I know you intended to visit?'

He did not lower his gaze. 'I assumed you wanted to see me as soon as possible. You said His Majesty your husband had an open wound; I didn't think a reply was necessary.' He paused. 'Does he still have that wound?'

I nodded, intrigued as I glanced at the threadbare sleeves hanging over his large bony wrists. He looked as if he had walked to Blois in that robe.

'Have you no belongings?' I asked.

'I brought a valise. I left it with the guard outside. Shall we see the king now?'

I nodded, starting to rise when the room melted around me. At that moment, the gift I had not felt in so long awoke. As I reached out to grip the edge of my desk, I heard him say, 'You know why I have come.' I met his gaze. He stood still, unmoving, as if nothing were amiss.

This strange man had come to court to tell *me* something.

'We 'll see His Majesty soon,' I said, and I motioned my ladies out, though it was unorthodox. I was the queen; I'd never met this man before. For all I knew, he could be mad.

I led him into my private cabinet, a small room with a glazed window, gilded desk, chairs, and a fireplace. I'd had the walls covered in fragrant cedar, with Henri's and my initials carved in gold on the frontispieces. My cabinet at Blois was one of the few places in France where the interlocked HD did not appear, and another man might have paused, even concealed a smirk.

Nostradamus didn't seem to notice the room. He sat on the chair I indicated, and after declining my offer of wine, he said, 'I was surprised by Your Grace's letter. I've sent you several messages over the years, but not once did you respond.'

'You sent me letters? But I received nothing. I assure you if I had, I . . .' My protest faded; I was about to lie. 'The truth is, I receive hundreds of petitions. My secretary alerts me to the most urgent or personal, of course, but I can't look at every one.'

'I see. My messages were not important, then.'

'Oh, no! They were simply overlooked.'

'No. They were not important.'

He wasn't saying I'd considered his messages unimportant, I realized, or that an oversight had impeded them from reaching my hands. He was saying – 'I'm saying they weren't meant to reach you,' he interrupted, and he smiled for the first time, revealing crooked teeth. 'God directs our paths. You know this; you too feel the invisible.'

In my stomach, I felt a flutter, my gift unfurling neglected tentacles.

'Catherine,' I said faintly. 'Please, call me Catherine.'

'That wouldn't be proper. You are my queen.'

Silence fell. 'Why did you send me letters?' I asked.

'Because I have had visions,' he said. 'Of you and the future.' He lifted his chin toward the door. 'I wrote them down years ago, before you came to France. The book is in my valise. If you'll permit, I'll recite the most important ones now. You see, my visions come to me . . .' He paused, seeking the right words. 'They come without warning. Many remain a mystery.'

'Yes,' I said softly. 'I understand.'

'I thought so.' He folded his hands. 'What I have to say won't be easy for you to hear.'

I suspected as much. I could feel the brooding in the air, emanating from a dark place in his mind that had nothing to do with his humanity.

'I am just a vessel,' he went on. 'This gift first came to me in my adolescence. I always knew I was different, even as a child, but I didn't understand how different I was until I was older. I fought it, at first. I despised the power it had over me. In time, I came to accept it. God has chosen me for reasons I cannot pretend to understand. Much of what I see I turn into verse. Poetry is music. The listener hears what he wants to.'

He closed his eyes and sighed, a long sigh that floated upward like smoke. Tension gripped me as a spasm crossed his face. I sat frozen, waiting, as the silence extended.

Finally, he spoke. '"The young lion shall overcome the old in single combat. He will pierce his eye in a cage of gold. Two wounds in one, the old lion will die a cruel death."'

I frowned. What did he mean? Lions were a symbol of royalty, of course, but the symbolism could apply to many things and he spoke of cages, of combat.

His eyelids quivered. He wet his lips. '"The lady shall rule alone, her unique spouse dead, who was first in the field of honor. She will weep for seven years and reign long."'

I felt a wave of profound despair. He sat quiet for a long moment, his words dying. Then he opened his eyes and murmured, 'I will go. I've done what I was called for.' He started to stand.

'No!' My voice rang out, shrill in the silence. I paused, took a shuddering breath. 'I . . . I don't understand. Are these prophecies . . . what do they mean?'

He did not speak. He held my gaze, his eyes sad, almost repentant.

'You must tell me,' I said. 'Please. Are you saying that I . . . I will outlive my husband?'

He leaned to me. Though we didn't touch, his proximity felt

like a caress. "'No truth can be determined for certain that concerns the future.'"

I started. 'Someone said that to me once, in my childhood. How did you know?'

'It's a common saying among seers.' He paused. 'Is there anything else you must ask me?'

I resisted the urge to demand a detailed explanation. He looked exhausted. Later, I told myself. Once I get to know him better, he can explain it all to me.

'We should go see my husband now,' I said. 'He has a flesh wound. And my children – I would appreciate it if you'd draw up their horoscopes. You'll be rewarded for your services.'

Nostradamus inclined his head. 'I'll do what I can. But I can stay just a short time.'

To Dr. Paré's astonishment, Nostradamus cured Henri's leg wound with a simple plaster of mint and mold. He then drew our children's horoscopes. The charts, to my relief, didn't show anything out of the ordinary, which was just as well, for he made an immediate sensation at court, a new seer always being much sought after until his first blunder. To his credit, Nostradamus didn't flick his fingers at the women who sidled up to him with love troubles or the dandies in search of fortune. Still, as with all novelties they couldn't understand, the courtiers wearied of him, and he of us.

I offered to accompany him through the Loire, with a stop at Chaumont to meet Ruggieri. When we arrived Nostradamus stepped into the hall and stiffened. Clad in expensive scarlet velvet embroidered with stars, Ruggieri rushed down the staircase, thin as ever, hair askew and eyes febrile as he kissed my hand. He beamed at the older seer. 'Your reputation precedes you.'

Nostradamus replied drily, 'Does it?'

We dined on roast quail. Ruggieri then took us to the observatory to gaze through his glass at the sky. When he insisted we stay the night, Nostradamus raised his hand. 'I cannot.'

Ruggieri pouted. Nostradamus turned heel and descended the staircase, without anything to light his way. Fearing he might trip and break his neck, I grabbed a candle, told Cosimo to stay put, and braved the stairs. By the time I reached the hall, I was out of breath, sullied from passing through cobwebs.

He was striding into the courtyard to my litter; he removed his valise from the interior and pulled up his hood. 'Seigneur!' I bustled to him. 'What is the meaning of this? Ruggieri is a trusted friend of mine since childhood. Why do you disdain his hospitality?'

He turned to me, featureless under his hood. 'I did not disdain his hospitality; I reject it. I cannot stay here. I am not comfortable.'

'Well, neither am I. It's not Blois, but I assure you the sheets are clean and floors swept.'

'No,' he said. 'I am not comfortable with him. I must go.'

I stared in bewilderment. 'Has he offended you?'

'No. But he will offend you. He will betray you.'

I gave a short, nervous laugh. 'Come now! I trust Cosimo with my life. You are tired. Let us go inside. We'll have some hot wine and –'

'My imagination never plays tricks.' He stepped to me. 'He plays with evil. And evil he will wreak. It is his fate.'

I lifted a hand to my throat. 'You actually think Cosimo . . . ?'

'I'll never withhold the truth, no matter how painful. Should you wish to see me, send word to my home in Salon.' A smile crossed his lips. 'Or I may come to you, should the need arise.'

Uncertain as to how to respond, thinking that if he ever spoke to others like this he risked arrest by the church or worse, I took a ring from my finger, its jasper stone bearing my seal. 'If anyone tries to harm you, tell them the queen of France holds you under her protection.'

He pocketed the ring. I stood under the moon as he shouldered his valise and strolled onto the road. I didn't think I'd see him again and I wasn't sure I wanted to. Mesmerizing as he was, he had struck an unbidden chord in me that I did not wish to hear.

15

Not a cloud marred the sky on the day of the first wedding of a dauphin to be celebrated in Paris in over a decade. Candles sparked fire off the nobles' finery, the breeze drifting through Notre Dame's open doors spiraling the draped silk banners. Depleted as our treasury might be, we would not spare expense for this important occasion.

I was beset by worry as François and his bride knelt before the altar. I'd protested the marriage at first; my son had turned fourteen, an age when most princes have awoken to their carnal appetite, but he continued to be plagued by crippling ear infections that nothing could assuage and he looked frail in his gem-encrusted robes. And while he appeared enamored of Mary, he treated her more like a beloved sister than a consort. Henri thought bed sport was just what our son needed, but I suspected François did not have the maturity, and I blamed Diane, her ceaseless vigilance over him having retarded my son's growth. She had kept him a perpetual child, coddling him to his detriment so she could keep him under her control.

Nonetheless, the marriage united Scotland and France; and the impaled arms of Valois and Stuart were displayed on the litters that brought us back to the Louvre, where we dined on tablecloths emblazoned with the thistle and fleur-de-lis.

Mary and my husband opened the dancing, while I sat on the dais and recalled when I'd been a bride, displayed beside my father-in-law for the first time.

Henri wore plum velvet studded with pearls. As he entered his thirty-ninth year he had grown more like his father, though his demeanor was subdued, mindful of his regality at all times.

François had laughed too loud and drunk too much. Henri scarcely touched wine anymore and when he smiled, it was with a near-imperceptible tilt of his bearded lips.

And the bride – how different she was from the naïve girl I had been! With her chestnut hair swinging past her waist and my seven gray pearls swaying about her slim throat, she reveled in her own beauty, her gaze casting shameless coquetry at Henri. I felt envious of her careless youth and vibrancy and turned my gaze to our guests.

At the Guise-Lorraine table, the aged dowager duchess, flanked by her favorite daughter-in-law, le Balafré's wife, and several Lorraine cousins, sat engorged with pride as she beheld her royal granddaughter; at the children's table their offspring mingled with mine.

Foremost among these was le Balafré's son Henri, an angelic boy with white-gold hair and sculpted features. He sat beside my own seven-year old Henri, who twirled the jeweled pendant I'd given him, his dark eyes impatient, for he danced well and longed to show off his grace. The bridegroom, François, watched Mary, even as my second son, almost eight-year-old Charles, gabbed in his ear. Nearby, my eldest daughter, Elisabeth, was serene in carnelian, overseeing ten-year-old Claude and five-year-old Margot. My baby, four-year-old Hercule, played with his food.

Like François, they too would wed someday and leave me, I thought. I must care for them while I could, plan their futures and ensure their happiness.

I eased back in my chair, reaching for my wine when I found myself staring into the austere visage of Queen Jeanne of Navarre at the table to the right of the dais. Her eyes were cold, regarding me with the same intolerance she'd shown years before when she'd come to Amboise and denounced my Catholic faith. Her mother, François I's sister Marguerite, had died several years ago, shortly after Jeanne wed Prince Antoine of Bourbon. Descended of thirteenth-century noble blood, the Bourbons were Catholic princes of France who stood next in the line of succession after my own sons. Jeanne and Antoine made an illustrious match but,

I suspected, not a happy one. A handsome lout preening in his unlaced doublet, Antoine drank heavily, his dark blond hair disheveled about his flushed face as he chatted up a painted court jade even as his wife sat a few chairs away, clad in the unadorned black of her Calvinist creed. I'd heard she had tried to convert Antoine to Protestantism to no avail; as I saw Antoine lean close to nuzzle the jade's throat, I felt a surge of pity for Jeanne. It was evident that Antoine did not care about religion or anything else that might come between him and his pleasure.

Still, she was so unapproachable that I'd barely exchanged three words with her, and as I tried to think of something to engage her in conversation, I found myself looking at her son, little Henri, heir of Navarre – a sturdy freckled child who'd inherited her red hair and his father's green eyes and saturnine features. He was six, a year older than Margot; and as I wondered why he wasn't seated with the other children, he turned in his chair toward me.

I was captured by his stare. In his curious eyes, not yet tainted by age or experience, I recognized myself, the girl I'd been: prematurely cognizant of the world but unaware of how much it could change. A rush of sympathy overcame me as I thought of how overwhelmed he must be by the activity and glamour of the occasion, and so I beckoned him. Jeanne started and leaned to him, whispering in his ear; he faltered for a moment before he rose and came to me.

He bowed with stilted precision, uncomfortable in his finery, his hair springing around his head in untamed spikes. He 'd been born under Aries, I recalled, thinking back on the birth announcement Jeanne had sent and the silver christening basin I'd dispatched as a gift.

I said softly, 'My child, do you know who I am?'

'Yes.' He fixed his gaze on his polished shoes. 'You are Tante Catherine.'

'That's right. I am Aunt Catherine. Come; let me give you a hug.'

As his gaze fled to his mother, I descended the dais and took him in my arms, feeling a compact body that didn't even tremble as I enfolded him.

It came upon me. I had never felt anything like it since my childhood, a sensation so powerful that it dissolved my surroundings and left me floundering in darkness.

Cannon fire bursts in the distance, echoing through a long valley blackened by drifting smoke, where charred trees bear only the shredded remains of autumn leaves. A man sits on a black destrier, a white plume in his dark cap; his beard is thick and coppery on his weathered face with its long nose and pursed lips, wide cheeks and close-set eyes full of purpose; he seems to command the very air he breathes. He sits his horse as though born on a saddle, nudges it with his knees to calm its nervous prancing.

A young page rushes up to him, dressed in green livery bearing an unfamiliar badge.

'They will not surrender,' the page gasps, and the man looks at him with a flash of impatience in his eyes. Then he tosses back his head and laughs. He says something I cannot hear and I try to move closer, to hear him, but he recedes, disappearing like smoke and –

My gasp brought me spinning back to the hall; as I struggled to regain my bearings, nausea filling my mouth and sweat chilling me under my gown, I felt the boy reach up to touch my cheek. 'Aunt Catherine?' he murmured, and I gazed down at his face, knowing then I had just seen him as he would become.

Jeanne strode to us and removed him with a jerk from my embrace. 'That is quite enough, madame,' she said, her eyes flashing as she took in the ruby and pearl crucifix pinned to my bodice, a recent gift from my son's bride.

'She didn't hurt me,' said little Navarre. 'She smells nice.'

'She smells of idolatry,' retorted Jeanne.

Despite the fatigue that always accompanied my gift, I had the stamina to chuckle. 'I see some things never change. I wanted to welcome the boy and ask him if he might like to sit with the other children. He is half Valois, lest you've forgotten; he shares their blood through you.' Ignoring her scowl, I said to him, 'Would you like to meet your cousins?'

Navarre looked toward the children's table. I thought he would refuse, cling to his mother, who obviously guarded his every move. To my surprise, he stuck out his chin. 'Yes. Can I, Maman?' he asked, raising his gaze to Jeanne.

What could she do? With a frigid nod, she watched as I took his little hand in mine – he had small hands for such a robust boy – and brought him to the table, where I presented him to young Guise, who yawned, and to my own children. 'This is your cousin of Navarre,' I told them. 'He's new to court. Please make him feel welcome.'

Margot smiled. 'You are Marguerite,' Navarre blurted, and she tossed her ringlets. 'I'm no daisy, cousin. Everyone calls me Margot.'

Henri thrust his chin out. 'And I am Henri, duc d'Anjou.'

'Now, now,' I chided. 'Be nice. Later, once the adults have finished, you can dance together, yes?' I looked into Navarre's upturned eyes. 'I hope you enjoy your time here with us,' I said, and again I felt my inexplicable kinship with him tug at my heart.

He gave me a smile, prompting my Henri to scowl. I inclined my head to Jeanne, who retreated to her seat like a thwarted lioness deprived of her cub.

The lingering effects of my vision started to fade, but I sat on my dais in quiet contemplation for the rest of the night, observing young Navarre awkwardly brave the dance floor while Margot spun like a pixie about him. Here, I thought, was a prince worth watching.

After the marriage, we retreated to the placid charms of Fontainebleau. The world may have seemed to pause for my son's wedding, but it had not, as the cardinal's latest reports confirmed.

Henri summoned me to his study. I found him at his desk, bruised shadows under his eyes. 'Mary Tudor is dying,' he said. 'Our English ambassador reports this child she claims to carry is a tumor. She'll not heed her physicians and spends her days weeping over Philip, as he left her to return to Spain as soon as he heard she was pregnant.'

'Poor woman. She's not had an easy life.'

'No, and when she dies neither shall we.' He scanned the dispatch in hand. 'The English favor her sister, Elizabeth, to be queen, though Mary holds her under house arrest.' He smiled sourly. 'Elizabeth has eluded incrimination in every plot against Mary, though all know she's an avowed heretic. If she claims the throne, she 'll move against us.' He thrust the dispatch aside, looking at me with somber eyes. 'Monsignor says we must offer Philip a new bride as soon as Mary Tudor is dead.'

Everything faded around me. All I could hear was one word. 'Bride?' I echoed.

'Yes. With Elizabeth set to be England's queen, we must ally ourselves with Spain.'

The golden light swirled with motes, terribly bright. Henri sighed. 'Catherine, if there were another way, I'd take it. But there isn't. Only one of our daughters is of age to wed.'

'But Elisabeth is only fourteen, and Spain is so far away.'

'She's a princess. She must do her duty, as we did.' He took my hand. 'You do understand?'

I nodded. 'I do. But promise me I'll be the one to tell her. She should hear it from me.'

'You have my word,' he said, kissing my cheek.

The remainder of that year passed like a flurry of leaves before the first winter storm. The constable and his nephew Coligny, whom I'd not seen in years, were sent to Philip II's court in Brussels to negotiate the terms of the marriage treaty. Soon after, I heard rumors that while traveling through the Low Countries, Coligny had become interested in the Protestant faith.

I didn't heed the talk. I was too immersed in the impending loss of not one, but two of my children, for upon hearing Henri's approval of a match between Elisabeth with Philip of Spain, the cardinal wasted no time in suggesting my daughter Claude for the Duke of Lorraine, a Guise relative. I raised vigorous protest, citing Claude's age, for she was just eleven. But to everyone's surprise, Claude displayed unexpected spirit. Plump and short, having inherited the less attractive aspects of our combined bloods, she came to me and declared, 'My lord of Lorraine and I have known each other since childhood. He is all I require in a husband.'

'But, my child, how can you know at your age?' I regarded her with a combination of awe and sorrow. I hadn't paid much attention to this daughter of mine, and I was taken aback to find she was almost a woman in thoughts and words, if not yet in body.

'I do,' she said. 'I see no reason to delay my betrothal. I don't want to end up like my cousin Jeanne of Navarre, married to some prince I care nothing for.'

I couldn't argue with her logic. Her reasons were sound and so I agreed to her betrothal, providing Lorraine agreed not to bed her until her fourteenth year.

Mary Tudor died in November. The half sister she'd kept under guard and almost beheaded for treason ascended to the throne of England as Queen Elizabeth I.

Within days, Philip of Spain accepted our offer of marriage.

In January 1559 Claude wed the duc de Lorraine. By February, Admiral de Coligny and the constable had hammered out our treaty, in which Henri gave Elisabeth to Philip II in marriage, as well as his surviving sister, my dear Marguerite, to Filbert of Savoy, one of Philip's principal royal allies. Peace with Spain was achieved after decades of strife; and as promised, Henri let me break the news of her nuptials to our daughter.

I found Elisabeth in the nurseries, seated by the casement.

Outside, the day was bright. Voices carried to us on the breeze. I moved to Elisabeth's side and caught sight of the group of figures in the gardens. One was unmistakable, a lyric of a girl tossing her mane much like the prancing palfrey whose reins she held. With a jolt, I saw my son François on the beast, clinging to the saddle pommel while Mary guided the horse about in circles. I was relieved to see an army of grooms close by.

'It appears Mary Stuart has taken it upon herself to help François overcome his fear of horses,' I remarked, with some asperity.

'He's improving,' said Elisabeth. 'He'll soon be ready for his first hunt.'

I turned my attention to the old notebooks piled by Elisabeth. She must have scavenged the coffers to unearth these childhood artifacts.

'Why aren't you with them?' I asked, shifting the articles aside so I could sit.

She raised solemn eyes, a book open in her shapely hands. Her fingers were bare, though she was of age to adorn them; her dark hair framing a face upon which life had yet to inscribe its harshest lessons. 'I wanted to see if I remembered my Latin.'

'Remember?' My laugh sounded too hearty to my ears. 'How could you not, my child? You always excelled in Latin. No one could best you.'

'I wanted to be sure.' She lifted her eyes. 'I'll have need of it in the Spanish court. It's why you are here, isn't it? To tell me I will marry Philip II?'

Raw pain went through me. 'Who told you?'

'Madame la Sénéchale. But don't be cross with her; I've suspected for some time. I realize how much pain she has cost you, Maman, but she isn't to blame for this. It is my duty to wed where I am told and she confirmed what I already knew.'

She understood; she knew how much Diane had cost me, though my rival had been like a second mother, always at her father's side. Her awareness that I'd suffered in the shadow cast by my husband's mistress made me feel as though I'd been hiding behind clear glass, my secrets in plain sight for all to see.

Her next words were spoken with equal calm. 'Will Philip take a mistress?'

'No,' I said at once. 'He's renowned for his rectitude.'

'He's still a king. He's much older, already a widower. And he has a son already, by his first wife.' I stared, dumbfounded, as she added, 'I ask because under the circumstances I wish to comport myself with dignity, as you have.'

A hollow opened inside me. I clasped her hand. 'He will love you. How could he not? You are young, beautiful; you are everything a king could want.' I couldn't tell if I spoke to her in that moment or to the dream I'd never had, but she smiled and closed the notebook, as if my words had brought her comfort. 'Will I marry here or in Spain?' she said.

'Here.' I felt as if someone else spoke through me. 'We will plan everything.'

'Good. I want my sisters and Mary to be my maids of honor.' She leaned to me. 'I know Philip won't come to fetch me, but I wish to greet his proxy as the queen I will be.'

'You will.' My voice splintered. 'I promise.'

She reached out and embraced me, a child of my Medici blood.

'Thank you, Maman,' she whispered.

16

Elisabeth's wedding was set for June, to coincide with that of Henri's sister Marguerite to Filbert of Savoy, who, unlike Philip II, would come to Paris. Philip sent word that he would dispatch his premier general, the formidable Duke of Alba, to act as his proxy.

To prepare a daughter's trousseau should be cause for rejoicing, but as I supervised the seamstresses, mercers, and shoemakers charged with outfitting her, and the packing of gowns, cloaks, shoes, and muffs (for winters in Castile, I'd heard, were brutal), I felt as though each article set another stone in the road that would soon take her away from me.

Philip had stated his desire for Elisabeth to depart as soon as possible. At thirty-two, he was anxious to beget another heir. The thought of my child in his austere realm haunted my nights. Adding to my dolor was the impending loss of my sister-in-law, who'd been my most constant companion after my ladies, though Marguerite expressed resignation to her union with Filbert. At thirty-six, the independent streak of her youth had mellowed and she yearned for permanency after a life of royal spinsterhood.

'Defiance cannot feed the heart forever,' she said to me. 'I must admit, I'm looking forward to my life in Savoy, where at least I'll be a woman in my own right.'

I wished her the best, for at her age it was unlikely she'd bear a child. When Filbert arrived, he expressed satisfaction with his bride-to-be. They made an odd pair, and I smiled at the thought of François's sardonic reaction at the sight of his bony daughter beside her portly betrothed.

Then, without warning, June was upon us, bringing with it the Spanish retinue.

Tall and gaunt, the dead lamb of the Order of the Fleece slung in gold about his neck, the Duke of Alba met Elisabeth in the Louvre's great hall. I noted at once the surprise on his jaundiced face. My daughter wore pale rose banded with gems; she recited her welcoming speech in perfect Spanish, and at its conclusion Alba graced her with a stiff smile that caused the Spanish entourage to exclaim, '*Hermosa!* Beautiful!' and explode into applause.

Festivities ensued. Though we were bankrupt, paying for the clothes on our backs through loans, we made certain no one would return to Spain complaining of their reception. The night before the wedding, I accompanied Elisabeth to her room and brushed out her hair. We didn't speak. There was nothing we could say anymore to breach the sorrow between us.

She reached up and took my hand in silence.

Two days later, I watched her kneel beside Alba in Notre Dame and marry Philip II. As Alba slipped the band over her finger, I closed my eyes. She was still in France and would always be my daughter, but in that moment she had ceased to be mine.

She belonged to Spain now.

We had the celebration jousts and marriage between Filbert and Marguerite to endure. Royal weddings are protracted affairs and Henri decided it would be best not to overtire everyone by having one marriage follow the next. Instead, we'd hold a celebratory joust for Elisabeth; clad in a new suit of gold-embossed armor, Henri would engage the winner.

I, in turn, tended to my children. I had to mollify François, who'd taken it into his head that as his father would joust, so must he. The idea of him in armor and bouncing around on a horse under the noonday sun was unthinkable; he had just had an earache and was still recovering, and I had to dissuade him of his foolishness. Then I marched off to see to Elisabeth, whose scarlet brocade required last-minute adjustments, and on to Margot, Charles, Henri, and little Hercule. By midnight, I was exhausted. I staggered into my rooms, undressed in a numb haze, and fell into bed. That night, I dreamed.

I float through a black tunnel. I cannot feel anything solid, and it is dark, so very dark, like the awful finality of a tomb. The lack of sensation suffocates me; I want to cry out but I have no voice with which to utter a sound. A flame flares in the distance. It draws me toward it, burning higher, closer and closer, warning me of something inescapable, something –

I was awoken by Lucrezia shaking me. 'My lady!'

Struggling out of my tangled, sweat-soaked sheets, I was overcome by a sickening dizziness. I knew this feeling; I'd last felt it when I embraced the little prince of Navarre. It was my gift. And then I heard Nostradamus's voice, as though he were in the room with me: *I will never withhold the truth* . . .

I pushed past my anxious lady. 'I must see my letters.'

The pile reproached me on my desk. I'd neglected my correspondence these busy past weeks. As Lucrezia lit the candles, I yanked up a chair, glancing at and discarding papers at my bare feet. It was here: I could feel it. I ignored messages from provincial governors and petitions from charities; missives from Venice and Florence were pushed aside as I searched, my anxiety increasing until I could hardly breathe.

Then I saw it. An envelope sealed with my ring's ensign. This was his letter.

I opened it. His words were concise: *Your Grace must take heed. Remember the prophecy.*

He had sent me a warning.

'*Dio Mio.*' I looked at Lucrezia. 'Something terrible is going to happen.' The letter slipped from my fingers. 'But I don't remember the prophecy. Nostradamus recited several to me when we first met. I don't even have the book he gave me. It's in Blois, in my cabinet. I left it there.'

I didn't sleep the rest of the night, pacing while my women sat in bleary-eyed attention. The moment dawn broke, I took to the corridors. Minor courtiers sprawled on the floors and in the alcoves, while our palace cats prowled for rodents.

Henri and I lived in separate wings. Diane still attended him on occasion in his chambers, and I never went to see him without sending word in advance. But she wouldn't be there this morning. She always kept her distance when we assumed center stage, still the hypocrite after all these years. Nevertheless, I found my husband amid a crowd of secretaries and pages, standing on a footstool in his linen drawers, the breastplate of his new armor fastened to his chest as his wardrobe master fitted the leggings. Le Balafré lounged in a chair nearby, long legs stretched out before him. When he saw me, the scar on his gaunt face twitched. There was no love lost between us; from the day I'd first arrived in France he 'd treated me with disdain.

I ignored him, forcing him to rise and make his obeisance.

Henri looked fatigued, his beard hugging the sunken length of his cheeks. 'Yes, Catherine?' he said, as if my appearing unannounced in his rooms were a daily occurrence.

'My lord,' I said, 'might we have a moment in private?'

He motioned about him. 'As you can see, I'm rather busy. Can't it wait until later?'

'No.' I felt Guise's stare. 'I fear it is of the utmost importance.'

'So is everything.' Henri sighed, waving his wardrobe master aside. One of the leggings didn't quite fit. He got off the stool.

'Besides being fitted for the umpteenth time,' he said, as his attendants left us, 'I've a mountain of papers to sign, the English ambassador to meet, Alba to see, not to mention inspecting the lists before the joust. Is this so important?'

'It is. I am here because . . . I think we 're in danger.'

He frowned. 'Danger? How?'

'I don't know.' I clasped my hands, hearing myself and knowing how I must sound to him. 'I had a dream last night and . . .' My voice caught. I could see the disbelief in his eyes. I went to him. 'Please, just listen to me. I fear for someone dear to us, perhaps in our own family.'

He dropped onto the chair by his desk, reaching down to unlock the bindings of the legging. It fell with a clank to the floor. He couldn't recline because of the breastplate and so he sat in erect discomfort. 'Very well, I'm listening. But that secretary of mine will be back any moment and I'll not be able to send him away a second time. He's been at me all morning.'

I told him about the dream and the letter from Nostradamus. I had to stop myself from blurting out the truth about my own past premonitions, as I'd never mentioned my gift to him and suspected he'd not appreciate hearing his wife declare she possessed occult powers.

When I finished, he folded his hands at his chin. 'And you think your dream and this prophecy of Nostradamus's portend some peril to us?'

'Yes.' I was relieved by the lack of derision in his tone. 'If you recall, he did cure your leg. And he told me he would contact me should the need arise.'

'Catherine,' he said, without a trace of mockery, 'this is absurd. You are overwrought because of Elisabeth. She must soon leave for Spain and you worry for her.'

'No, you don't understand. His letter was dated weeks ago. I only looked for it because of my dream. It's a warning. He wrote his prophecies down for me in a book, which he gave to me when he first came to Blois. But I left it there, in my cabinet. We must send for it.'

He regarded me as if I'd lost my senses. 'Send for a book? In less than three hours we are holding a joust to celebrate our daughter's union with the king of Spain.'

'We can still hold it. Just send someone we trust to the Loire to –'

'Catherine.' He did not lift his voice, but I could hear his impatience. 'Blois is closed for the season, as you know. My chamberlain holds the keys to our apartments and he has far too much to do without my dispatching him on this fool's errand.'

'It's not a –'

He held up his hand. 'You're asking me to send a trusted servant to Blois, a day's ride at best, to fetch a book he's never seen. You have hundreds of books in your cabinet. How on earth is he supposed to locate the one you want?'

I hadn't thought of that. I hadn't stopped to think about any of this, but I wasn't going to admit that to him. I squared my shoulders, fighting back a wave of inexplicable desperation. 'Then, I will go myself. Get me the keys and I'll take Lucrezia and a guard. I'll be back by nightfall.'

'And miss the tournament, where I'm scheduled to challenge the winner?' He looked at me with narrowed eyes. 'You can't be serious. It was a dream, Catherine. Nothing bad is going to happen if you don't get that book.'

Suddenly, I doubted myself. He was right: it had been a dream. A dream and a cryptic letter from a man I hardly knew, whose prophecies were thus far unproven.

And still, I knew. 'I realize it sounds mad, but I can feel it, Henri, in my heart. What if it's Elisabeth? We've asked so much of her and she's been so tired. What if she falls ill?'

'We're all tired. We're tired of England and Spain, of heretics demanding the right to worship, and bad harvests and poverty. We each have our burdens to bear. Elisabeth will bear hers as best she can. I'm not sending her away because I want to but because I must.'

'I know that. No one is faulting you. It might not be her. It might be a warning about someone else, one of our other children.'

'Catherine, there is no warning, no prophecy. You're overwhelmed like the rest of us, though you hate to admit it. You worry for Elisabeth, for you are a good mother.' He paused, softened his voice. 'Philip wants her in Madrid by November so he can present her at his Christmas court. You should use this time to give her support, not to rush off to the Loire because of something that man said to you years ago.'

'Henri, please.' I gazed at him, my tears breaking free.

He stood and took me in his arms. Against his chest, the chill gold of the breastplate pressed to my ear, he caressed my hair. 'There, now,' he murmured. He cupped my chin, lifted my face to his. 'It is no sin to weep.' He gave me a resigned smile as voices came from the antechamber, indicating his horde had returned. 'Let's get through the blasted tournament and if you feel like this tomorrow, we'll see what to do, yes? We'll go to Blois together, if need be.'

I exhaled in relief. 'Thank you. I . . . I love you.'

The words were out before I could stop them and he went still. Then he closed his arms around me. 'I love you too,' he whispered.

He didn't speak again as his servants erupted into the room. But as I departed I realized that I finally had from him what I'd always wanted.

No truth can be determined that concerns the future.

Hurrying to my apartments, I repeated old Maestro Ruggieri's adage, interpreting it as a sign that there was time to avert calamity if we were forewarned. Tomorrow, I'd send for Nostradamus's book, and the seer himself if need be, to explain it. One day wouldn't make a difference.

It was already midmorning and I dressed in my court gown and jewels, gathered up my other children and my entourage. We entered the rue de St. Quentin to the blast of trumpets. My ladies and I mounted the dais to join Elisabeth, Mary, and François under the canopy. Charles, Henri, and Margot sat below us on cushioned tiers. I sat on my chair, took a goblet of wine from a page, and settled in for a long afternoon. I'd always found the thundering of steeds down the lines, the breaking of lances, and the shouting of the crowds overly boisterous.

Four competitors were scheduled to joust today, with Henri engaging the winner. The crowd roared as Henri's boon companion, the scarred le Balafré, galloped onto the field on a massive white destrier. As he swiftly proceeded to unseat his first opponent, Mary leapt to her feet. 'Crack open his head, Uncle!'

I yanked at her skirts. 'Sit down! Are you a heathen to display yourself thus?'

She tossed her head; her Guise uncle won three more rounds. Le Balafré then challenged the duc de Nemours, who lost. I didn't even bother to try and restrain Mary as she shrieked her delight along with everyone else as Guise cantered about the arena, his scarred face flushed.

'Who will challenge me?' le Balafré cried, his gauntlet lifted. 'Who dares fight the victor?'

Montgomery, a captain of the Scottish guard, stepped forth. 'I will.'

There was uproar. Montgomery might be part of the privileged corps that protected my husband's person, but he was still a Scotsman. Le Balafré eyed him and nodded. He wouldn't show himself a coward even before an inferior's challenge.

Montgomery mounted a white steed. Guise and he positioned themselves at opposite ends of the list and charged. With a deft upswing of his lance, Montgomery slammed Guise's shield, throwing the duke from his horse and onto the field. 'Foul!' cried the spectators. 'Again!'

But there could be no repeat. Le Balafré had been routed and the subsequent blast of trumpets proclaimed that now my husband, the king, would challenge the victor.

I sat upright. Had this been a coliseum, they'd have unleashed lions on Montgomery. But Henri was a staunch champion and indicated he would joust against the captain.

Clad in his gold armor, he galloped forth on his dappled charger. He looked fit, younger than his forty years as he rode to his end of the list and dropped his visor. Silence fell. The heralds sounded, and king and captain leapt forward.

In that instant, I recalled words spoken at Blois over four years ago.

The young lion shall overcome the old in single combat.

I started to rise. Everything slowed around me, so that I could distinguish the clumps of earth torn up by the horses' hooves, hear the creaking of armor, and smell the anticipation in the air. I opened my mouth. A crash shattered my cry as lance struck metal in a deafening explosion.

The applause cut short. Henri was lifted from his saddle, his lance clattering to the ground. As grooms raced to him, I saw his foot tangle in his stirrup as he slid from his saddle. The men caught him in their arms. There was a stricken pause.

The first scream came from Mary – a petrified wail that seemed to echo for hours. I stumbled from the dais, shoving past gaping courtiers frozen on their tiers. When I reached the arena, breathless and panting, the nobles were bringing Henri toward me. His helmet was still on, the visor dented beneath his brow. They laid him on a bench, began to remove the helmet. I glanced at the field. Montgomery stood frozen, his splintered lance still in his hand.

Henri let out a moan as the helmet was pried from his head. I covered my mouth with my hands to stop my own terrible cry.

He will pierce his eye in a cage of gold.

My husband's face was white; there was very little blood.

From his right eye protruded the shards of Montgomery's lance.

17

We brought him back to the palace, where I stood at his bedside as Dr. Paré examined the wound. Henri had slipped into unconsciousness, his pallor so pronounced that blue veins could be seen under his skin. Paré prepared a poppy seed plaster and applied it to the injured eye before carefully wrapping gauze about the protruding shard. He then motioned Monsignor the Cardinal and me into the antechamber.

'Well?' barked Monsignor, his usually moderate voice shrill. 'Will he live?'

I spun to him. 'How dare you? You speak treason!'

He eyed me in disdain, dispelling any doubts I might have had about his nature. 'Madame,' he said, 'we have the realm's welfare to consider. His Majesty's wound could be mortal.' He spoke without any discernible emotion, as though Henri were some cur trampled by his coach.

My rage, never far from the surface where the Guises were concerned, rose to suffocate me. I was about to order him away when Paré said, 'Monsignor, the wound is grave, yes, but not necessarily mortal. We must first remove the shard before we can determine the exact damage.'

Cold spread through me. I had foreseen peril but had never imagined it would touch Henri. I turned away from Monsignor's calculating stare. 'We must do everything we can,' I said to Paré and I could not keep the panic from my voice. 'His Majesty's life is in our hands. Perhaps I should summon Nostradamus. He helped heal my husband before.'

'That was a flesh wound on his leg,' Paré said gently. 'Skilled as he is, Nostradamus is not a surgeon. Moreover, it would take too much time for him to get here and the shard must be extracted as soon as possible, before corruption sets in. I've operated before on the battlefield, but I'll need a model first, to experiment on.' He paused. 'I need heads, Your Grace. As many as can be gotten.'

'Execute ten prisoners and bring the doctor their heads,' I barked at Monsignor.

The cardinal drawled, 'May I suggest that one of those heads be Captain Montgomery's?'

I rounded on him. 'It was an accident. We don't kill men for accidents.'

'Montgomery is a Huguenot. It's no coincidence that he challenged my brother first. His Majesty has been a foe of the heretics; this was an act of Huguenot revenge.'

I stepped so close to him I could smell the expensive musk on his robes. He disgusted me with his limpid air and manicured hands, the ease with which he clothed his monstrous heart. 'Don't try me again,' I warned. 'Go. Do as I bid. Now.'

I didn't give a fig for Montgomery, but he would not die to suit Monsignor. As the cardinal swept out into the gallery, where I heard courtiers clamoring for news, Paré gave me a sad look. I couldn't bear to see the doubt on his face; so I left him and went into Henri's chamber. Pulling a stool by the bed, I sat and took my husband's hand.

He would live. He must.

The disembodied heads yielded no definitive answers, and Paré decided to trim the shard first, to facilitate curing the wound. The flesh about the injured eye was ugly, inflamed, and fearing the onset of corruption I sent a letter by urgent courier to Nostradamus's home in Salon, begging for assistance. While I waited for his response, I anchored myself at Henri's bedside, accompanied by my sister-in-law Marguerite and my Elisabeth. He drifted in and out of awareness; every time he woke, he found me there. I bathed his face and throat with rosemary water; I smiled and spoke in a cheerful tone. I never let him sense my dread or the fear that tightened about me like a noose.

By the third day, he was feverish and restless, his skin the color of sand. Nostradamus had returned word that he'd come at once if I needed him, but to his great sorrow, as Paré claimed, he was not a surgeon and could only offer his advice. In his letter he enclosed a recipe for a poultice he thought might help. Henri's eye was now a swollen morass and his attendants had to forcibly hold him down so Paré could change the soiled dressings and apply the poultice. Despite her resolve to stay with me, Elisabeth looked faint, so I sent her away with Marguerite, insisting they both rest.

Marguerite returned as soon as she'd seen my daughter to bed. Paré had finished and coils of fetid gauze sat in a basin at his feet. I smelled a rank odor that raised the hairs of my nape – the smell of pus, hallmark of a rancid wound. Icy sweat beaded Henri's brow. He 'd thrashed like an animal, bellowing in pain; now he lay so still I feared the worst.

I whispered to Paré, 'He's barely moving. Isn't there something else we can do?'

He murmured, 'I fear the shard may have penetrated His Majesty's eye and pierced the protective membrane of his brain. The poultice may help with the outside corruption, but if the shard goes any deeper . . .' His voice faded into a laden silence.

'What about the operation?' I said. 'As soon as the swelling goes down, you can remove the shard, yes?'

He shook his head. 'It would require trepanning the skull and at the moment His Majesty is too weak. Perhaps after we've seen some improvement from the poultice, or perhaps it might not be necessary at all. He might recover on his own.'

'With a shard in his eye?' I stared at him. 'Are you telling me this is all we can do?'

Paré gave a forlorn nod. I turned to my husband. Blood and pus had already started to seep through the new bandage. As I reached for his hand, his uninjured eye opened, with a startling suddenness. I leaned close to his parched lips.

'Marguerite,' he whispered, 'her . . . wedding . . . See to it.'

Behind me, I heard a desperate sob escape Marguerite. I didn't need to look at her to know that she too had succumbed to despair.

At midnight, Monsignor married Filbert of Savoy and Marguerite. There was no celebration. I embraced each of them, my voice as weary as my appearance, and returned to Henri.

Outside his doors, the struggle for power commenced. I knew it was happening. I knew the Guises and their sycophants met in closed rooms, drawing up alliances to safeguard their power. I paid their machinations no mind, not because I didn't care or rail within at their cruelty, but because I couldn't do anything to stop it, even if I'd had the strength.

My husband, with whom I'd lived for twenty-six years, was slipping away from me. All I could do was watch, helpless to defend him from the enemies within and without.

One by one, they came to say farewell. Our son François entered the room clutching Mary's hand, an immature fifteen-year-old boy and seventeen-year-old girl, whose sheltered existence had been shattered. With tears coursing down his face, François babbled that he didn't want to be king; he didn't want his father to die. Mary took him in her arms, meeting my eyes in silent fear. I wondered if the Guises had been at her already, terrifying her with a list of her future responsibilities as queen, to ensure she'd look first to them for counsel, before me.

Pale but composed, Elisabeth kissed Henri farewell and went to be with my younger children, whom I'd ordered to the Louvre. Charles wept that he wanted to see Papa and rejected all consolation, clinging to the hunting hound puppy that Henri had given him. I refused to let any of them be subjected to the sight of their father crying out in agony; I shrieked at Paré and he dosed Henri with enough opiate to fell a horse.

Still, he did not die.

He fought like the soldier he'd always been, even as the fever escalated. He did, at times, rally, gasping that a proclamation announcing his son François II's accession be sent out. I loved him then more than I ever had before. He had lived like a king and would die like a king, ensuring as best he could that France did not perish with him.

I was with him at the end, on a July afternoon of savage beauty. He'd been delirious, muttering incoherent words. As I knelt beside him, he turned his head and gazed at me with lucidity, the fever releasing his body so he might return to it one last time.

His cracked lips opened. He mouthed one word: 'Catherine.'

Then he closed his eyes. And he left me.

I surrendered his corpse to the embalmers, who would remove his heart and seal it in the alabaster casket by our unfinished tomb in St. Denis. I gave him up to the lamenting servants who'd attended him for years, to Constable Montmorency, who stood guard at his deathbed, and to the overseers of his funeral, the Guises, who donned white with premeditated haste.

I returned to my rooms through corridors that still rang with his footstep. My women rose in unison, eyes red from weeping. Lucrezia reached out. Something in my gaze stopped her. She must have seen that if I felt her touch, if I felt any touch, I would crumble.

I moved alone into my bedchamber. It seemed as if I'd been gone a hundred years. All my possessions were here: my Venetian silver brushes with the entwined HC on their handles, vials of perfume and unguents, my children's portraits on the walls. I saw it all, registered it in my mind, and still I felt like I'd stumbled into a foreign place.

Blinded by tears, I pressed my hand to my mouth.

Then I heard a rustle, the clack of heel, and turned to see her emerge from the shadows by the bed. Had she thrown a dagger, I couldn't have moved. Diane returned my stare. A ruby throbbed at her chest, affixing her long black cloak to her shoulders. In her hands was a silver casket.

'I've brought you these.' She set the casket on my dressing table, opened the lid with a flourish. Nestled within on crimson velvet were diamond pendants and rings, pearl earrings, ruby brooches, and emerald necklaces. 'I return these for delivery to the queen of France.'

'*Puttana!*' I struck her with all my might. She staggered back, my imprint livid on her cheek.

She lifted her chin. 'You've no doubt dreamed of doing that for years. I'm honored I can provide you with this final service.'

My breath came in bursts, my hands clenching again as I prepared to do what I'd indeed always dreamed of – rip apart that unearthly mask and see if she bled like everyone else.

'You could have me arrested,' she said, 'but I don't think His Majesty would approve.'

'You're not fit to speak his name!'

'I do not speak of Henri. I speak of our new king, François II. I've been a mother to him. If need be, he 'll protect me.'

Henri's body was being desecrated at that very moment by embalmers and she stood here declaring her immunity as if it were a virtue. I knew then that she'd never loved him. She was incapable of it. She was as lifeless as her pantheon at Anet.

'Madame,' I said in a low voice, 'I might see you impaled on the highest turret this very hour, and no one, not even my son, would be able to stop it.'

Her eyes widened. I saw then what I longed for: fear. Fear of me. And then all the rage and hatred, all the murderous intent, vanished. She was nothing to me now.

I took a step back. 'But I won't. Instead, I command you to leave court this very hour.'

'I had no intention of staying.' She moved past me, regal even in defeat. But she would carry the brand of my fingers on her skin till her dying day. The imprint would fade but the sting would remain – a reminder that I too had exacted payment in full.

She halted at the door. 'I have another service to render, one I think you'll appreciate. The intrigue and conspiracies, the bribing of favors, the constant plotting and quest for safety – I leave it all to you. No one is more deserving of it; no one will do with it what you can.' Her lips curved in an icy smile. 'But it's not as easy as you think. To be a woman alone in this world requires every weapon you possess, every last bit of strength and endurance. You cut away pieces of yourself without realizing it, until you have everything and nothing at the same time. It's all yours now, to do with as you will.'

She turned to the door. 'Madame,' I said. 'You do not have my leave.'

Her hand paused on the latch.

'You once took something of mine that was not yours. Now I want it back.'

'He is gone,' she hissed. 'I cannot breathe life into the dead.'

'You are presumptuous. He was always mine. He'll be entombed in our sepulcher, where one day I shall lie beside him, as his wife and queen. You, on the other hand, will be nothing. So don't try me. I am the king's mother. One word and you'll end up worse than any of your rivals.'

She glared. 'What do you want? Say it so I can go. I tire of this game.'

'Chenonceau. You will sign over the deed before you leave.'

Laughter erupted from her. 'Is that all? Take it. Convert it into a haven for your widowhood. I still have Anet. It was mine by my first marriage and Henri deeded it to me again, in case a day like this came. He knew you well, madame. He knew you for the merchant's daughter you are.'

She lifted the latch, thinking as always that she'd had the last word.

I had an inspiration. Wrenching open my dressing-table drawer, I pulled out a coin pouch and flung it at her feet. 'Here is my payment. You'll see you've made a profit, which is the only thing you ever cared about.'

She met my stare before she retrieved the pouch. Then she left without a backward glance.

My breath drained from my lungs. My knees crumpled under me.

On the floor, with my face in my hands, this time I grieved as a Florentine.

PART IV
1559–1560
The Tigers

18

In Florence when a loved one dies, we set out feasts. We invite our relatives, neighbors, and friends to eat and recount our times with the departed. We tell tales, some humorous, others sad, but always with the aim of keeping our loved one with us awhile longer. We allow the celebration of life to assuage our grief and guide us toward the future that awaits us.

I wasn't permitted any of this. No sooner did le Balafré and Monsignor institute our official forty days of mourning than I was obliged to assume my cloister in the Hôtel de Cluny, that crumbling old palace where royal widows confronted the vacuity of their lives. It was an archaic custom, designed to ensure the queen wasn't pregnant, for this could upset the established succession, particularly if she later gave birth to a son. Henri and I had not been together for weeks before his death; I knew I was nearing the end of my time of fertility, but none of this mattered. The Guises had ordained that I must bow to the custom and I had to submit.

Sequestered in rooms draped from eaves to floor in white, I donned the black mourning of Italy in defiance, taking the broken lance as my emblem even as my every move was reported by attendants handpicked by Monsignor. I should weep and wail against my fate; question God's will and my own helplessness before it, until pummeled by grief, I'd accept the inevitable and seek solace in a well-appointed convent or rural house. After all, I was no longer queen. Mary Stuart had assumed my place; and no doubt my crest was already being dismantled from the walls to make way for hers. I had a pension and my estate; like other royal widows had done before me, my time had come to retire from the world.

No one expected anything more of me.

And I considered it, long and hard. It would be so easy to do. I had Chenonceau. I could grow old among my vineyards and fruit trees and never look back. Why shouldn't I seize what little happiness I had left? Had I not sacrificed enough for duty? Unlike the duchesse d'Étampes, who'd died in poverty at Diane 's hands, unlike Queen Eleanor, who had left France after my father-in-law's death, unloved and unwanted, I could walk away from court and forge a new life for myself, unfettered by struggles that no longer concerned me.

Only the thought of the Guises' ceaseless ambition, of their hounding of my son as he huddled terrified of the unknown gave me incentive. I would not sit out my widowhood in safety while they ruled in my child's name. I had borne their insufferable dominion long enough; the time had come for me to stake my place at my son, our new king's, side.

If I did not fight for him, who would?

I stood, cast aside my veil. The sight of my face for the first time in weeks brought the ladies to a standstill. The sole personal attendant I'd been allowed, my Lucrezia, smiled.

'Your Grace,' one of them inquired. 'Do you feel unwell?'

'On the contrary.' My voice was hoarse from disuse. 'I am both fit and hungry. Please see that I'm served some meat today. I've a craving for it.'

'Meat?' she gasped. Broth, bread, and cheese were all widows should eat; widows were frail and meat incites the blood.

'Yes. And be quick about it. While I dine, you can pack my belongings for transfer to the Louvre. Send a messenger to tell my son, the king, that I am on my way. A poor mother I would be to deny him solace at this trying time.'

Thus did I cut short my mourning and took leave of the Hôtel de Cluny.

The world had changed. Overnight, the Tournelles had been abandoned to its ghosts, while the Louvre blazed with light from torches mounted on its facade, spilling liquid gold over laughing courtiers who, days ago, were full of grief. A fete was obviously in progress.

Lucrezia and I shifted through the crowds. Few noticed me, cloaked as I was, and music assaulted my ears as I climbed to the second floor and my apartments, where my household awaited. Anna-Maria rushed to hug me; Birago took me gently by the arm and led me to the table. Though he looked thinner than usual in his scarlet Florentine robe, his concern for me furrowing his angular brow, his presence was a reassuring reminder that I still had friends.

That night as we dined, he related that Monsignor the Cardinal and his brother, le Balafré, had seized control of the government, overseeing the Council, the treasury, and the military, and sending out proclamations announcing as much. They'd made themselves regents in deed, if not by title, usurping my son's rights as king.

'But François is fifteen,' I protested. 'He 's of legal age to rule. How could they do this?'

'He let them,' said Birago. 'He signed a paper giving them power to oversee his administration, but I don't think he understood what he signed.' He paused, lowering his eyes in obvious discomfort. 'Le Balafré has taken him and Mary Stuart hunting in the Loire Valley, claiming they needed time away from court.'

I sat stunned, even as my fist curled about my goblet. I wanted to hurl it across the room. I should never have gone into cloister; in doing so, I'd given the Guises the opportunity to make themselves de facto rulers. François was scared and impressionable; of course he'd signed a paper handing over the realm to them. He knew nothing of ruling and the Guises had been right there to ensure he didn't need to learn.

'There's one more thing,' Birago said, switching to Italian, which he did when he had something private to impart. I loved hearing our language in his cultured voice, though the news was not good. 'Monsignor instituted an edict against the Huguenots. The constable argued against it, saying the burning of Frenchmen would damage the king's reputation, but the cardinal would not heed him and sent him from court. His nephew Coligny also left but told me before he did that he hoped you might receive him when you returned.'

I was sorry Montmorency had left, for I needed everyone who opposed the Guises. I was also intrigued that Coligny had foreseen I would return. After all these years, he apparently still remembered me. Did he ever recall our afternoon in Fontainebleau, when we'd discussed Machiavelli and the Huguenots? He'd shown himself as someone who viewed the world without delusions of grandeur. Perhaps he could be the ally I needed to oust the Guises from power.

'I would like to see him,' I said at length. 'Do you know how he can be reached?'

'Letters can be exchanged, but I must warn you, rumor has it Coligny favors the Huguenots, that he attends their sermons and reads their books. Some even say he's converted to their faith.'

'Well, rumors are not fact.' I refilled my goblet. Strangely enough, I didn't feel fear, though it was to be as I'd suspected – a battle to the death with the Guises for control over François. I had done battle before, I told myself. I battled Diane for years. And like her, the Guises had no idea how far I was willing to go to protect my children.

After my meal, I penned my missive and entrusted it to Birago. 'Deliver this and then let it be known I wish to visit my children at St. Germain, as a loving mother should.'

Birago nodded, a knowing smile on his lips.

My children were under the care of their governors, Madame and Monsieur d'Humeries, and my sister-in-law, Marguerite, who was due to leave for Savoy. She and I shared a final supper together, after which I gave her the dented brazier in which we'd concocted my potions. 'Take it, and whenever you burn the lavender, think of me,' I said, and we embraced.

Henri's death and the absence of Diane (for she'd been a constant, if nothing else) had not affected my children as much as I'd feared. I found Hercule and Margot playing with toys, oblivious to the tragedy that had made their elder brother king. Even my eight-year-old Henri seemed untroubled, insisting that I let him show me his latest deck of hand-painted cards. He was well advanced in his studies, his tutor informed me, and excelled in all outdoor activities. Looking at his slim, lean frame, I couldn't help but think fate had played a horrid trick in making François my firstborn. Henri had suffered least from Diane's pernicious influence and would surely have made a better king, despite his youth.

I wasn't so reassured by my nine-year-old Charles, however. He demonstrated a deep sensitivity over the loss of his father, crying so disconsolately that I had to choke back my own tears as I assured him Papa was in heaven now, watching over us. Charles looked too thin and sallow, and I devised a new diet for him, rich in red meats and legumes.

Elisabeth was also pale and thin, but she had not succumbed to her grief, informing me she'd met with the Spanish delegation to tell them she would travel in December to Spain. She'd been spending time with Claude, now wife to the Duke of Lorraine, and they'd found consolation in each other. I didn't look forward to saying good-bye to Elisabeth in a few short months but she insisted that her father would want her to go.

I took refuge from the sorrow of losing her in my own plans. Several days after my arrival in St. Germain, I received an answer to my missive. Three short lines: *In two days, at dusk in the gardens. If I don't arrive by nightfall, leave. I'll send word.*

'Yes,' I told Birago. 'Tell him I'll be there.'

I stood under the palace's shadow, the fading sun bloodying the sky. Wind buffeted St. Germain's turrets, sweeping away the pall of smoke that hung over Paris. My advice to Monsignor had been ignored. His edict against the Huguenots was now in effect and in less than two weeks over one hundred heretics had met their fiery end in Paris.

The terror had begun. Birago informed me that hundreds of Huguenots fled for the relative safety of the south, desperate to escape the cardinal's agents, who rounded them up like cattle.

Time was running out. If I didn't put a stop to them, Monsignor and le Balafré would turn France into their private realm, murdering our subjects and silencing any noble who dared contest them.

I was anxiously looking toward a distant cluster of elms when he appeared on the path.

He moved confidently, a man of medium height clad in a black doublet, his red-gold beard framing his mouth. He was forty, my age, yet his expression seemed much older as he bowed before me. 'Your Grace, may I offer my deepest condolences?'

'Thank you, Seigneur. I'm grateful you could come.'

I was suddenly aware of my extra weight, of the strands of graying hair whipping about my face in the wind. I'd never allowed the shape-shifting reflection in my mirror to taunt me; like many wives I'd let myself grow complacent before my time. Now I felt the startling desire to be looked upon as a woman and I was ashamed by it. My husband had been dead little over a month. How could I wonder if I held some attraction for a man I'd met a handful of times?

'Madame, it is I who am grateful,' he said. 'I feared you wouldn't wish to see me.'

I frowned. 'We are friends, are we not? I know time has passed, but I've not forgotten your kindness to me when I first came to this realm or your services to my husband over the years.'

He smiled. 'We were much younger then.'

I was caught aback by something in his tone, almost like a reproach. Had he not remained in Paris to see me? 'I believe it was you, my lord, not me, who chose to keep his distance,' I reminded him. 'I'd have received you at court.'

He bowed his head. 'True. Your Grace knows that I never liked the court.'

'I do.' I paused. 'Even so, you are here now.' I regarded him in the silence that ensued.

He had changed, hardened in some indefinable way. He seemed wary, as if he'd learned it was best to conceal one's emotions. He was still attractive, even more so, in fact, as his age had finally caught up with his premature sobriety and lent him presence.

But my gift didn't stir. I didn't feel anything from him at all.

Doubt overcame me. What was I doing, meeting in secret with him? If the Guises found out, I'd risk whatever clout I had left, accused of plotting treason with a suspected heretic.

As if he could read my mind, he said, 'If you have any cause to regret this arrangement, I will leave at once, without any dishonor.'

'I'm concerned for you,' I replied, wincing inside that he'd seen through me. 'I understand Monsignor the Cardinal has set spies on you.'

'That's true. Since my uncle left court, Monsignor has turned his suspicions on me. I eluded his men tonight, as no doubt they'll inform him, but they watch me nonetheless.'

'And do they . . . ?' I drew a breath. 'Do they have reason to suspect you?'

'I make no secret of my disagreement with the Guises.' He looked at me as he spoke, without hesitation. I'd forgotten how often courtiers failed to look one in the eye and found his candor both refreshing and discomfiting. 'They will use your son to their advantage. Already they move to bring the Inquisition into France, though persecuting the guiltless will ruin our sovereign's name.'

He spoke the very words I wanted to hear, as if I'd given him my script. I wanted to trust him; and still, I vacillated. I feared plunging into the heart of matter.

'Many Huguenot pastors look to you,' he added, perceiving my doubt. 'They know you counseled our late king of tolerance and they've asked me to appeal to your sense of justice.'

'They know?' I said, startled.

He smiled. 'Nothing that happens at court remains a secret. And those of the New Faith abound, though not for long, if Monsignor has his way.'

He caught me off guard. I realized I still knew so little of this faith the cardinal was intent on destroying, or of those who practiced it.

'I'm flattered,' I said, 'but with my husband gone, I have no power. And I am a Catholic. However, unlike the Guises, I do not think persecution is the answer.'

He turned away, his profile etched against the encroaching night. 'Persecution,' he said quietly, 'is chaos.' Hearing a smoldering in his voice, I abruptly understood why the Guises watched him. He'd grown into his promise, possessing the innate qualities of a leader. Given the right opportunity, he could be magnificent – and dangerous.

He turned back to me. 'All over France, the cardinal's edict sets Catholics to plunder and murder. We may not adhere to the Roman faith, but we're still Frenchmen. Only you can persuade the king to rescind the edict, so we may live and worship in peace.'

We . . .

The question burned on my lips. I had to ask; there was no evading it now. 'Do you defend the Huguenots because you are one, Seigneur?'

He did not falter. 'I converted several years ago. I've not hidden it, but neither have I announced it at large.' His smile broadened, lending mischievousness to his face. 'You should know I requested my uncle's vacant seat on the Council and was denied. Monsignor and le Balafré will never allow me at their table. As it stands, I have no choice but to retire to my house in Châtillon to be with my wife and son.'

A wife: he had a wife. A wife and a son; a family . . .

'Forgive me,' I murmured. 'I did not know you were wed.'

'Charlotte and I married two years ago. We were betrothed in our childhood, but it wasn't until recently that we decided to wed. As we grow older, we come to value the simpler things in life. Family is the simplest and most precious of all.'

'I understand,' I said, though I didn't. Important and overriding all other concerns for me as it did, family had never been simple either as a Medici or mother to the Valois.

'She makes you happy?'

'She does. I've delayed returning to her because I wanted to see Your Grace.'

'You should call me Catherine.' I met his eyes. They were so deep yet at the same time so impenetrable, like icebound lakes. He could be the ally I needed; he could help me overturn the Guises and regain the kingdom. But not now. I was still too weak and he too vulnerable.

'You must know I do not go away by choice,' he added. 'Nor will I stay away forever.'

'I know.' I gave him a smile. 'I promise I'll do everything I can to get the edict rescinded and, as soon as I can, to seat you in Council. I believe we can accomplish much good together.'

He took my hand and raised it to his lips. His kiss was dry. 'Should you find need of me before then, for whatever reason, do not hesitate to send word. I'll come at once.'

I watched him stride back down the path and into the cluster of trees, swallowed by the night.

Though my plan had not gone as expected, for the first time since Henri's death, I felt hope.

19

In September, my son and his queen returned from their hunting trip. I waited in the courtyard, flanked by Elisabeth and Claude, wearing the black gown that had become my armor.

I was eager to see François. He must feel the loss of his father; he was the eldest, and Henri and Diane had often attended him. While he and I hadn't forged a bond because of Diane's constant vigil over him, I now had the opportunity to. At fifteen, my son might be a man by law, but emotionally he was much younger. He would need me to give him strength and steer him past those treacherous shoals that the Guises would dash him against.

My delusion was dispelled at once. He entered in an upholstered litter, escorted by le Balafré and our new queen, Mary. 'His Majesty is ill. Give way!' Le Balafré barked, and he led my son past us in a bundle of trailing furs, into the palace. Fluttering in distress, Mary started to follow. I snagged her by the arm. 'What is wrong?' I asked, alarmed by her pallor.

'My poor François,' she said, breathless. 'His ear became inflamed and he collapsed with a fever.' She pulled from me. 'I must be with him, madame,' and she left me standing there.

Raindrops splattered the cobblestones. Elisabeth slipped her hand in mine. Claude looked at me awkwardly; as Lorraine's wife, she was expected to attend Mary. 'Go,' I said to her. 'See to your duties. You'll come to me later to report on your brother's health. Is that understood?'

Claude nodded and scampered off, sturdy as a hen in her white velvets.

Elisabeth murmured: 'Come, Maman, let's go inside. It's cold.'

* * *

Following François's coronation – which was a modest affair because of his frail health – the Spanish escort arrived to take Elisabeth to Spain.

I insisted on riding with her all the way to snowbound Châtelherault. By the frozen river, she turned to her ladies, retrieving a squirming bundle and passing it gently to me. When I peeled back the ice-flecked wool, I encountered moist dark eyes staring at me from a fluffy white face.

'I haven't named her yet,' Elisabeth said. 'She's a puppy, but she won't grow much bigger than she is now. I'm told the breed is very long-lived and cleaves to one master.'

The little dog yipped, writhing in my embrace as she tried to get free of the wool long enough to lick my nose. I stared at Elisabeth in helpless silence.

'She's also rather noisy.' My daughter laughed. 'She'll bark at anyone she doesn't know and will make an excellent guard for your door.'

'She's lovely,' I said. 'I'll call her Muet, silent one, because she's so noisy.'

Elisabeth whispered, 'I love you, Maman. I'll write to you every day.'

I embraced her, Muet wiggling between us. Then I released her to her escort, standing on the riverbank as she embarked on her passage into the mountains. Countless people had crossed the Pyrenees; Spain was just across our border. We could visit every year if we liked.

Still, I stood there long after she disappeared, smelling her scent on the dog's soft fur.

The court moved to Blois after François again took ill, no doubt from the strain of his crowning, during which he'd been forced to stand and kneel for hours in a freezing cathedral, his chest bared for anointing. He'd never been strong, but I barely recognized the dreadfully gaunt adolescent huddled in bed, his sunken eyes glittery with opiate and fever.

I tried to reassure François and lend him encouragement.

I brewed special herbal drafts of rhubarb and chamomile; I sat and read to him. But whenever I mentioned the Guises or the edict, he moaned and turned his face from me, muttering he had never wanted to be king.

Mary didn't appear to enjoy being queen either. She was thin and agitated, worrying over François until I insisted she partake of other diversions. We walked the walled gardens of Blois together, played the lute and embroidered, establishing a delicate rapport that was shattered one afternoon as we sat in my rooms.

'Those Huguenots are vicious dogs,' she said without warning. 'They defied my uncle Monsignor's edict and ripped it from the town squares, though it is forbidden by law. Burning is too good for them. They should be drawn and quartered, their limbs left to rot on every city gate. My uncle says they cast spells on poor François to make him ill. He says they poison the wells and curse the harvests, so that our people thirst and starve.'

I looked up from my sewing hoop. I had not heard this particular brand of venom from her before. 'My dear, your uncle exaggerates. I assure you, they are not monsters. And I doubt there are so many as to bring about such calamity.'

Her eyes grew huge in her drawn face. 'You don't think heretics dwell under this very roof? The entire court seethes with them!'

In the corner on her cushions, Muet growled. Lucrezia came over to refill our goblets. I drank it in one gulp. 'You should heed less rhetoric,' I said, more sharply than I intended. 'François has always suffered from earaches and we've had bad harvests and too much rain for several years now. As a queen you must learn the value of tolerance with all your subjects.'

She gasped. 'You . . . you actually defend them . . . ?'

'I defend the innocent.' I fixed her with my stare. 'I want peace in France and prosperity for all. This is not Spain: we do not burn people here for differences of opinion.' I stopped her protest. 'Yes, it *is* a difference of opinion. Last I heard we worship the same Christ.'

She stood, trembling, her embroidery falling in a tangle at her feet. 'So it is true. You . . . you are . . .' She gulped, as if she were choking on the word.

I shot a look at Lucrezia, who stood immobile, decanter in hand. I forced out a chuckle. 'What? What am I? By God, you do not think that I, the king's mother, am a heretic?'

She didn't move, didn't meet my eyes. Her silence was answer enough.

I sighed. 'You disappoint me. I was born in the Roman faith and, I assure you, I will die in it. Just because I advocate tolerance doesn't mean I share the credo. Like you, I know almost nothing of these Huguenots, but I am sure of this much: they do not persecute us.'

'Yet you defend them!' Mary cried. She whirled about, marching away. I rolled my eyes in exasperation at Lucrezia. 'Have you ever heard such nonsense? Now my own daughter-in-law thinks I'm in league with the Protestants. Where could she have gotten such a preposterous notion?' Even as I feigned dismay, I knew what she would say before she spoke.

'Where else?' she said. 'Take heed, my lady, lest Monsignor find a way to consign you to the flames. It seems he will stop at nothing to achieve his ends.'

Five nights later, a pounding on my door awoke me. I fumbled for flint to light my candle when Lucrezia raced in. 'My lady, you must rise! We must leave at once!'

I slid from my bed; from her truckle bed at my side, Anna-Maria peered at me. Birago came in moments later. 'Blessed Virgin, what is it?' I asked, throwing on a shawl.

'The Guises say that Huguenot rebels march toward us. Monsignor orders our departure for Amboise. There is no time to pack. We must go as we are.'

I recalled my confrontation with Mary and wanted to break something. I searched Birago's face. 'Is it true? What do you know?'

He looked tired, his thin features drained from the long nights and days he spent acting as my spy in the galleries and passageways of the courts, trying to ferret out any useful information he could. 'All I know is that a Guise scouting party came upon the rebels in the forest and captured one. This man confessed that the Huguenots plan to siege Blois and take Their Majesties captive.' His voice lowered. 'The Guises have spies everywhere. I can't imagine how they failed to uncover this before now. In any event, we're expected in the courtyard. I wouldn't tarry.'

I dressed, grabbed my jewel coffer and sleepy Muet under my arms, and sped from my apartments. Courtiers were rushing from every direction, carrying half-packed valises as they stumbled down the tiered staircase in a panic. My women and I were swept along, staggering into the courtyard breathless and with our headdresses askew.

A contingent of guards blocked the château's iron gates. Grooms ran about with torches, casting a smoky glow over the women as they scrambled into carts normally reserved for transporting furniture. Men leapt onto horses; le Balafré's retinue cantered around the courtyard, yelling and inciting more panic. Fear ripened in the midnight air.

I caught sight of le Balafré herding Mary and François into a carriage. Thrusting my coffer and Muet at Lucrezia – 'Find a wagon!' – I dashed across the courtyard. I reached le Balafré with my heart in my throat. He gave me a cruel smile from his white steed, his lean figure encased in armor. 'I see Your Grace heeded our warning. You may ride with Their Majesties.'

I scrambled into the upholstered interior. When I looked up, Mary seared me with her stare. Smothered in furs, François groaned, 'What's keeping them? Do they expect us to wait and be killed?' and I banged on the rooftop with my hand. 'Go! Now! The king commands it!'

The carriage lurched forward, descending the steep château road and careening into the night.

'How can you call it a revolt?' I faced Monsignor and le Balafré in the lusterless light seeping through their study in Amboise, the sumptuous palace embellished by my father-in-law, where I had first struck my pact with Diane. Now I fought to strike another pact, having waited days for an audience, badgering Monsignor's secretary until he agreed to see me. 'You sent us racing from Blois when you know those men were disorganized and desperate. They let themselves be rounded up like lambs; they wanted to plead with the king and offer their grievances. They are starving, afraid; your edict has denied them the right to conduct business and they've lost their livelihoods. You can't blame them for seeking justice.'

Monsignor sat at his desk, his well-fed fleshy cheeks tinged red with anger. At his side, his brother, le Balafré, stood like a granite pillar, his unblinking gray-blue eyes fixed on me.

'An example must be made,' repeated the cardinal. 'Those poor men, as you call them, are traitors. They planned an attack on a royal château.' He raised his voice to cut short my protest. 'We have the documents to prove they were both organized and willing to do harm to Their Majesties. They planned to take them captive and kill my brother and me.'

'And they planned to legalize the Huguenot faith and sit their leaders on the Council,' intoned le Balafré, his voice inflexible as the gold-sheathed sword at his waist. He grimaced, his puckered scar distorting his lips. 'We are the ones who seek justice, madame, and after we have had it, we will have their leaders – all of them, including Admiral de Coligny.'

I returned his stare in silence, willing myself to stay seated, for now I knew that I fought for more than the lives of anonymous men ensnared by the Guises.

'What . . . what does Coligny have to do with this?'

'He is the mastermind,' replied Monsignor. 'We found a letter on one of the prisoners, conveying Coligny's order to capture the king. This was his plan. He is heretic as Satan.'

'If that is true,' I countered, 'then why send us such a pathetic lot?' I looked at le Balafré. 'You are a soldier, my lord. You fought beside my husband and you know Geneva and the Low Countries are full of mercenaries for hire. Surely, Coligny could have hired some.'

Le Balafré didn't answer; the cardinal's fist clenched on his desk. 'Madame, we have heard you out in patience,' he said, 'but I suggest you confine yourself to your household affairs. These men are rebels. They'll be put to the death and a warrant will be issued for Coligny.'

'Dear God,' I breathed. 'You are mad. You cannot kill those men. It could mean war with the Huguenots. Coligny is a noble-man, nephew to the constable. You cannot –'

'We can!' roared le Balafré. He took a step to me, his huge veined hand at his sword hilt. 'Do not presume to tell us how to rule. We are Guises, descendants of a noble line that puts your merchant's blood to shame. Our late king had no choice when they wed him to you, the niece of a false pope with nothing to commend her; but we do. Mother to His Majesty or not, one more word and we'll see you exiled for life, Medici.'

He spat my family name as if it were filth. For a heart-stopping instant, I couldn't move. I met his malignant stare and saw the revulsion he'd never fully displayed until now – the contempt for my lineage, my gender, my very person. I was horrified by the thought that during the twenty-six years I'd been with Henri, this man had nurtured such loathing of me. But I was even more horrified by his omnipotence, his undoubting belief that he was in the right, always, because he was a Guise.

Monsignor folded his supple hands at his mouth, in a vain attempt to disguise his smile. 'Madame, you look pale. Perhaps you should retire.'

I started to turn, not feeling the carpet underneath my feet.

'You will attend the executions when a date is set,' I heard le Balafré clip. 'The entire court is expected to attend. We will broach no absences save for the queen and Their Highnesses.'

I looked back at him. 'I wouldn't miss it,' I said and I left them with their eyes narrowed, pondering my meaning. Only once I'd clicked the door shut on them did I let myself feel the horror and fury that ran like poison through my veins.

We assembled in Amboise's inner courtyard. I wore a veil to obscure my face and sat apart; I was the only one to don black, while the court assembled in their finery on tiers, as if for a tournament. In the background came the muted roars of Amboise's caged lions in the menagerie.

Monsignor brought forth François in his royal robes and coronet, sitting him on a chair under a canopy, his oversized cap shadowing his waxen face. He looked frailer than ever, but as I started to rise le Balafré stepped forth to stop me.

'His Majesty is here because he will see the heretic traitors pay for their crimes.'

'Then I should be with him,' I said. I saw Monsignor nod, a pomander held at his nose. I could barely look at him as I sat next to François and noticed how my son gripped his chair's armrests, his knuckles drained to white.

Guards hauled in the first ten prisoners, their hands roped behind their backs. Their features were indistinct from where I sat but I saw they were young. My stomach knotted as I wondered who they were: landowners, farmers, or merchants; if once they'd dwelled in safety in their townships, where they bedded their wives, loved their children, and sought meaning in an incomprehensible world through a new faith that promised what ours had failed to give.

Condemned traitors weren't allowed to speak, but when the first young man caught sight of us above him, a collection of shadows, he called out, 'Mercy, Your Majesty! Have mercy –'

He didn't finish. The executioner swung his sword and sent the man's head flying. The next victim staggered on his predecessor's blood. He was forced to his knees. Leather-clad apprentices below the scaffold caught his severed head.

Another followed, and another. Blood flooded the scaffold, dripping to the cobblestones and snaking toward the keep, where the others sang as their comrades died – not somber Catholic prayers but the vibrant psalms of the Protestants. But as the pile of heads mounted and the air turned foul with the stench of urine, feces, and blood, their singing faltered and by dusk the guards were dragging the last of the fifty-two shouting and flailing to their deaths.

I did not look away. I did not close my eyes. Though my heart quailed and bile rose in the pit of my being, I forced myself to bear witness to the madness unleashed by the Guises. It was in those hours, as night fell and the cardinal started to turn green about the mouth, as one by one the nobles staggered away while le Balafré remained obdurate, directing the executions with militant precision, that my own resolve turned to stone.

I would destroy the Guises. I would not rest until I freed France of their menace. Forever.

My son let out a moan as the last prisoner was hacked to pieces by the exhausted executioner. I felt his icy fingers grip mine and heard him whisper, 'May God forgive them.'

I knew he meant the Guises; but what God might forgive, I never would.

And if I had my way, neither would the Huguenots.

20

Flambeaux lit the night, summoning curious fireflies to circle in the spring air. A pavane sounded in the distance, redolent of Florence. Canopied barges shaped in the fantastical images of proud swans and birds of prey glided past on the Cher, their painted oars stirring the river's silvery surface. Mary and François sailed there with a select group of attendants, holding hands and finding solace in a make-believe refuge veiled by hangings of gossamer. My other children, Margot, Charles, and Henri, sat in another barge with their governors, without a care in the world.

I'd managed to spirit them away following the executions, but only after the smell of the rotting heads garlanding Amboise's balustrades had caused Mary to faint and crowds of angry citizens clamored at the gates, flinging a dead dog at the cardinal's carriage when he attempted to leave the palace. As I'd hoped, with one act the Guises had unmasked themselves as tyrants, turning all but our most conservative Catholics against them; for if Monsignor and his brother could slaughter fifty-two men without even a trial, it did not bode well for anyone else who might think to oppose them.

And so Monsignor conceded to my request that a change in scenery was in order. He and le Balafré had to remain behind to restore some semblance of order, but he didn't want his precious Stuart niece or François falling ill; and I seized full advantage to divest ourselves of most of the court, as my château was too small. As soon as we reached Chenonceau I sent out my invitation. I now had the advantage and I stood at the window, watching my son and his queen sail past.

A knock came at my study door. Lucrezia said, 'He's here.'
She paused. 'Are you sure you know what you're doing?'

'Of course. Don't fret.' I gave her a smile as I gathered the
portfolio containing the document that I'd drafted with Birago.
'I'll be there in a minute. See that our meal is readied.'

She snorted and retreated. I eyed myself in the mirror. I'd
donned a new black damask gown with a high collar. Pearls
adorned my ears; rinses of walnut juice and henna had restored
the auburn in my hair, now coiled in a gilded net at my nape.
I'd shed pounds by riding for an hour every morning and
cutting back on my penchant for bread. In all, my reflection
assured that I'd succeeded in resurrecting something of the
girl he'd met in Fontainebleau. It was vital I appear vibrant
and strong.

Taking up the portfolio, I pushed open the door between my
study and the adjacent room.

Birago and Coligny stood by the hearth, goblets in hand. He
had accepted my wine and removed his cloak: good signs. At the
sound of my entrance, he turned. In the flickering of the candlelight, he didn't seem to have aged a day.

'Welcome,' I said, as he set aside his goblet and bowed over
my hand. Birago excused himself, leaving us alone. Coligny
had about him the aroma of horses and sweat, for he'd ridden
several hours to get here. Abruptly nervous, I motioned him
to the table.

I'd chosen this chamber because of its intimacy and saw that
despite her reservations Lucrezia had outdone herself. The sideboard shimmered with polished gold platters; a vase of lilies sat
on the mantel, while the central table was set with my Limoges
porcelain and Murano glass goblets.

A frown crossed Coligny's brow as he stood by his chair. His
beard was fuller, its brassy color radiant, as if he'd combed
pomade into it.

However, the candlelight deceived: I could see new harsh lines
scoring the corners of his eyes and he was much thinner.

'My lord,' I said, 'you must be hungry. Please, sit.'

'Before I do, I must ask you about what happened at Amboise. The Huguenot pastors are horrified, as is our brethren. I . . . I need to know.'

I faced him. 'What? If I sat there like Jezebel while innocent blood was spilled? Is that what you think?'

To my relief, he did not hesitate. 'No. I think that you did everything you could to stop it.'

'I did. Birago must have also assured you that I protested the warrant for your arrest. Fortunately, they'll not dare issue it now that Monsignor has seen the enormity of their error.'

'Too late,' he said in a low voice, and I assented.

'For those poor souls, yes; but I trust, not too late for us. Now, will you dine with me?'

We sat opposite each other. Lucrezia entered with our first course of roast goose garnished with artichoke hearts from my gardens. He looked surprised; I told him, 'I brought the seeds from Tuscany myself. There is no artichoke superior to the Florentine.'

'It's . . . delicious,' he marveled, tasting it. 'I'd expect such fare in a country home.'

'This is a country house.' I reached over to pour claret into his glass. 'I loathe meals at court. The food arrives cold from its long trek from the kitchens and is so spiced or drowned in sauce you don't know what it is. When I'm not at court, I eat what my gardens can produce. The goose was born and slaughtered here; even this wine is made from my harvest of grapes.'

He raised his goblet. 'To Your Grace's health.'

'Catherine,' I said, as our goblets clinked together. 'You must call me Catherine.'

We fell into silence as we received next a course of chicken basted in fennel. He ate with gusto; I was pleased to note he had rough table manners, a country boy at heart. It was one of the reasons I liked him. After years of mincing courtiers and back-stabbing mistresses, conniving churchmen and arrogant nobles, to me he personified all that was still gallant in France.

I breached the quiet. 'I want you to know that my son regrets

the events at Amboise. He did not realize how terrible a retribution the Guises would enact.'

He considered me. 'Was His Majesty's signature not on the
warrant of execution?'

I swallowed. 'It was. But François has been ill and the Guises
forced his hand. He didn't understand what he was doing. I saw
how awful he felt as he watched those men die.'

'Not as awful as their widows and children.' He sat back in his
chair as Lucrezia came in to remove our plates. 'Your Grace – I
mean, Catherine . . . I'm afraid that one deed has caused grave
mistrust among the Huguenot leaders. They deem the king as
bloodthirsty a tyrant as Philip of Spain, who slaughters Protestants
by the thousands in his dominions.'

He couldn't contain the anger that crept into his voice. His
trust in me was betrayed and I found as I drank down my wine
and poured another glass, my hands trembled.

'I am aware of how low my son's reputation has fallen,' I said,
'and that it will worsen unless something is done. But I take some
comfort in the fact that the Guises confront equal calumny.' I
reached to my side and slid the portfolio across the table to him.
'You will find here an edict I intend to see ratified by parlement,
allowing the Huguenots liberty of conscience. We can overthrow
the Guises and safeguard your brethren, but I will need your help.'

His silence weighed as he read my edict, which I'd spent days
preparing. An eternity seemed to pass. Then he said, 'What do
you mean by "liberty of conscience"? This says Huguenots won't
be disturbed if they abide by the law. But the law currently forbids
all gatherings for worship.'

'What I mean is that the law will change. By my edict,
Huguenots will be able to petition the king when wronged and
hold services in sanctioned temples designated for that use.'

He nodded. 'A shrewd move. It invalidates the Guises' edict
of persecution.' He set the paper aside. 'And you believe the king
will sign it?'

'François is under my care now. He understands the urgency
of our situation.'

Coligny took up his goblet. The candlelight fractured on the beveled crystal, shedding gilded fragments over the blond hairs on his hands. 'Are you considering legalizing the Huguenot faith?' he asked, as he lifted his eyes to mine. 'If so, you'll find opposition from many Catholic lords, as well as Rome and Spain. None wishes to sanction coexistence of our two religions.'

I started to evade the question, for I hadn't thought that far ahead; then I decided it was best to begin this venture with full honesty. 'I cannot say when, or even if, I'll be able to legalize your faith. As you've said, there are many obstacles and I cannot make a foe of either Spain or Rome. But peace in this kingdom is paramount to me. We've too much to lose otherwise.'

He sipped his wine, without taking his eyes from me. He did not speak and I thought perhaps I had disclosed too much. After all, he was still a stranger to me.

'How can I help?' he finally said.

I allowed myself a smile. 'You speak with the Huguenot pastors and other leaders, yes? Tell them of my edict. Let them preach to their congregations and counsel restraint, so there are no disturbances while I work with parlement.' My voice took strength, envisioning the country liberated at last from the Guises' terror. 'I do not blame the Huguenots for wanting revenge, but there must be tolerance if we are to survive.'

'And the Guises? The leaders want them removed from the government. They see the Guises as cold-blooded killers, who must pay for what they've done.'

'I agree. However, I cannot remove them by force, not yet. But I believe in this new enterprise as I've believed in nothing else, and I know that in the end France will have no peace while the Guises hold power.'

He leaned back, raking his hand over his close-cropped hair. 'I think I can speak for most of the leaders when I say peace is also our desire. But not everyone will bow to reason.'

'Oh? Explain.' I knew I wouldn't like it, but I needed to hear it. I must recognize and overcome all obstacles, no matter where they came from.

'Put simply, the deaths at Amboise have divided my brethren into two factions. One side wishes to live their lives without fear. The other wants the same, plus the removal of the Guises and a role in the government. This is not simple: some men will switch sides, depending on their circumstances. If you seek to worship freely, but then your house is burned, your crop razed, and your daughters raped by a Guise patrol, you're likely to change your stance.'

'So, we have religious and political issues to address.' I caught a shift in his eyes and added, 'I would seek to place Huguenots of influence on the Council. I do not believe our differences mean we cannot find common ground.'

He cupped his hand at his chin. 'When that time comes,' he said, 'I would welcome a place at court. We need to work together if we are to return France to her former glory.' And a genuine smile brightened his face, the first I'd seen all night. 'I believe you have our best interests at heart. I will therefore speak with the leaders and the pastors and see that no one acts in retaliation for Amboise. It will take time, though. They are scattered; no one dares congregate in these dangerous times. I'll have to meet with them one by one.'

'I ask for nothing more.' For the first time in weeks, I felt I might actually succeed in bringing down the Guises for good. I reached for the decanter, saying, 'I hope you'll like the chamber I've prepared for you. It's small but I've little extra room, as my children are here.'

'I'm sure it would be fine,' he replied, 'though I must decline your hospitality.'

The air in the room shifted. I bit back my protest. Of course he couldn't stay. I might see Chenonceau as my refuge, but neither of us could be sure there weren't Guise spies lurking about. And he had his own family to consider, whom he'd left to see me.

'Naturally,' I said, hiding my disappointment. 'I was thoughtless to assume otherwise.'

'No,' he said. 'I would stay, if I could. But my wife . . . she has been ill.'

'Oh, no. I hope it's not serious.'

'I'm afraid it is.' He averted his eyes from me. 'Charlotte is dying. She gave birth a few months ago to a daughter,' he said, his voice so low I had to lean to him to hear. 'The labor was hard but the child sound. Then Charlotte lost her milk; she couldn't feed the babe. Her appetite deserted her and at first we thought she had milk fever, but as time went on she did not improve. We hired a doctor and he found . . .' He swallowed. 'She has a lump in her breast. She wastes away before my eyes and I can do nothing.'

I knew all too well the helplessness of watching a spouse die, of praying for a miracle you fear will never come. I reached over, set my hand on his where it rested on the table. 'I will send to court for our royal physician, Dr. Paré. If anyone can heal her, he can.'

He went still. Then he withdrew his hand and stood. 'No. It is too late.'

That brief touch of his skin burned in me. I followed him to the bay window overlooking the night-shrouded gardens, where mummers entertained Mary and François in a spangled pavilion. 'She might yet be saved. While there is a chance, we must never lose hope.'

He turned so quickly we found ourselves face-to-face. I could discern darker flecks in his pale blue eyes, the supple lines at their corners, and slash of cheekbones above his lustrous beard. He was a few inches taller than me; his wine-tinged breath blew warm on my brow. 'You remind me of her,' he said. 'She too is brave and bold.'

Under my bodice, my heart started to pound. 'I . . . I am not her,' I whispered.

His hand slid downward, to my waist. 'No, you're not. She doesn't have your strength. You are the strongest woman I know, Catherine de Medici.'

The sound of my name on his lips sent heat rushing through me. No one had looked at me like this; no man had ever seen the strength in me as he did. I felt as though I might dissolve in his gaze, as if he had opened that place inside me where I'd locked the wreckage of my youth and my dreams – everything that life and time had made me surrender.

And I knew then that I wanted this man. I had wanted him all along.

Desire flared in me like a newborn sun, so overpowering that I tried to pull away. He didn't let me go. He brought me to him, his lips closing on mine, quenching my breath. I lost all sense of reason, of myself, drowning in the heat of being wanted for myself, for the very first time.

I heard him murmur, 'Just for tonight,' and it was enough. It was everything.

I led him through the darkened château to the staircase. Through the open windows that let in the soft evening air, the sound of music and laughter drifted to me. My children and Mary Stuart were enjoying their revel; they sounded for once like the young people they were.

Lucrezia rose from her stool, her eyes sharp in the moonlight sliding like silk through the mullioned window. I gestured. She gathered Muet in her arms and retreated without a word.

My bedchamber awaited; sun-dried linen sheets drawn back, the satin coverlet I'd embroidered by hand folded over. Anna-Maria was with the children; hearing the door click shut behind me, I moved as if in a dream to the candle in its sconce on my dressing table.

'No,' he said, 'leave it. Let me look at you.'

I felt as I had the night I first bedded Henri, at a loss as to how to act. I almost laughed aloud. I was forty-one. I'd been with a man before. I knew what couples did.

With that uncanny way he had of sensing my thoughts, Coligny said, 'Don't be afraid.' He untied my sleeves, removed my stomacher, bodice, and skirts, until my clothing lay strewn like foam at my feet and I stood in my shift, trembling, but not with cold.

In an instinct born of years as a wife, I turned to climb into bed. Then I heard clothing slide to the floor, the single clank of a metallic buckle. When I looked around, he stood naked, a taut silhouette of pallid skin.

I stared. He was beautiful but his body was nothing like Henri's, not that broad hirsute frame I'd known. This was a small wiry man, his muscles melded to the bone, standing with utter confidence and a wry smile that made my knees turn to water. His manhood rose upright from its thatch of bronze hair; his ribs showed under his flesh as he drew quick breaths. Lifting his corded arms to undo the gilded net at my nape, he released my hair and it tumbled over my shoulders.

'Like a dark sea,' he whispered and he melded his body to mine, laying me on the bed as with one hand he slipped my shift upward, over my head. All doubt evaporated when I felt his touch, transformed by some alchemy into exquisite, near-unbearable pleasure. He teased me with his lips and his tongue, and when I began to shudder and he entered me, I let out a cry I'd never made before: a spontaneous celebration of uninhibited joy that released my very soul.

I awoke before dawn. He was at the window, dressed. He turned as the sky unfurled behind him. 'I must go,' he said and he sat beside me, caressing tangled hair from my face. He looked into my eyes with sadness and I said softly, 'No apologies.'

His expression was gentle yet grave, once again the reserved courtier.

'We must never speak of it,' I said, and I touched his cheek. 'They would not understand. We have so much to fight for and they . . . they would say I seek peace with the Huguenots because I took you to my bed.' As I spoke I trembled with the first chill I'd felt since our night together and I had a fleeting fear that I might have surrendered something I'd come to regret.

'I will not tell a soul,' he said. 'Never forget that God has a plan for you. Without you, this realm will fall apart. You can save France, but never underestimate them. Remember, while you think you hold them at bay, they are still tigers and tigers know when to attack.'

He kissed me. 'I'll send word as soon as I can. Until then, do not risk yourself, even for me.'

I cradled his face, engraving it in my memory. 'Godspeed, Gaspard,' I whispered.

He gathered his cloak and left.

As I brought my hands to my face, his scent clung like rain to my fingers.

21

We left Chenonceau in late autumn, as the chestnuts changed colors and wild swans flocked to the Cher in search of last-minute food. I'd had time to bask in my secret, to relive it in my mind every night; I'd ridden with Mary and overseen François's health. I spent time with Charles, Henri, Margot, and Hercule, governing their lessons and their well-being.

At ten, Charles bore a startling resemblance to his father. He was tall as Henri had been, with the hooded Valois eyes and aquiline nose. He liked the same activities: riding, hunting, fencing, and hawking, and I had a special bow made for him so he could practice. Seven-year-old Margot was budding into a precocious beauty with her mass of red-streaked hair and feline eyes that seemed to miss nothing. She was indolent, however, preferring to preen before the mirror, and I put her on a strict diet, for like me she easily gained weight. In contrast, nine-yearold Henri was slim as a blade, with my olive skin and long-lashed dark eyes that contained a prescient light. Of all of them, Henri alone seemed to sense the change in me.

I enjoyed every moment of time alone with my children, but the idyll couldn't last. When the Guises sent word that the court was in Orléans preparing for Christmas, we packed up and left, the children chattering with excitement as I braced for another battle with the Guises.

Instead, we arrived to tragedy.

Marie de Guise, regent of Scotland on her daughter's behalf, had died after years of struggle against the Protestant lords, who now ruled the kingdom until Mary came home or named another regent. Mary was oblivious to the political discord plaguing her land, disconsolate over the mother she did not recall, and though the Guises declared us in mourning, they understood that with no means to keep Scotland safe, our alliance was now on paper alone. The Guise prestige had plummeted; few of the nobles invited to court that holiday season deigned to appear and tumult plagued the streets, with placards denouncing the Guises as bloodthirsty tyrants plastered on every corner. Their stranglehold on France was weakening.

I was left to care for the children and Mary. Her sorrow roused frenetic concern in François, who couldn't stand to see her distressed. The combination of her grief, undercurrents of intrigue at court, and daily visits from Monsignor proved too much and François fell ill again.

This time, the onslaught was merciless. Within days a monstrous fistula had formed inside his left ear and he writhed in agony, suppurating pus and soaked with fever. I ensconced myself in his chamber and held him while he shrieked and his physicians debated the feasibility of using a stronger dose of opiate.

'Fools!' I yelled. 'Look at him! Dose him now or by God I'll have your heads!'

Mary hovered nearby. I almost waved her out, thinking the sight of her would make François even more anxious, but she crept to his side and took his hand. I watched in awe as he went quiet, like a sick animal soothed by its master's touch. She had a more calming effect than any opiate, and so I left her in charge of his care so I could contend with the growing anxiety at court.

Every time I emerged from his rooms to change my clothing or take nourishment, I found a host of whispering courtiers and dagger-eyed ambassadors waiting in the galleries, searching my face for any sign that death was about to claim my son. François was childless; his heir was my third son, ten-year-old Charles. I could almost hear the court's avid speculation as they sensed the balance of power begin to tilt; and I took to creeping down hidden back passageways to my rooms, where I stayed only long enough to recover my strength.

One night, bone-weary from my vigil, I entered my apartments in a haze. As I passed the alcove, I sensed a presence. I whirled about. I couldn't contain my gasp when I saw Nostradamus materialize as if from nowhere. 'You scared me to death! How did you get in here?'

'Through the door,' he said. 'No one noticed.' He wore unadorned black, his collar high about his throat. He clutched a staff and held himself with an aged person's focused poise, yet I heard wry humor in his tone. 'You'd be surprised at how little attention old men get.' His voice softened. 'I am sorry for your trials, my lady. I would not have come this far to trouble you had I not felt the need.'

I took a step back. 'No. You must not say it.'

He tilted his head. 'If I do not say it, how will you know?'

'I don't want to know!' My voice cracked. 'My son is dying! If you have any care for me, you'll not speak of further suffering. I'm not you. I can't bear to know the future.'

'And yet you must, for I have seen you in the water.' His voice turned dark. '"The eldest branch dies before eighteen, without leaves and two islands in discord. The younger tree will rule longer, against those who would fill the realm with blood and strife."'

A black wave crashed over me. 'What . . . what does it mean?'

He shook his head. 'You ask and yet you know.' He held up his hand. 'I cannot give you something I do not possess. I do not hold the key. Only you do, for it is your path.'

He turned and walked out, leaving emptiness in his wake. I wanted to yell at him to come back. What good was a seer who spoke in riddles and disappeared like mist? How could his convoluted prophecies serve me now?

Then, without warning, I understood.

François was my eldest; he had no child. The islands in discord were the religions. And my next son, Charles – he would inherit. He would rule, much longer, against those who wished us harm. I knew who they were: the Guises, my mortal enemies. I had to fight. Charles would need me more than François ever had; he would need me to champion his rights, to thwart those who sought to rule through him and bring more havoc upon France.

Never forget that God has a plan for you. Without you, this realm will fall apart.

I was about to lose a son. But in return, I now had the chance to save his kingdom.

I called for Birago. 'Send out letters with my private seal,' I said in a muted voice. 'Write to the constable, to all the nobles who would see the Guises fall. Tell them the Queen Mother urgently requests their presence at court. Tell them it is a matter of life and death.'

He nodded. 'Is His Majesty . . . ?'

'Soon,' I whispered. 'We must be ready.'

Five days later, as I held his wasted hand, flanked by sobbing Mary and the grim-faced Guises, my son François II breathed his last.

He had not yet celebrated his seventeenth birthday.

PART V
1560–1570
The Tempest

22

I did not have time to mourn.

We returned to Paris with my son's corpse, where he was handed over to the embalmers and Mary, our widow queen, was escorted by her Guise relatives to her cloister in the Hôtel de Cluny. Overnight, a frozen hush descended, mirroring the December snows blanketing Paris.

I moved at once to protect Charles and my other children. No one was allowed to see them without my permission, especially the Guises, and once I proclaimed our official mourning I embarked on my second order of business.

'The lords will be here by tomorrow,' Birago informed me as we sat in my apartments at night, haggard from our labor. 'Letters have also been sent to Philip of Spain and Elizabeth of England, as well as the princes in Germany and the Low Countries, stating your case.'

'Good.' I undid my ruff, set it aside. 'Is there any word from Queen Jeanne of Navarre?'

He sighed. 'Yes. She wrote back to say she'll consider your offer to receive her, but she does not think she can bear weeks of difficult travel across France in the dead of winter.'

'Is that so?' I snorted. 'Well, that suits me fine. I've no desire to contend with her or that Bourbon husband of hers. I offered as a courtesy, nothing more.'

Birago ran a hand over his balding pate. Now in his late forties, he'd lost most of his hair and his bare brow emphasized his sharp features and deep-set eyes, which were always alert, watchful, like a bird of prey's. '*Madama,* much as I hate to say this I believe we should not dismiss Antoine of Bourbon so quickly. By law,

Charles must have a regent until he comes of age. Antoine is of royal blood; he stands in the line of succession after your sons. He is also of the Catholic faith and therefore could stake a claim to the regency against you.'

I forced out a curt laugh as I trudged to my chair. My legs ached from the icy chill permeating the old Louvre, which no amount of fires in our hearths could mitigate. 'Last I'd heard, Antoine's sole faith was wine and vice. I hardly think such a louse poses a threat.'

'When it comes to power, even the worst sinner can repent.'

'In other words, he could become a Guise weapon.' I sat, considering. 'Well, for now we can assume Jeanne has no intention of letting Antoine come to court. Like us, she must be aware that he has a right to the regency, and the last thing she'll want is her husband, the father of her son, making an alliance with the Guises, whom she detests as only a Huguenot queen can. I don't think we need worry on his account.' I paused. 'Any news of Coligny?'

As I spoke, I kept my tone neutral, not showing the surge of anticipation I felt when Birago replied, 'He wrote to say that the Huguenot leaders agree to refrain from further action until they hear the outcome of Your Grace's edict.'

'And of our request to attend us at court . . . ?'

'He cannot, for the moment. His wife is still quite ill, and he says he must be with her.'

I bit my lip, my enthusiasm fading into disappointment. Much as I yearned for him, I couldn't expect otherwise. 'So be it,' I said. 'We'll proceed without him. As soon as the lords arrive, call the Council to session. It is time I gave these Guises a well-deserved lesson.'

I sat at the head of the wide oak table as the lords filed in. I smiled at each in turn, noting the constable's vigorous nod and Monsignor's silken smile. Though not pleased to find himself surrounded by old foes at court, he didn't look like a man who was about to concede defeat.

'Where is your brother le Balafré, Monsignor?' I asked, and
he replied: 'He sends his regrets but felt he should inform our
parlement of our late king's funeral arrangements.'

'Oh?' I returned his smile. 'He should have asked first. I sent
word myself, days ago.'

The cardinal's fine features tightened, his conciliatory mask
slipping to reveal the despot underneath. A courtier first, his
instincts honed for survival, he knew what was coming.

The others waited. With Birago seated beside me, holding his
leather portfolio, I said, 'I grieve for my son François. God has
seen fit to take him from us and leave this realm to an underage
monarch, our new king, Charles IX.' I paused. My mouth was
dry. I took a sip of watered wine from my goblet. 'To learn to rule
requires time and France, as my lords know, is in dire need of a
steady hand. I therefore propose to declare myself regent until
Charles is of age.'

I saw gloating consent on the constable's weathered face; he
was now avenged for his exile by the Guises after my husband's
death. The others sat silent, almost quiescent; they did not worry
me. I was concerned only with Monsignor. Though I had him
cornered, he still had fangs.

His lips curled. 'I assume Her Grace will retain this Council?'

'Yes, with one addition. At the appropriate time, Admiral de
Coligny will join us.'

'Begging your leave,' Monsignor purred, 'but isn't he a
heretic?'

'My nephew is as qualified as any lord present,' growled
Montmorency.

'I don't question his qualifications,' replied Monsignor, 'but
rather his role against us.'

'I make the decisions now,' I interrupted. 'Coligny will serve,
pending the king's approval.' I looked at the others, found no
visible resistance. Rumors of Coligny's heresy might abound, but
it seemed he had not openly declared his new faith.

Monsignor steepled his long fingers before his face. As silence
fell, Birago took out the papers from his portfolio. 'Gentlemen,'

he said, 'I have here the official proclamation of Her Grace's regency, for your signatures.'

Hours later, I emerged to a cold supper. I devoured every morsel moments before Birago entered my room. Lucrezia cleared the plates as we sat by my fireplace.

'*Madama,* while we've won this day we are far from safe.' He stretched his feet before the fire. 'My spies tell me le Balafré never presented himself in parlement. He went to Champagne, to the Guise seat of Joinville, where he has many retainers. I fear he plots against you.'

'I expect nothing less. But at best Joinville is a week's ride from Paris. Whatever they plot, they cannot rouse an army without us learning of it first, yes?'

Birago nodded. 'Indeed. I've almost as many spies as Guise has retainers.' Then he paused. 'I know you hold Coligny in high esteem, *madama,* but seating him in Council might not be a wise decision. For now the Catholic lords accept your regency because they no longer trust the Guises, but they'll not be so amenable should Coligny's faith become common knowledge.'

In the quiet that followed his words, I heard the wind moan against the palace walls. Birago knew. My rooms were Lucrezia's domain: she'd seen Coligny enter with me. I didn't fault her. She must be worried; she wanted to protect me and confided in Birago, who was my adviser.

'Coligny holds significant influence with the Huguenot leaders,' I managed to say at length. 'We need their cooperation to implement my edict.'

Birago looked directly at me. 'I understand. However, I must ask that you not place your trust in him until he proves worthy of it.'

'Yes,' I murmured, 'of course. I am grateful for your candor.'

Birago left me. Scooping up Muet, I went into my bedchamber. As I prepared for bed, in my mind I traced his taut body, felt his hands buried in my hair, his mouth on my breasts . . .

That night, I did not sleep.

★ ★ ★

Christmas was a gloomy affair; Mary remained in her cloister and a subdued funeral cortege accompanied us to my son's entombment in St. Denis, after which I returned to the Louvre to assume charge of Charles.

I was gratified after the New Year when Monsignor, deprived of all power save his seat in Council, accepted an invitation to attend the Holy Council in Rome, which would assemble to discuss the spread of heresy in Europe. With the cardinal gone for what I hoped was months of theological debate and le Balafré kicking up dust in Joinville, I was at liberty to rearrange the court to my liking and institute a new regimen for Charles.

Like François before him, my ten-year-old son was over-whelmed by his kingship. He had a thousand questions, mostly about how much his life would change. 'Can I still hawk and hunt whenever I like?' he asked me as we stood in his scarlet-and-gold-hung rooms.

'Of course,' I said. 'Watch your fingers.' He fed tidbits of meat to a new peregrine falcon perched on a pole by his bed, a recent gift sent to him from Spain by his sister Elisabeth.

I smoothed the locks of tangled dark hair from his brow. 'Hunting and hawking are fine, my child, but you're king now. You must learn to rule. Birago will instruct you; he studied law in Florence and can teach you the proper ways of governance.'

Charles frowned. 'François said he hated being king. He told me the Guises were at him day and night and he never had a moment to himself. They even questioned him about how often he slept with Mary and got mad when he told them she was like a sister to him. Birago won't do that to me, will he?'

Guilt stabbed through me as I thought of how little I'd been able to protect my late son. François had been my firstborn, my triumph after years of barrenness; I could still recall how beautiful he'd been, a child delicate as a faun, and how he'd wailed for Diane whenever I assumed charge of him. Of everything she'd done, taking him from me was her cruelest act. In doing so she had deprived me of the chance to show François how much I loved him.

I forced out a smile, focusing on Charles. His infancy had likewise been overshadowed by Diane, but he was mine now. I would make him strong, healthy, everything a king should be.

'The Guises no longer have any power here,' I said to him. 'You needn't worry.'

He shrugged, seemingly absorbed in his falcon. Then he said with that uncanny insight that children sometimes display, 'If you're to be my regent, why can't you instruct me?'

I chuckled. 'Because I too have much to learn. Now, finish with that bird; Birago expects you in the classroom.' As I leaned down to kiss his cheek, he wrapped his arms around me. 'I love you, Maman,' I heard him murmur. 'Promise me, you'll never let the Guises hurt us again.'

Of all my children, he'd always been the least demonstrative, but I'd seen his desperate grief when his father died and knew he had a deep sensitivity. I held him close. 'I promise,' I whispered. 'They'll never hurt us. Never. I'd die first.'

I left him to check on Hercule, who had a mild colic, and then, after seeing to Margot and Henri – whom I'd set to a rigid schedule of studies – I returned to the task of ruling the kingdom.

I hadn't lied when I said I had much to learn. I'd never held power as queen consort in Henri's reign, save for my brief regency during the Milanese war, and I was faced with a near-destitute treasury, a troubled populace, and fractious government. Widespread starvation haunted France, the legacy of years of harsh winters and humid summers, so I had our royal storehouses opened and grain distributed. Birago suggested we reinvigorate taxation by putting the burden on our nobility rather than the mercantile class, but we were immersed in presenting my edict of toleration to the parlement, where it was hotly contested. It passed by a narrow margin; the Huguenots were now free to resume their businesses and worship in peace.

It was my first triumph as regent, and to celebrate our success I presented Charles at court.

Without extra money, we made do with what we had. Lucrezia, Anna-Maria, and I almost ruined our eyes and fingers altering the royal robes to fit Charles's spare frame. I dressed my other children with equal care; as our new heir, Henri sported a silver tissue doublet, which he accessorized in his inimitable style with pearl-drop earrings. Margot wore red satin and we squeezed Hercule into azure velvet and a jaunty cap.

Mary Stuart appeared clad in the white veil and gown of mourning. Though her cloister was at an end and the children clamored about her, to me she resembled a lost soul, shrouded in uncertainty. I dreaded the thought of contending with the thorny issue of her future, but I knew I must before the Guises did it for me, and so I wrote to Cosimo Ruggieri the next day to request an astrological chart, hoping to find clues to my immediate problems in the stars.

I had neglected Cosimo, leaving him to his business in his château at Chaumont, and I was shocked when he arrived by how thin he was. He looked as though he hadn't eaten a full meal in weeks, his face pared to bone and skin, his black eyes huge and gleaming with intensity.

As soon as he saw me, he released a dramatic sigh. 'I've done my utmost, but I'm afraid I'm not the great Nostradamus. I can't divine the future in a basin of water.'

I resisted rolling my eyes. We were off to a fine start. 'You don't see Nostradamus here, do you? Come, did you bring the chart? What does it say?'

I peered at the complex diagram he unrolled from a leather tube and set before me. He traced a line. 'See here: this eclipse in Leo means war.'

'War?' I looked up, startled by the certainty in his voice. 'Are you sure?'

'Yes. War is imminent. The stars do not lie.'

I swallowed the retort that his father would have disagreed. The Maestro had said nothing can be predicated for certain which concerns the future. And if nothing is certain, surely we can gain the knowledge to avert calamity.

'As soon as you take your rest, you must return to Chaumont,' I said. 'I must know how this war will come about. I need names, dates, places.' I was about to wave him out when I recalled the reason I'd summoned him. 'Did you see anything in the stars for Mary Stuart?'

He nodded, his intense black eyes unblinking, overpowering his gaunt face. 'I saw a marriage in her future that will bring about great misfortune.' He paused. 'I assume the name Don Carlos means something to you?'

I went still. Don Carlos was the prince of Spain, Philip II's son.

I went to Mary's apartments the next day. She looked better, with color in her cheeks and a new sheen in her hair. She'd even put on some much needed weight.

'I wanted to see how you fared, my dear,' I said as we kissed each other's cheeks. 'The cloister can be so difficult, but you seem to have survived well enough.'

'They insisted I could be carrying a child.' She smiled; we both knew, without having admitted it out loud, that my son never consummated their union. 'They also tell me I can rejoin the court, but François is gone. I feel as if I don't belong here anymore.'

I fell silent. I realized a transformation had taken place: our pampered queen had taken stock of her life in her widowhood, much as I had. I understood how trying this time of reflection was and resisted my sympathy for her. I had to do what I'd come here for, come what may.

'My dear,' I said gently. 'I'm afraid I've bad news to impart. Your Guise uncles . . . I've reason to believe they seek to wed you to Don Carlos, Philip of Spain's heir.'

She blinked. 'But he's mad. He's not fit for public life. Everyone knows that.'

'I fear his lack of reason poses no impediment as far as your uncles are concerned.'

Anger sparked in her eyes. 'I've just lost my François. They cannot think I'll consent!' We both glanced to the door, half-expecting her women to rush in. When they did not, she added in a taut voice, 'What can I do to stop it?'

I was again taken by surprise. The last time we'd had an actual conversation, she accused me of heresy. I twined my hands. 'You are still queen of Scotland, yes?'

She nodded, frowning. Then she froze. 'You think I should . . . ?'

I met her eyes, difficult as it was. I had fought with everything I had to stay in France; I connived to save myself. I expected the same from her; in fact, I anticipated it, for unlike me she had options. If she refused Don Carlos, her Guise uncles could offer her as a bride for Charles and I'd find myself trapped. This was why I couldn't falter. There was no other way.

'I don't remember Scotland,' she said, and it was as though she spoke to herself, to the curtains fluttering in the air coming through the casement. 'But it is my realm.' She lifted a hand to her face, her slim white finger now bare of a wedding ring. She turned to me. 'Maybe in Scotland, I will be happy again.'

I could have wept, for I knew that the loss of her prince had left a hollow in her that would never be filled. Despite all his faults, François's death had heralded the end of her innocence.

'You will,' I said, 'if that is your desire.'

Her smile was heartrending. 'I've had what I desired. Now I must do my duty.'

I took her in my arms. We had never been close, but I prayed for her safety.

For she was right: we both must do our duty. It was the price of privilege, of our roles as royal women. Before comfort, before hopes and dreams, our countries must come first.

Summer faded into autumn.

I wasn't present when Mary informed her Guise relatives of her decision, but I could imagine the uproar. Whatever transpired, however, was masked by stiff familial unity when she received the Scottish lords sent to escort her home.

On the day of her departure, mist floated over the landscape, veiling the drays and coaches of her entourage. To the cracking of whips, the assembly lumbered onto the road to Calais, where galleons waited to convey her to Scotland.

As her coach disappeared, Mary leaned from her window, her white-gloved hand raised in a final farewell.

23

A month later, I received word from Coligny, a brief note requesting I meet him in a small town called Vassy. 'It's near Guise territory,' Birago told me, 'a four- or five-day ride east from Paris. Why would he want you to go there?'

'I don't know.' I looked again at the paper in my hand before I met his worried eyes. 'But no doubt he has something important to tell me.'

'Then he can come here. It's not safe or wise for you to go to him. What if someone hears of it? He hasn't yet presented himself at court, and many of our Catholics still believe he had a hand in that Amboise affair.'

I couldn't tell him that the last time I'd seen Coligny he told me not to risk myself and would therefore not have asked this of me unless it was safe.

'He had nothing to do with Amboise,' I said. 'And I hardly think I'll be in any danger. But just in case I'll go in secret; we can say I'm visiting my daughter Claude in Lorraine. She is after all pregnant with her first child and it stands to reason that I'd wish to see her.'

'*Madama*, think about what you're doing,' he implored, but nothing he said could dissuade me. I was desperate to get away from the court, from the constant struggle and intrigues. I wanted to be a woman again, free of the entanglements of power.

Birago grumbled but ensured I had a strong guard; and on a chilly spring dawn I left the Louvre in a hooded cloak, a valise with my belongings packed behind my saddle.

I rode a sure-footed mare, my days of riding the hunt long past. As we cantered out the gates of Paris onto a wide stretch of road still paved with a few ancient cobblestones left by the Romans, I reveled in the snow-bitten air on my face; the vast land lying fallow around me and the azure dome of the sky, so unique to France. I'd been holed up in chambers for so long I'd forgotten the simple pleasure of being outdoors. Yet as we progressed, stopping at predetermined inns along the way, I also saw stark evidence of the havoc wrought by our religious discord. In one township, I saw a charred Catholic church, its relics and bell smashed on the ground; in another, a Huguenot temple – identifiable by its strange cross-armed crucifix, a resting dove at its base – had been defaced, the word heretic splashed in red over its splintered doors. The smell of blood and smoke hung in the air, like an echo.

There was famine too, especially outside towns, where the peasantry was isolated and left to scavenge in sodden fields; emaciated livestock stood hock-deep in mud and gaunt-cheeked children in rags, with sores on their legs, rummaged through trash heaps. It reminded me of the siege on Florence, of the senseless devastation of war, and, recalling Cosimo's unsettling words I regretted not having sent for him before I left, to demand that chart I'd asked from him.

By the time we reached the walls of Vassy under a drenching rain, I was saddened and more resolved than ever to ensure nothing like what the Guises had wrought during my son François's reign ever happened again.

I lodged in a house commandeered by Birago's network of informants; that night, I had my own large room, cleansed and readied only for me, and I sat in an upholstered chair before a stone-surround hearth when Coligny arrived.

He stood on the threshold, dripping water. As he cast back the hood of his dark cloak and revealed his bright eyes, I laughed. 'You didn't think I'd come!'

'No, I knew you would.' He strode to me, enveloping me in the scent of wet wool. His arms were around me in a minute, his mouth crushing mine with a hunger that incinerated my fatigue. Without words he undressed me, took me to the bed, and made love to me with a fervor that left us gasping, entangled like waves in a rough sea.

When we were done, I took the last of my cheese, figs, and bread from my valise and brought them back to bed, where we ate with our fingers, cross-legged and touching each other. I traced his beard, thicker now and more unkempt, marveling at its wiry feel; and finally, as he lay back on the pillows with his hands crossed behind his head, I said, 'So, why did you bring me here? What is so important that you couldn't come to court to tell me?'

He held out his hand. 'Come.' As I nestled in the crook of his arm, drinking in his musky scent, he whispered, 'I wanted you to see what you have done, the marvel of it.' His voice was passionate; I could feel joy emanating from him, a palpable heat.

'What?' I poked his ribs. 'Tell me!'

'No.' He threw his bony shanks over me. 'Wait. Tomorrow, you'll see.'

'I want to know now –' I started to protest, but then his lips covered mine and I forgot what I wanted. I forgot everything but the feel of him, moving inside me.

The next morning he took me outside Vassy to a barn in a forest clearing; as we approached, I heard song coming from within. I turned to him. 'It's . . . they're at worship.'

He nodded, leading me into the musty interior, where I came to a halt behind rows of women, men, and children, singing with their heads lifted. I'd only heard psalms in Latin before; only seen the bejeweled ostentation of our churches. I stood transfixed by the simplicity of this gathering: the odor of barn animals and straw in the air, the rafters where pigeons perched; and the singing in French, so exuberant and alive, so different from the stately inaccessible Latin chants I had grown up with.

Coligny smiled. 'This is a Huguenot temple. We worship where we can; we seek God not in ritual and incense, but in celebration of his Word. You made this possible. Your edict has brought us peace.'

I pressed my hands to my mouth, tears starting in my eyes.

'After the service,' he said, 'the people will want to meet you. They'll want to thank you.'

'They . . . they know I'm here?'

'They will, if you wish it so.' He grinned. 'There is nothing to fear. You can see for yourself we are not devils or traitors seeking to tear this kingdom apart. We are just ordinary subjects, beholden to you and to your son King Charles for bringing us –'

The thunder of hooves outside spun us around. The worshippers did not hear, engrossed in their song, but Coligny gripped my arm and pulled me to a nearby side door.

'Go,' he whispered. 'Now! Get away as fast as you can.'

As he pushed me from the barn I found my guard waiting, holding my horse by its reins. 'Your Grace must leave now.'

With my heart racing, I scrambled into the saddle, looking to the barn where I could hear Coligny's voice ring out. A woman wailed. The guard still had my reins; as he yanked my horse toward a thicket where he'd tethered his mount, I glimpsed men in chain mail galloping around the barn from the other side.

'Wait,' I said, and though I meant to sound imperious, my voice was a mere whisper.

'They're Guise retainers,' my guard said. 'Your Grace, please; I have sworn to protect you.'

'No!' I snatched at my reins; as I did, I saw the people pouring from the barn, Coligny's black-cloaked figure among them. Some ran into the surrounding trees, seeking refuge; others came to a terrified halt before the men on horses now circling the barn, pikes lowered as they began to strike. One flung a lit torch through the door and flames caught hold at once; I heard shrieking and knew there were still people within, now burning alive. In horrified disbelief I watched as the Huguenots outside fell, sharp pike blades scything off heads, limbs, spraying blood. Screams and futile pleas for mercy assaulted my ears; and when I saw that unmistakable figure on his huge white destrier, the ragged scar visible even under the shadow of his helmet, his arm flung out like an avenging devil's, I kicked furiously at my horse with my heels.

My gentle mare reared, almost throwing me. I whirled in my saddle to my guard to find Coligny on his horse; his gloved hand held fast to my mare's braided tail.

'I promised you would be safe.' He met my eyes; as I saw the pain and sorrow in his expression, I wanted to yell in despair. He motioned to my guard. 'Take her back to Paris,' and then he threw up his hood and spurred off, racing past the retainers and le Balafré, who continued the slaughter, their laughter defiling the air.

No one saw me as I fled with my guard through the trees.

'How many?' I stood in my apartments in the Louvre, still wearing the soiled gown I'd ridden in without stopping. My hair hung tangled about my face; Lucrezia pressed a goblet of mulled cider into my rein-chafed hands.

Birago looked at the dispatch he'd received from his informants while I was still on the road. 'At least one hundred, maybe more. Every Catholic in Vassy has risen up at le Balafré's command. They hang pastors from the trees and torch Huguenot homes and businesses.' He lifted his somber regard to me. 'It's what we feared. The duc de Guise has declared war on the Huguenots and on you. Forgive me. I have failed. My spies had no indication he planned this.'

'No, it's not your fault. How were you to know?' I moved with slow, heavy steps to my chair. 'No one could have foreseen this.' I started to drink from my goblet and then flung it across the chamber. It clattered against the wainscoting. 'There were women and children there,' I whispered, my voice shuddering, 'innocents who'd done no wrong. If he gets his way, not a single Huguenot will be left alive. I passed an edict granting them the right to worship in peace and he has broken it. I want him arrested. He will pay for this, by God.'

Birago said quietly, 'If you issue the warrant for his arrest, he could set all France aflame.'

'Then let him.' I met Birago's eyes without flinching. 'He is a traitor. He must answer these charges before the king – alone and unarmed. Prepare the warrant. It is time these Guises learned I am not to be trifled with.'

To the chorus of '*Vive le Balafré!* ' an endless line of soldiers carrying pikes and armed retainers entered the courtyard; at their head rode their leader in silver-chased armor.

Standing at my balcony I gazed upon the mass of armed soldiers and retainers filling the courtyard below. Even if I summoned our entire royal guard, I wouldn't command half these men. Through my teeth I said to Birago, 'Where is Constable Montmorency? We sent him with the warrant. Where are he and the lords who went with him?'

Birago pointed. 'There.'

I followed to where he indicated. The constable in his battered armor rode with the other Catholic peers. On one of their pikes dangled a shredded parchment: my warrant.

'I sat that old man Montmorency in Council,' I fumed. 'I gave him a place of honor at our table after the Guises deprived him of it. How can he turn on us like this?'

'We knew the risks,' said Birago, calm as ever now that the crisis was upon us. 'Now we must negotiate. Charles is your son and their sovereign. Le Balafré must have terms we can use to our advantage.'

'Yes, fetch Charles at once.' As Birago left, I hurried with my women downstairs to the great hall. I'd just reached the dais with the thrones under the canopy when Birago brought in Charles. My son looked frightened and pale; his personal guard flanked him – insignificant defense compared to the horde of insurgent Catholics that came tramping into the hall moments later. They parted to reveal le Balafré, striding toward us with unmistakable purpose.

I took one look at his scarred countenance and braced myself.

Birago nudged my son. I watched with a knot in my throat as Charles squared his thin shoulders and said with a surprising, hard clarity: 'My lord duke, you were ordered to come to us unarmed. You will send these men away.'

Le Balafré executed a mocking bow. He didn't glance at me, his eyes fixed on my eleven-year-old son. 'Your Majesty, I fear I cannot. Heresy overtakes France; it is my sworn duty as a Catholic to defend us from its corruption, with an army if need be.' He spread his arms; from among his officers, the constable stepped forth. I couldn't contain my gasp when I saw the disheveled figure beside him – a mop of dirty-gold hair atop his leering saturnine face.

It was Jeanne of Navarre 's husband, Antoine of Bourbon. As I met his smug eyes, I realized I'd made a terrible mistake. Birago had warned me this lout could pose a threat; now he was before me: a Catholic prince wielded by the Guises to wrest the regency from me.

I clenched my fists. How could I have been so stupid as to think Jeanne could keep her wayward husband at home, under her skirts?

As if he could read my thoughts, le Balafré gave me a cold stare. Then he said, 'I hereby announce the Holy Triumvirate, dedicated to upholding the Roman Catholic faith. I, my lord the constable, and Antoine of Bourbon will now see to our realm's defense. Anyone who is not with us is against us and will suffer accordingly.'

Antoine thumped his fist against his chest. 'The regency is mine! You stole it from me, but it is mine and I *will* have it.'

Beside me, I felt Charles tense. I'd promised to him to keep him safe from the Guises, and before I knew what I was doing, I retorted, 'We do not take advice from drunken fools.'

Le Balafré's voice was like a blade. 'You misunderstand. The prince of Bourbon doesn't need your permission to be named regent. Now, madame, shall you honor him and send the heretics to their just fate, or shall I?'

Charles made a strangled sound; without warning he screamed his response. 'I'll kill you for this! I'll hang you from a gibbet and cut you down while you still breathe. I'll rip out your guts!'

I pulled him to me, feeling him shudder. 'You have no right,'

I told le Balafré as I ran my hand over Charles's hair, as I might soothe a panicked animal. 'This is treason. You are a traitor.'

Le Balafré said, 'I am but a humble subject who seeks to protect France.'

Then he flicked his hand and his men closed in.

'What do you mean, they bring an army?' A guttering candle tossed misshapen shadows on the walls. I spoke in a whisper so as not to awaken Charles, who slept in the next room. My apartments had become our world; held captive in our palace, I kept thinking how right I'd been to send my other children to St. Germain before le Balafré arrived, for at least there, surrounded by their household governors and guards, they'd be safe.

'My informants saw it,' said Birago. 'The Huguenots are marching against the Triumvirate.'

I felt as though I couldn't breathe. '*Dio Mio,* Cosimo told me there would be war.' I paused, forcing myself to remain calm. 'How many Huguenots?'

'If the reports are correct, five thousand at last count.'

'Impossible! Where would they get the money to raise such a force, in so little time?'

'Indeed. According to my reports, they had assistance from Calvinist bankers in Geneva. The coin can't be traced, of course. But someone has been planning this for months. Such negotiations do not happen overnight.'

The world darkened around me. 'And Coligny . . . ?'

Birago lowered his eyes. 'No. My informants lost all trace of him after Vassy.'

I had to act. I couldn't just sit here and wait for everything I had fought for to erupt in flames. 'Well, there must be something we can do.' I considered. 'Can we get a message to them?'

He nodded. 'Do so,' I said. 'I will talk to le Balafré. I'll tell him that I wish to negotiate with them first. Remind him, he needs our royal leave before he engages them in battle.'

When the duke came to me, he laughed in my face. 'You think you can forestall a holy war, madame? By all means, try. They march toward St. Denis, where I'll meet them soon enough. But you go with my escort, for I know these heretics will never negotiate or disarm, not for you or the king or God himself.'

His escort turned out to be five soldiers and the constable, a feeble protective force that amply displayed le Balafré's disregard for my safety. On a sweltering morning I set out on horseback with Lucrezia to the plains outside the walls of Paris, from where the Huguenot leaders had sent word they would meet me.

I drew to a halt. There were indeed thousands of men camped on the brittle fields stretched before me, the sunlight illuminating a swarm of tents and armory of weapons – cannons and harquebus, lances, siege engines, and shields: enough to bring down the walls of Paris.

I was stunned by the display. I'd seen the Huguenots as a persecuted minority, subjects who needed my protection. Yet here sat an army that easily exceeded my own royal guard.

'The Calvinists certainly got their money's worth,' I muttered to Lucrezia. Beside me, the constable spat out, 'Look at this rabble of heretics.'

I looked at him in disgust, marveling he didn't drop dead of heat, encased as he was in his ornamental armor. It was impossible to believe he and Coligny shared the same blood. 'They are men and the king's subjects too,' I said.

He stared at me from under his salty brows. 'Men? The day they took Calvin to their heart, they ceased to be anything but devil spawn.'

My response was to kick my mare forth, toward a white pavilion adorned with a red cross – the badge of the Crusades, adopted by the Huguenots. My escort followed, the silence broken by the jangle of harnesses and clip-clop of hooves. A dust cloud rose in the distance; a group of riders came toward us. Again I came to a halt. Lucrezia whispered, 'It could be an ambush. What if they take you captive?'

'Nonsense.' I pushed back my veil. 'If le Balafré doesn't consider me worth anything, I hardly see how these men will think any different.'

A brash youth led the approaching Huguenots. He wore chain mail, his sleeveless white tunic belted at his waist. His company echoed his ensemble; I scanned their ranks but didn't see Coligny among them. The youth brought his stallion to a stop and passed disdainful eyes over the constable's ranks. Then he said to me, 'I welcome Your Grace to the Holy Brotherhood in Christ, champions of the one true faith.'

So, the Catholics had the Holy Triumvirate and now the Huguenots had their brotherhood. I wondered what Coligny would make of all this posturing. Then I wondered where he was.

'Where can I speak with your leaders?' I asked.

'In the pavilion,' the youth replied. 'But Your Grace must come alone.'

The constable barked, 'Her Grace goes nowhere alone. I'm ordered to report on every word that passes between you.'

'Then nothing will be said. You are free to return to Paris.'

As Montmorency dropped his hand to his sword, I intervened. 'Your leaders promised me safe passage.' I looked at the youth. 'Do I still have their word?'

He gave a wry smile. 'If the constable should doubt anything, let him doubt his own cause. We do not set women and children on fire or hang pastors from trees.'

Before they started the war right then, I hastened forward, alone, into the Huguenot camp.

The pavilion was a large canvas tent that offered some refuge from the heat. The youth handed me a goblet of water. Moments later, to my shock, Coligny walked in. He wore the same white tunic. He'd lost weight. Days of riding under the sun had streaked his hair with gold, enhancing the structure of his face. I could now see a familial resemblance to the youth as the boy bowed and disappeared. Coligny and I were alone.

'Your brother?' I asked, and he nodded. 'The youngest.'

'So,' I remarked, 'this is a family affair.'

I couldn't feign incredulity. In some part of me, I had known. A man like him would not accept the persecution unleashed on his faith. But why hadn't he told me? Why had he led me to believe he was only a messenger, without any true power? The questions burned unspoken on my lips; I didn't want to demean us with doubt.

I set the battered silver goblet aside. 'I've come to tell you, you cannot hope to win. The duc de Guise and his Triumvirate have twice your men. You must disarm and come to terms.'

He gave me a pensive look. 'Of all people, you must know this time, we must have justice.'

'This is not justice,' I exclaimed. 'It's war!' I stopped, forced myself to lower my voice. 'I would have made le Balafré pay for what he's done.'

His bearded lips curved in a mirthless smile. He moved to the table, piled with maps. 'Catherine,' he said at length. 'He rode into Paris at the head of a legion; he holds you and the king hostage and has blockaded the city. How did you intend to stop him, with no army of your own?'

My reason failed me. I found no dissimulation in him, no pretense. His hidden strength had found its purpose. He was a leader now: the Huguenot leader.

'Why didn't you tell me?' I whispered. 'Why didn't you trust enough in me?'

'It was never about trust.' He returned, kneeling before me to take my hands in his. 'You don't understand because you don't see how power corrupts. You still believe logic can solve all ills; that men will heed reason because in the end we are equal under God.' His grip tightened. 'But the Guises and your church see us as vermin. The suffering will never end until we show them they cannot murder and pillage without consequence. They leave us no choice.'

I looked down at his strong, bronzed hands over mine. 'I believe in God,' I said. 'I believe there are many ways to seek his light, not just those set forth by Rome. But I've seen war before, in my youth, and I do not believe it can solve anything. I don't think God pays attention to how many people we kill to prove a point.'

He was still.

'We can still find a peaceful solution,' I added, reading encouragement in his silence. 'My edict remains in effect; the Huguenots are still under royal protection. If you come with me to court, I'll seat you on the Council and –'

'No.' He pulled away from me and came to his feet. His expression hardened, crumbling my hope. 'The next time I see the duc de Guise, it will be in battle. The time for discourse is past.'

I had lost my gambit. I envisioned a desolate future, dominated by a religious war that would turn this realm, my adopted country, into chaos – a place of charred hamlets and ravaged harvests, of widows and orphans and despair.

I stood and met his eyes, my next words erupting from me in a desperate plea. 'I cannot protect you if you choose this war. France is a Catholic realm; for now, it must remain so. Your cause is not sanctioned by the king; you commit treason and I'll be forced to side with the Triumvirate against you.'

'I know,' he replied, with heartrending acceptance. 'I do not expect anything else; your coming here was enough. Now you must defend your son, the king.'

My voice broke. 'Then at least withdraw. Pick another place to fight your war. Le Balafré has all of Paris to draw reinforcements from. He will slaughter you. All of you will die!'

He stepped to me. As he reached out, I held up my hand. 'No. I can't bear it. Not now . . .'

He nodded gently. 'I understand. I will take your warning under advisement. Until then, my Catherine, pray for France.'

And before I could reply, he turned and walked out.

Le Balafré waited for me in the Louvre's courtyard. He raked his gaze over my mount and his mouth twisted. 'Those saddlebags look too flat to contain Huguenot heads.'

I returned his remorseless stare. 'You will release the king and me at once. Only then shall you have our leave to wage this war you insist on. It will be fought at our command, without unnecessary rapine or butchery. And Admiral de Coligny is not to be

harmed. Do I make myself clear? If he is captured, you will bring
him to us, where justice can be served.'

'Perfectly,' he said, and as I swept past him he let out a callous
laugh that left me in no doubt that if Coligny should fall into his
hands, my lover's life would be forfeit.

24

I retreated with Charles and my children to St. Germain. As summer blazed into autumn, I watched from afar as our army, led by le Balafré and the constable, chased Coligny, who'd heeded my advice and retreated, electing instead to seize every stronghold he could find with a preponderance of Huguenots ready to assist him.

By September, the Huguenots had claimed thirty citadels and taken the constable hostage in battle near Orléans. Le Balafré was enraged. Together with our new regent, Antoine de Bourbon, he set siege on the city, flinging boulders over the walls; razing the countryside and salting every well. Inside the city, the Huguenots were starving but they still dumped hot pitch from the battlements and sniped at their foes until snows blew in to bury the dead rotting beneath their walls and everyone's supplies began to dwindle.

Each report I received rekindled the horrors of my childhood. I'd never been as devout as I pretended; but in those terrible months I anchored myself at my prie-dieu every night before bed and every morning after I awoke, praying for Coligny's deliverance and le Balafré's demise.

Then in December word came that Antoine of Bourbon, king consort of Navarre, had been killed during the siege on Orléans. Jeanne de Navarre was a widow and she sent me a recriminatory letter that dared reproach me for having let the duc de Guise put Antoine in harm's way. I choked on my incredulity as I read these words. She acted as though *I* were responsible for her inability to keep her foolish husband out of the fray! But I understood her plight and sent his body to her for entombment, along with a stern warning that she refrain from lending money or arms to the Huguenots. I couldn't afford for her to become embroiled in the conflict. She was a queen; her aid would lend the Huguenot cause legitimacy and turn le Balafré's wrath against her. But as the days shortened and I paced, awaiting news of the war's progress, I found myself thinking of her stalwart heir, that boy who had touched me so deeply at my late son's wedding. Like my own children, he was fatherless, and the thought of his loss so tugged at me that I sat down one evening and wrote him a letter, offering him my comfort.

As I sealed it, I wondered if Jeanne would let him read it.

Shortly after the New Year, le Balafré launched a renewed attack on the Huguenots trapped inside Orléans. I sent Lucrezia into the courtyard every morning to greet the courier, and one frigid January day she returned panting from her race up the staircase, missive in hand.

My shock when I read it must have showed; from the desk where he took his morning lessons with Birago, Charles raised wary eyes. 'Maman, what is it? What is wrong?'

He had turned twelve – that precarious age between childhood and adolescence. He was growing tall but had become anxious and thin, and he had trouble sleeping. His rooms were adjacent to mine, so I could keep a close watch over him, and as I saw the fearfulness in his expression, I mustered an equanimity that I did not feel.

'It's le Balafré,' I said. 'He's been wounded.'

His eyes narrowed to slits. 'Will he die?' Before I could answer, he snatched the missive from me. '"The duc de Guise has been shot,"' he read aloud. '"The assassin has confessed that Coligny hired him. Your Grace must come at once."' His laughter burst from him in a malicious cackle. 'Coligny paid for le Balafré's murder. Excellent! I'll give him a medal for it.'

'No,' I said quickly, alarmed by his vehemence. 'You mustn't say that. Coligny would never hire an assassin. And for the moment, le Balafré is alive.'

Charles crunched the missive in his fist. 'With luck, not for long. When do we leave for Orléans? I want to see our proud duke before he dies so I can spit in his face.'

I couldn't stop my brittle chuckle as I pried the missive from him and ruffled his hair. 'You're too passionate, my son. You must learn to control your impulses.' I wagged my finger. 'And you'll stay here. Let me take care of this.'

The moment I stepped into the canvas field tent, the stench of pus and blood struck me with a near-visceral impact. I fought back memories of my husband's death as I stood over the duke's bed and watched le Balafré gasping for air, slowly drowning in his own blood, his right lung pierced by the bullet. He was delirious, unaware of me; at a stool by his side sat his wife, her proud beauty stricken by the specter of impending widowhood. She clutched the hand of her son, a golden boy not much older than my Charles, who would soon inherit his father's title of duc de Guise. His fine-boned face, exalted by the smoky sapphire eyes of his family blood, twisted in pain when the doctor murmured, 'I fear the hour draws near.'

Young Guise looked at me; in his pained gaze I saw the struggle to harness the maturity required of him and something else, dark and beyond his years. 'Your Grace, might we have this time alone to say farewell to my father?' he said in a voice made raw by his grief.

'Of course.' I shifted back. I felt like an intruder. I felt their eyes upon me, the disconsolate mother and son who knew how much I loathed the duke and longed for his death. To them, his loss was an abyss. To me, it was freedom. 'You must send for me if . . .' I began haltingly, and Madame de Guise hissed, 'See to it that the foul murderer Coligny pays for this crime!'

I retreated to a nearby cloth pavilion, where Lucrezia had set out mulled wine for us. As she went to monitor the entrance, I asked Birago, 'What did you discover?'

He sighed. 'Everyone sings the same tune. Le Balafré was shot in the back by one of his own attendants, one Poltrot de Méré, a renegade Huguenot who turned coat and joined our forces. Under torture, he confessed that Coligny hired him to infiltrate our ranks and kill le Balafré.'

My fingers tightened about the goblet. 'Is the confession reliable?'

'As far as such things go. They flayed Méré until his flesh hung in strips. He'll survive only long enough to suffer the final indignity of execution. You do plan to . . . ?'

'Of course. He shot le Balafré. He must die for it.' I paused. 'There is no other evidence?'

'If you mean witnesses or correspondence, no. And Coligny denies all complicity. He issued a statement that Méré acted alone.'

'Thank God,' I whispered, without thinking. When I saw Birago frown, I added, 'Méré is a turncoat; he may also be a liar who seeks to implicate Coligny. He can't be trusted.'

Birago gave me a wry smile. 'This newfound naïveté does not suit you.'

It was the first allusion he'd made that he knew of my secret and I recoiled from it. I didn't want to hear his judgment. I didn't want what I'd shared with Coligny sullied by his hard truths.

'You presume too much,' I retorted. 'I am not naïve. I just know Coligny would not do this. He is a man of honor, a Huguenot, yes, but not a criminal. This was an act of cowardice.'

Birago sighed. 'The siege was over, the Huguenots trapped. Le Balafré sent terms for surrender. Coligny agreed and the next morning le Balafré was shot. In my opinion, this is no coincidence. Coligny was about to lose everything he fought for.'

I met his stare. 'I don't believe it. Not from him. It's not his way.'

'You no longer know his way, *madama*.' Birago stepped close to me. 'He's taken up the Huguenot cause and gone to war against us. You must distance yourself. He cannot be received until his name is cleared. And if it is not, you must judge him a traitor and see justice done.'

I did not want to hear this; my very soul rebelled against it. I stood frozen, until Lucrezia suddenly turned from the entrance to whisper, 'My lady, a guard approaches.'

I murmured to Birago, 'Excuse me. We'll talk later, yes?' and turned from his knowing eyes to step into the night, pulling my cloak about me. I didn't need to hear what the guard relayed; I already knew. Le Balafré, my foe, who had degraded and insulted me since my arrival in France, was dead. The Catholic cause had lost its leader. And I was free to again resume my rule.

I walked over charred fields, smelling smoke and roasted meat from the soldiers' campsites and glimpsing the crumpled spires of Orléans like ragged teeth on the horizon. I paused to draw in icy air, lifted my eyes to the mist-wreathed moon.

Only then did I allow myself to consider the unthinkable: What if it was true? Had Coligny, in desperation over his imminent defeat, stooped to murder? Had he sacrificed his own ideals, that moral standard I'd always admired in him, to save his faith?

A shiver went through me. I didn't want to believe it. I recalled the pride on his face as he led me into the barn in Vassy, his anger and horror as those innocents died, but I didn't want to believe that one atrocity could so warp his soul. We'd striven together for peace, worked always to that end. If he was found culpable of le Balafré's murder, it would bring about the ruin of his name, pit Catholic against Huguenot in a never-ending feud. It seemed impossible that the man I knew, so cautious and intelligent, would risk everything on such a gamble.

Still, as I stood alone on these war-blackened fields, I had to concede that harsh as it might be, Birago's advice was plausible.

It could be the man I knew no longer existed.

As this thought drove itself through me, I knew I faced a terrible choice. If I brought him back to court, I'd set myself against the world I struggled to keep whole for my son. Much as I'd loathed le Balafré, I could already envision how this news would be received by our Catholics and Philip of Spain, how this sole act might sow a feud that would tear France asunder. Already it set an inexorable shadow over Coligny and his cause, one not even I could dispel. Our dream was over. Now I must do as Birago advised. I must save France.

I could not afford sentiment; I had no time for it.
I had a realm to protect.

On May 13, 1563, I celebrated my forty-fourth birthday.
Inundated with work since le Balafré's death, I scarcely heeded
it. In Paris the people huddled for hours in blistering winds to
watch his coffin pass, weeping and wailing as if he were a martyr.
Every noble of rank attended his spectacular funeral in Notre
Dame, with one notable exception: I ordered Coligny to stay put
in his estate of Châtillon, pending the outcome of the investigation into the duke's murder. To placate those Catholics clamoring
for his head, I had the assassin Méré torn asunder by horses in
the public courtyard of the Place de Grève, a distasteful spectacle
I did not attend.

The war was over. With Antoine of Navarre and le Balafré
dead, the Triumvirate was vanquished and I reaffirmed my
regency and my edict of toleration. I knew I had to do more. Our
conflict had devastated France; I had to restore the Huguenots'
confidence in my policy of tolerance, while the Catholics had to
learn to respect my rule.

'What if we go on a progress?' I asked Birago as we sat at our
desks, laboring over our correspondence. 'Charles will turn fourteen next year, almost of age to be crowned. Huguenot and
Catholic alike must see that they have a capable king. We can visit
all the cities where there have been disturbances and ensure the
terms of my edict are upheld.'

He nodded. 'An excellent idea, though it would entail months
of travel and much expense. How would we pay for it?'

'With loans, of course. The Florentine bankers are always sending me offers of credit. I'll bring the children and the court. Who
knows? I might even persuade Philip of Spain and my daughter
Elisabeth to meet us at the border. I haven't seen her in four years.
A family reunion would do us all good. And we should start
seeking a bride for Charles; he'll have to wed soon and Philip's
Hapsburg cousin, Isabel of Austria, would be the perfect bride.'

'Not to mention, she'd cement your alliance with the Imperial

Hapsburg family.' He chuckled. 'It would be a coup. However, the king's betrothal to a Catholic princess so soon after our war might give the Huguenots cause for alarm. You are well aware of how Philip has encouraged his nephew the archduke Maximilian's efforts to arrest and burn Lutherans in his domains in Austria. As Maximilian's daughter, Isabel no doubt shares her family's intolerance.'

'True.' I reflected for a moment. 'Very well, we'll not mention the marriage suggestion until something is settled. And I'll have the constable plan the itinerary. As you say, we'll be gone months and he's the last of the Triumvirate. I'm not leaving him here to stir up any trouble.'

There was a brief silence. Then Birago said, 'Have you made any decision about Coligny?'

I averted my eyes. 'You heard the outcome of the investigation,' I said quietly. 'Despite the Guises' copious bribes none of the judges found proof that Méré was hired to kill le Balafré. But if you're asking if I'll invite him to join us, I fear it wouldn't be wise, not at this time.'

I heard him let out a relieved sigh as he bent to his papers. In time, I had told myself. In time, I would figure out what to do with him. But not yet; I needed this time away from his magnetic presence, from the passion we had shared; I needed to come to terms with my own conflicted feelings over what had occurred between us.

Birago brought me back to attention. 'When would you like to embark on this progress?'

'Early next year,' I decided. 'I'll ask Cosimo for a fortuitous date. Now, let's finish these letters and assemble the Council. We'll need their approval before I go begging for money.'

We held Christmas at Fontainebleau, on which I spent lavish sums, determined to show off our prestige. Charles giggled in delight as belled falcons swooped over the garland-draped tables, while Hercule devoured as many sweets as he could. My daughter Claude came to visit from her husband's northeastern duchy of

Lorraine; she was heavy with pregnancy and content as wives seldom are, sitting with a serene smile as Henri and Margot led the court in the dancing.

Under the glow of torches, Margot's satin skin complemented Henri's catlike grace. I found myself blinking back tears as I watched them, seeing their father and grandfather in Margot's elegance and my son's sophistication. I felt blessed that night to have survived the war, to have spared them the worst. They were healthy and vital; they represented the future of the Valois. Everything I did, I did for them, and the hour when I was no longer here to guide them.

In the zeal of my motherhood, I still believed I could mold the future.

25

We departed the Loire in the spring.

At the last moment, I had to leave little Hercule behind in the Humeries' care, after he suffered a minor case of smallpox. He was recovering, but his doctors deemed him too weak to withstand prolonged travel. Dr. Paré attended him and reassured me he'd heal in time, though the pustules might leave scars and the fevers could affect his growth. I felt guilty for leaving him and surrounded him with additional physicians and attendants, ordering that should anything untoward occur, they were to send for me at once.

Margot and Henri did come with us, along with Birago and my women. I even had a new coach with embossed gold Cs on the doors and sturdy upholstery, in which I might conduct state business while on the road. We carried everything we might need – enough furnishings, set pieces, horses, mules, livestock, and servants to supply a small nation.

The network of informants supervised by Birago kept me briefed. Thus did I learn that Philip had sent word that he was considering my suggestion that we meet. I had no doubt he'd agree in the end and was overjoyed at the thought that I'd soon behold Elisabeth again.

We visited numerous cities, from Normandy's craggy shores through the vineyards of Burgundy and into the gilded fields of Auvergne. In late autumn, we came to rest in the quiet township of Salon in Provence. I'd not sent word in advance, but Nostradamus greeted me at the doorway of his house as if he'd been expecting me for weeks. He had aged visibly, his black robe accentuating his white beard and bald pate, even while that piercing prescience in his eyes had turned sharp and translucent as a diamond.

He bowed, gripping a staff of polished wood as straight as he was gnarled, and we passed into a foyer decorated with painted furniture. An energetic partridge of a woman bustled forth to remove my cloak. 'Your Grace does us honor,' she said, turning to wag her finger at him. 'Now, you mustn't have her going thirsty upstairs in that study of yours. I've left a decanter of ale on the table and expect you both in the hall before five for supper.'

I demurred. 'There's no need. I can dine later with the court.'

'Nonsense. Your Grace must stay. We wouldn't have it any other way. Come, my dear.' She beckoned Lucrezia. 'I've a nice pitcher for us in the kitchen.'

I refrained from comment, despite my amusement. I'd never stopped to consider that Nostradamus might have someone so forceful to organize his private life.

'Madame Saint-Tère thinks she owns me,' he complained as he led me up a flight of stairs which brought back vivid memories of another staircase in another land, where the air had also been drenched in alchemy. Nostradamus's study was a spacious loft, dominated by an impressive star-glass mounted on a tripod and shelving on the walls filled with tomes and scrolls. It might have been the room of any affluent physician with a passing interest in astronomy.

'I've been expecting you,' he said, as he moved with a pained gait to a side table and the decanter. 'I saw you in the water. A long trip lies ahead.'

I looked at the decrepit copper basin on his desk. 'What is this?'

'It's where I see my visions.' He paused, gauging my reaction. 'You look surprised. Surely you didn't expect a cauldron?' He chuckled. 'It holds water; that is all I require.'

He handed me a goblet. As he proceeded to search through his papers, I peeked into the basin and found it disappointingly empty. 'Please, sit. I've something for you.'

He slipped a scroll into my hands. As I unraveled it, I saw a chart depicting planetary movements, convoluted diagrams, and mathematical annotations. The air turned thick. I wondered if he transformed any atmosphere he inhabited, the way salt taints liquid.

'This chart,' he said, 'depicts a summary of ten years into your future. In it are important events marking your life. It's why you're here, yes? To discover if my prophecies hold true?'

A shiver trickled down my spine. It hadn't been my intent at all, or so I'd thought.

He clucked his tongue. 'You still doubt me. Did I not predict your husband's death? Did I not say you would reign, and do you not rule now for your son Charles?'

I stared at him. 'I thought you said you didn't understand your prophecies.'

'I usually don't, at the time. Only after the event itself comes to pass do they become clear.'

'I see.' I set the scroll on his desk. I didn't relish any more predictions, particularly if it meant I'd be left alone to decipher them.

Nostradamus said, 'You keep Maestro Ruggieri in your employ, I assume? He can interpret the chart. There's nothing arcane there, just my observations based on years of studying the alignment of the stars on the date and hour of your birth.'

I heard no condemnation in his voice and still I felt ashamed for not heeding his warning about my astrologer. 'Ruggieri isn't with me,' I said. 'Can't you tell me what it says?'

'That would take too much time. I can tell you, you must protect the prince of Navarre.'

My stomach knotted. I had a vivid memory of the boy I'd embraced and my vision of him years from now – proud and confident on a black destrier, a white plume in his cap . . .

'You must watch over him,' Nostradamus added, as if he could hear my thoughts. 'You are two halves of a whole. You need each other to fulfill your destiny.'

'The boy is almost twelve years old and resides with his mother,' I began, and I breathed deep, daring to question for the first time.

'Jeanne rules Navarre as though it were a world apart, which you might say it is, for it straddles the Pyrenees between us and Spain, and shields her from the trials that affect us. One day, her son will inherit. How can he be so important to me?'

'He is,' Nostradamus replied, in a tone of infuriating certainty that implied I needed no further explanation. 'Still, our future is fluid. If it were not, there'd be no point in living.'

Why must he always be so vague? And yet, if he knew about my future . . . I took up my goblet and drank. 'And my sons . . . ?' As I asked, I felt a profoundly private fear. My eldest, François, had died young. Were my other sons also destined for early graves?

'Your remaining children will survive to adulthood,' he said, to my relief. He rolled up the chart, inserted it into a leather tube. 'It will weather the journey better this way.' He held out his arm. 'Now, let us go dine. Madame Saint-Tère's roast lamb is a marvel.'

After a hearty supper, Lucrezia and I said our farewells. Wrapped in our cloaks on our way back to camp, we were quiet. After Lucrezia assisted me to bed, I lay awake and watched the moonlight slide across the ceiling. I had the uncanny sense that Nostradamus and I would never see each other again and that the chart had been his final gift, a map to a future I could affect.

I drifted off to sleep. And I dreamed.

I run down a stone corridor. A bell tolls in the distance. I am drenched in sweat. It is hot, a purgatory. Others rush around me, shadowy terrified figures. Fear curdles in me; I know something horrific is happening, something I cannot escape. A wail shatters the night. Another follows; then another and another, shriek after anguished shriek. Footsteps pound. I stumble and almost fall, recoiling as my hand flails out and grips a wet wall. The floor is slippery. I look down and see blood coating the flagstones, splashing the walls like frayed ribbons and dripping whorls – blood everywhere. I hear a desperate cry, 'No, not him!' and I realize it is my voice –

I awoke gasping, tangled in sweat-drenched sheets. The night was still, a frozen hush, but I could sense a vibration in the air, as though something struggled to adopt a nebulous shape.

Lucrezia rose from her cot. 'My lady, are you ill? Shall I call for a physic?'

'No. I had a dream . . . an awful dream.' I told her what I'd seen. 'It was so real. I can still feel the blood under my feet. I was trying to save somebody's life.'

She peered at me. 'Do you know who?'

I went still. I had foreseen death on the eve of my husband's accident, though I hadn't known it would be him. This dream had the same potency, the same inexorable certainty. I met Lucrezia's eyes. 'I don't know who, but I think . . . I think it was Navarre.'

'The Huguenot queen's son?' She rolled her eyes. 'You know she guards him like a hawk. You couldn't save him from anything because she's always there. Go back to sleep. You're weary and we ate too much at the seer's house. Plus, you're worried about whether Philip of Spain will let you meet with your daughter. Your nerves are playing tricks on you.'

'Yes,' I said, 'that must be it. I'm just overwrought, is all.'

She trudged back to her pallet. Slipping into my sheets, I pulled the coverlet to my neck. But I stayed awake for hours, reliving the dream in my mind. Though I thought I should consult Nostradamus, I knew I would not. He had told me everything he could, and I didn't need him to confirm that somehow I must get young Henri of Navarre to my court.

I thought of my dream for days afterward, but my letters to Queen Jeanne of Navarre were in vain. She refused to send her child to me, citing that my intention to meet with Philip of Spain, whose persecution of the Protestants horrified her, was 'an infamy.' She even went so far as to inform me that my abandonment of Admiral de Coligny after le Balafré's murder, even though he'd been acquitted, had earned me the epithet of Madame la Serpente among the Huguenots, and she would never trust me with the welfare of her heir, regardless that he stood next in line to the French throne after my sons.

Her insults enraged me. Ensconced in her mountain citadel,

isolated from the discord and slaughter that nearly destroyed France, she had no concept of the difficulties I endured. As for Philip of Spain, I had no idea if he'd even approve our meeting but knew it would serve me nothing to inform her as much. From the day my father-in-law had sought to use her as a pawn to win back Milan, she had acted as if I were to blame for every misfortune in her life.

Packing up our belongings, we journeyed farther into the south, where the Mediterranean beckoned with its azure warmth and the scent of thyme and rosemary soothed our wind-chapped senses. Finally, while we rested in the white city of Marseilles, where thirty-two years ago I'd first arrived in France, word came from Madrid. Citing another of the innumerable revolts by the Flemish Lutherans and other problems in his far-flung empire, Philip sent his regrets that he could not join us. I was thrilled at the prospect of a reunion with my daughter, though I would have to resign myself to discussing my marriage proposal for Charles with the Duke of Alba, whom Philip had appointed to act on his behalf.

Summer came upon us with infernal heat, adding to our short tempers. Everyone was sick to death of poor food, sour water, and inadequate lodgings. Charles developed a fever halfway to Bayonne and had to ride with me in my coach, grumbling the entire way. By the time we came to rest in the large manor requisitioned for our use, he was insisting he wanted to return to Paris.

I agreed. Nothing appealed to me more, but I reminded him that we'd come to see Elisabeth. I ordered the court to wear its best finery and surveyed the nearby area for a site to hold the welcoming festivities.

I selected a knoll by the Bidassoa River, whose murky waters flowed into Spain. There we assembled under a sun that seared us right through our canopies. Charles sat clad in his mantle of estate and coronet, sweat soaking his auburn shoulder-length hair. He was too weakened from his recent fever to do anything but scowl at Margot and Henri, who played chess and were seemingly unaffected by heat. At twelve and fourteen, they were blessed with a vitality that left them unscathed by the saddle sores, upset stomachs, and other ailments that beleaguered the rest of us. Sipping iced wine as I searched the direction from which Elisabeth would come, the heat adhering my sienna velvet gown to my hips like a pelt, I wondered if I'd be able to rise when the time came or if I'd simply melt in a puddle at my daughter's feet.

The distant blare of trumpets startled me to attention. Waving the court to its feet, I stepped out into the glaring afternoon. In the distance appeared the limp banners of a cavalcade. When I spied two figures riding at its head, I yanked up my skirts and dashed forward.

The cavalcade halted. I saw the spectral figure of Alba dismount and help my daughter from her horse. She stood hesitant for a moment. From behind her, another figure appeared – a slight man clad in unrelieved black, wearing an odd high-browed hat with an ebony-colored plume.

He took her by the hand and they began walking to me.

Her red gown was in the Spanish fashion, stiff skirts draped over the narrow farthingale that had gone out of style in France years ago, her auburn tresses coiled under a diamond-spangled cap. As I neared, breathless from my run, I saw her eyes sunk in shadows, her mouth taut and cheeks hollow, as if she'd suffered an illness.

The man beside her regarded me without expression. His skin was like polished ivory, a close-cut silver-blond beard covered his jutting jaw. I knew that jaw: I'd seen it countless times in portraits sent to our court by the Imperial Hapsburg family. I felt faint as I bent my knees in clumsy reverence. I was completely unprepared for this.

Elisabeth said, 'Mother, may I present His Majesty King Philip II, my husband.'

Philip inclined his head. 'Madame de Medici, a pleasure.' His greeting was spoken with perfect neutrality; as I met his gaze I glimpsed frigid pale gray eyes, shadowed by his hat's rim.

Elisabeth submitted to Charles's embrace and Henri's and

Margot's quizzical stares. They had been children when she left and seemed confused as to who this composed stranger was.

We then attended an outdoor feast. As we dined, I gauged Philip's response, watching the way his spidery fingers tapped on his thigh as each platter of roast pheasant, venison, and duck was set before him. He ate sparingly, without any indication that what he tasted was agreeable to him.

The entire court stared. Here was the dreaded king of Spain, a legend among Catholics. He was frugal in both his speech and appearance, far smaller than my imagination had made him, with delicate hands and an almost feminine timidity, as if he were ill accustomed to attention. Still, I saw his gaze turn again and again to Elisabeth like a bird of prey's and I had the disquieting sensation he had another motive besides a familial reunion.

I knew it was customary for Spanish queens to remain quiescent in public, but I didn't like the way my daughter's eyes were muted, as if she were detached from everything around her. Our conversation was impersonal, without intimacy; as the festivities continued, a pageant and feast every night, a hunt or sail on the river every day, I managed to find time alone with her when Charles, Henri, and the other gentlemen invited Philip and his suite to go hawking.

I summoned Elisabeth to the long gallery, with its mullioned bay windows overlooking the river. Behind us trailed our women, dogs, and Margot, who dragged her feet because I hadn't allowed her to join the court in its blood sport.

Before I had so much as inquired into her state of health, Elisabeth declared: 'My husband demands that all edicts of toleration be rescinded and Catholicism asserted as France's one true faith. All those who wish to convert must beg for absolution. Those who do not must die.'

Still standing, I came to a halt and looked her up and down. 'Why hasn't he told me this himself? He's been here for weeks, dining at my table. Are you to act as his ambassador?'

'I am his wife and queen. It is my duty to speak to you.'

'And so you presume to advise me, your mother, on how I should rule my realm?'

'It is not your realm. My brother Charles is king of France.'

I flicked my hand at Lucrezia, who herded Margot and the others out of earshot. I let a few moments pass before I said, 'I've looked forward to our reunion every day since you left. It pains me to think I've done something to offend.'

'You have let heresy take over France. That is what offends.'

I stared at her, at a loss. 'Blessed Virgin,' I said. 'What has he done to you?'

'If you refer to my husband, he's utterly devoted.' She paused; I felt her hand slip into mine. Her fingers were cold. 'You must listen to me.' She glanced over her shoulder to where the women gathered by the tapestries to play with the dogs. 'Philip will not approve of any compromise. He believes you'll never put an end to the Huguenot insurrection. If I hadn't intervened when le Balafré seized you and Charles, he'd have sent an army to aid the Guises.'

'You . . . you intervened?'

'I didn't want him to worsen the situation. But I may not be able to do so the next time.' She raised her eyes, looking to me for the first time since her arrival as I remembered her. 'I miscarried six months ago. I almost died. That was why Philip delayed his response about our meeting with you. He feared I would not be well enough to travel.'

I couldn't move. My eyes filled with tears.

'I realized then I may not live long,' she added. 'I decided I had to do what I could to maintain the peace between our countries. Philip hears of everything that transpires here and he was not pleased that you let Coligny go free after he ordered le Balafré's murder.' She led me unresisting to a nearby window alcove. I sat beside her on the cushioned seat, stunned.

'Maman, please,' she said. 'Are you listening?'

'Yes,' I whispered. 'I am. I'm so sorry. I wish you had told me. I would have come to you.'

'The loss of my child was God's will. I mean, about Coligny.

He should have been put to death. Why did you not command it?'

'He . . . he was acquitted.' I wiped my eyes with the back of my hand. 'I ordered an investigation, but no one could establish that he had any complicity.'

'That doesn't matter. There isn't a Catholic in Europe who believes in his innocence. If he didn't have le Balafré killed, he desired it, and he led a rebellion against his king.'

'Not his king,' I protested. 'He led it against the Guises. My child, you have no idea what they had done, what they would have done had le Balafré not died. Your brother and I would still be his captives while he and Monsignor ruled the country.'

'Be that as it may, you cannot play both sides forever. In the end, you must choose.'

In my mind, I saw him as he 'd been in Chenonceau, chiseled sinew and bone, his breath warm as he bent over me . . . My voice caught in my throat. 'Don't you see? He did what he did for France. I cannot condemn him for what I myself would have done, given the chance.'

'Then you risk everything. He raised an army. What makes you think he won't do it again?' As she spoke, she did not take her eyes from me, as though she peeled back layers of my skin to expose the heart of my secret. She let out a gasp, rose swiftly to her feet.

'Dear God, you love him.'

I gripped her hand. 'No,' I heard myself say, the lie keen as a blade on my tongue. 'I care for him because in times of great trials with the Guises, he cared for me. It's not what you think.'

She went rigid. 'He is a heretic. He's not worthy of your care. There will never be peace while he and his kind live. You must rid France of them, once and for all.'

'You think that because of their faith, I should see them dead? They are people, Elisabeth: people, not monsters. I cannot kill thousands of French subjects.'

'They are damned.' She pulled her hand from me. 'You must protect France from those who defile it. Philip is right: you have lost your faith. You must beg God for strength.'

'And you have become too Spanish!' I said angrily. 'You forget that in France, we do not put our subjects to death without cause.'

'What more cause than heresy and revolt and the defense of our Holy Church? You must –'

Her voice cut off. Turning about, I saw Philip coming down the gallery, alone.

'It is too hot for hawking,' he said as he came before us. 'I thought I should return so we could converse. We haven't had time to speak, madame, and we've important matters to discuss.'

I caught a warning in Elisabeth's eyes, but as I looked at his tidy figure and thought of the dogma he'd instilled in my daughter, I was beyond caring. 'Your wife has said quite enough, my lord. Indeed, we should converse. I would hear your opinions from your own lips.'

Rays of scorching midday sun fell through the windows at our feet. I stood and we began to walk down the gallery, our shadows blending on the polished wood floor.

'You expect too much of me,' I began, without preamble.

'Oh?' I heard a sarcastic surprise in his tone. 'You've always declared yourself a devout Catholic. Now is the chance to make good on your words.'

'I *am* devout,' I retorted. 'But I never said I'd wage holy war on the Huguenots.'

He came to a halt. I saw fire leap in his icy eyes. 'The holy war has already begun. The question now is who shall win. It is in my interest that you do, given the alternative.'

I regarded him. 'I see you prefer candor.' I turned and resumed walking the way we'd come, forcing him to follow. The gallery stretched empty before us; my daughter and her women had left. 'Let me elucidate the matter for you,' I said. 'France is at peace. We've had our difficulties, but they are over, which I believe should be cause for rejoicing. After all, your concern is for our welfare, is it not?'

'That is not an explanation, madame. It is an excuse. You have not earned peace as much as prolonged the inevitable.'

I stopped in midstep. 'My lord, tell me: What would you do,

with half your nobility professed heretics and the other lusting
for blood? It is not so easy a situation, I can assure you.'

His smile was almost mechanical, an inflexible lift of his colorless lips. 'You know what I would do.' He leaned to me, his breath
tinged with garlic. 'The heads of a few salmon are worth those
of a thousand frogs. Exterminate the Huguenots and then you
will have peace.'

I stared. 'Are you suggesting I should instigate a massacre?'

'I am suggesting you utilize the tools every prince has at his
disposal. You are a Medici. You must know of men who will do
your bidding for a price?'

I took a step back. 'Is this how you would treat your subjects
in Spain?'

His eyes narrowed. 'I would never let my subjects go as far as
yours have. Now, I wish to discover how you intend to deal with
them. It is the only reason I am here with my queen.'

'Yes, I've seen how much influence you hold with my daughter,'
I riposted before I could stop myself. 'And I believe we've said
all there is to say. Should the Huguenots betray us again, I'll
decide with my son, the king, what we shall do, for rest assured
we'll not tolerate further sedition. But what you propose is
unconscionable.'

I turned to leave. He gripped my arm. When I whirled to him,
I saw the face I knew lurked under his impassive mask – the face
of hatred and intolerance, like bones beneath his skin. 'Take their
heads,' he hissed, 'and I'll give my Austrian cousin as queen for
your son, princesses for your other sons, and crowns for the lot.
I am prepared to be generous. But if you fail me, Madame de
Medici, you'll reap the consequences.'

I looked at his hand. He withdrew it, as if scalded. 'Send your
cousin first,' I said, 'and I'll consider the rest. Until then, I bid
you good afternoon, my lord.'

I proceeded down the gallery, feeling his eyes like arrows in
my back.

I'd met ruthless men in my time, men who killed and relished
it, men whose taste for mayhem ran like venom in their blood,

but none unnerved me like Philip II. He was everything I'd fought against. He was my uncle Clement, le Balafré, and Monsignor; he was all the destructive, dogmatic men who saw no other way but their own, who carried darkness in their souls and expected – no, demanded – that I do their bidding because I was a woman.

Never, I vowed as I exited the gallery. I would never be a man's pawn again.

I would rule France as I saw fit, come what may.

Once again we stood on the banks of the Bidassoa, a cruel wind razing the sky. Though it was late July, the heat had given way to gusting, premature autumn, and I embraced Elisabeth as she readied for departure. 'You must take care,' I murmured, thinking back to when I had lost a child in secret. 'Remember, many women who've suffered miscarriages go on to deliver healthy children.'

'Yes, Maman.' She glanced at Philip, already mounted and surrounded by his men. Her mouth parted, but a harsh cawing drowned her voice. We both looked to a nearby linden tree. Two ravens perched on its lowest bough, releasing harsh cries.

Then they went silent, regarding us with their black baleful eyes.

She whispered, 'An omen,' and as I started to protest, for I found her superstition yet another unwelcome legacy of Spain, the solemnity of her expression stopped me.

'You will think about everything we discussed?' she asked.

I resisted the urge to rebuke her. I didn't want conflict to mar our parting. 'I will.'

She gave me then the first genuine smile of her entire visit. For a moment, the stern queen vanished and she was my child once more, the daughter who'd given me such comfort. 'I love you, Elisabeth,' I said. 'If you ever need me, I'll walk across the Pyrenees to be with you.'

We embraced and she turned to her horse, the wind clutching at her cloak.

I remained at the river's edge until the cavalcade vanished and Charles muttered, 'They're gone. Can we go inside? I'm famished.'

I nodded and turned away, overcome by sorrow.

Above me, the ravens took flight into the storm-chased sky.

26

We embarked on the long trip home, the luster of our progress peeling away like the gilded *C*s on my coach. As I stared out the window at the passing landscape I didn't see the peasants laboring to reap the harvest or barefoot children and women, running to the sides of the road to cheer our passage. All I heard was my daughter's voice, intractable in its conviction.

You can't play both sides forever. In the end, you must choose.

I had already chosen. I'd chosen sacrifice over comfort, obligation over pleasure, duty over passion. What more must I choose?

My hands bunched into fists in my lap. I would not accept Philip of Spain's threats. I would not condone him dictating my affairs. I would continue to strive for peace, no matter the obstacles. I would not hand over chaos as legacy to my sons; I would not send legions of French men and women to the flames because of their religious beliefs.

And I would not forsake Coligny. I had denied him, and myself, long enough.

We reached Blois under an early snowfall; after I saw the court established I issued a proclamation reaffirming my commitment to tolerance between the faiths and ordering the nobility to attend our Christmas court without fail.

Among the invitations was one for Coligny.

We greeted them in Blois's painted hall, Charles and I on the dais as the lords and their wives queued up before us. The hall was hung with tapestries, lit with expensive scented candles; I sought to convey an air of festivity by slinging garlands and spangled boughs from the pilasters, but as each lord came and went, I felt increasing concern.

'They're all wearing white ribbons or gold crosses,' I hissed beneath my breath to Birago. 'What is this new fashion?'

'Huguenot for one, Catholic for the other,' he said, his brow furrowed.

I remembered the night long ago in Fontainebleau, when I'd tried in vain to identify Huguenots among us. Then, I'd seen brilliant jewels and gorgeous clothes; I'd heard only laughter and wit. Now it felt as if the very air were about to tear apart, and the expressions before me were somber.

'Since when has this court found it necessary to declare their religious affiliation?' I retorted, forgetting Charles sat right beside me. 'It's unacceptable.'

'Issue a decree against it.' Charles let out a terse laugh. 'But best do it fast, before another war breaks out. For look: here come our Catholic peers.'

I tensed in my chair. The Guise family entered. Le Balafré's widow was veiled, while her fifteen-year-old son, the new duc de Guise, wore a pure white satin doublet. The other Guise relatives were headed by Monsignor the Cardinal. One look at his malicious smile assured me he was responsible for this theatrical scene, to remind us that they would never forget le Balafré.

'I did not know you were back from Rome,' I said as the cardinal bowed before us and kissed Charles's extended hand. 'I trust the Holy Council went well?'

'Splendid,' he replied. 'His Holiness has pronounced anathema on all heretics.'

Charles glowered. 'Christ's blood,' he said, without bothering to lower his voice, 'why must you always ruin everything?'

I gave a nervous chuckle, about to remind him the Guises were our guests, when I caught sight of a figure walking toward us.

Silence plunged over the hall.

He too wore white. Harsh lines cut into his brow and bracketed his once-supple mouth; silver threaded his thinning hair. And his eyes were enameled by reserve, rimmed in shadow.

I said softly, 'My lord Coligny, welcome. Are you in mourning?'

'I am. My wife, Charlotte, has passed away after a long illness.'

'God rest her soul,' I murmured. Even as I struggled against a guilt-ridden leap of hope, he turned to Charles. 'My wife died before she could see me exonerated of the heinous charge leveled on me. Your Majesty does her memory honor by recalling me to court, where I can assume my rightful place and restore my name.'

The implicit accusation froze me. Did he blame me for his exile? I'd been looking forward to seeing him again, to reestablish our rapport; I expected nothing more, for I knew it would be far too dangerous to revive what we had lost, but I had not anticipated his coldness, the precision with which he had launched his address to my son, as if I were not sitting there.

Before I could react, Charles descended the dais to stand next to Coligny.

'You are welcome here,' I heard him say, and he turned to the court, squaring his thin shoulders. I'd crafted a speech for him, but instead of my words he spoke of his own volition, his voice ringing out with a certainty that caught me off guard.

'I would see this season of celebration marked by goodwill and reconciliation between the noble families of my realm, for we are all brothers in Christ.' He returned to Coligny, took him by the shoulders, and kissed him on the mouth. As I watched, paralyzed, he motioned to the Guises. 'Come, greet your brother.'

Coligny stood waiting. Though it was a spontaneous gesture by Charles, Coligny looked as though he 'd been waiting for this moment all his life. I glanced at Birago, found the same consternation on his face, and found myself both proud and alarmed. While my son wanted to be seen as a king, he should have consulted Birago or me before choosing this occasion and method.

'I command it,' Charles said; and before the sea of appraising eyes, Monsignor came forth and pecked Coligny's cheek. The duchess followed. I half expected her to throw back her veil and thrust a knife into his ribs but she leaned to him to accept his kiss before she stepped aside.

Young Guise did not move. Coligny started to shift to breach the distance between them when Guise spat, 'Murderer! I'll see you pay for my father's death.' He pivoted to Charles. 'Your Majesty, I fear I must retire.'

Charles flushed red as Guise executed a curt bow and strode out. I vacated my seat. 'No,' I whispered. 'Let him go. You've made your point. Now, say what I wrote for you.'

Charles went rigid. 'Don't tell me what to do,' he muttered, and then he said, 'Let there be no more talk of heretics at this court. We are all Frenchmen first!' And just as I started to think he would ignore my request, he said to Coligny, 'My lord, we forgive all trespasses against us and trust henceforth you will serve us faithfully. We hereby assign you a seat on our Council, where you shall advise us on matters pertaining to this realm.'

Coligny bowed. 'Your Majesty honors me beyond my worth.'

Charles smiled and strode into the banqueting chamber, followed by the courtiers.

Coligny looked at me. 'I came to see my name restored. I didn't expect this.'

I had just witnessed the first act of independence from my son; as I struggled to absorb the implications, I abruptly felt mistrust of this man, who seemed to sow discord wherever he went.

'I once told you I would seat you on the Council,' I managed to say.

'You did.' He paused. 'I must beg for your forgiveness.'

I met his eyes – those eyes that seemed to have changed more than anything else. 'No,' I said, 'no apologies. Let us leave the past where it belongs.'

'We cannot. We must confront it, for only then can we find peace.'

I did not know what peace he meant and did not want to. I had made a mistake. I wanted him gone from this court, from my life. The weight of what we'd been to each other, of all that had passed between us, seemed to crush the very breath out of me.

'I sinned out of despair for my wife,' he said. 'I was lost, frightened, and I abused your trust. I never meant to bring you pain. I will not stay here if you do not wish it so.'

I couldn't believe my ears. 'You still say it is my choice? Mine? After everything, you'd still place the burden on me? It seems you've forgotten how this all started and how it was broken. I was not the one who took up arms; I was not the one who –' I cut myself short. I could see in his face, in the way his jaw tightened, that he knew.

'I shall go,' he murmured, but as he started to bow I said, 'No.' He went still.

'No,' I said again. 'My son asked you to serve us. That is his decision and I will not countermand it.' I lifted my chin. 'You wanted my forgiveness. I grant it.'

'Then,' he replied, 'I will do everything I can to prove worthy of it.' He offered me his arm. Biting back tears, knowing that what we shared had been lost forever, I set my hand on his sleeve and let him escort me into the dining chamber.

There are many ways to betray one 's heart.

I had turned forty-seven, suffered disillusionment and far more devastating losses; I refused to mourn something that could never be. I'd basked in illusion, carried it with me as something precious, but now I swept up the fragments and put them away; and slowly, as winter gave way to spring, I came to accept that Coligny and I had no further meaning to each other, save as mother and adviser to our king. We saw each other in Council every day; we passed each other at the evening fetes but avoided each other's eyes and restricted our conversation to state business. I knew he often left court to travel to Châtillon and see his children; without my asking, Birago had bribed a servant in Coligny's household to keep us informed of his doings, and while part of me balked at Birago's belief that Coligny needed watching, I was more at ease knowing he dwelled under our eye.

He wasn't the only person I had to consign to the past. One July afternoon, as a citrus-scented breeze drifted through my casement at Fontainebleau, I received word from Salon.

Nostradamus was dead.

I couldn't imagine him gone. His incredible aura of wisdom, his ability to see into depths rarely glimpsed, had seemed impervious to the bane of mortality. Deeply saddened by his loss, I belatedly recalled I had his last gift, still enclosed in its tube. I sent the chart to Chaumont, asking Cosimo to interpret it and promising to visit as soon as I could.

News of another death was more welcome. At sixty-six, following years of seclusion in Anet, Diane de Poitiers breathed her last. I learned of it via a letter from a tax collector. For a moment I was plunged into the memory of the last time I'd seen her, of her frigid face as she confronted the loss of her prestige, and I took savage comfort that in the end, I was the one who thrived. I had outlived her to command a power she never had. Returning word to the tax collector to sell everything she owned, I closed that painful chapter of my life.

In August I received word that my daughter Elisabeth had delivered twin girls. I was overjoyed; so was Philip, who ordered weeks of festivities in Madrid. I sent them matching gold standing cups inscribed with the babies' names, moved by the decision to christen one of them Catalina in my honor, as well as a long letter to Elisabeth, teeming with advice and herbal remedies to assist her in her recovery from the birth.

We made our annual move to Amboise, where I inspected the aging lions François I had kept there. The creatures dwelled in such squalid neglect I ordered our court architect to design a splendid new enclosure, with a paddock where they could roam. Charles loved the lions and spent hours watching them let out their deafening roars. I was troubled by his suggestion that we set them to baiting a bear and instead put him to work with the keepers, heaving huge chunks of fresh venison with a prong into the paddock, where the beasts tore into them with relish.

Charles had reverted to his habitual self. He was now sixteen and of age to rule; I was no longer his official regent, but he showed no repeat of that spark of independence he'd displayed at Blois. He still had his schedule of lessons and Council meetings but spent his free time with his falcons and weapons. At Amboise, he and Henri even devised their own armory, where they could hammer out iron and bronze. The exercise strengthened their physiques and camaraderie, even if Margot sniffed that they smelled like blacksmiths and twelve-year-old Hercule was always getting underfoot and scalding himself.

I'd been distraught upon our return to discover my youngest son had suffered permanent disfigurement from the pox. He had deep crevices all over his face; his nose was deformed and the disease had stunted his growth, so he barely increased in height even as his spine distorted almost into a hump. Dr. Paré had warned me that while he would improve with care, it was unlikely he would ever sire children, as the pox at such a young age affected testicular development. I couldn't help but see him as a changeling with his wiry hair, porcine eyes, and dwarfish physique, struggling to master basics when at his age his siblings could already translate Latin into Greek. I believed the pox had retarded his intellectual development as well and asked Margot to tutor him, as of all of us she was the only one he seemed to feel any affection toward. As always where he was concerned, I wrestled with guilt. My last born, he'd suffered more than his siblings from my frequent absence, and though I tried to engage him, he was disinterested in me both as a person and a mother, preferring Margot whenever possible, and scampering after his brothers as if he sought to prove he was as good as them. Charles disdained him as a freak, but Henri found him amusing and allowed him to play in the armory with them. And he was still a Valois prince; in time, with the proper attention, he could be molded into an appropriate supporting role, as no one expected he'd ever inherit.

Thus did I immerse myself in the cares of my children and the realm, unaware that the world I labored to create was about to be shattered.

'My lady.' Lucrezia reached through my closed bed curtains to shake my shoulder.

Within the bed's darkness I struggled against lassitude. I'd been overseeing a refurbishment of Amboise's lower gardens and I was exhausted. At my feet, Muet growled.

'What is it?' I hauled myself up onto my pillows.

Lucrezia took Muet. 'My lord Birago and Monsignor are here. They say it is urgent.'

'At this hour?' Groaning, I slipped my feet into my slippers, took the robe Anna-Maria handed me, and coiled my hair at my nape with a comb. I limped into my presence chamber, resisting the pain in my right leg. I'd developed it a few days ago and suspected sciatica. I'd hoped a good night's rest, aided by the tincture of poppy and vervain I'd concocted in my kiln, would alleviate it, but judging by my shuffle I'd need a cane soon, like poor Nostradamus.

'Well?' I looked at Monsignor, dressed as if for office in his scarlet robes and skullcap; I ignored him as much as possible at court, though he still held a seat in Council as France's premier prelate. I was not happy to see him in my rooms, in the middle of the night.

Birago was ashen. 'It's Coligny. He . . . he approaches at the head of an army.'

'What?' I stared at them. 'Are you both mad?'

Monsignor looked almost pleased. 'I wish it were the case. This time, he's gone beyond any ability of yours to save him.'

'This is preposterous.' I snatched the goblet of cool water Lucrezia handed me, directing my words at Birago. 'You have an informant in his household, yes? Surely he would have –'

'Obviously not an efficient one,' interrupted Monsignor, and Birago wrung his hands. That one gesture made my heart miss a beat. 'But why on earth would he bring an army?'

'As you are aware, madame, there 's been disagreement in Council over Philip of Spain's decision to send armies into the Low Countries,' said Monsignor, his curt tone implying I'd been spending my time pulling up weeds in the gardens, rather than attending to matters of state.

I nodded impatiently. 'I am, and as you are aware, I refused Philip leave to bring his men through France. They were forced to march through Savoy instead. What has that to do with it?'

'Everything.' Birago wet his parched lips. '*Madama,* forgive me. At the time I thought Coligny lifted protest against our allowance of further repression in the Low Countries, that it was merely his expected stance over Spain's ongoing repressive policy. But I was wrong. He . . . he believes we allow it because we are planning the same thing here.'

I stood as if petrified, my mouth agape.

From his robes, Monsignor withdrew an envelope. 'I too have informants, madame. I planted spies among the heretics who witnessed meetings between Coligny and the other leaders. He preached a call to arms; he recruited Jeanne de Navarre to his cause and petitioned Elizabeth Tudor in England to finance his army and stockpile the Huguenot port of La Rochelle with munitions. Among his accusations are that you seek further alliance with Spain through a marriage for the king and will exterminate his faith at Philip's command. If we don't act, he'll have every heretic in France at your door. You cannot pretend anymore that he is your friend.'

'You . . . you knew this? You knew and you didn't tell me?'

He shrugged. 'Would you have believed me if I'd come to you without proof? I needed evidence, as time and time again you chose to give him the benefit of your doubt. He took every precaution; our interception of his correspondence alone was painstakingly difficult. He uses codes we've not seen before, but in the end our suspicions were confirmed that he's been plotting for months. He fears that if they don't strike first, we will.'

I heard Philip in my head: *The head of a few salmon are worth a thousand frogs.*

I knew in that instant this was *his* doing. He'd warned I would reap the consequences if I failed to fulfill his requests. Somehow, he'd infiltrated the Huguenot ranks and sowed panic.

As if Monsignor read my thoughts he added, 'You'll find in that envelope a letter from Spain, detailing your meeting in Bayonne and advising the Huguenots to prepare for death. I had no idea you and Philip had had such elucidating conversations. I'm sorry I missed them.'

'We spoke once. Once! And I refused him any concessions. I agreed to nothing.'

Monsignor sighed. Taking the envelope from him, Birago said, '*Madama,* this is my fault. I should have known; I should have acted as Monsignor did. I . . . I was deceived. My informant was a double agent; the intelligence he sent revealed nothing of interest.'

'Never mind that now,' I said, through my teeth. 'Coligny knows we cannot afford to keep a standing army. Would he dare to engage us in battle when we are defenseless?'

'Not if Monsignor and I can help it,' said Birago. 'We've dispatched Constable Montmorency to Paris to ready our retainers and issued a call to arms to all our Catholic nobles. Coligny has ten thousand at his command. We can defeat him with a full force behind us.'

I wanted to scream out my order for his arrest. I had forgiven him. I had seen him acquitted of a nobleman's death and brought him back to court, where he'd sat on my son's Council. I'd even grieved over the passion we once shared. Now another Huguenot revolt was upon me and Coligny was once again the leader. He chose to believe Spain's lies rather than come to me. Just as before, he'd not trusted in me but instead crept behind my back to foment chaos.

He was determined to destroy us all.

I clenched my jaw. I didn't even feel the pain in my leg anymore. 'We leave for Paris at once. If it is war he wants, then by God war I shall give him.'

27

For the next six months we battled the Huguenots, waylaying them in flooded fords and isolated hilltops, fighting or withdrawing. When they overran Catholic cities, the first to suffer were our women, raped and hacked to pieces before their children. Churches were burned, relics looted, priests roasted over fires in mockery of the Inquisition. But we could be just as cruel; when we took cities held by Huguenots, our soldiers delighted in skewering them on pikes and festooning the gates with their heads and limbs.

I barely slept, watching over my children and a bewildered Charles, who couldn't understand why we were at war again, even as France transformed into a nightmarish vista of charred fields, devastated villages, and desolate hamlets, populated by widows and orphans.

Once my initial anger over Coligny's betrayal ebbed, I sought compromise. I dispatched innumerable letters requesting a meeting, reminding him of our agreements and promising a full pardon if he laid down his arms and presented himself to court to discuss his grievances.

My efforts were in vain.

The Huguenots distributed pamphlets throughout their embattled towns, paid with Tudor coin and printed in Geneva. Birago's informants brought me one. *Madame la Serpente and her son the Leper King,* it read, and I shuddered in rage to see the depiction of my son as a depraved, disease-ridden monarch bathing in children's blood, and of myself, corpulent and rapacious, sitting on a throne with my foot on a pile of decapitated Huguenot heads.

Then word came that Coligny had welcomed Jeanne of Navarre in the southwestern seaport stronghold of La Rochelle. Jeanne had traveled incognito through our war-torn country with her fourteen-yearold heir; taking him by the hand, she mounted La Rochelle's ramparts to exhort the Huguenots in his name to fight against us to the death. Coligny then lifted the prince's standard aloft and shouted: 'Behold France's true savior. When Henri of Navarre is king, we will be freed of Valois tyranny!'

I was beside myself; haunted by Nostradamus's warning that I must protect young Navarre yet unable to stomach that he'd been exalted as the future of the Huguenot cause, his right to the throne placed above my sons'. Jeanne earned my undying hatred for this deed, but the full force of my enmity, the cauldron of my rage, I flung at Coligny. He had betrayed my trust and gone to war against me, and now he committed the ultimate offense: he defamed my flesh and blood.

This time, I would have vengeance.

I put a price of ten thousand livres on his head and ordered our troops to siege La Rochelle. I didn't even argue when Henri requested to join our forces, to serve under the constable. He was almost sixteen, strong and beautiful; his regal presence would harden our men's resolve and Montmorency would keep him safe. I had a gold suit of armor made for him and he declared that if he captured Coligny, he'd send me his head and forfeit the bounty. I laughed at his fervor; I was sure he'd never get that close. Later, he wrote from camp, telling me of his budding friendship with young Guise, who was a year older than him and at his side day and night.

As autumn neared, La Rochelle resisted every attempt to bring it down, and again I sent out terms for peace. We were running out of money. I would accept none from Spain, despite Philip's offers, while the Huguenots had an endless supply from England.

Elizabeth Tudor had become a serious participant in the outcome of our war. She now held Mary Stuart in imprisonment, after Mary made a disastrous second marriage and the suspicious death of her husband led the Protestant lords of Scotland to revolt against her. She fled to England to throw herself on Elizabeth's mercy; horrified, Elizabeth put her under guard. I couldn't summon much sympathy for her; Mary's fate was of her own making, yet seeing as Elizabeth had seen fit to support Coligny and I needed her to desist, I sent a letter reminding her that Mary was still an anointed queen. I hoped to alert her to the fact that she'd best attend to the trouble in her own realm, rather than abet traitors in France. My tactic worked. Within days her ambassador waved Elizabeth's ubiquitous flag of truce, requesting that I offer the English queen a marriage proposal. I smiled. She knew such diplomatic exercises could take years, given the age difference between her and my sons. She'd prolong her consideration, accept my gifts and blandishments, while Coligny would soon find his coffers depleted of her gold.

I immediately called the Council to session. I anticipated Monsignor would cajole me to accept Spain's assistance rather than court the heretic of England; I was prepared to counter with a letter of credit from my Florentine bankers.

But when I entered the chamber, I found Charles waiting there with Birago.

I looked at them in puzzlement. Charles said in a broken voice, 'Maman, we've word from Spain. My sister Elisabeth, she . . . she has miscarried and . . .'

I held up my hand, stopping him. Without a word, I staggered back to my apartments, where sunlight burned. Dropping at my prie-dieu, I lowered my head and waited for the deluge.

Nothing came. Not a single tear.

All I could remember were the hours after her birth when I'd held her, spellbound, her enormous eyes fixed on me as if I was everything she wanted to see. I could still feel her perfect skin, smell her clean infant's scent, and touch the wispy tendrils of her dark Medici hair . . .

Lucrezia came to me, her eyes red from weeping. 'His Majesty says he'll cancel the Council session and institute forty days of official mourning,' she said.

'No.' I forced myself to rise. Behind her in my rooms I saw my dwarf Anna-Maria crying into her handkerchief. 'No,' I whispered. 'Tell him I'll be there. I just need a moment . . .'

It was then that I remembered the ravens at Bayonne. Elisabeth had called them omens and she had been right. She had given Philip of Spain two daughters, and no son.

When I returned to the Council chamber, it was full. The lords stood in unison. With a voice that scarcely trembled I said: 'God has seen fit to take my daughter. Our enemies should not be quick to rejoice, however, or suppose my anger over their betrayal will lessen. Philip of Spain is a widower, as grief-stricken as we, but in need of a wife, for he has his succession to consider.'

I turned to Monsignor. His soft face was suffused with triumph; he had longed for this day, to witness me so sundered by loss that I'd entrust Charles and the kingdom to his safekeeping. Though he must despair over his Stuart niece's misfortune, Mary remained a viable bride, promising the crown of Scotland to any Catholic prince who cared to rescue her. That prince could never be Philip. He must remain tied to us lest he decide he'd had enough of my equivocation and invaded our war-racked country.

No matter how much I wanted to give up I could not.

'I want my daughter Margot to take her sister's place,' I said. 'And you, Monsignor, will present my proposal in person to King Philip. To prove my constancy, I'll accept four thousand of his men to aid us in our war against the Huguenots. But that is all I am willing to concede.'

I drew up my chair. 'Now, gentlemen, we must find a way to level La Rochelle.'

That night, I extinguished all the candles and sat on the floor. I waited a long time, an eternity, it seemed, but grief found me, as it always did.

The world went black. I saw and felt nothing more.

Until the vision.

28

A bearded man gallops across a burnt plain roiling with dying and wounded soldiers. It is the throes of a battle nearing its end; cries shatter against the black whorl of the sky. The man's horse is panting, its flanks flecked with spume. He looks over his shoulder, digs his spurs into the animal's ribs. From the melee, another rider races toward him, clad in gold armor, a sword bright as a razor in his gauntleted fist. Relentless, he slashes at figures in torn white tunics. His blade seems to strike a thousand places at once, beheading a man here, thrusting another through the chest there, disemboweling a charger and sending its rider tumbling to the ground. But he is intent on the one who eludes him, who even now begins to vanish into the haze.

'Traitor!' The man in gold screams. 'You will die! You will die for France!'

I struggled to open my caked eyelids. When I succeeded I found a group of shadowy figures crowded about my bed. A hand pressed a chamomile-soaked cloth to my brow; I cracked my mouth open to talk. My voice issued hoarse, raw. 'Water . . . I need water.'

'God save her, she's talking!' Lucrezia bent over me.

'Of course I'm talking,' I muttered. 'Did you think I was dead?'

The people about the bed assumed identities: Anna-Maria, her head only reaching the height of my daughter Margot's waist. Dark shadows ringed my daughter's blue-green eyes, as if she hadn't slept in weeks.

'You look terrible,' I muttered.

Margot gave a weak smile. 'And you've begun to recover.' To my bafflement, Lucrezia started to cry. 'We thought we had lost you,' she whispered, grasping my hand in hers.

I frowned. Anna-Maria nodded; with a start, the pain of Elisabeth's death crashed over me. For a second I wanted to close my eyes and fall back into oblivion. But I couldn't; I had to organize our new expedition against La Rochelle, see to the envoys and ambassadors who seemed to always be a half step behind me. I had to –

I went still, looking at the somber faces. 'How long have I been here?'

Lucrezia put a goblet of water to my lips. 'More than a month.'

'A month!' I pushed her hand aside. 'That's impossible. What happened?'

'A fever.' Lucrezia took away the goblet and rinsed the cloth in a basin at my bedside. She returned it to my forehead; it felt cool, flooding my parched senses with the tang of the herb. 'A tertian fever. We found you on the floor in your rooms. The physicians could do nothing. They bled you, but you didn't wake. We 've been taking turns watching over you. Oh, my lady, the sweat came out of you like rivers, cold as ice. Yet you didn't move. It was like a living death. When you started speaking just now . . . we thought it was the end.'

'What did I say?'

'You spoke of a battle, of a rider fleeing and a man in gold. It sounded like . . .' Her voice trailed off into silence.

I could feel the scores on my arm from the bleedings. I didn't tell them that what I had was no ordinary fever but rather a recurrence of my childhood ailment. And with it had come my gift.

A crash at the door jolted everyone about. 'Is she awake? Is she speaking?' Charles came to my bed, his brow smudged with powder from the latest armory he'd set up in the Louvre. He leaned over me, his person pungent with smoke. 'Maman, is it true? Did you see it?'

I looked past him to see Margot peering behind his shoulder. She must have slipped out to fetch him. 'What,' I said, 'am I supposed to have seen?'

'Their defeat!' His voice trilled. 'We attacked La Rochelle. Birago and I organized everything while you were ill. Philip's

Spaniards joined us. We blockaded the city and routed the Huguenots. They run for their lives.'

'Gold armor,' I whispered. 'Henri had gold armor. I gave it to him. *Dio Mio,* is he . . . ?'

'He's fine. He went after Coligny; he followed him for miles on horseback. He told Guise he'd made you a promise. But Coligny got away.' Charles paused, staring at me. 'You saw it, didn't you? Did you also see the constable? He's dead. He died on the field, fighting to protect Henri. We had him buried in St. Denis, close to Papa. The constable always loved Papa. I did right by putting him there, didn't I?'

Montmorency: Coligny's uncle. I saw him as he'd been on the day I first met him in Marseilles: a titan, blocking out the sun. He'd been my friend and foe, veteran of three reigns and staunch defender of our faith, which he'd put above himself. Now, like so many others, he was gone. I couldn't say I was deeply saddened by his death, not after what he'd done with the Triumvirate, but I felt the weight of the years as I never had before, every link with my past severed so that I seemed to stand alone, with a surfeit of memories no one else shared.

Overcome by lassitude, I said, 'Yes, you did right. I didn't see him. I didn't know.' I felt myself slipping away, this time into dreamless sleep. 'Forgive me. I'm so tired.'

Charles kissed my cheek. 'Rest, then. And don't worry. The war is over. Soon we can issue a pardon and go back to living as we were.' He patted my hand. 'Oh, I almost forgot. Happy birthday, Maman. We must celebrate when you feel better.' He turned and swaggered out.

Margot stood still, regarding me with an almost fearful look in her eyes.

'My birthday,' I mused, 'my fiftieth.'

As I drifted off, I didn't know how I felt about the fact that Coligny still lived.

Once I left my bed we announced an amnesty, allowing the Huguenots exercise of their religion in designated towns and occupation of four cities, including La Rochelle. The settlement also pardoned all rebel leaders. I chose to make an occasion of it by honoring Birago's efforts on our behalf with the title of chancellor.

I then disbanded our army. My son Henri came home from the front. He looked fit as ever, triumphant from his first foray into blood-soaked manhood. He was accompanied by Guise, broad-shouldered and golden as a god. They were like opposite sides of a coin: one dark, the other light; exploding upon the court like comets, bringing raucous antics in their wake.

I was pleased. My sons had taken initiative during my illness and done their Valois blood proud. None could say they weren't everything a prince of France should be.

As for Coligny, no one knew where he'd gone into hiding. I did not rescind the price on his head but I let it be known he was included in the general amnesty, providing he refrained from any further acts of treason. Though he'd been defeated, he still had his brethren's respect and I didn't want more trouble from him.

Instead, I set myself to building a future where he no longer had a place.

'Philip says no to Margot.' I glanced at the dispatch in hand. 'Monsignor claims he did his utmost to persuade him, but it seems Philip is too full of sorrow over Elisabeth to consider another wife at this time. However, he does agree to Charles's betrothal to his sixteen-year-old cousin, Isabel of Austria.'

I looked up in triumph at Birago. 'Spain will stay married to France. Our Austrian envoy has sent a miniature of the bride for Charles to see. I trust you've already spoken to him?'

Birago rustled in the satin box on my desk, the gold chain of the chancellorship slung about his concave shoulders, adding authority to a bony face carved by years of tireless service. As I watched him hold up the small gold-framed painting, I was overcome by sudden remorse. This stalwart Italian of mine had never strayed from my side and he had paid the price. I often forgot that he had never wed, that I knew nothing of his private life. To me, he lived in an industrious world regulated by quill and parchment, fulfilling his duties and overseeing a vast underworld of spies and intelligencers, striving to keep me and France safe.

'Such white skin and blond hair,' he mused. 'She'll make a lovely bride.'

'Indeed,' I remarked. 'Well, perhaps now that we've seen to Charles we should go about finding you a bride, yes? There must be some lady at court who's caught your fancy.'

He smiled, exposing his brown teeth. 'I fear I'm too old for such things.' I detected a melancholic note in his voice, and before I could say more, he added, 'I have spoken with Charles about the marriage and he had one essential requirement: that she be unassuming. In other words, he said, as unlike his sister Margot as we can find.'

I laughed. 'Charles does adore Margot, but I agree with him: one of her is quite enough. And Isabel fulfills his requirement, according to our envoy. She's of strong Hapsburg stock, virtuous and pious. She'll give him no trouble and many healthy sons, God willing.'

Birago replaced the painting in its satin box and I turned to gaze out the window to the Tuileries, where workmen were converting the barren soil into an Italian grotto. Distant hammering sounded from the Hôtel de Cluny, which I'd ordered demolished so a new palace could be built in its place: my Hôtel de la Reine. Building had become my latest passion. Since my illness, I'd been obsessed with it. Birago said it was because architecture exalted the soul, but I believe that in truth it gave me something tangible to revel in, a visible display of my power.

'What of the Princess Margot?' Birago asked, wincing as he righted himself. 'It's disappointing that Philip won't have her, but there are always other alliances.'

I nodded, going to my chair to caress old Muet; as she nuzzled my hand with her nose, still spry at twelve years, I heard Nostradamus as if he whispered in my ear: *You are two halves of a whole. You need each other to fulfill your destiny.*

I paused. My heart did a slow tumble in my chest. 'What about Navarre?' I looked at Birago, who regarded me as if I'd spoken in a foreign tongue. My voice quickened with excitement. 'Margot and he are both nearing their eighteenth year; they'd be perfect for each other. When Jeanne dies, he'll become king of Navarre, and remember, Coligny exalted him as a Huguenot savior. But if we marry him to Margot, he cannot go to war against us, and Huguenot and Catholic will be united through their persons. They are cousins, after all; they share the Valois blood through Jeanne's mother, François I's sister, and Margot will bear him Valois heirs.'

Birago rubbed his chin pensively. 'It's an interesting solution, but I doubt our Catholic lords or Rome would ever approve. Monsignor says His Holiness is so keen to eradicate heresy he would excommunicate all Protestant princes, including Jeanne of Navarre. Marrying Margot to Jeanne's son will not be viewed as the act of a true Catholic queen.' He gave me a cynical wink. 'And we've had enough accusations about your lack of religious zeal already.'

'Bah!' I waved my hand. 'I don't care what they say about me! But what if Navarre would agree for all children born of the marriage to be raised Catholic?' I was convinced now, the idea shining like a beacon. Surely this was what Nostradamus had meant. With Navarre as my sonin-law I could both protect and mold him, depriving the Huguenots of a royal figurehead to rally behind and forcing both sides to lasting compromise.

'In time,' I went on, 'we might even persuade Navarre himself to convert. He's young, impressionable; and if he and Margot live here, at court with us, who knows what we might achieve? At the very least, Navarre won't take a stance against us.'

'All well and good,' said Birago, 'but what about Coligny? Do you think he'll agree?'

The mention of his name darkened my mood. 'I hardly see how his opinion matters either way,' I retorted, yet even as I declared my defiance I braced myself for Birago's next words.

'His opinion matters greatly,' Birago said, 'as you well know.

He may be disgraced and unwelcome at court, but he still holds great standing with the Huguenots and he'll protest any arrangement that binds Navarre to the Catholic cause. He also holds tremendous influence over Queen Jeanne, whose approval you'll need to conclude the marriage.'

There was nothing I liked less than being reminded of my limitations. 'Leave her to me,' I said. 'As for Coligny, every Catholic in France would leap to earn the reward I put on his head, if I give the word. He's in no position to gainsay me. He owes me his life.'

'I'm relieved to hear it. I feared you might still nurture affection for him.' He met my eyes with a knowing look I couldn't avoid. 'After all, not too long ago you were still . . . friends.'

'That was before he broke his word and nearly brought us to ruin. Whatever affection I had for him is gone.' As I spoke, I pushed aside my doubt. I would always retain a remnant of emotion for Coligny; it was unavoidable, after everything we had shared. But never again would I let passion cloud my reason.

I passed my hands over my skirts, eager to start my plan. 'We mustn't tell anyone save Charles. I'll need his consent, of course, but I don't want word getting out until I return from Chaumont. Is that understood?'

'Yes, *madama*. My lips are sealed.' He did not need to ask why I wished to consult Cosimo.

'Are you certain? There must be something.' I paced the observatory at Chaumont as Cosimo examined Nostradamus's chart, my stomach empty and my back and buttocks aching from the ride in my coach from Paris. All I wanted was a roast pheasant, a goblet of claret, and to rest my bones in the bedchamber readied for me.

'I see only the marriage with the Austrian.' Cosimo raised sunken eyes.

In his forties, he'd grown emaciated, moved with the furtive scuffle of a hermit, and had developed a disconcerting tic, his left shoulder twitching in tandem with a quiver in his cheek. The château itself also felt abandoned, the many rooms and halls shuttered, the staff I'd appointed to serve him dismissed. The smell of mold was so pervasive, Lucrezia had set herself to lighting fires in the hearths and dusting the mantels, while I climbed the stairs to the observatory, where Cosimo spent his waking hours.

'Cosimo,' I said, repressing my impatience, 'Nostradamus claimed that chart contains ten years of my future; he told me I must protect Navarre. I already know about the Austrian. Don't you see any other marriages there?'

I looked at the chart, which swirled with intersecting colored lines and planetary illustrations I couldn't have deciphered to save my life. I had the unbidden thought that perhaps I should not trust his judgment in this matter. After all, did he possess any real power beyond interpreting vague portents and devising appropriate days for coronations, or did he seize on opportunistic moments of lucidity, random occasions when he managed to pierce the veil between this world and the next? After knowing Nostradamus, I found Cosimo's demeanor disconcerting, as if he sought to personify the shadowy character he thought a seer should be.

He sniffed. 'The chart is arcane. Nostradamus obviously didn't study in Italy.'

'Of course he didn't. Do you see Margot's sun sign, at least? She is a Taurus.'

'Let's see.' He traced a line. 'Yes, her life passage moves through this quadrant.' He tapped the paper. 'According to this, she will marry a Sagittarius.'

I gasped. 'Henri of Navarre is Sagittarius!'

His cheek twitched. 'I said passage, not union. And an eclipse in Scorpio here signals blight.'

'Blight?' I paused. 'What does that mean?'

'It's unclear.' His lips pursed. 'As I said, this chart was devised by one unskilled in such matters. Perhaps if you tell me what you wish to know, I can better assist you.'

I drew in a deep breath. I might as well tell him everything or we'd be here all night.

'I want to know if I should arrange a marriage between Margot and Navarre. I need to find a way to bind Catholic and Huguenot in peace and I think this might be it.'

Cosimo regarded me with one skeletal hand caressing the strange pendant at his chest. I'd noticed it when I arrived – a silver amulet depicting a horned creature, a hole piercing its middle.

'You could marry Margot to this prince,' he said, 'but peace will not come so easily.'

'Of course not; I realize one marriage won't solve everything. But if I can manage it, the Huguenots will have to lay down arms for the foreseeable future. Navarre will be one of us; they'll have no prince to support their cause. All I need is Coligny and Jeanne's consent.'

'And do you think they'll give it?' he asked.

I snorted. 'I think they'd rather die.'

'Then perhaps they should.' He turned to a nearby cabinet, removing an oblong lacquer box. He set it before me. Inside, arranged like tiny corpses on black velvet, were two perfect mannequins: a man and a woman, genitals delineated. I lifted the male form with a mixture of awe and repulsion; it felt almost like living flesh.

'One for him and one for her,' Cosimo said. 'With these, you can bring Coligny and Jeanne of Navarre under your control and make them do whatever you desire.' He withdrew a cloth bag from the box, containing silver pins. He held one up. 'You must first personify them by attaching an article from the person: a hair, a piece of clothing, anything that belongs to them. Then you invoke your will. It's like prayer. You can light candles too, red for domination, white to purify, yellow to vanquish. When you wish to exert power, drive these pins into the limbs. You can cause pain, illness, and incapacitation. Even death.'

With one long finger he pried back the velvet lining to reveal a secret compartment. Unhooking its tiny latch, he uncovered a small vial filled with white powder, much like the one his father had given me in Florence.

The candlelight sent distorted shadows across his hollowed face. 'They call it *cantarella:* a combination of arsenic and other secret ingredients. It was said to be the Borgias' favorite poison. Few know how to create it. It can cause illness, madness, and death. Mixed in food or wine, it is untraceable. No one will ever know.'

I met his unblinking stare. The male figure dropped from my hand into the box. It sprawled over the female, like macabre toys about to copulate. I snapped the lid closed, as though they might leap out.

'Now,' Cosimo breathed, 'you have everything you need. You cannot fail.' He took off his amulet, sidled close to slip it over my head. It hung against my breast, heavier than it appeared. 'Evil against evil,' he said, 'in case they seek to counter you.'

I held back my smile at the thought of Coligny resorting to black magic. Cosimo's stare unnerved me; he was quite serious in his suggestion that I invoke spells and poison my opponents, and I had the sense I'd best not refuse his bizarre gifts. Whatever he'd been doing in this château had addled his brain; he had crossed into a place where I did not wish to follow.

'You should be careful,' I said, eager now to eat and depart. 'If you were ever overheard, you'd risk arrest and prosecution for witchcraft.'

His laugh was brittle and too high-pitched. 'Who will ever hear me but you, my lady?'

I nodded and took up the box. He led me onto the torchlit landing. 'I leave tomorrow at first light,' I said. 'If you divine anything else in the chart, you must send word.'

His eyes seemed to go right through me, as if he intuited the unspoken rupture between us.

'I'll devote myself to it entirely.'

I didn't look back as I descended the stairs, but I felt his stare, stalking my heels.

★ ★ ★

'You look splendid.' I stepped aside to allow my new daughter-in-law full view of herself in the mirror. Isabel of Austria had arrived a week before to a lavish reception, which she endured with stoic gratitude despite her swollen eyes and the handkerchief she clutched to her nose as she sneezed every few minutes. She'd caught a nasty cold during her travels, but when I suggested we postpone the wedding until she recovered, she shook her head.

'No,' she stated in her accented French. 'I must marry as planned. Then I bear a son.'

She seemed confident and I now watched her scrutinize her reflection without vanity, her fair brows furrowed inward as she adjusted the coronet on her dark gold hair. She wasn't as attractive as her portrait. Her oval face was marred by the jutting Hapsburg chin and her blue eyes were too small and serious. If she felt frightened or overwhelmed, she didn't show it. Judging by her expression I'd have thought she was going to one of her three daily masses.

Resplendent in crimson brocade, her bosom displayed to the limit of decency, and her gorgeous hair spangled with jeweled combs, Margot exclaimed, 'Why, you look pretty!' as if it came as an unexpected surprise.

I threw her a stony look. At eighteen my daughter had shed the last vestiges of her childhood to reveal a startling beauty; her slanted eyes seemed to absorb whatever color she wore and her naturally titian hair was the envy of every woman at court. She had become our official muse, to whom the poets dedicated reams of overblown verse. I'd perceived a predatory light in her eye as the gentlemen paraded before her in the hall, their muscled thighs in skin-tight hose, their oversized codpieces bobbing; and I did not like it. I needed her to remain a virgin and had insisted her women accompany her everywhere. I also received reports on her activities and knew she dutifully practiced her dancing, music, and poetry; sat for portraits and endless dress fittings – all the expected activities of a princess. Still, her passion for life reminded me of her grandfather François I, kindling my fear that despite my efforts she would find a way to whet her appetite, though I'd yet to discover any proof.

'This dress' – Isabel plucked her overskirt – 'it is not – how do you say it – too rich?'

Margot giggled. My other daughter, Claude, squat and fat in violet velvet and pregnant with her second child, elbowed Margot.

'It's perfect.' I smoothed her cloth-of-silver skirt embroidered with pearl fleur-de-lis. 'It suits your complexion. You have such nice skin, my dear. Doesn't she, Margot?'

Margot blew air out of the side of her mouth. 'I suppose so,' she said, and flounced to the dressing table to examine Isabel's jewelry. 'Oh. These are nice.' She snatched up a set of ruby earrings. 'Look how well they go with my dress. Red is my best color. Everyone says so.'

'Take them,' Isabel said, before I could protest.

Margot plucked off her opals and clipped the rubies on her ears. As she gazed into the mirror, I thought there couldn't have been more marked difference between her narcissistic adoration and Isabel's indifference. As if a malign being whispered in my ear, I knew with absolute certainty that one particular admirer had told Margot to wear red.

'Aren't you going to thank her?' I said, and Margot kissed Isabel. 'Thank you, dearest sister. I adore them.'

As she skipped back to Claude to show off her trophies, I bent over to rub the stain left by her slipper on Isabel's hem. Isabel touched my shoulder; I looked up. 'That's not important,' she said. 'No one sees dirt on a bride, yes?'

She won me over with those words, testament to the common sense she'd learned as merchandise on the royal marriage market. 'Indeed,' I said, and I winced as I straightened up. My kirtle was laced too tight. I shouldn't have asked Lucrezia to yank the stays an extra notch in the futile hope of restoring something of my vanquished figure.

'You too look splendid,' she said, gesturing at my reflection.

I had no choice but to turn to the mirror. I beheld a short, stout woman in an almost-black shade of violet, my hair covered by a peaked coif, my dark eyes pleated at the corners. I'd donned sedate emeralds for my ears, an onyx brooch beneath my ruff and my black pearls. But nothing in the world could restore my youth, and I turned away.

Bells tolled. Isabel's regal mask settled back over her face. 'It is time,' I said, and I took her hand, leading her from the chamber to wed my son.

Under the vaulted ceiling, we assumed seats in the royal pews: Henri and Hercule to my right, Margot and Claude and her husband to my left. Courtiers and nobles filled the chapel to capacity, the heady aroma of perfume mingling with the harsh smoke of the candelabrums and torches on the walls, and occasional whiff of horse droppings caught on some lord's boots. Clad in his crown and royal robes, Charles knelt beside Isabel at the altar as Monsignor the Cardinal performed the interminable ceremony.

I watched Margot out of the corner of my eye and caught her gaze straying to the pew occupied by the Guises. Young Guise certainly merited notice in his scarlet doublet, which highlighted his intense blue eyes and white-gold hair. He'd grown a mustache and beard that added gravity to his years: for a heart-stopping second, I saw the falconlike reflection of his dead father, le Balafré, and a tremor rippled through me.

Both he and Margot wore red.

All of a sudden Henri's lips were at my ear. 'There's a ghost with us. Look. Coligny is here.'

I froze. 'He . . . he can't be.'

'Well, he is. Can't you feel him? He stares at you even as we speak.'

Blood rushed to my head. I couldn't hear or see anything. This couldn't be happening. I wasn't ready. I'd known this day must come, but I wanted to orchestrate it at my convenience, after I'd set in motion my plan to wed Margot to Navarre. I didn't have the players in place yet. Queen Jeanne still eluded me; I'd invited her to court to celebrate Charles's marriage, but she'd sent her regrets, saying that she was ill. I'd assumed Coligny would also stay away, as I had not lifted my restriction on him. He would not risk his safety. Henri must be mistaken.

I braved a glance over my shoulder, past the bored courtiers eager for the ceremony to conclude and festivities to begin, past the whispering ladies and matrons fanning themselves despite the chill, onward to the darkened recesses, where a collection of figures was standing.

There in the shadows he stood, his eyes gleaming like arctic fire in his careworn face.

'See?' said Henri. 'I told you so. The dead are with us.'

'How could you?' I remonstrated as Charles changed for the banquet. 'He hasn't been officially pardoned! How could you invite him here?'

My son whirled to me, knocking aside the kneeling page who'd removed his gem-encrusted slippers. 'You said our settlement pardoned *all* the Huguenot leaders!'

'That's different. They acted under his command; the leaders followed his direction.'

'I don't see a difference. A pardon is a pardon. I'll not go back on my word as king. I invited him because it's my wedding and I want him to know we bear him no ill will.'

I stood open-mouthed, so taken aback I had no idea what to do. It was like that day in Blois: whenever Coligny appeared, my son transformed into someone else. I saw my own weakness in him, the trusting person I had once been. I knew Coligny's lure, how he could attract and convince others, for I'd felt his power. I could still feel it. Only now, I knew better.

'Did he write to you?' I asked, and Charles gave me a startled look. Then he spat, 'Yes, he wrote to me. What of it? And I wrote back. I removed the price on his head and assured him he had my protection. I mean it too. The war is over. I want peace and I *will* have it.'

'If you want peace, then you must be the one to send him away. Your bride is a Catholic princess, cousin to Philip of Spain. She cannot receive him.'

'She'll receive him if I say she will.' The page scrambled out of his way. 'I'm sick to death of this enmity between the religions. Coligny is a peer of France; he deserves to be at court. It's the perfect time for us to make a lasting peace.' He paused, looking at me through narrowed eyes that reminded me of his father. 'You told me not to mention the marriage with Navarre and I agreed. Have you changed your mind? Would you rather we kept killing each other?'

'Of course not,' I replied, and I couldn't keep the anger from my voice. 'But you know Coligny waged war against us. He refused all compromise until he had no other choice.'

'He didn't wage war against me. I didn't make agreements with Spain.'

I resisted the urge to grab him by his collar and shake some sense into him. I had no authority over him anymore; at twenty years of age, he was firmly our king. I'd kept him under my care as long as I could. I now saw that in doing so I'd inadvertently sowed his resentment.

I softened my tone. '*Mon fils,* I agree with the sentiment, but this is neither the time nor the place. You must send him away for his protection. The Guises are here. You risk his life.'

'If Guise or anyone else touches a hair on his head, they'll answer to me.' He yanked his cap from the cowering page. 'Coligny stays. In fact, I'll reinstate him in Council. He can serve as a Huguenot adviser, as he used to before the damn war.'

He stalked past me to the door. 'I'll see you in the hall.'

Charles disappeared right after the feast, leaving Isabel and me to preside over the nuptial festivities. I reasoned he'd gone off to change his clothes, as he detested finery. Left on the dais with Isabel, I watched Margot, flushed by wine and the fawning compliments of the gentlemen. She seemed oblivious of Guise, who sat with Henri. If he in turn took notice of her, he had an expert facility for disguising it, smiling and nodding as Henri whispered in his ear and a court strumpet refilled their goblets every chance she got. Indeed, Guise appeared engrossed in whatever Henri was saying, unaware he was being watched by the handsome Spaniard Antonio de Guast, who'd served under Henri's command during the war and now acted as his bodyguard.

The Spaniard's dark stare gave me pause. I'd seen that look before, countless times among the women at court who assessed each other like combatants in the arena: it was covetous and jealous, and it made me wonder at the depth of his relationship with my son.

A high-pitched squeal wrenched my attention to Hercule, already bedraggled in his new clothes, snatching morsels from platters as a group of ladies – flown on wine – hastened after him, slapping his buttocks with their feathered fans. He was almost sixteen and a disaster. He'd shown no improvement in his studies or deportment, despite Margot's pains, and I winced as I caught Isabel watching his antics with a rigid frown.

I couldn't blame her. It was her nuptial feast, her introduction to our court, and all semblance of decency had degenerated the moment the tables were dismantled. Courtiers slipped into the shadows by the pilasters to nuzzle; the musicians' kettledrums and pipes sounded in tandem to shrieks of drunken laughter as dancers swirled on the open floor. In my father-in-law's time, such behavior was unheard of; as full of wit and hedonism as his court had been, the women never shoved their bodices past their shoulders to expose their nipples, nor had the men leered and cupped themselves as if in a brothel.

I reached for the decanter to refill her goblet. 'The court,' I started to explain. 'We haven't celebrated in some time. We 've been at war and they're overly exuberant . . .' My explanation faded as the sparse color drained from her face, her eyes fixed forward.

I followed her stare. Around us, the court's laughter sputtered and died.

Charles marched to the dais, his long hair falling to his shoulders, his billowing chemise sleeves rolled to his elbows, exposing sunburned forearms. At his side was Coligny.

In a ringing voice my son said, 'Admiral de Coligny wishes to greet my queen.'

Coligny bowed. The last time we'd been this close was five years ago. To my surprise, he seemed smaller than I remembered, his chiseled features marked by deprivation. His eyes were still lucid, still penetrating, but he looked haunted by everything he'd seen and done in the name of his faith, a man compelled by doctrine to sacrifice his ideals.

He's getting old, I thought. He's a weak and aging man. There's nothing for me to fear.

'Seigneur,' I said. 'Welcome to court.'

'Thank you. Your Grace looks fit. I trust you are –'

'I'm fine. May I present my new daughter-in-law, Her Grace Queen Isabel?'

As he started to bow, Isabel stood with a rustle of skirts. She inclined her head, forcing him to step aside so she could leave the dais. With a perfunctory curtsy to Charles, she exited the hall. I could have applauded. Her nerve, it seemed, was tempered with steel.

'Her Majesty complained of a headache before you arrived,' I said, noting the embarrassed flush on Charles's cheeks. 'She's had a long day and needs to rest.'

'Of course,' said Coligny. 'I understand.'

'The admiral has agreed to serve at court,' Charles informed me, with a defiant lift of his chin. 'He says he'll be honored to regain his seat on the Council and assist us in forging peace.'

'Is that so?' I forced out a smile. 'Well, let us first ensure there's peace with your new bride, yes? This is your wedding night.' I braced myself for his retort; instead, Charles mumbled, 'Yes, of course. I shouldn't neglect her.' He clapped Coligny on the shoulder. 'I've had your old apartments readied. You can worship freely there and receive your Huguenot friends.'

'Your Majesty is most gracious.' Coligny lowered his head.

'Good. And we'll hunt together in the morning.' Charles started to follow Isabel; I snatched him by the hand. 'Let me accompany you.' I glanced at Coligny. 'We should speak more at length, Seigneur. Perhaps tomorrow, after the hunt?'

His reply was inscrutable. 'If you wish.'

I turned away, moving with Charles through the courtiers. After seeing him to Isabel's rooms, I returned to my own.

'Is it true?' Lucrezia asked. 'Is he back?'

'Yes.' I went into my bedchamber and shut the door. By the light of a candle, I pried up the loose floorboard under my bed and removed Cosimo's box. I didn't open it.

But I thought about it. I thought about it for a very long time.

The following afternoon, I waited for him in my study, sitting at my large desk where hidden levers could be released to expose secret drawers, in which I stored important documents. On the desk itself I'd placed a portfolio and the royal seal – manifest symbol of my power.

He walked in, his unadorned black doublet fitted to his lean frame. He had retained his figure and the sight of him caught at my breath. We had not been alone since Blois.

He spoke first. 'I know you are angry with me.'

I regarded him coldly. 'Do you fault me?'

'No. But you've nothing to fear. I would not undertake another war, even if I were in a position to do so. No man desires peace more than I do.'

'I've heard such words before.' I fixed him with my stare. 'Yet you still chose to believe the worst of me. Why should I think that anything has changed?'

'I don't expect you to. I only ask that you let me prove myself.'

'Prove yourself? I've given you more than one occasion, if I recall, and you did not think it worth your while. Were it not for my forbearance, you'd be a hunted man.'

A spark surfaced in his eyes. I'd forgotten how self-contained he could be, how unrevealing of his self. Now that he was before me I recognized that mastery he'd always had over his emotions, a talent I only now was beginning to grasp. With him, everything ran under the surface. Everything was hidden.

I sat forward in my chair. 'I pardoned you once. I can do so again. Contrary to what you may think, I've no desire to persecute your faith. I never have. Indeed, I hope to soon arrange a marriage between a Huguenot and a Catholic. What say you to that?'

'My faith has never opposed such unions. I believe yours, however, does.'

'Yes, but this is no ordinary marriage. I wish to wed Margot to the prince of Navarre.'

To a less discerning eye he would have appeared unmoved. But I noticed the subtle tightening of his posture. 'I don't see how this matter concerns me.'

'I will tell you how it does. You carry influence with Jeanne of Navarre, do you not?' I paused. 'And you say you wish to prove yourself. Very well: I want you to sign this letter to her, requesting that she come to court with the prince. It will show her that you believe the enmity between our faiths can be resolved and that you support my marriage suit for her son.'

This time, I saw it in his eyes. At last he revealed the suspicion lurking under his impervious facade. 'I fear Her Grace of Navarre has been quite ill. Traveling will be difficult for her.'

'She wasn't too ill to travel to La Rochelle,' I rejoined, unable to conceal a flash of anger. Did he think me a fool? 'I hardly see how a trip to Paris can be an inconvenience. Unless I'm mistaken, she would be only too happy to see you reinstated at court and, I assume, welcome the chance to end the discord between our faiths. After all,' I added, 'her son is in our line of succession, but he could be removed. The pope has declared anathema on all Protestants and would excommunicate Jeanne of Navarre, thus opening her realm to invasion by a Catholic power. I could convince His Holiness to reconsider, should circumstances warrant it.'

The air thickened. I didn't believe Navarre posed any real threat to the succession: I had other sons, should Charles, God forbid, die without an heir. Still, if Jeanne was excommunicated, her kingdom would be forfeit to its nearest Catholic neighbor: us or Spain. I had no intention of wasting my resources trying to overtake her realm, but Philip would, and Coligny knew that he himself had contributed to it by his wars. I wondered if he ever regretted his actions, if he ever looked back to that hour when he'd betrayed our alliance over Philip's lies.

If so, he would never say it. And no matter what, this time he must submit. Promises were not enough. He had to prove he was capable of bowing to a higher authority than his own.

'Is that all?' he said at length. 'This is what you offer me: a bribe?'

I let out a short laugh. 'Come now, it's a friendly arrangement. We were friends once, yes?'

He ignored my question. 'Will you expect the prince of Navarre to convert?'

I paused. *How* did he know?

'His conscience is his own,' I said carefully. 'Yet if we show our people that princes of different faiths can live together in harmony, perhaps they too will follow suit.'

He did not speak. I reached to the portfolio, retrieved the letter. 'Just sign. After that, I'll ask nothing more of you. If Jeanne refuses, so be it.'

I inked a quill, extended it to him. He hesitated for a moment, but he did not read the letter. Then he leaned forward and appended his signature, so close I might have touched him.

I sanded the letter. 'We'll celebrate our Christmas court in Paris this year; you're welcome to stay. Our next Council session will be held after the New Year.'

'By your leave, I'll spend Christmas at Châtillon with my wife and children.' His mouth shifted into what might have passed for a smile. 'I wed again in La Rochelle. God has seen fit to bless me again at this late stage in my life.'

I could not look at him. 'Congratulations,' I heard myself say. 'I hope you'll both be very happy. Good day, my lord.'

He bowed. As soon as he left, I pressed a trembling hand to my mouth. Birago slipped in.

'He signed,' I said. 'But I want him watched. I . . . I don't trust him.'

Birago retreated, clicking the door shut.

I looked at the letter, at the tight curlicues of his signature, and felt torment prowl the fissures of my heart, like a howl seeking its way out.

PART VI
1571–1574
Scarlet Night

29

The letter worked; Jeanne returned word that she would come and I went to inform Margot.

She sat staring at me as if I'd uttered an obscenity before she said, 'If this is a joke, it's in very poor taste.'

'I assure you, it's not. Queen Jeanne and her son will arrive in May. We'll meet them at Chenonceau. If all goes as planned, you and Navarre shall marry in August.'

She came to her feet. 'I think not. He's a Huguenot, a heretic. He's unworthy of me.'

I regarded her from my chair, unable to rise owing to another flare-up of my sciatica. I didn't enjoy doing this to her; for all her outward maturity, to me she was still my child, whom I must sacrifice for the good of the realm. But few of us marry for love; as royal women, we must fulfill our duty and Margot was more fortunate than most, for she wasn't being sent to a foreign court.

'You forget he's a prince,' I said, keeping my tone gentle but firm, 'and he will one day be king of Navarre; he's therefore most worthy of you.' I preempted her protest. 'And in case you're thinking of running to Charles, you should know that he has given his consent. He too believes your marriage can bring Huguenot and Catholic together.'

Her eyes widened. 'You actually think this marriage will bring us together?'

'Why shouldn't it? You may not share the same religion, but you'll bear him sons and –'

'You want him to convert,' she interrupted. 'This isn't about resolution; this about winning your battle with Coligny. You want to crush him with my womb.'

Her acuity caught me by surprise, though I should have anticipated it. I would have to persuade her by appealing to her sense
of purpose.

'Jeanne of Navarre is gravely ill,' I said. 'When she dies, her
son will become a Protestant king, overseeing a Protestant state.
The Huguenots look to him for leadership. I'll not have him
plunge France into chaos. He must be brought into our fold. Who
better to do this than you?'

'As simple as that,' she replied flippantly. 'It all comes to pass
because you wish it so? I wonder what will happen when Jeanne
discovers your intent. She'll not be pleased, I suspect, and
Navarre might have a thing to say about it as well, considering
he must revere his faith.'

'What can he know of faith? He was a child when Jeanne
started filling his ear with Huguenot nonsense. After all is said
and done, he'll learn one sermon is as good as another.'

She laughed incredulously. 'You can't honestly believe that!
You know Jeanne is pledged body and soul to her faith and has
taught her son to do the same. After all these years of war, how
can you not understand that their way of worship is as important
to them as ours is to us?'

'We worship the same God,' I snapped, stung by her insight.
This was not going as I'd planned. When had my daughter paid
such close attention to doctrine? She was a dutiful Catholic, yes,
but I'd always thought she viewed religion much as I did: as a
necessary institution we must conform to because the alternative
was chaos.

'You are a Valois princess,' I added. 'As Navarre's queen, you
can bind him and his faith to us. It is your duty, and a small price
to pay for a future of peace.'

Her expression wavered. Had I finally touched her pride? While
Navarre might not be her ideal, how could she resist playing a
pivotal role in our welfare?

Our eyes locked. To my disconcertion, I still saw no indication
that I'd convinced her. She looked at me as if she were seeing me
for the first time and didn't quite like what she found. Then she

said quietly, 'Very well. I'll do as you ask. But you can't make me love him.'

'You'll fare better without love. We Medici always do.' As soon as I spoke, I regretted it. I'd remembered Papa Clement's phrase exactly, used it to the same horrid purpose. I saw her flinch, take a small step back. I wanted to console her, to somehow ease the harsh reality of what I'd said. But I could not. I would not lie to her nor pretend the task I set before her was anything other than what it was: an act of submission, which could entail the loss of her youthful dreams.

'You should pack for Chenonceau,' I murmured, and with a curtsy she turned and walked out, leaving me sitting there, an awful feeling in the pit of my stomach.

That night after I retired, I tossed and turned for hours.

I loved Margot. Of all my children, she and Henri were my brightest, combining the best of the Medici and the Valois bloods. Why did I now condemn her to a loveless union, when I knew how much misery it entailed? Had the past years of war and struggle hardened me so much that I didn't think twice about sacrificing her happiness? Maybe this marriage wasn't meant to be. I could still put a halt to it, go to Charles and –

Sharp rapping came at my door. I glanced at the candle; the hours notched on its side had dissolved in a molten pool. It was too late for visitors. Then I heard Lucrezia say, 'Your Grace, Margot's lady is here. She says Her Highness is in danger.'

I hobbled down the darkened galleries in the west wing of the Louvre, which I'd shut down for repairs. I was panting, my sciatic leg throbbing, as Lucrezia and I came before an open door.

'*Putain!*' a voice yelled. 'I'll flay you alive for this!'

At the crack of a lash, I forgot my pain and barreled in. Margot cowered by a coffer, her scarlet bodice in shreds, her lacerated arms raised to protect her face. Charles stood over her with a hunting whip. By the shuttered window, Henri held a dagger to the throat of none other than young Guise. His distended blue eyes met mine as my son dug the stiletto against his neck, drawing a bead of blood that trickled down his strong white throat.

'Shall I do it?' hissed my son. 'One less Guise makes no difference to me.'

Margot cried out, 'No! Leave him alone. It's not his fault. I asked him to meet me here!' ·

Only then did I notice that once again both she and Guise wore red. And I understood, with a sickening knowledge that curdled inside me. She was Guise 's lover, had been his lover for months. Their choice of color was obvious, a declaration I should never have failed to notice.

Charles lashed out with the whip, cutting into her shoulders. Her wail propelled me forward. I wrenched the whip from him. He whirled on me, snarling like one of his dogs. I saw something terrifying in his eyes, a demon blazing at me, and I backed away, saying to Henri, 'Let Guise go.'

Henri withdrew his blade. A spasm shook Guise. 'Madame,' he said, 'I am wronged.' His gaze shifted to Henri; my son's face darkened. 'It is I who am wronged,' Henri said in a quavering voice filled with an emotion I'd never heard from him. 'You have played me for a fool and I will never forget it.'

'I did not intend to,' said Guise softly, 'but you wanted something from me that I could not give.'

Henri started to lunge. I lifted my voice, detaining him. 'No.' I looked at Guise. 'You will leave court at once. Return to your family estate in Joinville and stay there.'

He bowed, gathering his doublet about him. He shot a look at Margot before he walked out. Henri called after him, 'If I ever catch you with my sister again, I'll see you dead!'

I signaled to Lucrezia to close the door and bar it from any intrusion. With the whip still in my hands, I turned to my sons. 'What is wrong with you? She is your sister. How could you –'

'She's a whore,' spat Charles, his lower lip spraying blood, cut no doubt by his own teeth. 'She's about to be betrothed to Navarre and she goes and fucks Guise behind our backs.'

I suppressed my horror as I gazed at his twisted expression, his shoulders, thickened with muscle from his daily labors in his armory, hunched about his neck.

'Go,' I said. 'Let me take charge of this.'

'Yes,' said Henri. 'Let Maman take charge. I daresay Guise won't come near Margot again.'

Charles barked sudden laughter. 'Yes, and he'll stay away from you too, brother. No doubt, your pretty bodyguard Guast will be pleased.'

Henri froze. Then he grabbed Charles by the arm and steered him out, leaving me with Margot. She forced herself to her feet, her hair catching in the clotted blood on her shoulders.

'Is it true?' I said. 'Did you let that Guise whelp take your virginity?'

'No.' She was trembling uncontrollably. 'I . . . I only wanted to see him, to . . . to say good-bye.' Her voice choked on a sob; she buried her face in her hands. 'I love him. I love him with all my heart and now I've lost him forever because of you.'

I found myself unable to move. She had nearly cost me everything by giving herself to the heir of a family that was my most relentless foe; yet I could not blame her entirely, for it was my fault. I had underestimated the depths of her passion; I hadn't realized how dangerous it could become. In a man, such impulse was permissible, even admirable; but in an unwed woman, especially a princess, it could spell her doom.

'You must never see him again,' I heard myself say, and my voice was flat, cold. 'Do you understand me? Never. Guise is dead to you now. As you must be to him.'

She raised huge tearstained eyes, full of a pain that I almost couldn't bear to see. I extended my hand to her. 'Come, we must tend those wounds. Can you walk?'

She nodded and together with Lucrezia I took her to her apartments.

The next day, I wrote to the duchesse de Guise to inform her that the recently widowed Madame Porcein would make an excellent match for her son. The widow in question was in fact twice his age, but I assumed he'd informed his family of his predicament and there would be no objection. There wasn't. Guise wed his bride in a hasty ceremony the very next week.

I went to inform Margot. Guise had not fought for her; he did not lift a single protest that she was his one and only love. The stunned expression on her face said everything.

'Now,' I added, 'you can devote yourself entirely to Navarre. You will marry him, get him to convert, and bear sons that you can rear as Catholic princes. It is your destiny.'

'My destiny,' she echoed. She smiled darkly. 'Is that what you call it? You and Charles have taken everything from me. You have destroyed me. I hate you both. I wish you were dead.'

I eyed her where she sat taut on her bed, like a wounded animal about to strike.

'So be it,' I said, and I yanked open the door. 'But whatever you feel, you will do as I say.'

Storm clouds hovered over Chenonceau, a fanged wind ripping at our standards and our clothes as we waited for Queen Jeanne's entourage.

My hands were numb in their lynx-lined gloves. A few steps away Margot stood in a primrose satin gown, her sable hood crumpled about her head like a ruined veil. The bruises had faded, but she was not speaking to us, her face a mask of stony indifference.

Heralds blew a shrill note. Moments later, the entourage from Navarre straggled toward us. I surveyed the ranks, a small collection of black-clad lords on horseback escorting a coach. I stepped forth to open the door. 'Madame, I am so pleased to –'

My greeting died in my throat.

Queen Jeanne sat sunken among her pillows, wrapped in a fur mantle; she was mere flesh pasted over bones, her coppery hair lank and eyes ringed in shadows.

One of her men eased me aside to help her out. She leaned on his arm as she faced me, so frail it seemed she'd be carried away by the wind. But even in her weakness she had not lost her impudence;

she gave me a ghastly smile and whispered, 'In case you're wondering, Madame de Medici, the answer is no: my son is not coming.'

Jeanne sat erect in the airy blue-satin suite I'd appointed for her. She'd not left the room in weeks; I was terrified she would die before we'd reached an accord and I'd had my own physicians attend her. She looked better, frail color in her pale cheeks, though her hacking cough and her infuriating obstinacy persisted.

'I said no. I'll not bring my son here until I am completely satisfied.'

I lost all patience. 'What more do you want of me?' I cried, pacing the chamber. 'First, you insist on a ceremony that will be neither Catholic in appearance or ritual and I assured you they can wed outside Notre Dame, after which your son and his entourage can attend a Huguenot service while we hear mass. Then you asked that if Spain makes a threat against Navarre, I must pledge my surety of troops and I agreed. Finally, you requested Coligny's support of the marriage and I told you he does, as you yourself saw by his letter.'

'I saw his signature on a letter, yes. But how do I know the letter was his?'

'Of course it was his!' I paused, lowering my voice. 'I wouldn't play you false. I've told you before: our children must wed. They are ideal for each other and together will show the world that while we may not worship the same way, we need not go to war over our differences.'

'When did you decide we can live in peace?' she said tartly. 'After or before you put a price on Coligny's head and destroyed the Huguenot stronghold of La Rochelle? Or was it when you brought in Spaniards to fight against us?'

I clenched my hands at my sides. 'Did you come all this way to remonstrate with me?'

Phlegmy laughter rattled her chest. She gasped, pressed a handkerchief to her mouth. The cloth came away stained with blood. She tucked it into her cuff as if it meant nothing.

'I wanted to see you again,' she said. 'I wanted to lay eyes on the infamous Catherine de Medici and find out if everything they say is true, if they call you Madame la Serpente because, like a snake, your bite kills your enemies.'

Red heat overcame me. How dare she sit there in her Huguenot weeds and accuse me, when she'd abetted our enemies? I took a step forward, not caring in that moment if she consented to the marriage or dropped dead at my feet. She flattened against her chair.

I paused. I did not expect this recoil or the frantic clutch of her hands at her skirts. As her dilated gaze met mine, I realized she was afraid. Afraid of me. She actually believed I was as monstrous as the Huguenot pamphleteers claimed. She'd heeded innuendo and rumor, though she knew what it meant to be a woman alone, with a realm and children to protect.

My mordant sense of humor got the better of me. With a chuckle, I said, 'Well, now you've seen me. Do I look as evil as they say?'

'The fact that you make light of it confirms everything,' she replied.

'Then think what you like; it makes no difference to me. I offer your son a royal bride and your realm protection from Spain. No other will give you as much.'

She eyed me in silence. Then she thrust out her chin. 'You can't manipulate me. I'll not call for my son nor give you an answer unless I am allowed to meet with your daughter – alone.'

I considered. Margot was here, of course. But could I trust her? I rued the hour I'd admitted my plans to her, for now I must rely on her. Jeanne wouldn't budge; she'd write another batch of sepulchral warnings to her son and he'd lock himself up in her castle. My hope for ending our religious dissent would fall apart. War would erupt, as it inevitably did, and I'd again be at the helm of a realm devouring itself whole.

Unless . . . The idea crept through me like a cat. I still had Cosimo's gifts.

'Fine,' I said to Jeanne. 'I'll send Margot to you this afternoon.'

I went downstairs to my study. Once inside, I locked the door and removed the box from a hidden cabinet in the wall. Opening the lid, I found the dolls resting on their velvet bed.

I lifted the female form.

You must first personify them by attaching an article from the person.

All I needed was a wisp of Margot's hair.

Despite her anger with me and her habitual melancholic drifting about the palace, Margot radiated health, her color high from days in the gardens, her hair a mass of sun-lightened curls.

'You look lovely,' I told her, and her turquoise eyes narrowed as I reached out to tuck a stray ringlet of hair over her shoulder. 'Now, remember to answer her questions, but don't reveal too much. We mustn't overtax her.' I cupped her chin. 'Do you understand?'

She scowled. 'Yes. I'll be the perfect, dutiful daughter-in-law and say as little as possible.'

'Exactly.' I propelled her to the staircase. 'I'll await you in my study.' As she lifted her skirts to mount the stairs, I closed my fingers about a strand of her hair.

In the study, I pulled the curtains across the windows, set two candles and the doll on my desk. I felt ludicrous, standing there about to coil my daughter's hair about a wax figurine in the hope of compelling her to fulfill my will. I steeled myself and took up the doll. I lit the candles and paused. What now? I had the pins. Should I press one into the doll to enforce my desire? No, that might hurt. I could see Margot talking to Jeanne and crying out in sudden pain.

What if I knelt? Would that be sacrilegious? It must be. Best not.

I extended my hands over the candles. Closing my eyes, I whispered, 'I, Catherine de Medici, invoke upon thee, Marguerite de Valois, my sole desire. You have no other will than mine. You will tell Jeanne de Navarre everything she wants to hear and nothing to cause doubt.'

I opened an eye. I felt no brooding presence, no subtle thickening in the air or ripple along my skin, as I'd felt every time my gift had stirred or I'd met with Nostradamus. If I had a facility for magic, it wasn't revealing itself. I picked up the doll again, cradled it in my hands, and repeated my chant. I recalled reading somewhere that blood was essential to spells. I opened the box, retrieved a pin and jabbed my finger. A dark red bead welled. I watched it seep over my nail to spatter the doll's face. I went still, straining to hear the thump overhead that would herald Margot's precipitous drop onto the floor.

Nothing.

I again whispered my chant, removed the amulet from inside my bodice, and pressed it on the doll. Evil against evil, Cosimo had said. Then I waited, reasoning that spells, like scents and potions, needed time to brew, to blend and create the desired result. After what I hoped was sufficient time, I blew out the candles, gathered the objects, and returned them to hiding. At the last minute, a twinge of guilt caused me to unravel the amulet from my neck and also hide it in the box, next to Maestro Ruggieri's old vial. Then I whisked back the curtains, propped the window open. Sitting at my desk, I smoothed out a fresh sheet of parchment and inked my quill.

That was the moment I began these confessions.

Hours fled by as I revisited the past, filling page after page with memories. When Margot knocked at my door, I looked up in a daze. She entered. 'The queen wishes to see you.'

I tucked the pages into a portfolio. A strange calm stayed with me as I went to Jeanne 's rooms. I found her at the gilded desk, a quill in hand. She'd donned a blue gown and pearls – unusual extravagance. She turned in her chair. She looked serene, as if she'd taken a rejuvenating tonic. If this was due to my magic, it had imparted unexpected consequences.

'Madame, I don't know how you managed it, but your daughter is as virtuous a princess as I've had the privilege to meet.' She extended the page to me. 'Here is my consent. Providing you fulfill the terms we discussed, I believe she 'll make an excellent wife for my son. She says she can think of no greater privilege than to be Navarre's queen and live in our realm.'

I hadn't believed the spell would work. How could such an insipid ritual bring about the impossible? Yet it seemed it had, though I'd not been specific enough. I needed Margot and Navarre to live in France; under no circumstance could he return to his country, where he'd be surrounded by Protestants warning him against us.

'She says she cannot embrace my faith,' Jeanne went on, 'but when I told her my son would want their children raised Protestant, she replied that as his wife, she owes him her obedience.'

I had to bite my lip lest I burst into caustic laughter. Margot was truly my daughter! She'd refrained from rousing Jeanne's suspicion yet had managed to promise something she knew I would never allow. The loss of Guise still burned inside her; she would do anything to thwart me, it seemed, but the marriage would proceed and soon Navarre would be under my control.

'I'll come with you to Paris,' Jeanne added, to my disbelief. 'Margot has asked me to help with her trousseau. I'll also write to my son. You did say you'd like them to wed in August?'

I nodded, searching her face for a sign of deceit. I found none. She'd never been good at concealing her feelings. 'Yes, in August,' I said, and I exhaled in relief. 'We'll arrange the most glorious wedding France has ever seen.'

'Not too glorious,' she chided. 'My faith is a simple one. Now I must rest. We'll meet tomorrow to plan the details. We can share lunch, *al* – What do you Italians call it?'

'*Alfresco*,' I said. 'Yes, that would be nice.'

As I left her, I couldn't help but marvel that fate, the supreme joker, had thrown together such a pair of mothers-in-law.

30

Upon taking up residence in my newly completed Hôtel de la Reine, Jeanne dove into the wedding arrangements as though she'd never been ill, dragging me around Paris to view this bolt of fabric, that pair of candlesticks or piece of cutlery. In a store on the Left Bank, she so admired a pair of supple Italian gloves fringed in gold that I bought them for her. She accepted them in childish delight, proof she wasn't immune to vanity. I found it fascinating to watch her become the woman she might have been if her religious devotion hadn't shackled her heart.

The moment word came that her son had departed Nérac, I ordered banns posted, inviting everyone in the realm to Paris to partake of the grand event. Everything was going as planned until I received word one evening that Jeanne had collapsed.

I hurried with Margot to the *hôtel* through a dank mist. We found the downstairs hall filled with men in dark clothing, all Huguenots. They turned toward us as if on cue, bowing stiffly.

From among them stepped Coligny.

He looked healthier than the last time I'd seen him, his face more rounded and rested, his spare frame heavier and his eyes alert, piercing.

Time in Châtillon with his new wife had done him wonders, and as he bowed before us a surge of dread iced my veins.

'I didn't know you were back,' I said. 'You should have sent word, my lord.'

'Forgive me. I'd only just arrived and taken residence in my town house when I heard Her Grace of Navarre was ill. I thought it best to come here first, to offer my services.'

I detected an undertone in his voice, something I couldn't quite place. How serious was this collapse of Jeanne's? Were we to be plunged into mourning before her son arrived?

As if he read my thoughts, Coligny said, 'She is too weak to come downstairs.'

'Then we'll go to her.' I motioned to Margot. Coligny led us through the Huguenots, all of whom drew back in marked silence. My nervousness grew. Jeanne was my guest. Did they think I'd do her harm?

In the bedroom, Jeanne lay propped on pillows, her face paler than her sheets. That flare of life that had sent her racing through Paris had consumed her.

She murmured, 'Madame, my hour draws near.'

'Nonsense.' I patted her hand. It felt cold and brittle. 'You've overextended yourself. You'll be back on your feet soon. We have a wedding to plan, remember?'

Her gaze shifted to Margot. 'Come closer, my dear. There's something I must say to you.'

Margot leaned to her colorless lips. I heard her whisper. My daughter nodded. 'Yes,' she said. 'I will. I promise.'

Jeanne sighed. As her eyes closed in exhaustion, her pastors emerged from the alcove. Turning to the bedroom door to leave, I caught sight of the gold-fringed gloves I'd given her, flung on a table near the hearth. They were turned inside out, the fingertips cut off.

'I'll send our court physician Dr. Paré to attend her,' I said to Coligny outside the room. 'She'll need expert care and –'

'By your leave, that won't be necessary.' His voice was aloof, as if he spoke to a meddling stranger. 'I have already called for an experienced doctor; he'll be here by nightfall.'

Taken aback by his tone, I nodded curtly and left. On our return to the Louvre, I queried Margot. 'She asked me to protect her son,' she replied.

'Protect him?' I frowned, recalling Nostradamus had uttered the same words to me. 'Why?'

Her eyes lifted to me. 'Didn't you see it on their faces, in the way Coligny spoke to you?'

I froze. That was what I'd heard in Coligny's voice but failed to place: suspicion. Suspicion of me. 'You can't be serious,' I said with a brittle chuckle. 'Jeanne has been sick for years; everyone knows it. Coligny himself has mentioned it.'

'She seemed well enough the past few days.' Margot's stare bored into me. 'You bought those gloves for her, didn't you? Why did they cut out the fingertips?'

I knew why. It was an old trick devised by the Borgias: poison was applied to the inside of a glove and the wearer never knew until it was too late. They'd cut out the tips to examine them.

My voice faltered. '*Dio Mio,* they're mad. How could they think I'd harm her?'

'You are a Medici; they have always doubted your sincerity.'

'Do you doubt?' I asked, and I held my breath, dreading her reply.

'No,' she said quietly. 'But I am not a Huguenot.'

Jeanne de Navarre died the following afternoon. I took Margot's advice and sent Paré to perform the dissection of Jeanne's corpse, which revealed extensive corruption in her lungs, confirming she'd perished of her ailment. After some hesitation – for I feared he'd cite her death as reason to cancel our arrangements – I wrote a letter of condolence to her son and had her body embalmed and dispatched to Navarre for entombment.

To my relief, Navarre returned word that he would not delay his departure, and in mid-July he entered Paris under a sky scorched white by the sun.

Unrelenting heat had descended upon us; people slept on rooftops and crammed the banks of the Seine seeking relief, while cutthroats, beggars, and thieves abounded in the near-anarchic atmosphere of a city crammed to overflowing with thousands of Huguenots and Catholics who'd come from all over France to witness the wedding. As Navarre rode in with his Huguenot suite, those of his faith lifted a cheer loud enough to drown out the few Catholics who dared shout derogatory epithets, so that it seemed all Paris reverberated with acclaim for him.

I watched his approach from my balcony. I was eager to behold him again, to see with my own eyes if he'd grown into the proud man of my long-ago vision. As he dismounted in the courtyard, a short, compact figure dressed in black, I beckoned Margot, who looked pristine as a cloud in light blue silk, pearls roped through her tresses and coiled about her collar.

We descended into the hall. It was filled with courtiers, a gaudy menagerie interspersed with the black mourning of Navarre's entourage. Scanning the Huguenot nobles, I saw no sign of Coligny. I was relieved. The last thing I wanted was his dour visage spoiling the occasion.

Navarre stood by the dais with Charles and Hercule, the former in a bright gold doublet and plumed hat, the latter in carnelian satin. Charles spoke fervently to his Bourbon cousin, while seventeen-year-old Hercule, looking overdressed and dwarfish, gazed at Navarre curiously.

I heard Charles exclaim, 'I tell you, it was the best hunt ever. I killed the boar with one shot. One shot! Coligny said he'd never seen the like. Didn't he, Hercule?'

My youngest son shrugged. I saw Navarre toss back his head and laugh, his unruly flame-red hair spiked round his sun-reddened face. As I approached with Margot, he turned to us.

I almost came to a halt.

He looked exactly like the man I'd envisioned from the boy, all those years ago, down to the laughter shining in his close-set green eyes.

His gentlemen shifted closer to him. Just beyond their circle I glimpsed my Henri, resplendent in mauve velvet, his mane flowing to his shoulders and a pearl dangling from one ear. A sardonic smile curved his lips, his arm resting casually on his friend Guast's shoulder.

I held out my arms to Navarre. 'My child, how you've grown.'

'Tante Catherine,' he said, inclining his head. 'It's been a long time.'

I pulled him into my embrace. His compact body was hard; he reeked of sweat. His black doublet was faded and unfashionable, without adornment or slashings of any kind; but as I drew back and assessed his eyes with their thick, almost girlish, lashes, his strong jaw and clever mouth, that unruly thicket of hair and impressive breadth of his shoulders, I thought he had a bucolic masculinity rarely seen in our French dandies.

'You're the very image of a king,' I said. 'It does my heart good to see you.'

'I'd rather be a prince and have my mother alive,' he replied.

'Yes, of course. The poor dear, she was so proud of you. I'm sure she smiles down on us at this very moment. Come, greet Margot.'

I stepped aside. Margot stumbled on her hem as she came face-to-face with Navarre. I saw color flush her cheeks as she muttered, 'Cousin,' and leaned to kiss his stubbled cheek.

'It's Margot, right? Not Marguerite?' he said softly, with a grin. 'Or have things changed since the last time I saw you? Best let me know now, eh? We've a lifetime together ahead of us.'

She hesitated. She'd clearly not expected his sense of humor. 'Margot is fine,' she said stiffly. 'Or call me whatever you like. It's not as though I've a choice.'

I laughed loudly. 'Aren't they charming?' and looked about at the watchful courtiers.

Everyone broke into applause. Charles cried, 'A toast!' He snatched two goblets from a page, sloshing claret to the floor as he thrust one at Navarre. He extended the other to Margot, leaving me to reach for my own. Hercule skittered forth and almost overturned tray and page in his lunge for the last goblet. Henri's smile widened; he did not move from his spot.

Charles raised his goblet. 'To my cousin Navarre and my sister Margot!' He downed the wine; everyone followed suit. 'Now, let's eat!' With a flare of his coat, Charles turned to lead the court into the banqueting chamber. As I reached for Navarre's hand, for I intended to sit him next to me, Margot said, 'Forgive me, my lord, but my head aches. I shall retire.'

I glared at her. She ignored me, curtsying to Navarre and crossing the hall with her disgruntled women, who were obliged to attend her. Navarre arched his brow; I chuckled. 'A new bride's nerves: nothing to worry about. She's overwhelmed.'

The moment the feast ended, Charles got up and left, as usual. Navarre and I had barely spoken, for Charles monopolized the conversation, asking Navarre about everything from the weather in his realm to his preferred ways of hunting. I noticed Navarre answered amiably but never revealed more than what he'd been asked; and while he'd drunk more than seemed humanly possible he still appeared sober as he lounged in his chair, regarding the court's antics with interest. At his seat beside Charles's empty throne Henri picked his teeth with a silver utensil, while Hercule set himself to consuming an entire platter of sugared almonds.

The dancing was about to start; courtiers lined up for the saltorello, an exuberant dance that allowed our ladies to show off their legs and our men their agility. A group of painted women – professional courtesans with plunging cleavage and rouged lips – sauntered in front of the dais; one brazen beauty sporting a diamond glued to her cheek winked.

Navarre sat upright from his slouch; even Hercule stopped stuffing himself with almonds.

'Who are those ladies?' Navarre asked me, his voice thick with indolence and wine.

'They are members of our court,' I said.

'Are they, by chance, ladies of your household? I've heard it said you hire the most accomplished women to serve you; they're called the Flying Squadron because they ride the hunt like amazons.' His eyes glittered. 'I do like to hunt. I like it very much.'

From the corner of my eye, I saw Henri press a hand to his mouth in stifled mirth.

In truth, I'd never heard of this so-called Flying Squadron; but plenty of women at court made a living off men, so if the name fit, why dissuade him? I wanted our guest to feel at home.

'You should go to them,' I said. 'They're always eager for new companions to hunt with.'

He stood, passing his hands over his rumpled doublet. I met Henri's eyes and almost burst out laughing. Jeanne may have regaled her son with sordid tales of our licentiousness, but it seemed she'd only piqued his interest, for he now regarded our lacquered whores as if they were choice haunches of venison he couldn't wait to taste.

I snapped my fingers at Hercule. 'Accompany your cousin.'

Hercule darted to his side. The instant they left the dais, the prostitutes enveloped them, red-nailed hands everywhere as they guided them away.

I leaned back in my chair. Henri sidled beside me. 'Flying Squadron? That is rather quaint. Your idea, I suppose?'

'Hardly.' I pinched his cheek. 'Who knows what monstrosities Jeanne told him about me? But he's just lost his mother and if he has need of feminine comfort, who are we to deny it?'

'Those sluts are no doubt up to the task, but I wonder what Margot will think.'

'I doubt she'll care,' I confided, taking up my goblet. 'Did you see her leave the hall as if she wore a crown of thorns? You'd think I was marrying her to Satan himself.'

'She pines for Guise.' He turned his hooded eyes to the hall. 'And he apparently pines for her. I've heard he's outraged we'd dare marry Margot to a heretic and will protest the wedding.'

I shot him a look. 'He'd best not. I've forbidden him from coming to court until he's sent for. If he continues to cause mischief, he'll find himself confined to his estate for the rest of his life.'

'When has that ever stopped a Guise?' he replied. 'They're as bad as Coligny.'

I felt disquiet as I saw his expression darken. His sudden aversion to Guise unnerved me, for until the altercation over Margot they'd been friends. I preferred it that way; Guise was not somebody I wanted left on his own, considering his father had been le Balafré.

I said, 'Well, I'll not have Guise or anyone ruin this for us. Look, isn't that your friend Guast over there with those young men? Why don't you join him?'

'I'm tired of Guast. He's greedy; he's always asking me for

something. Now he wants a monkey, as if I bred them in my chamber on trees.'

'Give him your brother Hercule,' I quipped, and Henri let out a laugh. 'Maman, you are too wicked!' He leaned over to kiss me and sauntered off to his covetous friend.

I sighed. My leg hurt. I wanted my bed. I rose, moved through the court, and up the staircase. At the last minute, I decided to check on Margot. I knocked on her door; one of her ladies admitted me.

Moonlight slivered through the casement. My daughter sat before it, still in her gown, the ghostly light haloing the pearls in her hair. My heart softened at the sight of her. She looked small and alone. I remembered she was only nineteen, still a girl in many ways . . .

'You'll look tired tomorrow if you don't get some sleep,' I said.

'Who cares how I look? If I want to stay awake, I will. Or do you deny me that, as well?'

I stepped to her. 'My child, you've so much life ahead of you. Try not to grow bitter before your time. These first pains of love: they go away in time. They fade and we forget.'

'How would you know? You've never loved anyone.'

'That's not true,' I said, and all of a sudden I felt so old, so tired. 'You think you know me, but you don't. I have learned that we either accept what life gives us or we die. It's that simple.'

'Then I'd rather die.'

'But you won't.' I leaned over her immobile form, set my lips on her dry cheek. 'You will live. You can do nothing else. You are my daughter.'

The wedding day approached. I kept watch over Navarre through Birago's spies, pleased to hear he'd taken to the divertissements of Paris with gusto. If he was bereaved over his mother, he made a fine show of hiding it, drinking in our taverns with his Huguenot comrades until all hours and bedding every whore in sight. He wasn't seen anywhere near Coligny – which pleased me more than anything else, until Birago came to me.

'It's His Majesty,' he said as I sat in my study attending to my endless correspondence. 'One of my informants saw him slip out through the servants' quarters, dressed in a hooded cloak. As he often goes out like that for his own amusements, no one thought to mention it at the time. It was only after he was seen again, just two days ago, that the man came to tell me.'

'Did he follow him?' I asked.

'Yes. His Majesty met up with Navarre and they . . .' He coughed into his hand awkwardly.

'I can imagine,' I said drily. 'I hope it was an expensive brothel, at least.'

'No, *madama*,' Birago lifted troubled eyes to me. 'They did not go to a brothel. They went to Coligny's town house on the rue de Béthisy.'

I sat in utter silence. Then I said, 'Do you know what they did there?'

'I'm afraid not. My spies are diligent, but I've not succeeded in penetrating Coligny's personal rooms. I did manage to bribe a cook in the kitchens, but of course he's heard nothing.'

I felt as if I couldn't draw enough air into my lungs. 'How many times have they met?'

He blinked his watery eyes. 'At least two. Charles elected to go to him, after Coligny declined the offer of his old apartments at court. Coligny said he was more comfortable at his town house, as he brought guests to the wedding he could better accommodate there.'

'Guests . . .' I echoed. I recalled the faces of the men I'd seen when I went to visit Jeanne on her deathbed. I had recognized several prominent Huguenot nobles but at the time, given the circumstance, thought nothing of it.

'Find out everything you can,' I said. 'I need to know how many of these friends of his are lodged in that house and what they plot. For they plot something, I have no doubt.'

'Yes, *madama*. What about Charles? Should I speak to him?'

'No. Leave that to me.'

Birago nodded and walked out. Feeling a sharp pain in my hand, I looked down.

I had crushed my writing quill to splinters.

* * *

I went straight to my son's apartments. I found his room in chaos, clothing and hunting paraphernalia strewn about, his hound gnawing on a meat bone while Charles stood poised near the door, hurriedly donning a cloak. If I'd come a minute later, I'd have found him gone.

He spun to me. His face blanched. 'What . . . what are you doing here?'

'I came to see you. Do I intrude? Are you going somewhere?'

'I . . . I was . . . There's a new pack of deer near Vincennes, and Navarre and I . . .'

I planted myself at the door. 'Don't lie to me. You're going to see Coligny, aren't you?'

He shrank back, his expression one of utter stupefaction. Then he said nervously, 'Coligny? Why would you think that? I'm not going to see him. He doesn't like to hunt anymore.'

'Perhaps not deer,' I replied. 'I know about your meetings with him. I know you've been going to his house in secret with Navarre.' I paused. His eyes had grown wide, his mouth working as he struggled for an excuse. 'There's no need to hide it from me,' I added. 'You've made it clear you mean to rule as you see fit. Just tell me the truth and I will leave court today.'

'You . . . you cannot leave,' he stammered. 'We've Margot and Navarre's wedding to attend.'

I let out a taut laugh. 'What wedding? If you want to go make pacts with Coligny, you risk everything. At least grant me the mercy of not having to bear witness to it.'

His expression unraveled. 'But I didn't agree to anything! I just listened. I swear it.'

'Listened to what?'

I watched the color seep from his face. He regarded me with such a terrible mixture of bewilderment and fear for a moment I wondered where I had erred, how I'd failed to recognize that my constant care of him would never defeat the influence of a man like Coligny. My son was vulnerable; he'd lost his father at an early age, watched his elder brother suffer under the Guises, and endured years of warfare; since he'd taken a whip to Margot

I'd sensed something broken inside him. Now Coligny preyed on his weakness, on his desperate desire for lasting peace and his struggle to be seen as a king not dependent on his mother for guidance.

'What does he want of you?' I said. 'I'll not fault you, I promise. I know how you feel: I know how he can convince us to believe almost anything. Just tell me.'

He kneaded his cloak, his gaze darting about as if he might find an escape. 'He . . . he . . .' I saw him swallow. 'He wants me to exile you from France,' he burst. 'He says you'll bring more destruction on us, that you may have poisoned Jeanne of Navarre and you'll force Navarre to convert. If that happens, he says the Huguenots will have to go to war in Navarre's defense.'

I felt rage boil up and forced it back, keeping my voice inflectionless, as though what he had just confided came as no surprise. 'He said all that, did he?'

'Yes! But we didn't believe him. Navarre told him so. He said, "I will marry Margot and I swear to you nothing on this earth will persuade me to convert."' Charles flung himself at me, clutching at my hands. 'Forgive me. He asked to see me and I couldn't say no. But I know I was wrong to let him say those things to me.'

I looked down at his fingers entwined with mine. 'Yet you were going to see him again,' I heard myself say, and I marveled at my ability to conceal the fury and fear building inside me.

'To tell him no. I was going to tell him that I will never send you away.'

I pulled my hands away, took a deliberate step back. He gasped as though I had struck him.

'No, don't leave me,' he whispered. 'Maman, please. I . . . I fear him. He tells me I mustn't listen to you, that you lead me astray.' He shuddered. 'I want so much to believe him when he says I can be a great king, but he looks at me strangely, as if he doesn't see me. He promised he'll help me bring France peace and glory, but I don't think it's me he wants to guide.'

My poor son. Coligny had hypnotized him, twisted him up in lies and deceit. But Charles was more perceptive than I'd been.

He already sensed he was just a means to an end. Coligny did not care about my son. He wanted Navarre, his champion prince, the heir of his dead queen; Navarre, who had a blood-right to the succession. He wanted Navarre to inherit France. It was why he'd signed the letter to Jeanne, why he sought to undermine me. If he could push me aside, the Huguenots could wage war until no one was left to challenge Navarre's right to the throne.

'Charles.' I touched his shoulder. 'You must promise never to see him again. He cares nothing for you. He is a liar. He has always been a liar and a traitor.'

His mouth quivered. Tears welled up in his eyes. 'I promise,' he whispered. 'I do.'

I pulled him close. 'Don't cry,' I murmured. 'I am here. I will keep you safe, always.'

I called for Birago and left Charles under his supervision, with guards at the door. I then returned to my study, where Lucrezia had closed the shutters to block the worst of the heat.

I sat for a long time in silence, reliving the past.

I saw him again as he'd been at my nuptial banquet, a solemn youth in ivory, with beautiful eyes. I remembered the dusk of St. Germain, when I sought his help against the Guises; and later, at Chenonceau, when his body entered mine. Every word that went between us, every touch, passed through me. And when I was done and the memories lay at my feet like crumpled papers, I realized there weren't many, only a few in fact, though it was enough to fill a lifetime.

Night descended. Lucrezia slipped in to light the candles and inquire about my supper. Nothing formal was planned tonight, so I had her serve me in my rooms. I didn't eat much. With concern she asked if I needed anything else.

'Yes,' I said to her. 'Tell Henri I must see him.'

He came soon after, clad in loose crimson pantaloons and an unlaced chemise that revealed the curls on his sculpted chest. His hair tumbled like a dark mane to his shoulders; his eyes were bright from the evening's wine, reminding me of his grandfather François.

'It's like Hades in here,' he said. 'Do you have a ribbon?'

I undid a lace from my sleeve. He tied back his hair, roving to the table. He picked at the remains of my roast pheasant with his long fingers. 'Margot is being impossible. I asked her to dine with me tonight and she sent back word that her head ached. Does she take me for an idiot? She never has headaches. All she wants to do anymore is sit in her rooms and mope.'

I watched him take up the crystal decanter and pour wine into a goblet. He drank, eyeing me. 'Well?' he said, and calmly, without any anger, I relayed everything I had discovered. When I was done, he sighed. 'My, my: what a tangled web.'

I shifted on my chair. 'He's determined to destroy us so he can –'

'Turn his heretic devils on us.' Henri smiled. 'Well, if Charles missed their meeting today, we can assume he's been forewarned.'

'For now. But it's not enough. He'll find another way. He always does.'

I unfastened my ruff and tossed it aside. My son was right; the room was stifling. I wanted to crack open the casement, but my apartments sat on the first floor over the gardens and I couldn't risk being overheard by courtiers who took to the shadows to make love or spin intrigue.

'You could kill him,' Henri said, and I glanced sharply at him. He returned to the decanter. 'There is a way. No one would suspect you had a hand in it.'

The room went still – that kind of stillness like the gathering of clouds before a tempest.

'What way?' I asked quietly.

'Guise. He blames Coligny for murdering his father. He 'd bathe in his blood given the chance. Of course, he'll need direction. We don't want him knifing Coligny at court.'

'And you could . . . ?'

'Persuade him?' He traced his finger around the goblet rim. 'Of course. Guise and I may have our differences, but when it comes to Coligny we understand each other.'

I looked about my room. It was full of familiar objects, my children's portraits on the walls among the most cherished. I paused on the painting of my Elisabeth, so lifelike it seemed she was here. Something ominous grew in the back of my mind, a terrible force.

There will never be peace while he and his kind live.

'What do you suggest?' I said, and I was surprised at how easily I accepted it, how I felt as though a great burden I hadn't realized I carried had been lifted from me.

He braced one leg behind him, the goblet balanced on his knee. 'It must be done anonymously, so Guise will need a time and place. Coligny has some sort of routine, I assume?'

I bit my lip. 'I don't know. Birago can find out, but we cannot risk an uproar before the wedding next week. Afterward . . .' I considered. 'What if I summon him?'

Henri arched a brow. 'Do you think he'll come?'

'I do,' I said, and I could already envision him before me, unyielding in his black doublet. I wanted to confront him, I realized. I wanted to hear him admit the truth to my face, for once in his life. 'He suspects me of killing Jeanne and is anxious for Navarre. Without Charles's support he'll fear he's losing his influence. Yes, I think he'll see me. He can't do anything else.'

Henri's eyes glittered, like serrated jewels. 'When?'

'I'll send word. Tell Guise I'll pay whomever he hires for the deed but make sure he understands he undertakes it of his own accord. If it comes to it, I'll deny all complicity.'

Henri quaffed his goblet. He leaned down to kiss my cheek, enveloping me in his musky scent of claret, salt and sweat, and the jasmine essence he used to perfume his throat and wrists. 'Trust me to take care of Guise,' he said and he untied his hair, dropping the ribbon in my lap.

Left alone, I finally undid my own hair. Light flickered in my bedchamber; the candles were lit, the covers turned down. Lucrezia and Anna-Maria waited.

But I knew sleep wouldn't give me solace this night.

To the clamor of bells, we assembled on the dais outside Notre Dame 's doors rather than in its cool interior, suffocating in our finery. An ocean of people converged around the platform, Huguenot and Catholic together, united for the moment by the event. My daughter and her groom knelt on cushions before the makeshift and secular altar. Margot wore violet; Navarre had opted for complementary mauve, his copper hair springing up about his matching cap.

Monsignor intoned the oratory. It was designed for brevity, so we might escape as soon as possible, but halfway through Charles started to shift in his throne, his spidery fingers tapping his chair arm. 'On, on,' he muttered. 'Can't he just bless them and be done? It's infernal out here.'

I agreed. Perspiration dripped under my coif and my purple damask. Everyone else was equally sick with heat; even young Guise – seated opposite us in a tier with his mother the duchess, his uncles, my daughter Claude, and her husband of Lorraine – seemed relieved when Monsignor finally asked, 'Do you, Marguerite de Valois, princess of France, take Henri de Bourbon, king of Navarre, as your lawful husband, to cherish so long as you both shall live?'

I held my breath. Margot did not move. The silence lengthened.

Charles spat, 'Damn her!' and leapt up to push Margot from behind, forcing her head forward and upsetting her diadem, which slid precariously from her brow. Her cheeks turned scalding red as she righted herself. 'She agrees,' crowed Charles, and Monsignor repeated the question to Navarre, who laconically assented. 'I do.'

It was over. As the populace threw wilted flowers into the air, we assembled behind Margot and proceeded into Notre Dame. During the stampede to the pews, I felt a touch on my arm and turned to find Henri. 'Congratulations, Maman. Coligny didn't stop the wedding.'

'Shh!' I rebuked as trumpets sounded a ponderous note. 'What of the other matter?'

'He agrees.' My son leaned close. 'There 's someone in his employ – Maurevert, I believe he's called. You might be interested to know he once served in the Huguenot army, a turncoat like the man who shot le Balafré. Ironic, don't you think?'

'Yes, yes. But remember: not until I send word.'

I sat beside my daughter-in-law, who looked drawn from the heat. She'd thus far shown no signs of fertility, though Birago had assured me that Charles did not neglect his spousal duty. I had begun to worry over her constitution; I needed her to bear a son that would put Navarre at even greater distance from the throne.

'After mass, you should retire,' I advised. 'There's no need for you to overtire yourself.'

She nodded in weary gratitude, turning her gaze back to the altar. Margot knelt alone. Navarre attended a Huguenot service in a nearby temple.

Isabel sighed. 'Such a beautiful bride, but so sad.'

'Let her get with child,' I retorted, impatient with her moods, 'and she'll know happiness soon enough.'

Two days later, I summoned Coligny.

31

He entered my study and bowed, as if the heat didn't affect him at all, a black ruff cradling his bearded chin, every button of his doublet fastened and his cloak draped over his shoulders. I'd always appreciated his magnetic attraction; now I felt it aimed at me like a curse.

I motioned. 'Sit, my lord. There's no need for ceremony.'

'If Your Grace doesn't mind, I would prefer to stand.'

'Very well.' I felt his gaze follow me as I paced to my desk. I let the silence build, until he said, 'I assume I've been called here to some purpose?'

I turned to face him. The corners of his mouth twitched, as if he subdued one of his rare smiles. Was he amused?

'Yes,' I said. 'I have called you for a reason and I believe you know what it is.' I paused, watching him. His face was immutable, like stone. And he wasn't sweating. The morning sun already broiled Paris but he didn't shed a drop.

'I'm afraid I don't understand,' he said.

'Oh? Are you telling me you have not been meeting with my son and Navarre, counseling them on how to best rule this realm?'

He frowned. 'Are you accusing me of disloyalty? If so, you are mistaken. I did meet with His Majesty and Navarre but only to discuss issues concerning the defense of France.'

'We are at peace. Who are we supposed to be defending ourselves against?'

'Spain,' he said, and I laughed aloud. 'Not that again!'

He met my eyes. 'You may not think Spain worthy of fear, but you have not heard from the countless refugees fleeing Philip's massacres in Flanders and the Netherlands.'

I stared at him, forgetting in that instant that I'd decided his fate. I felt almost pity for him, wondering how he could remain mired in fear of a menace that had failed to materialize.

'You surprise me,' I said. 'I'd have thought that after all these years you'd have seen through Philip of Spain's threats by now. He likes to pretend he'll fall upon us at any moment, but he hasn't so far and I, for one, doubt he ever will. He has more pressing concerns.'

'And you always underestimate your foes,' he replied, with unexpected intimacy. 'You made the same mistake with the Guises, I believe.'

I refused to let the gentle rebuke in his tone affect me. 'You are right: I have underestimated you.' Before he could react, I added, 'I know you didn't advise Charles against Spain. You advised him against me.'

I watched his expression falter. It was astonishing. He'd lured my child to his house to turn him against me and yet he looked as if he'd never thought I might find out.

'I fear you misunderstand,' he said. 'The king and I did speak but I never counseled him against you. I merely told him –'

'That I might have poisoned Jeanne and will make Navarre convert.' I smiled as I saw the impact of my words drain the color from his face. 'Oh, and I must be exiled from France, because I'll bring the realm to ruin. Is that all, my lord? Or did I miss something?'

He didn't shift a muscle. He met my stare and said in a low voice, 'I loved you once. Yet now you accuse me of conspiring against you?'

It felt as though my heart twisted in my chest. 'How can you say that? You deceived me, believed lies told of me, waged war against me. You never loved me.'

'Oh, I did. I loved you so badly I did what I never thought I could.'

The sadness that rose in his eyes riveted me. 'Or have you forgotten how I saved you from le Balafré?'

'Le Balafré? What . . . what has he to do with this?'

'Everything. I had him killed, you see. I did it for you.'

I stood as if melded to my spot. 'You declared yourself innocent of the charge. I ordered an investigation. You swore you had nothing to do with it.'

'I lied.' His voice quavered, as if he held back a near-overwhelming emotion. 'I lied because I thought . . . I believed at the time we would find our way back to each other, once it was over. But I was wrong. You went on progress and when you came back, everything had changed.'

I did not feel my hand rise, not until I was pressing it to my lips.

'I am to blame,' he said. 'I know that now. I never let you know how I felt. When I saw you again, two years had passed and my wife was dead. I felt such guilt at her passing. I watched her agonize for months and all I could do was long to be free of her. But when she finally went, I was so alone. I had nothing but my children and my faith. Then you summoned me to Blois and I saw we would never be who we were, and it was as if something died inside me, forever.'

'Dear God.' I turned away. Even as I fought against it, a terrifying hope began to rise in me. 'You never said a word – not even then, at Blois, when it might have made a difference . . .'

'I know. What good would it have done? You had changed. I thought it best to let you go.'

His words shuddered through me. I whirled around, stabbed my finger at him. 'I did not change,' I said, my voice trembling. 'You did. You believed I'd agreed with Philip to persecute your faith and you went to war. It wasn't me who did this to us: it was you. It was always you!'

He bowed his head. He looked as if he might weep. I thought that if he did, if he begged my forgiveness for what he'd done, for the betrayal and the pain he'd caused, I would let him live. I would send him back to Châtillon and his children, deprived of all power but unharmed.

I would not stain my conscience with his blood.

Then I heard him say, 'Sometimes we must strike first, before we are struck in turn,' and I froze, meeting his eyes. In them, I saw what I had for so long anticipated – and dreaded.

Silence fell between us, taut like the pull on fabric before it shreds.

'You admit it,' I breathed. 'You admit everything.'

'I do. I fought for the only thing I had left: my faith. You and I had reached an impasse. Where you saw compromise, I did not. But believe me, I never meant to become your enemy.'

'And yet,' I said, 'here we are.' I drew back, lifting my chin. 'You will resign from the Council and leave Paris. You are unfit. Be grateful that I spare your life, for no other monarch would.'

'If His Majesty commands it, I will submit.' He stepped close to me, his voice so low it was almost inaudible. 'You make a mistake if you think I am of any account. My faith will prevail, with or without me. We will fight for Navarre and a Huguenot France. Nothing you do can change that.'

'You . . . you think you can threaten me?' I whispered. 'If so, then you are the one who is mistaken, for come what may, *I* will prevail.' I took one last look at him, engraving this moment in my memory so I would never be tempted to rue this day. 'We are done here, my lord.'

He bowed and walked out, without a single glance back.

A cold pit opened in my stomach. I turned to my desk, retrieved the sealed note I had written that morning. I called for a page. 'Bring this to my son, Prince Henri.'

After that, I went about my business. I wrote my letters, bathed, changed one black gown for another, and sat down to dine. At one in the afternoon as my supper was being served, in the street winding from the Louvre to the rue de Béthisy a shot rang out.

Lucrezia was clearing the table when Henri came to me. Leaning to my ear he whispered, 'They got him. But he's not dead. He had men with him; they saw the house from where the shot was fired. When they broke in, a harquebus was on the table. It had Guise's insignia on it.'

I looked at Lucrezia, standing still with the water pitcher in hand. I waved her out, shoving back my chair angrily to stand. 'He's a fool! I told you, I wanted it done anonymously.'

Henri heaved an exasperated breath. 'He wanted them to know who had avenged his father.'

'Then he's put us all in danger. Coligny threatened me; he said he'd fight for Navarre. Now, instead of a corpse, we have a wounded leader who'll demand justice.'

Henri frowned. 'They say the shot went through his shoulder. Maybe he'll die.'

'Not soon enough.' I struggled for calm, for control, even as I felt myself tumbling into an abyss. 'We must send our Dr. Paré to him. Then I'll take Charles and visit.'

Henri gaped at me. 'But they'll all be there, his men, the other Huguenot leaders . . .' His voice faded into understanding. 'I see. We must act as if we had nothing to do with it.'

Turning from him, I called for Birago. As he hustled away to get Charles, I said to Henri: 'Keep Guise out of sight. At dusk, bring him to the oleander grotto in the Tuileries.'

We went by coach to the rue de Béthisy, flanked by armed guards.

A crowd of Huguenots already stood vigil outside Coligny's house. In less than an hour, word had spread. By nightfall, I feared, all of Paris would be in tumult.

As we descended from the coach, someone yelled, 'Murderers! Papist fiends!' and Charles cringed. I raised my chin. No one dared forbid us entrance, and in the main hall of the house we found more Huguenots, all men who went silent at our appearance. To my disbelief, Navarre stepped forth, his hair disheveled and chemise unlaced, as if he 'd just woken from a nap.

'How is he?' I asked.

Navarre searched my face. I almost looked away, wondering if he'd see the complicity etched on my features. 'He was shot in the shoulder. It's bad, but we're told he'll survive.' He glanced at Charles, then back at me. 'You shouldn't have come. It wasn't necessary. They already know who did it. You should be issuing a warrant for Guise's arrest.'

'We will, when we know all the facts. Now, take us to him.'

Navarre led us to the staircase. The Huguenots parted as we passed. No one said a word.

Upstairs, Paré bustled to me, older now, but with the same brisk efficiency he'd shown when attending to my husband and eldest son in their death throes. 'The wound is deep,' he said in a low voice. 'I've extracted the bullet and set the bone. He lost a finger and his elbow is shattered, but if he rests and keeps the dressing clean, in time he will recover.'

Charles had stepped to the bed where Coligny lay. Supine on the narrow mattress, he looked very small, almost insignificant.

Until he raised his eyes to me and I saw them smolder with all the force of his will.

Charles said softly, 'My friend, I promise to find the culprit and exact full retribution.'

Coligny did not take his stare from me. Everything around us faded.

'Your Majesty,' I heard him whisper, 'I suspect no other than Guise.'

I moved to the bed. 'Paré says you will recover. I am glad, for I remember when le Balafré was shot. The doctors said if the bullet could have been extracted, he might have lived.'

Coligny smiled. 'As I said once to you, my life is of no account.'

As his smile knifed through me, I suddenly understood. It all came into monstrous focus. He wanted to die. He wanted to perish for his faith, for then he'd wield greater power than he ever had alive. He too had learned his lesson from the murder of le Balafré.

He had seen the devotion martyrs could engender.

I met his burning stare. 'My only regret,' he said, and he turned his eyes to Charles, 'is that my wound prevents me from serving Your Majesty at this perilous time.' His hand reached up to grip Charles's; even as I watched, horrified, Charles bent down and Coligny whispered, pressing as he did something into Charles's palm.

Then he collapsed upon his pillows, his face ashen.

Charles turned to me and held out his hand. 'Here is the bullet.'

I glanced at the shredded nub. 'We must let the admiral rest,' I said, and I could feel Coligny watching us as I took Charles by the hand and guided him to the door.

Our guards surrounded us. In the coach, seated opposite each other while we lurched over cobblestones, I asked, 'What did he say to you?'

Tears swam in Charles's eyes. 'Nothing,' he murmured, and the moment we reached the Louvre, he rushed past Birago into the palace. Birago met my stare.

'Come with me,' I said to him.

In the oleander grotto, delicate bushes transported from Florence sat in tubs filled with native soil, waiting to be replanted. Their red and white blossoms were brazen, their scent as overpowering as their distilled essence could be lethal. Hedges ringed beds of rosemary and marjoram; scattered throughout were enamel salamanders, frogs, snakes, and grinning satyrs.

Two men approached us. One moved with a grace I recognized at once; the other was taller, broader. My throat tightened when he swept back his cloak's hood. With his handsome, chiseled features, white-gold hair, and those deep blue eyes he had the beauty of a young lion.

Beside him, Henri was a dark panther, rubies glimmering about his bare throat, his hair loose about his shoulders and the beginnings of a goatee sharpening his chin.

'You are in grave danger,' I told Guise. 'You should not have failed me.'

His eyes met mine. His voice when he spoke was husky, made for the bedroom. 'I know. Already the heretics surround my *hôtel*. They wave cudgels and knives, and scream for my head. I'm fortunate His Highness was with me or they'd have fallen on me like locusts.' His full lips parted in a disdainful smile. 'I hope there are no heretics hiding in the bushes here.'

As Henri let out a laugh, I retorted, 'It is no joking matter. If we don't act quickly, we could face another war, only this time they'll burn down Paris.' I motioned to Birago. 'Tell them.'

Birago was like a gnarled branch in his velvet robe, wisps of hair on his liver-spotted pate, yet he spoke with authority. 'Over six thousand Huguenots are here; many came for the wedding but have yet to leave. Should they decide to seek retribution for the attempt on Coligny, they'll do far more than wave cudgels and knives at our gates. They could storm the Louvre itself.'

Guise stood silent. 'Then let me make amends,' he said at length.

I stared at him. 'I gave you a time and place to do the deed, and you bungled it. What makes you think I'd entrust anything more to you save safe passage to your estate in Joinville?'

'I don't expect you to trust me,' he replied with surprising calm. 'But I assure you that this time, I will not fail. Unlike Lazarus not even Coligny can rise from the grave.'

Henri stepped to me. 'Maman, I will go with him. We will kill everyone in the house.'

Without warning, I heard my dead father-in-law's voice in my head.

That is the way of life, ma petite. *Sometimes we must strike first* . . .

I pressed a hand to my chest, turning toward the Seine, its acrid stench intermingling with the sweetness of my garden. I couldn't deny it anymore. If he recovered, Coligny would fight me – to the death. It was his life or mine.

I turned back around. They shifted in the shadows: Guise a statue of ivory, Henri sleek and part of the night, Birago a wavering reflection of my own self.

'All of them?' I whispered, and the faces of those I'd seen in the house flashed before me. They had wives, children. Could I live with their deaths?

'All of them.' Guise recited the names impassively. 'Coligny's son-in-law Teligny, his captain Aubigne, the nobles Rochefoucauld, Souissy, and Armagnac: they are in that house and they must die. The Huguenot cause will never recover.' He paused, glancing at Henri, who made a deprecatory gesture. Guise returned his gaze to me. 'You have Navarre. I suggest you keep him under guard until this is over. It goes without saying he can never return to his realm.'

I hesitated, looking at each of them. My heart pounded in my ears. I thought of what they were asking of me, what I would set in motion if I agreed, and then, just as I began to doubt, I remembered Coligny's words: *We will fight for Navarre and a Huguenot France* ...

It was him or me. It had always been him or me.

I felt myself nod. 'Tomorrow night,' I said quietly. 'You can act then.'

Guise bowed. With a wink at me, Henri pulled up his hood.

'What day is tomorrow?' I asked, as they disappeared into the lengthening shadows.

'Sunday the twenty-fifth,' said Birago. 'The Eve of St. Bartholomew, patron of healers.'

The next day, at twelve o'clock of another scorching afternoon, I received word that Navarre had returned from his morning visit to Coligny. My son Hercule had joined him in his apartments and I dispatched our court prostitutes there, to ensure they had enough flesh and wine to lull them for hours, so they'd fail to notice the guards at their door. When Henri returned from his evening patrol to report that there had been no disturbances in Paris, though Huguenots still crammed the alleys and lanes around Coligny's house, I went to see Charles.

As I spoke to him, he sat on his bed with his hound beside him, juggling the shred of bullet back and forth in his hands. 'So, it's true,' he said when I finished. 'Guise shot him.'

'No.' I leaned forward in my chair. 'I told Guise to do it. My only regret is that he failed. I met with Coligny in the morning; I had hoped to save his life, but he threatened me. After I pardoned him for acts no other would, he admitted he was responsible for le Balafré's murder and he would fight to put Navarre on your throne. I decided I had no other choice.'

Charles lowered his head; a low broken sound came from him. 'Why do they hate us so much?' he whispered. 'I don't understand. Why, when all we ever wanted was peace?'

'It's not all of them. Charles, look at me.' I cupped his chin, raised his face to me. He had emulated Henri and started to grow a goatee, but in that instant all I saw was the boy he'd been when le Balafré and Coligny first went to war, with the same stricken bewilderment in his eyes. 'It's not all of them. There are many Huguenots who revere their king, who desire peace as much as we do. Do you understand? We must do this to save them.'

A tear rolled down his pale cheek. The bullet slipped from his hand to the floor as he nodded, hugged his knees to his chest, and coiled up next to his dog.

I left him in Birago's care. In the corridor, I found Henri waiting. 'There's to be no change in our plans,' I told him. 'Guise's anger for Coligny still burns hot; I don't want him going any further than the men in that house.'

'I'll oversee everything.' He gave me a reassuring smile. 'Trust me, Maman. After tonight, you'll never have to worry about the Huguenots again.'

His words left me unsettled, though I didn't know why. I could not turn back, I told myself as I returned to my rooms. I could not afford to indulge doubt or regret. I had to do whatever was necessary to preserve France. Other rulers before me had done away with their enemies; and Coligny was a traitor. He deserved to die for what he'd done.

Still, I barely tasted my food, sitting in silence while my women moved about sorting odds and ends, until I thought to ask, 'Has anyone seen Margot?'

Anna-Maria shook her head. 'No, my lady. She has been keeping to her rooms, but I heard that she planned to dine with Queen Isabel this evening in her apartments.'

It sounded reasonable enough and yet I found myself thinking it would be better if Margot stayed with me tonight. Isabel retired early. Who knew where my daughter might stray? I didn't want her going to see her husband or brother Hercule and finding guards at their door.

'I'll fetch her,' I said. 'I feel the need for company. Lucrezia, come with me. Anna-Maria, stay here and ready a truckle bed for her in my room.'

I pulled my velvet shawl about my shoulders, opened the door, and stepped with Lucrezia into the corridor. On the walls, the torches sizzled, casting more smoke than light. I glanced at Lucrezia; she returned my look with a wariness that made me again aware of what was happening beyond the palace walls. It was almost as if I could see the armed men following Guise and Henri as they galloped down Paris's dark streets to the house on rue de Béthisy, where a gravely wounded man lay in his bed, unaware that death approached.

'It'll be fine,' I said to Lucrezia, and, I think, to myself. 'You'll see. It will all be fine . . . '

As we wound through the long passages of the old palace, I was struck by the silence. There were no official entertainments planned tonight, so the court had no doubt scattered to its own diversions, yet the Louvre was preternaturally hushed. It disconcerted me; I was used to seeing groups of women swishing past in gem-spangled gowns and lithe men prowling the shadows. We were overcrowded with guests of rank invited to the wedding; yet now it seemed as if the entire palace stood empty.

I glanced again at Lucrezia. 'It's like a tomb. Where is everyone?'

She shook her head. 'I don't know.' Something in her tone, almost like an expectant fear, brought me to a halt. 'Lucrezia, what is it?'

'It's nothing,' she began, and she paused, gazing at me from within the shawl she had pulled over her head. 'I thought you knew. Rumor is, His Majesty is unwell and ordered an early curfew.'

'Unwell?' I frowned. 'But I left Charles only a few hours ago. He was upset but not . . .'

Trust me, Maman. After tonight, you'll never have to worry about the Huguenots again.

As I recalled Henri's cryptic words, a sudden gasp escaped me. I began walking, more quickly now, a hand at my throat. Lucrezia hastened after me. We traversed a courtyard littered with gravel and other refuse, the fountain in the center a mess of rubble, part of my ongoing renovations; I stumbled and felt Lucrezia grip my arm. She pointed at my feet. Looking down, I saw I still wore my soft-soled indoor slippers.

'I should have changed my shoes,' I said. We skirted the fountain and moved toward an arcade illumined by sconces, where a staircase led up to Isabel's apartments.

It was then that I heard the mournful toll of a tocsin.

'Saint Germain-l'Auxerrois,' Lucrezia explained, to my relief. It was the church across from the Louvre; at this hour, I was usually abed myself, writing or reading, so I'd failed to recognize it. But as the bell continued to ring, signaling an emergency, fear seized me. I went still, my shawl clutched about me, Lucrezia reaching for my hand when –

A pistol shot exploded. I met Lucrezia's stare. Another shot came and then a scream tore the silence, followed by another – anguished wails that reverberated into the night, punctuated by distant shouting, clanking steel, and the frantic pounding of footsteps.

Then the unearthly silence fell anew.

'Margot,' I whispered. 'We must find Margot before –'

A round of harquebus shots into what seemed the very space above our heads cut off my voice. Lucrezia gasped as I stood swaying, buffeted by the cacophony coming from the palace.

In a flash at the corner of my vision, something streaked past us.

I jerked around, grasping Lucrezia. A lone man raced through the arcade – a youth with tousled hair, in a black doublet and hose, his mouth wide in soundless terror, hands extended as if he pushed through glass. Behind him followed a group I recognized at once as men of our court, dressed in leather jerkins and black masks, carrying pistols and knives. I watched them gain on the youth as he darted about a column, skidding to a halt when he realized too late his mistake and doubling around the way he'd come. He sprinted into the courtyard, dodging one of the men who leapt at him, nearly colliding with the fountain as he came running, running – straight to me.

His hands seemed to stretch out impossibly, fingers clawing at the air. I felt my own hand lift, reach for his. A splash of scarlet gushed from his mouth. He fell on his face inches from where I stood, a dagger stuck in his back.

With lupine howls, two of the masked men kicked him faceup and plunged their daggers repeatedly into his chest. Then one looked up and saw me. He froze.

'*C'est la reine mère!*' he exclaimed. I met his white-rimmed eyes through his mask; then he yanked out his blade and ran off with the group, laughing boisterously as if they were at a fete.

I looked at the corpse at my feet, the stunned green eyes already glazing over. On his blood-soaked doublet was a red shield, embroidered with interlocked chains in silver thread.

The shield of Navarre.

You are two halves of a whole. You need each other to fulfill your destiny.

I gasped. 'No, not him.' A primal urge overcame me. I bolted to the staircase, Lucrezia behind. As we climbed the stone stairs, my lungs burned, my skirts catching wetly at my ankles. Glancing down I was horrified to see smears of blood in my wake; I had somehow trailed my skirt edges in that poor boy's blood.

I heard Lucrezia panting as we reached the third floor. Here there was unsettling stillness. Though I could hear rounds of shots in the distance, raucous yelling and terrified shrieks, they seemed unreal, muffled by the tapestries lining the passage. We staggered to the gilded doors of the queen's apartments; I saw a red cross splashed on the wood, the paint still dripping, and banged on the doors with my fist, wondering why there were no guards present, even as I knew in the dark whirlpool of my mind that I needn't fear; my daughter-in-law would be safe. Secret orders had been given. Only those who ventured out risked death.

'It's me!' I cried. 'Open up!' My voice echoed eerily. I heard a bolt scrape over a lock and the door opened, revealing Isabel in her robe, her hair escaping its net at her nape in sweat-dampened strands. I stared in bewilderment at the white cloth with a red cross tied about her left forearm. Before I could say a word she grasped me by the shoulders. 'Get inside, now! You're not wearing the sign. They'll kill you without it.'

I pulled away before she could force me into her rooms. Behind her I glimpsed the pale faces of her women, kneeling before her prie-dieu. 'What sign?' I said, and hysteria crept into my voice. 'What is happening? Tell me this instant.'

'The sign.' She jabbed her armband. 'It shows you are a Catholic. Don't you know what they're doing? They're killing the heretics. Everyone without the sign dies.'

Lucrezia let out an anguished moan. I looked at her and felt as if I'd gone mad. 'No, it cannot be. I told them only those in the house. This can't be happening. It can't.'

The sound of screaming spun us around; we froze as we saw three women running as if crazed down the passageway by the staircase, around the corner into the long gallery that led to the king's wing. Men followed, carrying pikes. The women's desperation seemed to bounce off every wall, magnifying until I couldn't hear anything else.

The screams were abruptly cut off.

'Get inside,' Isabel repeated. 'We'll be protected here. The sign and God will protect us.'

I turned back to her. 'Where is Margot? Is she with you?'

Isabel shook her head. 'No. She didn't come to dine. She . . . she sent word that she was going to visit with her husband.'

'*Dio Mio*, she's with Navarre.' I thrust out my hand. 'Give me your armband.' Isabel stared at me, petrified. 'Quick, woman,' I barked and she fumbled at the cloth, untying it.

'My lady, please. You mustn't! Navarre is a Huguenot; they'll kill you too.' Lucrezia grabbed hold of me as I knotted the cloth about my left sleeve.

'They won't kill me.' I lifted my eyes to hers. 'I'm the Queen Mother. They think I . . .' My voice faltered, cracked at its seams. 'They think I ordered it.'

'I'm going with you,' Lucrezia said.

'No. It's not safe. I'm better off alone. You stay here with Her

Grace. Bolt that door and don't let anyone in. Do you hear me? No matter what, don't let anyone in.'

As Isabel took Lucrezia by the hand I turned away, back down the passageway under the flickering torches, toward the corner where the screaming women had run. Alone now, it was as though every sense in me heightened, so that even the most muted sounds of death coming from the opposite ends of the palace were distinct, assaulting me like an inescapable tide.

And as I walked through the palace where my worst nightmare was taking form, where I'd lived with my husband, raised my children, and fought for my country, I remembered the dream I had the night after I saw Nostradamus for the last time. I recalled the shadowy figures, the bell and the screams. I saw myself again, trailing blood. I'd not understood at the time, but now I did.

In seeking to kill one man, I was about to bring about the deaths of thousands.

And I might be too late to save the very prince I'd been told I must protect.

I blundered into the long gallery, my heels skidding on the wet floor. I didn't look down; I focused on putting one foot in front of the other, trying to ignore the shrieking coming from a room nearby, deafening me.

'Navarre,' I whispered. 'Navarre must not die.'

I came to the end of the gallery; to my right, an open arcade led into the privy garden. I drew to a halt as I caught sight of a group of naked Huguenots. Soldiers in our livery were hauling them together, their clothes discarded in a heap, the men yelling and struggling, the women covering their faces with their hands and crying. The soldiers thrust pikes through them, scything them like wheat. I watched them fall upon each other, some still alive, others dead, and then the soldiers began stabbing indiscriminately, plunging their pikes into that mass of flesh.

'Not Navarre.' I started to pray. 'Please, God, not him.'

I kept moving. I knew that if Navarre was alive, the only place he could be was in the king's apartments. No matter what happened in the palace, no matter how much madness was unleashed, no one would dare harm him if he was with Charles. I prayed Margot had somehow gotten wind of the plans and that was why she'd not visited Isabel, going instead to bribe or order away the guards at the apartment doors so she could take Navarre to safety.

More bodies began to appear along the corridors I passed through, stripped of clothing, throats cut, sightless eyes wide and bellies spilling entrails. I kept seeing my daughter sprawled among them, her gorgeous hair matted with blood; and as I discerned a keening that seemed to come from nowhere, I realized it was me, my voice seeping in hushed anguish from my lips.

When I heard a burst of laughter behind me, I whirled about. Drifting among the corpses behind me were our court prostitutes, clad in their best finery, their bosoms glistening with pearls and rubies, their skin powdered and white armbands dangling crucifixes and rosaries. They were whispering to each other, pointing at a past client or lover, now butchered at their feet. As one tapped a corpse with her high-heeled slipper, I choked back bile.

I lost track of my surroundings, though I'd come this way a thousand times before to see my son. I paused, forced myself to focus, to recognize a familiar furnishing, a painting, a statue to guide me. I felt trapped in a warren as I turned abruptly and started down a dark passageway, avoiding the larger rooms and galleries, weaving around black pools of blood. My hem sloshed; incarnadine splashes crested the wainscoting almost to the eaves; discarded and broken weaponry was strewn everywhere, as if our entire armory had been ransacked. Then I saw Charles's initials on the far oak doors and heaved a sigh of relief. I was near his private rooms.

I tripped against something. As I gasped and drew back, I could not tear my gaze from the stunted little body blocking my path, its crooked back riddled with stab wounds. I felt my scream unspool in my throat before I realized it wasn't my dwarf, not my precious Anna-Maria. It was male, one of Charles's favorite jesters, whom my son liked to see tumble and juggle balls.

I flung myself around him, rushing now to the doors. As I

squeezed through them, I was relieved to see five of our royal guards posted outside Charles's bedchamber. Their expressions were impassive, yet as I neared I saw one's hand tremble as he gripped his halberd. These men were Swiss mercenaries, hired and paid well to serve the king alone; they'd obviously been standing here protecting my son and listening to the horrors taking place in the Louvre.

They parted and let me into the antechamber. Birago was slumped on a chair, his head in his hands. He looked up, his eyes filled with sadness.

'Are they here?' I asked, my voice a mere thread.

He motioned to Charles's bedroom, where I'd left my son what seemed like a hundred years ago, asleep and in his care. 'Guise and his men came,' Birago said, and he spoke as if in a trance. 'He ordered me out. His Majesty was in a rage. I begged him to stay calm, but when Guise told him they were keeping him inside for his own protection, it . . . it unhinged him. He started shouting he'd never take orders from a Guise again, that he'd see him dead first.'

Birago regarded me helplessly. '*Madama,* he was like a man possessed, yelling that he'd kill Guise and every other Catholic who dared harm his Huguenot guests. Then Margot ran in. She said Navarre and Hercule were trapped in their rooms and about to be killed. Guise tried to stop her, but she struck him across the face and begged Charles to save her husband. She was so frantic that Charles ordered that Navarre and Hercule be brought here, to his rooms.'

As Birago spoke, the will that had propelled me through the palace drained away. 'They're safe,' I heard myself whisper. 'Thank God, they're safe.'

Birago forced himself to rise. 'Navarre's suite, his friends and attendants – I think they are dead. Navarre had blood on him when they brought him here, and he was crying. He accused Charles and you of instigating a massacre to force him to convert. He said Coligny had been right all along, that you'd contrived to set Guise loose to kill every Huguenot in France.'

His words knotted like rope about my throat. 'But he's alive?' I said, and as Birago nodded I turned to put my hand on the door. It was unlocked. I stepped into the bedchamber.

Charles's hound rested in front of the door. As the candlelight from the antechamber spilled in around me, it snarled. Hercule huddled near the alcove, his pitted face splotched with tears. When he saw me, he drew his knees up to his chest, his eyes bulging in fear.

I looked to the bed. Charles reclined against the carved head-board with Navarre in his arms. He held a dagger to Navarre's throat. Navarre watched me approach, his sleeve torn at the shoulder. Even on his black doublet, I could see blood glisten.

Margot appeared from the shadows. 'Are you happy now?' she said, and I turned to meet her eyes, filled with rage. 'You did this. You turned my wedding into carnage.'

'I . . . I did nothing,' I said. 'You know, I am not to blame.'

'Yes, you are. You wanted Coligny dead and now we all have his blood on our hands.'

'Be still,' I hissed at her, and I turned back to Charles. 'My son, please. Let him go.'

Charles shook his head, pressing on the knife. A trickle of blood oozed down Navarre's throat. My son shuddered. 'He must convert or he will die. Guise will kill him.'

'No, listen to me. He shares our blood; he is Margot's husband. Guise will not hurt him.'

Charles coiled his arm tighter about Navarre, his blade so near to the throbbing vein in Navarre 's neck I had to stop myself from lunging at the bed to save him. 'Guise told me he'd come for him,' my son quavered, his voice thick with tears. 'He said he was a heretic and must atone for everything his kind has done to us. I must save him; he must renounce his heresy.'

I took another step. The hound growled, showing its teeth. 'He will,' I said. 'I promise you. He'll do whatever you ask of him. Just let him do it freely.'

Charles hesitated. As his grip wavered, the knife scratched an erratic line on Navarre's flesh. He let out a gasp. Charles whispered,

'He must say it.' His other hand cupped Navarre's chin. 'Say it! Say it or I'll slit your throat before Guise does!'

Navarre looked at me – in his eyes I saw such hatred and powerlessness I almost couldn't bear it. 'Do it,' I said to him. 'For the love of God, convert to save yourself.'

His throat convulsed. He uttered, 'I . . . I abjure all others save Rome. I am a Catholic!'

As Charles sagged, the dagger falling from his fingers, I leapt forth to pull Navarre away. He staggered from me into Margot's arms. She held him, weeping as I'd never heard her weep before, as if our entire world had shattered.

I said, 'You've no reason to fear. I will protect you.'

Navarre's bitter smile contorted his mouth. 'Like you protected the thousands who have died? Madame, though you may wish it so, this night will never be forgotten.'

I met his icy eyes. I didn't speak. I had achieved what I'd sought from the moment I decided to wed him to my daughter. He would live as a Catholic prince; his children would be born Catholic, raised Catholic. I had safeguarded our future, deprived the Huguenots of a royal leader.

But I knew I had lost him, perhaps forever.

32

Three days later, we gathered in Notre Dame to celebrate Navarre's conversion. As he knelt before the altar to accept the Host proffered by a gloating Monsignor, I stared at Navarre's back, not wanting to see the triumphant smiles of the Catholic peers and courtiers who'd survived the night already being recorded in infamy as the Massacre of St. Bartholomew.

As horrified as I was, I did my best to present an impassive facade, unwilling to display any shame or fear over what I'd done. The very peace I had struggled to obtain through Margot and Navarre's union hovered on the brink of disaster; France was in more danger than ever before, and so I labored without cease, nailed to my desk penning explanations to England, the Low Countries, and other Lutheran powers, even as I received their thunderous condemnations alongside gleeful congratulations from Rome and Spain.

Outside Notre Dame, Paris was a city awash in blood. Once the slaughter had begun, few bothered to note who was Catholic or Protestant. The populace took advantage of the moment to strike at each other with impunity and hundreds of innocents were caught in the mayhem. Bodies floated like debris down the Seine; alleyways and bridges were littered with corpses. Fear of plague loomed like a specter, and as those who survived fled with whatever they could carry, I ordered mass graves dug outside the city walls, where the dead were dumped, quicklime slathered over them to hasten decay.

My son Henri came to me, haggard and apologetic. I listened in silence as he related how he, Guise, and their men entered Coligny's town house and caught the Huguenot lords unaware.

322 C. W. Gortner

As these men died fighting to protect their leader, Guise stormed up the staircase. He yanked Coligny from bed, stabbing him multiple times before he flung him out the window. Drenched in blood, Guise, triumphant, looked down on the cobblestoned street below as one of his retainers hacked off Coligny's head. Guise then hung it from his saddle like a trophy and rode through the streets, inciting the mob. Any Huguenot not hidden behind fortified doors fell to the Catholic wrath, executed in a frenzy of hatred and violence.

'I swear to you, I tried to stop it,' Henri said, his voice trembling. 'But the secret orders Guise left in the Louvre were in effect and his retainers had started killing those not wearing the armband. I didn't know what to do. It was a nightmare I could not escape.'

I nodded. I didn't have the strength to berate him. I had never seen him like this; at least he showed remorse, his terrified expression proof he'd not willingly engaged in slaughter. His youth and inexperience had misled him. In his zeal, he'd gone further than he should have.

'You went against my wishes to connive with Guise,' I said quietly, 'but you are not to blame. This was *my* mistake. I should never have tried again after we first failed to kill Coligny. Go now. Watch over Navarre and see to it that Guise departs Paris at once. He's to stay away until I decide otherwise. He has gone too far.'

After my son left, Birago arrived, gaunt with exhaustion from his attempts to control the chaos. He informed me that Huguenots throughout France were bolting across our borders into Geneva. There, I'd been branded as Queen Jezebel. Printed pamphlets declaimed every vile rumor told of me: I was the Italian serpent, a monstrous being who'd schemed with Spain to exterminate their faith. When once I might have been outraged, quick to protest my innocence, I told Birago to do nothing. Let all the calumny fall upon me, if it would absolve my sons.

As for Coligny, my lack of feeling toward his savage death was too private to admit to even my intimates. Alone at night in my rooms, as I heard the servants scrubbing the corridors outside my doors, I kept waiting for grief to overwhelm me, for a pain so visceral it would thrust home the enormity of my guilt. I feared my heart had turned to stone, calcified by strife and betrayal until I could no longer feel a thing. When I learned that Coligny's mutilated body still hung on the makeshift gibbet where Guise had left it, I had it taken down and his head brought to me.

Only after the soldier parted the burlap sack and stepped away, leaving me to gaze at the lifeless face, cleansed of gore so that it resembled a wax rendering of someone I'd once known, did the ice inside me crack. I saw no trace of the dangerous vitality I'd once loved and come to fear, no recognition in that frozen expression of the pride I'd reveled in. I reached out a quivering hand to trace his cold white lips, twisted forever in a grimace of pain, and my anguish welled up, like flame in my throat.

I turned away. 'No,' I whispered. '*Dio Mio*, no . . .'

Lucrezia waved the soldier away and gathered me in her arms, holding me as I rocked back and forth, repeating the denial over and over again. I knew then that something in me had died with him and I would never be the same. There was nothing left of the girl I'd been, nothing of the naïve adolescent who'd first come to France. He had been there from the beginning; he had known my innocence. Of everyone in my life, only he had touched the person I hoped to be.

Now he was dead, by my command.

I sent his body to Châtillon for burial and ensured his widow and children received a pension for his years of service, though he'd died a traitor, his property forfeit to the Crown. It was my atonement, my final gift to him – the only way I knew how to say farewell.

Now, as I watched Navarre make his way back to us, his stony expression unrevealing of the price he'd paid for his life, I could restrain myself no longer in public. I felt it build inside me – an eruption of exhaustion, anxiety, and relief so overwhelming that when he reached our pew and sat beside Margot, who turned bitter eyes to me, I threw back my head and laughed aloud.

I was still a Medici and I would survive.

★ ★ ★

We moved to St. Germain, leaving the Louvre to its ghosts. I fretted over Charles, who'd suffered an attack of fever. Dr. Paré examined him and reported that while serious, the fever would abate. However, Charles had told him he could not sleep. Paré recommended a daily dose of diluted poppy and that we keep my son as free from overstimulation as possible, for Paré believed he was suffering a nervous affliction brought on by the recent events.

Navarre came with us; outwardly, he was not a captive. He'd renounced his heresy, and while Henri kept close watch over him he seemed resigned. He had his own apartments; he rode daily, practiced archery, and even spent time with Margot. She must have told him Charles was ill and to my surprise he took to visiting my son. Several times Birago told me that Charles and Navarre had spent the afternoon gambling and laughing like friends. It was such an odd development that my suspicion got the best of me and I made an unannounced visit, to determine for myself the extent of this newfound friendship.

I found them seated at a trestle table, drinking wine and playing cards while Margot and Hercule were nearby, heads together. Since the massacre, my youngest son had cleaved to her, slavishly grateful for her intercession that night, which he believed had saved his life, though it was doubtful that he'd been in any real danger.

At my entrance, they both froze. Charles looked up sharply.

'Isn't this nice?' I said brightly, my voice sounding too loud in the closed room.

Margot's expression turned to stone, as it always did these days when she saw me. I ignored her as I stepped to the table where Charles sat in his fur-trimmed robe, pale and shrunken opposite Navarre's robust person. Looking at Navarre 's compact muscularity, the high color in his face and thick red-gold goatee he sported, I had the sudden presentiment that I'd made a mistake. I had fought to save him because of a vision years ago, because Nostradamus had warned this prince was vital to my destiny. What if I was wrong? Navarre was still a Huguenot at heart; I had no delusion that an enforced conversion at knife point had purged him of his faith. In time, I'd told myself, he would fully embrace his conversion; but as I saw his easy smile at my appraisal, I wondered if instead I nurtured another menace to the safety of France.

I flicked my hand at the stack of coins at his side. 'It appears you're winning.'

He shrugged. 'I wasn't until today.'

'No, he wasn't,' said Charles, with febrile enthusiasm. 'But today, fortune is with him.' He and Navarre locked eyes across the table. 'Isn't it, my friend?'

'Indeed.' Navarre reclined in his chair, taking up the goblet at his side. 'His Majesty is generous. Another king wouldn't so freely allow someone like me to win.'

I sensed a laden undercurrent in their words. I shot a penetrating look at Margot. She had her hand on Hercule's; both watched me with intense interest, like hounds awaiting the command to leap at their prey.

I returned my gaze to Charles. 'Don't lose too much,' I muttered, and I reached to his brow, for he looked unnaturally flushed all of a sudden. As I touched him he flinched, and I felt heat rising off his skin. 'You have a fever,' I said. 'Remember what Paré advised: you mustn't overexert yourself. I think you've done enough gambling for today.'

Charles started to protest; instead, Navarre rose. 'Your mother is right,' he said, and he gave my son a tender smile. 'I wouldn't want you to fall ill on my account, cousin. Perhaps we can play again tomorrow, after you've had a good night's rest?'

As I heard the compassion in his voice, my heart lurched. He sounded as if he truly cared for Charles. 'We can't tomorrow,' Charles said. 'We 're going hunting at Vincennes, remember?'

Navarre paused. 'Oh, yes. I'd forgotten.'

I forced out a chuckle, dropping my hand to Charles's shoulder. 'I don't think it's wise to spend the day on horseback until this fever abates, yes?'

'But I promised!' Charles jerked from me. He stood awkwardly, yanking the voluminous folds of his robe about his slender frame. Beside Navarre, he looked like a child in a king's garb; even his voice was petulant. 'I'm better and I want to go hunting. I'm sick of being shut inside.'

'We'll see,' I repeated, and I said to Navarre, 'If you feel the need for exercise, my lord, there's no reason Henri can't take you. I'm sure Margot can see to Charles's diversion for one day. Can't you, my dear?'

I heard my daughter mutter, 'Do I have a choice?'

I smiled. 'Good, then it's settled. Tomorrow Henri will take Navarre to Vincennes and if Charles feels better by the evening, we can all sup together as a family.'

Navarre met my stare. I saw nothing in his regard, not a single emotion I could identify, as if his eyes were made of opaque glass. 'I'd be delighted,' he said.

As soon as he left with Margot and Hercule and I saw Charles to bed, I returned to my rooms and summoned Henri. He arrived rumpled from being awoken from his afternoon nap.

'What is it?' he asked, sensing at once my tension.

I paced my chamber, trying to make sense of the inexplicable dread inside me. I told him about my visit. 'It was almost as if they were plotting something.'

He laughed. 'If it were up to Margot I'd have no doubt. She despises us because we made a mockery of her wedding vows by killing her Huguenot guests – as though she ever cared a fig for heretics. But poor Charles just wants to make amends. He feels terrible about that night; after all, he forced Navarre to convert. Besides, what can Navarre do to us? The Huguenots are routed and running for their lives. And Navarre is no Coligny.'

I retorted, 'He could still turn against us!' and then I bit my lip, regretting this admission of my private fear. But it was done now, so I added, 'I know he's Margot's husband. He owes us his life and I've no evidence against him, but I don't want him so close to Charles.'

Henri nodded. 'What would you have me do?'

I considered. 'Take him hunting tomorrow as planned, but make the day long enough that you'll have to stay overnight in the Château of Vincennes. Birago will take care of the rest.'

His eyes widened. 'Maman, you're not going to . . . ?'

'No,' I said sharply. 'Of course not. I don't want him killed. But I must be sure he won't turn against us either. I'll keep him under guard in Vincennes for a time. Margot can join him there; once he gets her with child, then we'll know his loyalty.'

Henri grazed my cheek with his lips. 'To Vincennes it is.'

I waited out the next morning in my study, attending to my correspondence even as my thoughts kept drifting. Finally, after several hours in which I barely finished two letters, I rose to take my midday meal when Birago rushed in.

'You must come at once,' he panted. 'His Majesty has taken a turn for the worse!'

We raced to Charles's room. It looked as if a fierce wind had blown through it, chairs and tables thrown about, platters knocked from the mantels and coffers overturned. I stared, dumbstruck, at Paré as he forcibly held my son down by his shoulders. Charles thrashed on the bed, red-flecked foam gurgling from his mouth.

Birago wrung his hands. Paré was trying to get a leather strap between Charles's teeth but my son let out a guttural shriek and arched backward with such force that he sent Paré flying away from the bed. I gasped as my son's spine contorted at an impossible angle, bowing until his head nearly touched his feet, his nightshirt splitting across his chest. As Paré scrambled back to him, Charles started convulsing again. I lunged forward with Birago, gripping Charles's arms while Birago held his feet and Paré forced the strap between his lips. The power my son exhibited was inhuman; it took all of my strength to press down on him, my breath stalling when I saw his eyes roll back into their sockets. Blood seeped from his nose.

He abruptly went still, his chest heaving with a gurgling sound.

'What is it?' I gasped. 'What is wrong with him?'

'I don't know,' Paré replied in a hushed voice. 'I brought his afternoon draft but Their Highnesses Margot and Hercule were visiting, so I left the draft and came back later. Their Highnesses were gone and he was asleep. I tarried outside and then I heard him choking. When I ran in, I found him like this. He seemed better this morning . . . He had no fever. I checked.'

'Margot was here?' I looked at Birago. He whispered, 'Look at his chest.'

I glanced at my son's torso, exposed under his torn nightshirt. An amulet dangled against his white skin, the archaic design beaten into tarnished silver. I froze. Paré had risen and moved to the mess near an overturned table. I saw him pick up a goblet, bring it to his nose.

He recoiled. 'Almonds.' He dropped the goblet, lifting his eyes to me in horror. 'It's some type of arsenic! It was in his draft. Dear God, the king has been poisoned.'

'That's impossible,' I whispered, but I recognized that amulet. It was the one Cosimo had given me; the last time I'd seen it was at Chenonceau on the day I'd cast my only spell. I'd put it in the box with the wax figures and never worn it again, bringing the box with me from one palace to another, lost among my other belongings.

Paré collapsed to his knees. 'I didn't do it. I swear to Your Grace, it wasn't me.' And as I heard his abject terror, when his composure had never wavered even when overseeing my husband and eldest son in their final hours, everything around me started to keel, as if the room slowly capsized under a dark roaring ocean.

'Margot,' I whispered, and I stumbled from the room.

I barged into my apartments, startling my women as I moved into my bedchamber and searched my cluttered dressing table. The box was gone. Whirling about, I stormed to Margot's chambers. She sat on the window seat with Hercule; as she stood in a flurry of skirts, I took in her startled expression, which after weeks of flinty indifference was an admission in and of itself. I eyed her white satin gown, the grape-sized pearls in her hair, and thought she dressed as if for a celebration. Then I looked at Hercule. He recoiled, his face blanching.

And I knew.

'Where is it?' I said. I didn't take a step to her, thinking I might kill her with my bare hands.

She turned to a nearby coffer and removed the box, bringing it to me on extended hands. Inside, I found the wax dolls lying in dishevelment; as I heard my heart pounding, I sprung the latch under the lining, opening the secret compartment to reveal the vial Cosimo had given me. It was empty; a tentative sniff summoned the terrifying scent of almonds.

'How . . . how could you do this?' My voice was a mere whisper.

'Cosimo,' she said, and there wasn't a hint of fear or regret in her voice.

'You . . . you had Cosimo . . . ?'

'I wrote to him. He told me to look for the box. It wasn't hard. You didn't exactly hide it.'

I couldn't move, the box heavy as marble in my hands. 'Why?' I heard myself say.

Her eyes gleamed. 'Charles wants to die because of what you've done. You killed his subjects, set all of the Huguenots against him.' She paused, for effect. 'But most important, you killed Coligny, whom he loved like a father.'

'That is a lie!' I hissed. 'This has nothing to do with Charles. You did this because you loved Guise and I forced you to wed Navarre, and now you think that I . . .' I cut myself short, meeting her knowing gaze in stunned realization.

'What, Maman?' she purred. 'Because you plan to kill Navarre next? That's why you sent him hunting with Henri, isn't it, so you can do away with him in the forest and say it was a hunting accident? There'll be no chance of him becoming a Huguenot leader then. You will usurp his realm, rid yourself of the rest of the Huguenots, and wed me again where you please.'

'She hates us,' muttered Hercule under his breath, as if I weren't in the room. 'Maman hates us and didn't warn us about the massacre. She wants us all dead.'

I stared at my daughter in horrified disbelief. What had I done to create such a twisted being? I loved all of my children as best as I could; I'd fought to keep them safe. I'd been distant as a mother during much of their infancy, yes, but only because Diane stole them from me. But after my husband died, they were mine again and I never wavered in my defense of them. How could Margot, so full of beauty and promise, have become this vile stranger? I tried to summon my rage, to blast her into humiliation, but the truth coiled inside me and I could not evade it.

She would do anything for revenge. She was a Medici; her curse was my blood.

'I gave Charles the amulet and the poison,' Margot went on, as though she could read my thoughts. 'It's what Cosimo advised: earn his trust by showing him what you are capable of.'

I felt the box drop from my hands but didn't hear it hit the floor.

'And that's not all,' she said, with a slow malicious smile. 'Charles was going to let Navarre escape at Vincennes. But then you came and took away his last hope for redemption. Now he thinks Navarre will die. That's why he took the poison. He can't bear his own guilt anymore.'

I looked at her face, at those remorseless eyes, and I grabbed her with my fists, shaking her until the pearls unraveled from her hair and pebbled across the floor. 'He thinks Navarre will die because you filled his head with deceit! Do you know what you've done? *Do you?* Your brother is dying because of you.'

She laughed in my face. 'It's *your* poison, *your* amulet. Everyone will say you did it, just like you killed Queen Jeanne, just like you used me to wed Navarre so you could lure the Huguenots to Paris to kill them. They'll say you poisoned your son and no one will ever trust you again!'

Hercule cowered. 'Not me,' he blubbered. 'I didn't do it. It wasn't me.'

I pushed Margot aside, took a deliberate step back. 'As soon as I see to your brother,' I said to her, 'I'll deal with you as you deserve.'

I put my youngest children under guard and sent soldiers to Chaumont to arrest Cosimo, who was apprehended and brought to the Bastille.

At nightfall, I went with Birago to see him. As I entered his slimy cell, deep in the fortress, I shuddered to see my astrologer bound to a chair, nude save for a tattered loincloth. In the shadows on the wall hung an array of prongs and other instruments of torture.

Cosimo looked like a cadaver, bruises marring his sallow skin. All the life inside him seemed to rush into his eyes at the sight of me, bringing back the memory of the little boy I'd met outside his father's house. I had known him since childhood; we weren't far apart in age. He was a fellow Italian, a Florentine. I had a moment of paralyzing doubt. What if this was part of Margot's vengeance? What if she'd found the box on her own, spewed her venom in Charles's ears to tip an already unstable mind into insanity, and then schemed to accuse Cosimo?

Birago murmured, '*Madama*, we must proceed. His Majesty's life depends on it.'

I nodded and Birago took his seat at a small table, removing from his satchel the paper and quill he would use to record the session. Cosimo stared at me, unblinking, searing me with all the memories between us, even as Birago's resonant voice filled the small cold room.

'Cosimo Ruggieri, you are accused of conspiring to effect His Majesty's death by poison. Her Grace is here to determine the recipe for the antidote. If you provide it, she promises that you will leave here with your life.'

Cosimo did not move, did not indicate he'd heard anything.

'Cosimo,' I added, 'you know I've no wish to harm you. Just tell me what I have to do to save my son. You know the poison's ingredients. What is its antidote?'

His cheek twitched. Birago made a brusque motion to the table. 'If you do not speak, the truth will be forced out of you. Every poison has its cure. You know it and you will tell us.'

Cosimo's mouth twisted. His laughter cracked forth like shards of metal. 'You still don't understand, do you? The gift you've refused to acknowledge in yourself, I devoted my entire being to attaining. And everything I learned, everything I discovered, I put to your service. I did what you did not have the strength to do. I am your instrument.'

My skin crawled. 'You . . . you are deluded. How dare you set claim to my life?'

'Because I am yours!' His ribs protruded as he strained against his bindings. 'You never thought of me; you left me alone and ignored me, but I . . . I was always yours. While you paid heed to your fool Nostradamus, who only gave you poems and rhymes, I probed the darkest realms to bring you your heart's desire. But you disdained me. You forsook me and now –'

'*Enough!*' I struck him with all my might, rocking him back in his chair. I saw his eyes snap wide, blood spurting from his broken lip. 'Did you tell my daughter about the box? Did you set her to destroying my son's trust in me by making him think I'd murder Navarre?'

His laugh came again, high-pitched and taunting, spraying blood. 'Yes! I did it all! And now you can vent your fury on me; now you can become the queen you were born to be: so powerful and fearsome you'll be remembered forever. I have always known who you are, though you never loved or believed in me.' He thrust his face at me. 'Or do you believe the lance that took your husband's life was an accident?'

I froze. 'No. That's . . . it cannot be true.'

His smile was macabre. 'Can't you feel it? It's all around us, every moment; it binds us forever. Every step you've taken since that fateful day was foretold. You will be queen until your death; you will save France from destruction; but the bloodline you fight with every breath to save, the barren seed that is your family – they are damned.'

Birago stood, trembling with fury. 'He is mad. We must bring in the torturer.'

I remembered the warning issued by Nostradamus years ago outside Chaumont: *He plays with evil. And evil he will wreak. It is his fate.* I met Cosimo's eyes. 'Either you tell me how to save my son or I promise before this day is done you will beg for my mercy.'

He whispered, 'I do not need mercy anymore. And there is nothing you can do. It is too late.'

'Then,' I said, 'it is too late for you.' I turned to Birago. 'Cut off his tongue and hands, so he can never practice his foul art again. If he survives, put him on a galley to Italy.'

I went to the door. Cosimo screamed, 'No! Don't leave me, my *duchessina*!'

This time, I did not look back.

At midnight Birago came to my rooms to report that Cosimo had perished during the ordeal, his body dumped in one of the pits outside the city, with nothing left to mark his passage.

He then asked of Charles. From my chair at the hearth, I said emotionlessly, 'Paré attends him. There is nothing more we can do. Go rest. You look tired. We'll speak tomorrow.'

'*Madama*,'he said softly, 'you cannot believe the ravings of that wretch. Your husband's death was an accident. You were there. You saw it.'

My breath caught in my throat. 'I can hear no more. Go now, please.'

He retreated, leaving me to stare into flames that whispered secrets.

You will save France from destruction; but the bloodline you fight with every breath to save, the barren seed that is your family – they are damned.

Cosimo had never been a seer, but in that moment I believed him. None of my sons had children. Though Charles had been married for over two years, his queen showed no sign of fertility. And when Charles died, only Henri would be left to safeguard the throne, for it was painfully clear the pox had corrupted Hercule and he could never rule. Like an animal in a maze, my mind kept returning to the day in Provence when Nostradamus told me each of my sons would reach adulthood. He had not said they'd die childless, and yet now that threat was before me, an inescapable reality I could not ignore.

If Henri failed to sire a son, Navarre would inherit. The future would hinge on a Huguenot prince who believed I was his foe, whose mother I was accused of poisoning, whose friends had been butchered in my palace, and whose conversion I had forced. Everything I had fought for, the legacy of peace I sought for France and my bloodline, would be crushed under his heel.

Forcing myself to my feet, I walked to the window to stare into the night. The windswept trees in the gardens wavered against a sable sky blurred by a thousand stars. Looking at the distant constellations, sparkling like ice, I wondered if I had struggled, plundered, and clawed my way through a labyrinth of my own making, when all along my future had been preordained.

I turned to my desk, gazed for what seemed an eternity at the sheaf of paper and quills.

You need each other to fulfill your destiny.

Then I sat down and wrote out my instructions.

Henri arrived two days later, dressed in dirty hunting gear.

'It's done.' He yanked off his gauntlets. 'I took him to where we'd sighted a stag in the forest the day before. I sent our men away to surround it, and once we were alone I turned to him and said, "Go. Before one of us decides to kill you."'

He stalked to my sideboard to pour a goblet of wine, downing it in a single gulp. 'No doubt he's halfway to his kingdom by now.' He set his goblet down, spun back to me. 'If you wanted to let him go free, why didn't you just send him away with Margot?'

'It had to look as if he fled. The Catholics, Guise: it's the only thing they'd accept.'

'Yes, and now I'm the fool who let him escape.' Henri stared at me. 'Why did you do this?'

I lifted my eyes. He knew me so well. Of all my children, he saw into me as none had. I fought against the urge to tell him everything, reminded myself why I had to deceive him. Charles was bedridden with fever, but the convulsions were abating; Paré thought he might yet live and frantically sought an antidote. Cosimo was dead; Margot locked in her rooms. I had to bury the truth. Henri must never know what Margot had done; he must be kept ignorant, free of all blame. And while I was so angry at Margot I could barely look at her, she was still Navarre's wife. She must be protected. If anyone was accused of poisoning Charles, let it be me.

'All you need to know,' I said carefully, 'is that you must leave France.'

He went pale. 'You . . . you want me to leave? Why?'

'Because Birago tells me many of the Huguenots who fled to Geneva after the massacre are now plotting to return and move against us. They blame you for the massacre as much as they do me and Guise. I want you out of harm's way. I shall write to your aunt Marguerite in Savoy; she'll be delighted to receive you. It's not only your welfare I'm concerned for; I'm sending Hercule away as well, as soon as I secure Elizabeth Tudor's agreement to receive him as her suitor.'

Henri grimaced. 'That'll be a sight to see, our Hercule pawing Elizabeth Tudor.' He looked at me intently. 'This is rather sudden. First, you have me shut up Navarre in Vincennes and then you tell me I must threaten his life to force his escape; now I hear Charles is gravely ill.' His eyes glinted. 'Why would you send me away when I might soon be king?'

I met his eyes. 'Charles is ill, yes, but he may have many years yet to live. You must heed me. You must go and wait for me to summon you. I beg you.' My voice caught. 'You . . . you cannot stay. If you do, you risk your life.'

His eyes narrowed. 'My life? How? And don't tell me again it's those damn Huguenots.'

'Not the Huguenots.' I lowered my gaze. 'It's your brother. Charles has more than a fever. Paré says he suffers from a derangement and thinks the dead haunt him for what we did.'

'Then let me talk to him. He's my brother. He must know I could hardly stop Guise and several thousand of his own Catholics hell-bent on slaughter.'

'No, you can't try to talk sense to him right now. He's not himself.

He's threatening to send you to England instead of Hercule.

I'd rather die than see you in that heretic isle. Elizabeth has opened her ports to our Huguenot refugees; her realm seethes with them. Any malcontent could do you harm.'

A frown creased his brow, to my relief. Much as he might feign otherwise, Henri was fully aware of the consequences of the massacre and I knew he was still furious at himself for ceding to Guise that night, for it made him look as if he'd willingly allowed thousands to die.

'Hercule had no part in it,' I continued, 'and so Elizabeth will play her usual coy game with him. But not with you; she has been told that you were at Coligny's house that night.'

'And that's all? There's nothing else?'

'No.' I forced out a smile. 'It'll only be for a short time, I promise. We can write every day.'

He hesitated a moment before he nodded. 'I suppose I could use some time away.' He chuckled. 'No doubt Savoy will be less funereal.' He kissed my cheek. 'I hope you know what you're doing with Navarre. God knows what he'll do once he feels safe again.'

'Indeed,' I said under my breath, and I watched him saunter out.

Left alone I sank into my chair. I did not think. I simply put my face in my hands and wept as I hadn't in years. I mourned a thousand losses: for the child I'd been and the family I'd left behind, for the country I barely recalled anymore and the country I now fought to save. I wept for my dead children and my living ones, who'd grown up infected by the poisonous hatred of our religious wars. I wept for my friends and my enemies; for all the lost hopes and illusions.

But most of all, I wept for myself and the woman I had become.

Two months later I sat at Charles's bedside as he coughed up pieces of his lungs. He had not yet turned twenty-four, but Cosimo's poison had slowly done its work, rotting him from the inside out so that he lay drenched in sweat tinged with his own blood.

His fingers clutched mine. His eyes were closed, his chest barely lifting with each shallow breath. Earlier he'd signed a document bestowing on me the regency until Henri returned. His wife, Isabel, was already in mourning, anchored at her prie-dieu; only Birago and I, and his faithful hound at his feet, attended him as he drifted in and out of consciousness.

A little after four in the afternoon, his fever abated. As fitful rain pattered against the château walls, he opened his eyes and looked at me. He whispered, 'Forgive me.'

PART VII
1574–1588
The Beloved

33

I paced my chamber in the palace at Lyons, kicking against the gem-encrusted hem of my burgundy velvet gown, turning back to the window every time I heard clamor in the courtyard.

Autumn had come to France. Burnished leaves hung on the oaks and opal splendor bathed the hills. Four months had passed since Charles's death – four long and difficult months, during which I'd buried him, sent his widow to Chenonceau, and labored to secure the realm. Now I had received word that Henri had passed through Avignon and moved up the Rhône, escorted by Hercule, whose importance had grown since becoming our new heir.

Soon my beloved son would claim his throne.

I turned from the window to see Birago shuffle in with his ubiquitous portfolios. I grimaced as he set them on my desk. I should have felt compassion; Charles's death had left him bereaved and greatly aged, and he sought to assuage his grief by devoting his every waking hour to work. But I was in no mood today for his mournful visage or litany of responsibilities I must attend to.

'Whatever it is can wait,' I said to him.

'But these dispatches are from England. Queen Elizabeth demands we join her in protesting further Spanish aggression in the Low Countries. She says –'

'She'll not allow Hercule to pay her suit unless we throw our gauntlet into the ring. She's been delaying our request for months with the same excuse. If she so wants our support against Spain, let her give something in return.'

'But this trouble could spill over into France. We cannot –'

I stamped my foot. 'Do I look as if I'm dressed for the Council?'

Birago drew himself erect, or as erect as he could get these days. 'Forgive me. I see I've come at an inopportune time. It seems affairs of state must wait.'

He limped out. Lucrezia freed my veil from a snag on my ruff. 'I feel like a veal haunch at a banquet,' I groaned. 'Is all this truly necessary?'

'Absolutely. Do you want His Majesty to see his mother in her old widow's weeds?'

'I don't care. I just want him to arrive and –'

Cannon salvos drowned out my voice. My women hurried behind me as I charged into the corridor, moving with more speed than my girth and cumbersome gown should have permitted.

As I emerged into the courtyard, I spied Margot with her women. She wore a nectarine silk gown with a ruff so wide it framed her head, her face powdered and her elaborate coiffure sprouting plumes, her throat and bosom glittering with tourmalines. I'd released her from captivity in her rooms but insisted she be attended by a posse of stern matrons chosen by me.

'That gown is becoming,' I said as I went up to her. My fury against her had started to ebb; Charles was dead, and with Navarre gone she dwelled in limbo, a wife and queen in name alone. Nothing could excuse her behavior, but I knew well how bitter disillusionment can be.

She gave me a sarcastic smile. 'I might as well dress up, seeing as the entire court looks at me as though I were some pitiful widow. Poor Margot, they whisper, abandoned by her husband, without even a child of his to call her own.' She paused, her chin lifting slightly as she realized she'd just confessed an inner weakness to me. 'Speaking of which, have you heard from my husband? I understand he reached his kingdom to his subjects' great rejoicing and renounced his conversion. He's a Huguenot again. I wonder how long it'll be before he declares war on us.'

I wanted to feel sympathy for her, but of course she would never allow it. 'Why should he?' I retorted. 'He 's next in line to the throne after Hercule. I should think he 'd want to retain good relations with us.' I pinched her arm. 'And let me warn you now: no more mischief. I've kept your secret and now I want you to let Henri reign in peace.'

'Oh, you needn't worry about my secret,' she riposted, 'not when Henri has a secret of his own to keep.' Leaving me with these cryptic words, she swept back to her matrons.

She was impossible; no matter how hard I tried, she never failed to get a rise out of me. I deliberately dismissed her from my thoughts as I strained to see past the sea of courtiers. I would not let her mar my good mood. I was fifty-five and had endured many losses. Today was my glory. Today all things were possible.

Henri III was here. At last, we would have a king worthy of France.

Sensing my joy, Lucrezia said, 'We can go closer to the gates if you like, so you'll be the first to welcome him.'

'No.' Tears stung my eyes. 'Let him enjoy this moment. It belongs to him.'

But when I finally caught sight of him riding into the courtyard with his gentlemen, so proud and erect in his saddle, I couldn't contain myself. I shouldered through the crowd, my arms outstretched. 'Henri, *mon fils*! Henri!'

He dismounted and I flung myself into his embrace, inhaling an unfamiliar musk. His dark hair tumbled in a perfumed wave from his cap, his body taut as a lyre under his violet doublet. I clasped his face as he kissed me on my lips. '*Chère Maman*,' he murmured, and with his arms about me he turned to the waiting crowd. 'Today,' he declared in a ringing voice, 'I pay homage to my mother, who has steered this realm past many shoals so I might live to see this hour.'

And as everyone broke into applause, I let my tears fall unheeded down my cheeks.

We returned to Paris, traveling in procession so that the people could see Henri. He rode at the head of the cavalcade like the king I'd always dreamed he would be, dressed in mauve brocade shot with silver tissue, his gestures regal yet expansive as he greeted the multitudes thronging the sides of the road to cry out: '*Vive Henri III! Vive le roi!*'

In the Louvre I held a banquet in his honor, festooning the hall with evergreen boughs, the symbol of constancy. I sat on the dais beside him and Hercule; at either side of us in the hall stretched adjoining tables occupied by Guise, whom I'd allowed back to court in honor of Henri's accession; Monsignor, his uncle; and our other Catholic nobles. Margot presided over a separate table with the noblemen's wives and other prominent ladies of the court.

Henri sat on his throne, a coronet on his brow. He was generous with the courtiers who lined up to greet him, recalling their names with an accuracy that reminded me of his grandfather, François I. We dined on roast boar, swan, peacock, and pheasant; after the feast, a troupe of dwarves enacted a comedic play. At its conclusion, Henri motioned and his bodyguard Guast tossed a pouch of coins. The dwarves dove to the floor, losing their wigs as they fought among themselves for the largesse, causing more uproarious laughter.

Henri yawned. 'In Savoy, everyone of rank retains a theater group. No one keeps fools anymore.' He turned to Hercule, who gaped at the quarreling female dwarves as if he might eat them. 'What do you think, little ape? Should we dismiss the fools?' His tone was affectionate; he had never showed any malice toward Hercule, but my youngest son flushed hotly and spat, 'I'm not your little ape anymore. I'm the dauphin now!'

Henri smiled, returning his gaze to the crowded hall. The musicians tuned their instruments. As the courtiers began selecting partners for the upcoming dance, he abruptly said: 'Monsignor, a word about Madame de Lorraine-Vaudémont.'

I had no idea whom he spoke of. From his other side, Monsignor inclined his emaciated face to me, betraying he eavesdropped on everything. 'His Majesty refers to my cousin of Lorraine, whom he met recently in Savoy, where she serves as lady-in-waiting to the duchess.'

'Yes, she was enchanting,' Henri said. 'I'd like to bring her to court. See to it.'

'I would be honored,' replied Monsignor, mellifluous as always when he gleaned an advantage. He may have lost most of his teeth and his hair, but his mind still clicked like a well-oiled machine, and I started to lean to Henri to inquire further about this Madame de Lorraine-Vaudémont when I saw him slide his gaze to Guast, who hovered like a rugged shadow at the foot of the dais. Henri let out another yawn. 'I'm so tired. I believe I will retire.'

'But the dancing,' I protested. 'The court expects you to open the floor.'

'Let Hercule do it. He can dance with Margot.' Before I could detain him, he rose and descended the dais, walking from the hall with Guast close behind him.

I avoided Monsignor's pointed stare, my disquiet increasing as I searched for Margot. She'd abandoned her table for a couch near the pilasters, where she reclined surrounded by admirers.

As if she felt my stare, she lifted her eyes and gave me a cold, knowing look.

I rose before dawn. Henri and I were scheduled to discuss the agenda for his first Council meeting later in the week, and after a hasty breakfast I gathered my portfolio and met Birago in the corridor. He was leaning on his cane, his lined face revealing his discomfort.

'Your foot is badly swollen,' I said. 'Is it the gout again?'

He grimaced. 'I fear I ate too much at the banquet. But I took a draft and –'

'And you must rest today,' I interrupted. I held up my hand as he started to protest. 'No. Go back to bed, old friend. It's just a private meeting with my son. I'll come see you afterward.'

He assented gratefully and limped off, while I made my way to my son's apartments. Rounding the gallery into the royal suite, I found a guard at Henri's door.

'His Majesty has not yet risen,' he told me. 'He gave orders that he wasn't to be disturbed.'

'Well, it's time he got up. Move aside.' He knew better than to detain me and I strode into my son's antechamber to find the room submerged in dim shadow, the rising sun seeping under the edges of the curtains at the windows. A decanter and two goblets sat on the table; a half-open door in the wainscoting led into the bedchamber. I stepped toward it in sudden apprehension; it was so quiet I could hear snoring from within. Peeking inside, I saw the bed directly in front of me, its scarlet tester curtains open, revealing Guast's muscular nude body in slumber, one of his hirsute arms thrown over rumpled pillows.

Stifling a gasp, I started to step back.

A sound spun me around. Henri came toward me from an alcove in the antechamber. He wore a loose white silk robe, his thick hair tumbling about his shoulders. Without his court finery, he looked younger than his twenty-three years, though the chest I glimpsed under his parted robe was chiseled, dusted with curly dark hair just like his father's.

'What are you doing here?' he said, and there was a humiliated anger in his voice.

'Never mind that,' I replied. 'You should have locked the door. What . . . what is this?'

He stepped past me and pushed the bedroom door shut. 'I left orders with my guard. You are the only one bold enough to ignore them.' He moved to the table, reaching for the decanter. As he poured a goblet, he looked up at me. 'As for what "this" is, I think you know by now.'

I clutched the portfolio to my chest, dumbfounded.

He drank from the goblet, his eyes fixed on me. 'Well? Aren't you going to say something?'

I didn't want to ask. I didn't want to face it. He'd always been dauntless – fierce in war and his pride of place, worthy to bear his father's name. He had been the most gifted student of the family, more disciplined than Margot, quicker than Elisabeth, more avid than Charles. I believed he had the best of the Medici-Valois blood and had staked my hope on him, thinking that at long last France had a strong king. He'd made mistakes; he was impulsive and headstrong, but he was young and could learn restraint. And just as with his brothers, I was here to guide him.

But I had never envisioned this.

'How . . . how long?' I finally managed to utter.

'For as long as I can remember.' He moved to the window to pull back the curtains. Brilliant light flooded the room. He turned back to me. 'I met Guast during my first campaign against the Huguenots, if you recall. He helped me through a . . . very difficult time. Since then, he has been my companion. Were it not for him, I might have fallen prey to one of those Huguenot assassins you say are so eager to spill my blood.' He paused. 'Guast is the most loyal person in my life, after you. I want to give him a title. He deserves a reward for all his care of me.'

'You cannot,' I said at once. 'Everyone will know. Put him up in a country château; pay for his expenses out of your privy purse, but not here, not at court.' As these words escaped me, I marveled at myself. Here I stood on the day after my son's arrival, confronted by something I had no practice dealing with, and already I was thinking of ways to hide his secret.

'Maman,' he said softly, 'you, of all people, must know how impossible it is to forsake those we love.'

I heard Margot sneer in my ear: *Henri has a secret of his own to keep.*

'Love?' I echoed. 'You love him . . . ?'

'Indeed, or at least as much as we can love anyone. Margot is right, you know, hateful as she can be: when she lost Guise, she told me we are not like other people. She said we can't truly love because we 're incapable of giving without always expecting something in return.' He gazed at the closed bedroom door. 'There was a time when I thought I could love that way, but I was wrong. Still, what I offer, Guast accepts. I suppose that qualifies in some manner as love.'

'This is my fault.' I lowered my eyes, feeling a deep inner pain I'd never admitted aloud. 'I was not there during your or your sister's childhood to show you how much I cared. I should have never let Diane raise you. I should have fought that she-wolf for you.'

'I do not blame you,' he replied, with an understanding that made me want to weep. 'Besides, no one did this to me. No one is at fault. There are many men like me.'

A knot formed in my chest. 'What do you think the court will say? The ambassadors, the nobles? Do you think they'll understand?' My voice quavered as I tried in vain to hold back my emotion. 'Our enemies will use this against you; they'll see it as a weakness. Think of Guise: he's our premier Catholic lord now and the church forbids –'

Henri's face and voice sharpened. 'Don't cite Guise or the church to me. I've bathed in tears for the one and blood for the other. I'm done proving myself. I am king now and I will rule in deed as well as name – me, and no one else.'

I went still. 'I . . . I don't understand.'

'Let me explain.' He guided me to a chair. The portfolio slipped from my fingers. After pouring claret into a goblet, he pressed it into my hand and bent over to retrieve the portfolio. He set it on the table and knelt before me in a swirl of his robe, taking my other hand and regarding me with such tenderness I felt tears fill my eyes.

'What I mean,' he said gently, 'is that I am not my brother Charles. I want to rule on my own, Maman. I am king of France now. I need to make my own decisions.'

I felt faint, sitting utterly quiet as he lifted my hand to his lips in a brief kiss. 'You must be so tired,' he went on. 'You've spent the last fifteen years fighting to save us all from destruction. You lost Papa, two sons, and many friends; it is time you surrendered your burden. I am king now. Isn't this what you want: a son who can rule the country you've sacrificed so much for?'

I nodded numbly, the goblet untasted in one hand, my other limp beneath his.

'I know why you are afraid,' he said. 'I know that is why you let Navarre escape. You wanted him safe, in case we should fail. While he is wed to Margot, there is still hope he might convert again, should the time come for him to inherit.'

I flinched. He hushed me. 'Don't deny it. I don't reproach

you. You love France and both of my brothers died without heirs. Hercule is unfit, and now you think I'll disdain my duty. But you needn't fear. I've no intention of letting my love for Guast interfere with my reason. In fact, I will wed as soon as possible and get my wife with child, so no one can question my manhood. For no matter what they think, I am a man. I have the tools like any other.'

Once again, he'd seen right through me. I had thought to conceal the truth with intrigue and lies, and in the end I had hid nothing. The only thing I'd managed to keep from him was Margot's terrible act of revenge against us.

'Think of it.' He smiled. 'You'll soon have a grandson of our blood, not a half-breed with a heretic for a father. I've even chosen my bride: I will wed Louise de Lorraine-Vaudémont.'

'But she's a Guise,' I exclaimed. 'You cannot bring her family back into our lives.'

'She 's not a Guise; she 's descended of the house of Lorraine, niece to my own sister Claude's husband. She's lived in Savoy since she was twelve. She barely knows the Guises.' He pressed my hand, silencing my next protest. 'And she understands. We spent time together in Savoy and she knows about me. She told me I'd do her honor by making her my queen and she 'll do everything to prove her worth. All she needs to do is bear a son; and if there's one thing you can say about the Guise-Lorraine families it's that they do not lack for children.'

He had already discussed this with Louise. He had planned it even before he arrived. My mind spun; I felt as though I'd just stepped off a precipice into the unknown. I knew instinctually that if I resisted, if I tried to dissuade him, I'd achieve only his mistrust. This was his first official act as a king and I must honor it, difficult as it might be.

I set my goblet aside and leaned to him, taking his face between my hands, inhaling his scent of musk mixed with the expensive ambergris he used in his hair.

'Are you truly certain about this girl?' I asked.

He nodded. 'Will you see to it, Maman? Will you do me the

honor of arranging my marriage? I can think of no one better
suited to the task.'

I looked into his eyes, so dark and expressive, so like my own
in my youth it was as though I gazed into a mirror. 'Yes,' I said.
'I'll take care of it. You rest now. Go back to your Guast.'

He kissed me and stood. As I pulled myself up and reached
for the portfolio, which contained my recommendations for his
Council, he said, 'Leave it. I'll look it over later.'

I smiled and left, and made my way straight to Birago's rooms.
He was on his couch, a skullcap on his liver-spotted pate, his
portable desk at his side, immersed in work as always.

I told him everything. When I finished, he sat quiet for a spell
before he said, 'Perhaps it's for the best.'

I stared at him. 'You can't be serious. He wants to marry a
Guise!'

'Technically, as he told you, she's a Lorraine. And she's hardly
a threat.'

'Oh? And what if he's wrong? What if Monsignor takes her
under his wing, like he did with Mary Stuart?' I lowered my voice.
'She knows about Henri; he told me so himself. Together with
Monsignor, she could make him a laughingstock, turn this entire
court upside down.'

'*Madama,* I trust Monsignor no more than you but Louise de
Lorraine-Vaudémont brings nothing to this marriage save her
person. And men of Henri's predilection are not incapable of the
act with a woman. Were it so, half the marriages in this world
would be childless.'

I looked hard at him, wondering if I'd failed to note the same
affinity in him. I'd never heard a single hint of impropriety in all
the years he had served me and I'd come to see him as a gender-
less being, though of course he must have had needs. The thought
that I might not know my intimate as well as I supposed brought
a curt laugh to my lips.

'You honestly think she'll turn a blind eye every time Guast
takes her place in Henri's bed?'

'Yes. Every royal union is the same, regardless of the spouses' tastes, and serves the same purpose: to breed heirs. After His Majesty, Prince Hercule is next in line to the throne and we know he can never rule or sire children; after him, there is Navarre. Under other circumstances I'd agree Louise is less than ideal, but we need this time to bring stability to the realm. There is a new king on the throne; our deficit is immense, the harvest poor, and the Huguenots sneak back over our borders. We can't afford to argue his choice of a queen, so long as he has one.'

'You try my patience,' I said tersely. 'I know all too well how much we endure. Have I not been at the helm of this country these many years?'

'*Madama,* no one questions your devotion. But we now have a king of age to rule and he must do so.' He paused. 'It is always difficult for the lioness to let her cub leave the pride but in the end she must. And the cub must learn to be a lion in his own right. What the king needs now are experienced advisers to guide him and a queen who'll take what he can give. But if you try to thwart him, he could dig his heels in. Remember Charles; we can't afford the same mistake.'

I scowled. 'Very well, but only after you find out everything you can about her. And she comes alone, without favors, and without brothers and uncles seeking favors. I won't have the entire Guise-Lorraine clan invading this court. Understood?'

'Perfectly. What of Monsignor? He'll expect a seat on the Council for this.'

'He can expect alms from beggars. After he brings her, he will return to his diocese and tend to his flock. I'll not abide him in my presence. The only Guise I trust is a dead one.'

Six days later the cardinal himself came to say good-bye.

I dined in my apartments when the chill overcame me. I looked up to see him standing at the wall, his translucent figure wavering like red smoke against the tapestry. He lifted a hand. I glimpsed a sardonic smile on his face. Then I blinked and he was gone.

Lucrezia shuddered, went to close the draperies at the window. 'I feel a draft.'

'It wasn't a draft,' I said. 'Monsignor is dead.'

My ladies went still. I continued with my supper.

The next morning word came that Monsignor had caught a fever on his way to Savoy and taken to his bed. At the very hour I'd seen him, he died. He was forty-nine years old.

I didn't grieve his passing; I was not that much of a hypocrite. But I liked to think that in coming to see me, he had finally acknowledged my victory.

34

We held my son's coronation in February; two days later, he wed Louise de Lorraine-Vaudémont.

Birago's investigation had uncovered an astonishing virtuousness. Even Claude, who'd recently given birth to her second daughter and couldn't attend the wedding owing to a mild case of fever, endorsed Louise. Our twenty-one-year-old bride had led a sheltered life; she'd been a companion for her father before his death and then departed for Savoy to attend my own sister-in-law, Marguerite.

I had nothing to object to, save her connection to the Guise family. Still, as she came down the aisle to the altar, a fine-boned girl clad in lavender, I wondered how she would hold any lasting appeal for my son. Nevertheless, Henri seemed genuinely delighted with her, plucking a pink rose from the garland overhead to tuck into her fair hair. Color flushed her cheeks; she lifted her brown eyes adoringly to him as he kissed her and the court burst into applause.

From across the aisle, Birago caught my eye and winked.

After the wedding, I dedicated the summer to the selection of the Council with Henri, while Birago guided him without remonstration, so obsequious that my son didn't appear to realize that he was in fact under tutelage. Despite my initial apprehension, Guast remained in the background, even after he had gained his title and a lavish new wardrobe, while Louise garnered praise for her quiet dignity. Birago reported that my son visited her bed at least twice a week.

In late July, word arrived that my daughter Claude's health was failing. She was only twenty-seven, but the ordeal of giving birth

and ongoing struggle with childbed fever had taken their toll. I
made immediate plans to go to her. At the last minute, as Lucrezia
and I mounted my coach, Margot appeared with valise in hand.
'My sister is ill,' she said. 'I wish to see her.'

I bit back the retort that she'd never cared for Claude before.
In fact, my second daughter had led such a quiet life in Lorraine,
far from our entanglements, at times we forgot her altogether.

When we arrived at her home, Claude was resting; not wishing
to disturb her, I had her worried husband show me to my rooms.
As I sat on a padded chair, my aching feet propped on a stool
while Lucrezia unpacked my coffers, he brought in little Christina
and Charles, my daughter Claude 's two eldest children.

Four-year-old Christina was a replica of Claude at that age, with
the same plump body and doe-brown eyes. Her brother Charles
took after the Lorraine-Guise side with his slim height, a rash of
adolescent pimples marring his pensive face. I could see they were
awed by their legendary grandmother, of whom they'd no doubt
heard many tales, but then Christina abruptly wrapped chubby
arms about my neck. 'Grandmaman, you're so old!'

She couldn't possibly remember me. Though I'd sent gifts and
money for the children every year, never forgetting a birthday or
Christmas, I'd never seen them, for when Claude came on her
rare visits to court, they stayed behind. Nonetheless, Christina's
innocent declaration brought tears to my eyes. Then Charles
cleared his throat and said, 'Welcome, Madame Grand-mère.'

I gave him a smile. 'My child, you're so big. Almost a man, eh?
Come, I've some presents for you.' My granddaughter beamed.
I said, 'Lucrezia, show Christina her new dress. I believe it's the
perfect shade for her complexion.'

As Christina squealed over the rose velvet dress my women
had created for her out of one of my court gowns, Anna-Maria
brought me a volume bound in maroon Florentine leather that
I'd ordered made in Italy especially for Charles, its cover inscribed
with his name in gold leaf.

I handed it to him. '*The Prince* by Machiavelli,' I told him. 'My
favorite book. I think you are of age now to appreciate its wisdom.'

He fingered the book as if it were a jewel. 'Thank you,' he breathed, his eyes glowing just as my own late son's, his namesake, had when given a new falcon or pet hound. Only this Charles was clearly a scholar; the veneration with which he retreated to the window to open the book demonstrated he would never find satisfaction in swords or armor.

I leaned back against my chair and closed my eyes, content with the simple joy of having children about me again.

Later that evening I went to see Claude. I took one look at her emaciated form and placid smile and my heart sank. Still, I tutted over her, dug out my battered pot and herbs and commenced to cook up rhubarb drafts, while Lucrezia marshaled the servants.

Every morning for two months I awoke, bathed my daughter, and assisted her to a chair at the window overlooking the gardens. Sometimes, I read to her aloud. Other times we sat as she gazed into the gardens, smiling when she heard her young daughter laughing with Margot.

'Margot is so full of life, like a child herself,' Claude said to me. 'She'd be a good mother. You must see that she reunites with her husband. She needs a child of her own.'

I smiled, blinking back tears at the thought of how perceptive she was and how little any of us had truly known her.

One afternoon in August, I awoke from a doze to find her eyes fixed on me. Never beautiful, she had acquired an evanescent grace, her large grayish eyes overpowering her fragile face. In a quiet voice, she said, 'I'm tired, Maman.'

My throat knotted. I was about to lose this daughter of mine, whom I'd paid least attention to, whose stoic devotion to her family had spared her the excesses of ours. I belatedly saw that of all of us Claude had been the wisest. She'd known best how to escape the pain and fury that characterized our lives.

I started to rise, to help her back to bed. She shook her head. 'No, I want to stay here by the window. Call the others.'

One by one they filed in: her bereaved husband, who loved her as few men love their wives; her favorite servants; the devoted nursemaid who cared for her infant daughter, Antoinette, and her son Charles, his chin quivering. Christina played in my rooms with Anna-Maria, for I would not let her witness this; it was too traumatic for such a young child.

Then, as I stood gripping Lucrezia's hand, Margot entered, bringing me the memory of her and Claude when they were girls in the nurseries, the one bold, always hungry for acclaim, the other stolid and plain, content to stay in the shadows.

'I was never a sister to you,' Margot said as she knelt before Claude. 'Please forgive me.'

'There is nothing to forgive.' Claude placed her hand on Margot's cheek. 'You must be kind to Maman. Respect and support her, for you are her only daughter now. Promise me.'

'I . . . I promise.' Margot turned away. She met my eyes and for a brief moment we reunited.

We waited together. Toward dusk, Claude kissed her husband and closed her eyes.

After the funeral, at my insistence, Claude's husband took his children to their grandparents' home near the Guise family seat in Joinville. Left in the house with the servants, Lucrezia, Margot, and I packed up Claude's belongings as a donation in her name to the convent of St. Claire, which she had patronized.

The night before our departure, I stood in my rooms overseeing the packing of my coffers when my gift stirred. I went still, my hand poised in midair; around me, the walls dissolved.

I stand in a torchlit corridor outside the great hall; I can hear the strumming of lutes and thumping of kettledrums interspersed with laughter and though I cannot see them I know the court revels. I look about. Why am I here? Then I catch sight of six men coming toward me in masks and hooded cloaks, led by a broad-shouldered figure whose face I can't see under his mask. Beside him, his own cloak bunched over his hump, is Hercule. They move past me; I catch a gleam in Hercule's eyes as he glances at the leader, the flush of anticipation on his pitted features. I reach out to grab him, but my hands pass through him as if he were made of smoke.

They enter the crowded hall. On the dais Henri lounges on his throne, wearing a gorgeous red and gold doublet. He's smiling, watching someone; I follow his gaze and see Guast blindfolded in the center of the hall while laughing court jades turn him round and round. Guast's hands splay out as he tries to snag one of the jades. In the revelry, no one notices the men nor do they see the leader motion Hercule forward. But the jades draw back, their laughter faltering, when Hercule plucks off the blindfold and smiles into Guast's astonished face.

'Time to die,' my son says, and as my mouth opens to yell a warning, the jades shriek and Hercule yanks out a dagger from his cloak. Guast throws up his arms. The blade catches the light before Hercule plunges it to the hilt into Guast's stomach.

Silence falls. Hercule stands, panting, his black hair sticking up like quills. Guast looks in disbelief at the knife in his gut. Black blood gushes from the wound and he crumples to the floor.

Henri's scream rends the air; as he staggers from the dais, the leader gestures and the other men yank Hercule away. The courtiers follow in a stampede, until only Henri is left, alone.

I see him drop beside Guast, heedless of the blood pooling around him . . .

My chamber rushed in around me like a deluge. I was on my knees, my own cupped hands extended before me. Lucrezia bent over me, her pallid features frightened. 'My lady, what is it?'

'God help us,' I whispered. 'Hercule has killed Guast.'

We reached the Louvre at midnight, after two frantic days of travel. In the courtyard, torches sputtered against a miasmic fog. As we dismounted and grooms raced forth to collect our baggage, I told Margot to go straight to her rooms, while I moved into the palace.

It felt deserted. I saw no courtiers pass as I trod the dimly lit passages, heard no sounds. The air was cold, still; guided by the sconces at intervals on the walls and silent guards flanking the gallery, I made my way to the royal apartments, where, to my relief, I found Birago waiting.

'I've been here since it happened,' he said, his face waxen with fatigue. 'He's locked the bedchamber from the inside and won't let anyone in.'

'And Hercule . . . ?' I whispered.

'Fled the court. I've sent out search parties but thus far no one knows where he is.'

'Keep looking. He can't have gone far.' I drew my cloak closer about me. 'See that the fires are lit and then bring up a hot meal.' I waved my hand at him. 'Go. I'll take care of this.'

'*Madama*,' he said, 'you should know: the body . . . it's still in there with him.'

I nodded, biting back a shudder as I went to the bedchamber door and knocked, overcome by a vivid memory of the last time I'd been here and seen Guast sleeping naked in the bed.

There was no answer. I knocked again, louder this time, hearing it echo as though the entire palace was empty. 'Henri,' I said. 'It's me. I am here. Open the door, my son.'

I discerned muffled movement, the metallic clank of something being kicked aside, and then he spoke, his voice devoid of emotion. 'Go away.'

'No. Henri, please. Let me in. I . . . I want to see him.'

There was a long silence. I started to think I'd have to order the door broken down. Then I heard the key turn in the lock. Seizing a nearby candle in its holder, I pushed open the door.

Despite the cold, the stench hit me with a visceral force. I caught sight of an unlit candelabrum on the sideboard, went to touch my candle flame to the candelabrum's tapers; as the tapers flared, chasing away the shadows, I saw Henri on the edge of the bed, his lank hair falling over his face. He wore a shimmering red and gold doublet, the same one I'd seen in my vision, only the sleeves were undone and his chemise cuffs hung shredded and bloodied over his wrists.

Laid out on the bed behind him was Guast's bloating corpse.

My heart cracked in two.

'He . . . he didn't say good-bye,' Henri said in a bewildered voice. 'I kept telling him, he couldn't leave without saying good-bye . . .' He lifted his face; I almost couldn't bear to look into his haunted eyes. 'Why, Maman? Why would they do this to him?'

'I don't know,' I murmured and I stepped to him. 'My son, you must say good-bye. He will hear you, even if he can't respond. Then we can bury him as –'

He moaned, covering his face with his hands. 'I can't! I can't let him go into the dark. He hates the dark. He . . . he always wants a candle left by the bed at night.'

'We'll put one with him,' I said, and my voice sounded so calm, even as I battled my sorrow that he must endure this grief and suffer the kind of loss that never truly goes away. 'Come with me.' I reached out. His fingers were slack, icy; he had dried blood on them. I imagined him carrying Guast from the hall, up the staircase, through the gallery to this room . . .

His hand tightened on mine. 'I want them all arrested and put in the Bastille – Hercule and his savages, all those involved. But most of all, I want Navarre.'

I froze, met his distended stare. 'How – how do you know?'

He rose, went to his sideboard, and retrieved something. He held it out to me: it was the dagger that had killed Guast. There were bloodstains along the length of the blade; forged on its hilt, to my disbelief, were Navarre's interlocked chains in silver.

'It's his emblem,' Henri said, and his voice turned cold. 'He set the little ape to it, but it was his deed. He did it. He killed my Guast. I want revenge.'

Without a word, I reached for the dagger; it felt heavy in my hands. When I heard someone cough discreetly behind us, I turned with a startled gasp. It was Birago, carrying a covered tray. As the smell of hot food wafted to us, tears started in Henri's eyes. Leaning on me, he let me guide him from the fetid room as if I were the last thing in his world he could hold on to.

Hours later, as dawn broke over the frozen winter sky, I returned to my rooms. Dosed with rhubarb and poppy by Dr. Paré, Henri had been put to bed in another chamber far from his own, while Birago took charge of Guast's body and the cleansing of the king's apartments.

Lucrezia and Anna-Maria were waiting for me. So was Margot;

she sat on a footstool cradling my decrepit sixteen-year-old Muet in her arms. As I entered slowly, so tired I swayed on my feet, Margot set Muet on her cushion. 'Hercule is at Chambord,' she said. 'I let it be known in certain quarters that I wanted to speak to him. A few bribes were all it took.'

I eyed her. I had learned the hard way that Margot never acted without a reason. Why would she voluntarily bring me this information? 'Chambord is a hunting château,' I said. 'It's always empty this time of year. Why would he go there alone?'

'Because he 's not alone. He has others with him. Chambord can accommodate them.'

'Others? Exactly how many are there?'

'Rumor has it he's raised an army and he intends to use it against Henri.' Though she feigned impartiality, for the first time since her terrible act of vengeance I heard a tremor of fear in her voice. 'Hercule is an idiot,' she said. 'He doesn't realize what he's doing. I . . . I don't want him harmed. There's been enough blood spilled in this family already.'

'Is that so?' I met her stare. 'Well then, tomorrow we will go to Chambord. And I suggest that if you truly care about Hercule, you'll find a way to make him see reason before it is too late.'

35

Escorted by guards, we traveled to the Loire Valley. I questioned Margot at length and found no hidden motivation, no reason other than a genuine desire to save Hercule from Henri's wrath. I wondered if our shared grief over Claude had opened her eyes to the fact that we were all she had, that without us she truly would be alone. This bond she'd developed with Hercule since the massacre defied explanation, but I took her concern for him as a sign she wasn't as heartless as she seemed. Hercule had suffered since childhood, pitted by the pox, a figure of ridicule at court, now thrust into a position he was unfit to occupy. Recalling the words she'd let slip to me on the day of Henri's return, I wondered if maybe she saw something of herself in her younger brother, for in certain ways she too was an outsider, married but without a husband, childless and adrift in a world where she could no longer play the part of pampered muse.

Whatever the case, I needed her now. If anyone could talk sense into Hercule, it was she – a thought that was reinforced when our coach came up the road to François I's hunting preserve and I beheld a sea of tents and hundreds of men mingling outside the château.

The coach came to a jarring stop. Margot and I dismounted before a leering battalion. There were more men here than I'd ever imagined Hercule capable of gathering – enough to siege a city. I smelled unwashed flesh, gauged rapacious eyes. Society's dregs, who thrived in back alleys, willing to commit any crime for a price: this was my son's army, a larcenous band of impoverished foreign mercenaries, footpads, killers, and common thieves. Even with his allowance, Hercule didn't have nearly enough funds to satisfy this despicable lot.

I paused. Someone with means had definitely paid for this. Could it be Navarre? Ever since I'd seen the dagger, I'd been suspicious. He had never struck me as reckless; and the hooded men and now this band of thieves: it felt staged, as if I was deliberately being led down a false path.

Inside the château, broken casks and flagons, gristle and bones, were strewn over the inlaid floors; the walls were stained from the smoke of open fires, our prized tapestries torn down and used for bedding. Rangy hounds scavenged in the detritus.

Margot pointed. Turning about, I saw Hercule coming toward us, looking even more dwarfish within Chambord's immense vaulted hall. I half expected him to start stammering that he hadn't done anything on purpose, that he'd been forced to do it, but he maintained a stubborn silence until I said coldly, 'Your brother is furious and so am I. What possessed you?'

His face colored. We stood inches apart. Tensing his shoulders, he muttered as if by rote, 'If you threaten me, I'll march my army on Paris.'

I guffawed. 'You'll do no such thing! You will dismiss your so-called army and come back to court to beg forgiveness on your knees.'

He glowered; Margot stepped between us. 'Hercule, listen to me: you cannot send an army against Henri; it would be treason.'

His mouth worked. When he finally spoke, he blurted his words at me as if he feared he might not be able to say them, 'I'll dismiss my men when I get the recognition I deserve.'

I knew at once these were not his words; he didn't have the nerve. He'd been primed by someone with more of a stake in this than the murder of a favorite. No one would have spent this kind of money or time preying on Hercule's sense of inferiority without an ulterior motive.

'How dare you think you can dictate to me?' I said in a low voice.

He chewed his lower lip, glancing at Margot. I'd had enough. Grabbing him by the arm, I yanked him to the nearest window alcove, shoved him onto the seat, and stood over him. 'Where is your paymaster now, eh? Do you think he cares anything for you? He'll use you to his purpose and once he's done he'll sacrifice you without a thought. Who is he?' I thrust my face at him. 'Tell me this instant. Who is he? Why is he doing this?'

He flinched, his eyes bulging. Margot hustled to us. 'Stop it! Can't you see he's scared?'

'Good,' I retorted. 'He should be. He has no idea of what I might do.'

Her voice fractured. 'Leave him be! He's not to blame. He didn't —'

'Guise,' whispered Hercule. I turned slowly to him. 'Guise told me to kill Henri's friend.'

I went cold. Margot started to hush Hercule; I thrust out a hand, detaining her. She glared, but Hercule was already talking, desperate to unburden himself. 'Guise came to me. He said Henri sins against God and nature. He said France would never abide a catamite king or a heretic to succeed him. He told me I would be rewarded. He . . . he even gave me the dagger.'

Tears spilled from his eyes; though he tried not to, I saw his gaze shift to Margot, who went stiff as stone.

I looked at her. 'Did you know about this?'

She flinched. 'Of course not. I was with you, at my sister's deathbed. Would you accuse me of wielding the knife when I wasn't even in Paris?'

I held her gaze. 'Henri wants to put Hercule in the Bastille. If you knew anything about this and you kept it from me, I assure you, you will join him there.'

'No!' Hercule scrambled from the window seat to fall at my feet. He grabbed my legs, wrapping his arms about me as he started to sob like the deluded child he was at heart.

Margot said haltingly, 'I told you, I don't know anything.'

I reached down, pulled my son to his feet. I wiped his tear-stained face with my sleeve. 'Don't cry. I'll keep you safe but you must tell me what Guise promised you.'

His eyes widened. 'You promise you won't let Henri put me in the Bastille?'

'I do. Now what did Guise say?'

'He . . . he said Henri is cursed and will never have a son. He said I'm his sole heir because . . .' He faltered, lowered his eyes.

I cupped his chin. 'Because, what? What else did he say?'

'Navarre. Navarre and his heretics: Guise says they must die. Then I can be king.'

Fear sliced through me. I'd known since the massacre that one day I would have to contend with Guise, but I had not expected him to fall upon us as his father had before him, to inflict deliberate havoc so he could plunge us into war with Navarre. For there could be no doubt that was his intent: he had sought to implicate Navarre in Guast's murder to sow suspicion and doubt.

'Thank you, *mon fils*.' I forced myself to kiss his thick lips. 'Remember,' I said, 'Guise is not your friend. He is nobody's friend. You must never see him again.'

Hercule nodded, regarding Margot in abject misery. She in turn watched me. 'What will you do?' she said and for the first time I heard the tremor of uncertainty in her voice.

'Leave Guise to me,' I replied. And I meant it.

I disbanded the rabble in Chambord (which emptied my personal privy purse of funds) and returned with Hercule and Margot to Paris. As we rode into the city, where the bite of snow hung over the clutter of spires and turned the streets to frozen mud, I formulated my plan.

Henri met me in the Louvre. I did not like the way he looked; he was still gaunt, dressed head to toe in black. He had shaved his goatee and his hollow cheeks emphasized a relentless intensity in his eyes. But at least he was up. Birago had told me he had appeared to overcome the worst of his grief and had even begun to visit Louise, though as I glanced at her on a stool in the corner, remote as a shadow, I wondered just what these visits entailed.

My youngest son dropped to his knees before Henri's impassive figure and confessed everything. After he was done, Henri waved him out without a word. Then he looked at me. I was relieved to hear the old spark of defiance in his voice. 'So, my idiot brother was led astray by Guise, who killed Guast because he thinks I am unable to rule or sire an heir.'

'It's more than that,' I said, and I met his eyes. 'Guise wants you to fail utterly. He used the knife with Navarre's emblem to confuse us, to make you turn against Navarre and plunge us into war.' I paused, forming my next words with care. 'I think we should sign a treaty with Navarre. He needs protection from Spain and we can provide it. He'll cooperate.'

A vein in Henri's forehead throbbed. He abruptly stood, flicking his hand at Louise. She hastened from the room. He paced to his desk. 'A treaty with Navarre,' he said. He let out a dark chuckle, turned back to me. 'I know why Guise hates me. Maybe instead of finding accord with Navarre, I should just take Guise's arrogant head.'

'No, that is the last thing you should do. If we kill our premier Catholic noble, it will pit all the other lords against us. And we have no proof save Hercule's word; Guise made sure of that. But he's forgotten that I've lived through this before; I know he craves a religious war, just like his father, le Balafré, before him. He used Hercule as bait, but he'll think twice about going any further if we find accord with Navarre, who can rally thousands of Huguenots when it suits him.'

Henri's eyes narrowed. 'And you think Navarre will receive you after what we did to him?'

'I'll tell him I want to bring Margot to him. He'll understand my purpose; after all, he's heir to our throne after Hercule. He doesn't want Guise to succeed any more than we do.' I lowered my voice. 'And while I'm gone, you must try to get Louise with child.'

He hesitated, with a near-imperceptible wince of distaste. I did not press him. I thought again of that mousy queen he'd sent from the room and remembered the sight of Guast, strong and nude in his bed. I didn't want to admit it, but deep inside I already sensed the worst and realized I must make plans for it. However, until the day came, I must be seen to support the illusory facade that Henri had constructed around his marriage.

He nodded curtly. 'Fine. But promise nothing I might come to regret later.'

'Of course.' I moved to him. He accepted my kiss in silence.

I found Louise in the antechamber, a rosary in her hands. I paused, eyeing her. 'You should rely less on prayer and more on effort, madame. Do I make myself clear?'

With a furtive nod and curtsy, she disappeared back into Henri's room.

36

I prepared for my trip; I could be gone for months and so I waited to tell Margot. When I finally summoned her, she seemed relieved.

Henri had gone with Louise to Vincennes, leaving me to close down the Louvre for the winter. Standing in my rooms, surrounded by my coffers, I sent my women to fetch us a meal, to refresh us after a long morning of work. Alone, I trudged into my bedchamber to get my Muet. My personal articles were stored in sandalwood chests and I'd left my old dog dozing on her cushion on a chair. She would not accompany me on my trip, blind and deaf as she was, but rather stay with Anna-Maria. I thought I'd sit and pet her awhile; but as I moved to where she lay curled up, her tail over her snout, I realized she was very still.

I froze to my spot. When I finally reached out to graze her white fur, which was still as pliant and full as in her youth, I felt ebbing warmth. She had died moments ago.

My world caved in. She was the last living memento of my daughter Elisabeth, her only gift to me; and as I stood over that little being I saw all those I had loved and lost, felt the weight of my struggles crush me, and the cry that broke from me was a desolate howl.

Lucrezia and Anna-Maria ran in. 'No,' I heard myself say as they came to a halt beside me. 'Not my Muet . . .' Lucrezia embraced me. Anna-Maria started to cry. At the sound of her grief I reached for her and we wept in each other's arms like children.

Later that afternoon, we enveloped Muet in one of my shawls and took her to the Tuileries, where the gardeners labored to break the frosted ground. My hands trembled as I held her shrouded form; I could not surrender her and Lucrezia had to pry her from my fingers. I turned away to the leaden sky, the wind lacerating me as I heard the shovels begin to replace the dirt.

'Good-bye, my Muet,' I whispered, and my tears ran cold on my chilled careworn cheeks.

I was fifty-seven years old. I had contended with death all my life, burying a husband and four children, killing a lover and countless foes, but this small loss undid me.

If death had come for me that day, I would have welcomed it.

It took us three weeks to traverse France; when we finally entered the snowbound courtyard of his castle in Nérac, Navarre stood waiting for us.

He'd not ridden out to witness the celebrations his people had prepared for our arrival, nor had he seen the astonishment on their faces when they caught sight of Margot on her palfrey, dressed in a crimson gown trimmed in gold and an ermine-lined cloak. But I knew he'd been apprised of the stir she created and he greeted us with a sardonic smile, dressed in a plain black wool doublet and baggy breeches that reached to just above his knees. His build was compact, strong; his coppery hair messed atop his head like a storm-tossed thatch and his full beard exalting his long nose. His green eyes gleamed with mirth as he kissed Margot on the lips. She wrinkled her nose. Though he wasn't unattractive, I could smell his pungent male scent even from where I stood and understood why Margot disdained him. Evidently, Navarre wasn't in the habit of regular bathing, while she was fastidious when it came to hygiene.

'I'm overjoyed to see you again, my dear,' he drawled. He eyed the wagons of luggage coming into the courtyard behind us. 'Did you bring all Paris with you?'

He didn't wait for her response, turning to me with a broad smile, as if we'd only just seen each other last week. 'Tante Catherine, welcome to my humble realm.'

I immediately detected the change in him. He might act indifferent, throwing on that devil-may-care air that had made him the darling of Paris's whores, but I sensed a newfound self-assurance. Safely ensconced in his mountain kingdom, surrounded by his Huguenots, Navarre had come into his own. This time, it was I who was the guest in a hostile court.

I smiled in return. 'My son, how fit you look. The air here suits you.'

'It should.' He guffawed. 'It is my air, after all.' He took Margot by the hand. 'Excuse me, *our* air. Everything I have is now yours, my queen. Come, I've prepared a suite for you.' He paused. 'I hope it's satisfactory. I fear I cannot compete with the splendors of the Louvre.'

I heard Margot reply, 'I never expected you to,' and she took his arm to let him lead her into the castle, leaving me to trail behind and ignore his Huguenot councilors' pointed stares.

Navarre delayed our official business, citing the upcoming Christmas celebrations. He organized a progress to show Margot off and his people regaled us with garlic stew and freshwater trout. As I jostled along in a litter behind the royal couple, I beheld a robust folk who regarded me with misgiving. Protestant to their core, to them I was the monstrous Queen Mother, instigator of the massacre, and some even went so far as to hold up two fingers as I passed, to ward off my evil eye.

I was less interested in how they felt about me, however, than in observing how they interacted with Navarre. That they loved him was undeniable. Everywhere he went, his subjects crowded about him and he never failed to heed them, showing no visible fear for his person as he listened to their complaints with a single-minded attentiveness. It was clear to me that since leaving France, he 'd worked hard to shed his indolent image in favor of the mantle of a stalwart king, aware that his people's admiration was his best defense. Though I felt guilty for thinking it, I couldn't help but compare his affable manner with my Henri's aloof complexity. While my son had to shield himself from those who might do him harm, Navarre went about seemingly without a worry, his joie de vivre a beacon to anyone who crossed his path. Even Margot melted in his presence and began to display the coquettish air of her youth. I saw no sign that they had ever shared a bed, but watching her bat her eyes at him made me think it wouldn't be too long before, smell or not, he won her over. And once she got with child, it would bind Navarre even closer to us.

Nevertheless, I'd never spent a colder winter in my life. The snow fell for weeks on end, blanketing everything, and while I huddled in his stone fortresses before the fire, Navarre strode about in shirtsleeves as if it were midsummer. His resiliency and cavalier attitude soon began to grate on me, for he behaved as though this were indeed some endless familial visit. And my aggravation only increased when I received word from Birago that Elizabeth Tudor had finally granted Hercule leave to pay her suit and Henri had dispatched my youngest son to England in a galleon loaded with gifts. I was irate that I wasn't there to oversee Hercule's departure and nervous about how he might behave so far from home.

Margot, on the other hand, had settled in. One afternoon after I awoke from a nap, stiffer and colder than when I'd first lain down, I went into the hall with Lucrezia in search of warmth and I found my daughter in the middle of the bare floor, directing what appeared to be a small army trudging past her with armfuls of boxes, furnishings, and tapestries. Seated on a new gilded chair by the hearth, Navarre twirled a goblet, an insouciant grin on his face.

'*Dio Mio*,' I said, 'what is this?'

'What does it look like?' Margot snipped. 'I'm redecorating. All this stone and freezing brick – it's barbaric. I'm a queen now and I must live accordingly.'

I glanced at Navarre. He shrugged. 'She'll empty my treasury at this rate,' he muttered, 'but at least we'll starve in style.'

That night, dressed in one of her fantastic wigs and revealing court gowns, Margot presided over a fifty-course feast in her newly decorated hall, delighted there wasn't a lady present who could outshine her. Later I heard she and Navarre finally shared a bed, assuaging my fear that they'd go the rest of their lives without acknowledging the true purpose of their union.

The next day, Navarre sent word that he wished to see me.

I entered his private study – a masculine wood-paneled chamber Margot had not succeeded in overhauling during her rampage; it boasted a wide window that overlooked the snowcapped mountains, a threadbare rug underfoot, and racks of antlers displayed on the walls.

He motioned to a chair. Pouring two goblets of hot mulled cider, he handed one to me and said bluntly, 'I wish to conclude our agreements. I don't like having my life disrupted any more than it already has been. Tell me what you came here for, and if I can I will grant it.'

I took a sip of my cider, taken aback by his directness. 'I wish for us to reach accord,' I began. 'I believe we share a common belief in peace.'

'So the time has come for us to put the past to rest?'

I started. 'Do you mock me?'

'Not in the least. But you're not here for peace; you came to strike a pact. You want my allegiance and surety of my troops should you need them against Guise; in exchange, you promise that I will remain in the succession. Am I correct?'

As he regarded me calmly, awaiting my answer, I realized that raw potential I'd first glimpsed when he was a child had come into its own. He still needed finesse, but if he avoided a young king's natural inclination to indulge in heroics, in time Henri of Navarre would be a magnificent ruler. This thought both excited and unsettled me; he was the perfect bulwark against Guise's machinations, but he was also still a heretic.

'Yes,' I said, with a lift of my chin. 'You are correct. It is why I am here.'

He moved to his desk. 'I appreciate your candor. But seeing as I'm not the one who seeks bloodshed, what would I gain by submitting to your terms?'

'You'll stop Guise. All you need do is –'

'Convert?' He chuckled. 'Why should I? You don't want me to inherit France. You just seek a temporary savior until your son sires an heir. Then you'll disown me.'

'That's not true,' I retorted. 'You have no idea of everything I've done for you.'

'Oh, I know,' he said softly. 'Others may claim you live solely for power, but I know you do only what you think necessary to safeguard your sons' kingdom. We are not so different, you and I – though our methods do not always agree.'

I stared at him. 'What do you mean by that?'

He looked at me intently. 'I mean, I know you saved my life that night. You let me live and then you let me escape. I didn't understand at the time why I was alive, when so many others were dead, but I do now. For some reason, you and I are meant to play this game. It is why I stay married to your daughter, why I haven't requested an annulment. But there comes a time when a man must stand for what he believes in, regardless of the cost. And I must stand for my faith.'

He turned around, opened his desk drawer. 'Besides, my conversion will do no good. You see, Guise has accepted payment from Spain to form a Catholic league against me.'

Dread surged in me as he handed me a fragment of paper. I willed my eyes to focus.

My lord the duke has acknowledged the offer of fifty thousand gold écus pledged by His Catholic Majesty toward the eradication of heresy. Your Majesty may rest assured the duke will do all in his power to prevent the naming of the heretic Navarre into –

The rest was torn off. 'Where did you get this?' I said, and I couldn't hide the tremor in my voice.

'My patrols sometimes catch illicit couriers at the border; they find the most interesting things in their satchels. You can't imagine what people will entrust to a stranger. Unfortunately, this particular courier got away with the rest of the dispatch.' He smiled. 'As you can see, regardless of which faith I choose, Guise will not rest until he sees me dead.'

I forced myself to swallow. 'How . . . how do you know this is true? Any envoy worth his salt can falsify information to suit his master.'

'I know it's true because I know Guise. And so do you.' He

came from around the desk, took my hand, and lifted it to his lips. 'Now, Tante Catherine, I believe your son has need of you. Perhaps after you've dealt with Guise, you and I can meet again.'

He walked out. As his footsteps faded, I closed my fist over the paper in my hand.

I reached Paris by mid-November, after an absence of nine months. Birago rode out to meet me, crablike in his black damask, his gnarled hands clutching his staff as he got into my coach.

'There's disquiet in the streets,' he said. 'Plague broke out and His Majesty shut himself up in Vincennes with the queen. The sickness is confined to the poorer quarters of the city but he refuses to return to Paris until he can be sure he's safe.' Birago paused, coughing into his hand. He looked dreadful; jaundiced and hunched over, his shoulder bones poking under his robe.

'Anything else?' I asked quietly. I should never have gone for so long; I shouldn't have left the burden of watching over my son and the kingdom to this frail old friend of mine.

'That other matter you mentioned,' Birago said. 'While I've seen no evidence of payment from Spain, Guise has been meeting in secret with the other Catholic lords. It appears he could be forming a league with Spain and Rome, modeled on his late father's Triumvirate.'

'So,' I mused, staring toward the spires of Notre Dame, 'le Balafré rises again. Keep watching him. I want to know everything he does, everywhere he goes, and everyone he sees. When the time comes, I will deal with him.'

Anna-Maria was overjoyed to see me. As we embraced and Lucrezia and I removed our traveling cloaks, I thought of how much I relied on these two women. They had been my most constant companions since my arrival in France, always at my side when I needed them, forsaking husbands and children and homes of their own.

That night I sat before my mirror. Along with rheum, bad circulation, and a recurring knot in my chest that sometimes left me breathless, my hair had gone completely white. I'd had Lucrezia crop it, for I always wore a veiled coif in public and saw no further need to tend tresses. I hadn't minded at the time, relieved at long last of the weekly dyes with walnut juice, the hot irons, and fanciful coiffures. Yet as I now beheld my sallow image with its wintery fuzz I couldn't help but mark the insidious advance of my decrepitude. My chin was slack, the lines at my brow and about my mouth deeply etched; and my dark eyes, once my most notable feature, were sunk in permanent shadow, luster-less, the skin at their corners pleated like crepe.

Anna-Maria came with my bed cap. I said quietly, 'Do you think I'm too old?'

She met my gaze in the glass. Of the three of us, she most resembled her younger self, her piquant face barely scored, her small size and bustling movements lending her the illusion of eternal youth. She smiled. 'You can never be too old, my lady, not when France needs you.'

I reached up to clasp her hand in mine. 'Yes,' I murmured. 'That's what I thought.'

I went to bed, falling into exhausted sleep. I dreamed.

Blood drips from my ceiling. I lie prostrate in my bed; I can feel my lips straining wide to cry out but I cannot hear my voice. The drips of blood seep from the painted eaves and fall one by one onto my coverlet. Death is here. It surrounds me. I can smell its iron essence, almost taste its salt and bitterness. I flail; I try to inch away but the drops come faster now, faster and faster, turning into a rain, cascading about me, falling into my open eyes, my mouth –

'My lady, wake up!' Lucrezia was shaking me, stooped at my bedside.

I struggled upright, drenched in sweat. '*Dio Mio,* I had the most awful dream.'

She peered at me. 'You were shouting. You woke us in the other room.'

'What time is it?' I muttered and she glanced at the extinguished candle by my bedside, the hours notched into its side. 'Almost dawn. Go back to sleep a while longer.'

'No. I . . . I must get up. I'm due at Vincennes today to see Henri.' I arose quickly, the vestiges of my dream clinging to me as she helped me into my robe. She went to stoke the hearth, set a decanter by it to warm the morning wine. 'Should I get you something to eat?' she asked and I heard a catch in her voice. 'Lucrezia,' I asked. 'What is it?'

She went still; I turned to see Henri on the threshold. He was thin and pale, clad in an unadorned black doublet, his hair loose about his shoulders.

'It's Hercule,' he said in a low voice.

My throat tightened. 'But Hercule is in England, wooing Queen Elizabeth.'

'No. She refused his marriage suit, so he went to the Low Countries, where he got involved in a Lutheran revolt. He was taken prisoner. Birago paid his ransom. He arrived a few days ago but he . . .' Henri's voice faltered. 'Maman, you must help him. Dr. Paré says he is dying.'

I stood immobile, thinking I must have heard wrong. 'Dying?'

'Yes. He suffered a wound on his leg; corruption set in. I made everyone swear not to say anything; I wanted to tell you myself. But you were tired after your travels. You needed to rest.'

I reached for my robe. 'Take me to him.'

Birago was by the bedside with old Paré. They regarded me with sad eyes, their faces drawn with exhaustion. They must have been here all night, watching over my son so I could sleep.

I stepped to the bed. Veins could be traced under Hercule's translucent skin. His voice was hoarse, barely above a whisper. 'Maman, you are home.'

I set my hand on his brow. 'They tell me you're hurt. Let me see, yes?' I spoke gently, feeling the fever blazing off of him. His face spasmed in fear. 'Don't let them do it. Don't let them take my leg.'

'They won't. I promise.' As I spoke Paré eased back the sheet.

I had to stop myself from gasping aloud at the sight of the festering wound on his right thigh; the flesh so inflamed it looked about to burst. Vicious red streaks spread like tentacles to his swollen groin.

'I've seen this on the battlefield,' Paré said. 'Left untended, the corruption enters the blood. He was very sick by the time he got here and I dared not cut. Now –'

I stopped him. 'I don't blame you. Go. Fetch me hot water, fresh cloths, and poppy.' I swept a pile of garments aside from a nearby stool and sat, taking Hercule's hand. 'I'm here,' I said. 'All will be well, you'll see.' I reached out with my other hand to stroke his cheek. Though his unkempt beard was thick and wiry, it could not disguise his alarmingly gaunt face.

'Maman,' he said, 'I'm so afraid.'

Tears blurred my vision. He was flesh of my flesh, last child of my love for my husband. He'd never had a chance; the stigmata of illness had left him helpless in a world that knew only cruelty. And I had failed him. I should have protected him. I should have kept him safe.

'Don't be,' I said. 'You are safe. I love you. Your brother and your sister Margot love you.'

I stayed with him for the next six days, cleansing his wound and dosing him with massive quantities of poppy and rhubarb. He grew so thin, his bones showed under his flesh; I knew nothing could save him, so I made sure he was as free of pain as possible. When he began to breathe shallowly and his leg turned black I clambered into bed and cradled his head against my breast. I sang to him, the nursery rhymes every mother hums to her child; and he melted into me, soothed by my voice, by the constant motion of my hands stroking his hair.

When he finally went limp, my heart broke into a thousand irreparable pieces. I engulfed his lifeless body and wept for him as I never had during his life, for the wretched fate that had stolen away his promise before he'd ever had the chance to fulfill it.

I had lost my son. Henri had lost his heir.

And if Guise had his way, France would lose everything.

★ ★ ★

I left his corpse to be embalmed and went to see Henri in his apartments. He rose from his chair, searching my face. 'Is he . . . ?'

I nodded; as he moaned and turned away, I said: 'We must make plans.' My tone was detached, concealing the anguish that threatened to overcome me. More than ever before, I had to remain strong. The danger posed by Henri's lack of a Catholic heir was paramount.

'Plans?' He looked up with undisguised fear. 'What plans? What am I supposed to do now?'

I met his gaze. 'We invite Navarre to court. He is now your heir presumptive. Though Navarre has told me he 'll never convert again, we must persuade him to reason.'

He raked a trembling hand through his hair. 'Invite him to court? He's a heretic! Guise will never let him be named heir. He'll kill him first.'

'Perhaps.' I paused. 'But Louise is still young, as are you. If you get her with child . . .' My voice faded as a burst of frenetic laughter escaped him. Then he went still.

'You don't understand,' he whispered. 'I've tried. God knows, I've tried. I touch her and touch her . . . and I feel nothing. I'm not able to . . .' He swallowed, looked at me with stricken eyes. 'It's not her fault. It's me . . . I cannot be aroused by a woman.'

His words crumbled the last remnants of the illusion he had built between us. I did not remonstrate. I did not cajole or encourage him. Like me, he could not feign desire. We were not made that way. I had to accept that there would be no child of his loins.

All we had left was Navarre. He had to save us from Guise.

I reached out and Henri staggered into my arms. He was still my son. He was still our king.

And while he lived, there was still hope.

'Trust in me,' I said. 'I'll keep you safe. I'll fight for you to my last breath.'

37

Henri and I rode out from Paris to welcome Navarre. We both wore mourning for Hercule, whose body rested in the Abbey of St. Denis. We had delayed his funeral, waiting for an answer to our invitation. Finally, after weeks, Navarre sent word expressing his desire to be with us in our hour of grief. Soon he'd be here; together, we would find a way to contend with Guise.

As the entourage straggled into view, coming over the vale, I peered at it uncertainly. It was pitifully small, even by Navarre's impoverished standards – a mere clutch of horses and carts. Then the group neared and Henri's hands clenched on his reins.

'I see Margot,' he said tersely. 'Navarre is not with her.'

In the Hôtel de la Reine my daughter stood in her knee-length chemise, her soiled outer garments discarded at her feet. Her tired women heaved jugs of hot water into a linen-lined tub. I waited, tapping my foot. The women curtsied and left. With a sigh, Margot stepped into the tub.

'God's teeth,' I burst out, 'where is he? Does he not realize he could be heir of France?'

She splashed the rose-scented water over her voluptuous breasts. To my chagrin, her belly remained flat. 'He sends his regrets, but he was obliged to reconsider your offer when his Council raised objection. They don't think it's safe for him here. And in order for him to be made heir, he'd have to abjure his faith again, yes? Such a decision, he says, cannot be made lightly. He wrote you a letter.' She motioned to the heap of valises by the bed. 'It's in my bag.'

Her tapestry bag lay open, revealing perfume vials and

cosmetics. I found the folded parchment with Navarre's seal under her enamel hand mirror.

I send Your Grace fond greetings and my regret that I cannot attend the court and His Majesty my cousin in this tragic time. I grieve deeply for the loss of His Highness Hercule, duc d'Alençon; however, matters of state compel me to remain within my realm until my Council deems otherwise. I trust Your Grace has not forgotten our last conversation, in which I gave you a word of caution, for loyal Huguenots in France continue to inform me that a certain lord persists in his assembly of unauthorized power, which can only result in a threat to His Majesty. You will find in me a fellow monarch who fears greatly for my cousin the king's welfare, and one who sincerely hopes Your Grace and His Majesty will see fit to curb this lord's ambitions before it is too late. Until said time, it is unlikely I will gain my Council's leave to travel to France.

'He doesn't trust you,' Margot said, her eyes fixed on me. 'He thinks Guise will murder him just like Coligny. Nothing I said could convince him otherwise.'

'You should have tried harder.' I folded the letter, shoved it in my gown pocket.

'Easy for you to say,' she retorted. 'I'm sick of trying with him! He treats me like chattel. The moment you left, he went back to his wine and his hunting and refused to grant me a single sou for my expenses. I'll not stand for it. I am his wife, his queen.'

I regarded her in disgust. 'You haven't changed a bit. Your youngest brother is not yet buried and you think only of yourself. If Navarre refused to come, you should have stayed.'

She sat upright so fast she sent water sloshing over the sides of the tub. 'Don't you dare use Hercule against me!' To my disbelief, tears started in her eyes. 'He was the only one who loved me. None of you cared about him; none of you lifted a finger to save him. You let Henri send him off to England and now he is dead. This is your fault. It's always your fault! Before your family, before God and everything else, you put France first and look at where it's gotten us!'

I was stunned into silence by her cruelty, and her uncanny echoing of my own guilt.

'I did everything I could,' she went on, emerging from the tub. 'I told Navarre you'd make him heir if he came to Paris and heard mass. I begged him in Hercule's memory to put aside our differences and what did he do? He laughed at me. He's always laughing, acting the merry monarch for all it's worth.'

Snatching a towel, she wrapped it about herself. 'I've had enough of him. I stayed at his miserable court and smiled until my teeth hurt. I endured his ministers' insults and their solemn dirges, played the dutiful wife while he slept with every slut he could find before taking a mistress from among my own women. He's heartless. He sent me to the border without so much as a farewell; his guards didn't accompany me past Provence. They let me ride through France with my few attendants like a widow. He can rot for all I care. I'm never going back to him.'

I arched my brow. Grieving or not, here was the Margot I knew – the defiant and foolish woman, heedless of anything that did not touch her own self-interests.

'I think not,' I said. 'In fact, I suggest you not make yourself too comfortable, for as soon as our official mourning is over, I'm taking you back to him myself.'

I didn't wait for her response, turning around to stomp out. I should have known Navarre wouldn't budge from his citadel, that he wouldn't risk becoming our prisoner again or falling prey to Guise. But if he didn't come to me, then I would go to him.

I had a crown to offer, and no matter what the cost, he must convert and accept it.

I ensured Hercule's funeral was lavish in the extreme; Margot sobbed as the coffin was lowered into the vault, but within days she was entertaining guests at my *hôtel*, the candles and laughter burning far into the night, defying her dramatic assertions of grief.

Finally, the end came to our forty days of mourning. Henri and Louise were scheduled to open the court at the Louvre and I went to the *hôtel* to escort Margot to the festivities. I found her in black velvet and a ruff so high and wide it framed her head, her bodice sheared at the shoulders, nearly exposing her bosom. Ropes of pearls hugged her throat; her eyes were lined in kohl, her lips rouged scarlet.

'You look like a harlot,' I rebuked. 'Cover yourself this instant.'

She glowered, grabbed a length of diaphanous shawl. Throwing it about her shoulders, she paraded out to the waiting coach, leaving me to trudge behind.

In the Louvre, beeswax tapers shed golden light over the courtiers. The hall wasn't nearly as crowded as I'd expected; our ongoing penury and the instability of our succession had sent many of the nobles bolting to their estates. But as Margot and I took our places by the dais I glimpsed several Catholic lords, their bearded mouths barely concealing their sneers.

Tension hung in the air, palpable as the smoke rising from the hearths and smell of roast boar being served. As a page ladled meat onto my platter, my stomach lurched and I pushed the plate away. Lifting my gaze to the court, I caught sight of a lone figure standing in the shadows under the pilasters, his scarlet cloak draped across his broad shoulders.

With a start, I found myself staring at Guise.

I'd not seen him since the massacre. Against the red of his cloak, his doublet was a dark velvet skin molded to his muscular torso, his white-blond hair cropped close to his scalp, like a soldier's, his lean face proud. At thirty-five years of age he had fulfilled the dangerous promise of his paternal blood, though he exuded a sensual vitality his father, le Balafré, had lacked. I could understand why my daughter had grieved over him, and as I thought this I glanced at Margot.

She reclined in her chair, a smile on her lips. My heart began to pound. I glanced to the dais, where Henri sat with Louise; in her finery she was pale and remote as a shadow, a rosary dangling from her wrist. My son caught my stare; following my gaze over the sea of courtiers toward the pilasters, he went rigid, all color draining from his face.

I tried to eat, but the meat tasted like raw wood as I felt Guise's eyes bore at me. Margot chattered with a lady at her right, reaching again and again to the decanter to refill her goblet, pretending she didn't know her former lover was in the hall even as her gaze slipped furtively to him. I sensed something between them, an unspoken communion of intrigue. I sat on the edge of my chair as Henri rose to his feet. Hercule's death had endangered the Valois bloodline, which had ruled for nearly two hundred years, and Henri and I had crafted his careful speech.

Clad in his purple mantle and sapphire coronet, he spoke with fluid elegance, his voice echoing into the hall as he declared his sorrow over Hercule and the need to continue to heal the realm of discord.

'And let my foes thus take note,' he concluded, and I saw his eyes focus on Guise. 'I'll broach no dissension in this trying time. France must come first, above all else. In that spirit' – he gestured to Margot – 'I hereby appoint my sister's husband, my cousin and namesake Henri of Navarre, as heir-apparent to the throne, providing he agrees to the terms I shall set and until such time that Her Grace my queen gives birth to a son, God willing.'

The court responded with fervent applause. Just as Henri started to sit, Guise stepped forth.

'Your Majesty,' he declared, with a ringing command that brought everyone to a halt. 'We rejoice in your willingness to put your kingdom first, but I fear France requires a stronger solution than your choice of an heir.'

Henri froze. I stood quickly. 'My lord duke, we've just announced our –'

'Madame, I am not deaf,' he interrupted. He walked purposefully to the dais. When he reached it, he withdrew a parcel from within his cloak. I couldn't take my eyes off his large veined hands, which had stabbed Coligny and thrown him from a second-story window.

Guise brandished the parcel. 'I have here pleas from the lord mayors of cities that share a border with Navarre. He raids them with impunity, removing our Catholic officials to replace them with heretics. While we mourn the loss of our dauphin, he's seen to it that every city surrounding his realm answers only to him.'

I shot a look at Margot. She returned my stare, her eyes cold as onyx.

Henri did not move, did not speak, his stare on Guise. I saw something come over his face: a hardness that made his jaw clench and drew back his lips to show his teeth.

'Your Majesty,' Guise went on, 'Navarre plays you for a fool. He will never agree to your terms. When he takes your throne, he intends to unleash heresy upon us all.'

When Henri finally spoke, his voice was icy. 'You should know better than most how easy it is to falsify evidence where there is none. If this is true, why haven't I heard of it before now?'

'I only received the news myself a few days ago from a trusted source.' Guise's measured calm frightened me. Unlike le Balafré, he had learned self-control. 'I came at once to warn you, but it is a long ride from my estate in Joinville. However, if you doubt, read them for yourself.' He set the bundle on the dais. 'You'll see that we can never have peace while Navarre lives. He threatens our faith and the stability of –'

Henri cut him off with a lift of his finger. 'You should refrain from saying anything more, lest you go too far. You are fortunate you are not under arrest, given your past deeds.'

I saw Guise's jaw edge under his beard. 'You think wrong of me. I am your loyal subject, but now is the time for action, not words. We must finish what we started.'

'And you,' Henri said, 'sound more like your father every day. You should tread carefully henceforth. I'll suffer no Guise to rule my kingdom.'

In the silence that fell I could hear my own anxious breathing.

'I do not seek to rule France,' Guise said softly. 'I seek to save her.'

Henri flicked his hand. 'I will read these letters. Until then, I command you to return to your estates and stay there. I've been patient thus far, but even I have my limits.'

Guise turned and exited the hall, the spurs of his boots clanking in the hush. As Henri retrieved the parcel and stalked into a nearby antechamber, I snarled at Margot: 'Come with me.'

As soon as we entered the antechamber, Henri spun to Margot. 'Is it true? Has your husband played me false?'

'How would I know?' She smoothed a crease in her sleeve. 'I'm not with him at the moment, am I?'

'Then how did Guise find out about this?' He thrust the parcel at her. 'How is it that he knows what I do not?' He paused. His eyes turned to slits. 'It was you, wasn't it? You knew Navarre would seize those cities but didn't say a word to us. No, you told your lover instead.'

She arched her brow. 'Did you think I'd help you, after you let them take Guise from me?'

He stared at her, trembling; for a terrible moment I thought he would strike her. He dropped the parcel at her feet. 'Because you are my sister,' he said, his voice quivering with rage, 'I'll not punish you as you deserve. But you're hereby banished from my court. You're not to stay in Paris another day nor return to Navarre.' He looked at me. 'See to it.'

He walked out. I turned my eyes to Margot. In that instant, I truly felt as though I could hate her. 'Did you plot with Guise against us?'

She tapped the parcel with her foot. 'Read for yourself; the letters are mine.'

'Dear God,' I whispered, 'why?'

She smiled. 'Hercule is dead. I don't care who inherits, so long as we perish.'

I stepped back from her, from the calculated malice in her eyes. I heard Cosimo's words, haunting in their prophecy: *But the barren seed that is your family – they are damned.*

And as if she could hear them too, Margot lifted her chin, in triumph.

January came upon us in a maelstrom of wind and snow. Bundled up in sable and wool, I stood in the courtyard to see Margot off.

She would be taken to the Château of Usson in Auvergne – an isolated manor that could be well guarded, the only place besides the Bastille where she could do, or come to, no harm. She did not say a word when informed.

She emerged from the palace flanked by guards and moved toward her palfrey. I watched her mount the wood block and swing onto her saddle with graceful ease, her strength apparent in her every gesture as she took up the reins and turned to me.

I felt all of a sudden as if I might weep. I did not want to understand her; I did not want to know how this chasm had opened between us. But I did. She loved with her soul; she'd given herself entirely to the man we had denied her. It did not matter whether Guise would ever appreciate her sacrifice. What mattered was that she had never forsaken him.

'Remember who you are,' I said to her. 'Remember, the blood of kings flows in your veins.'

She gave me a bitter smile. 'How can I forget? It's my bane.' Kicking her heels into her palfrey, she cantered off, the guards close behind.

Within moments she had vanished into the swirling snow.

The harsh winter gave way to famished summer and a drenching autumn. Even as the harvest again moldered in the fields and riots broke out in Paris over the price of bread, Birago's network of informants sent daily reports of Catholic lords congregating at Guise's estate, of retainers being summoned and weapons stockpiled – all paid for by Philip of Spain. From the opposite side of the country came equally disquieting news, of more cities overtaken by Navarre, of thousands of Huguenots rallying to his standard and the seizure of every piece of artillery from every castle he could overtake. War was imminent, a war to the death; and trapped in my rooms as rain heaved against my windows, I penned letter after letter, asking Navarre to meet me before it was too late.

One evening as I sat with my fingers raw from holding my quill I heard the door open. I looked up to see Henri. He'd retreated to Vincennes following his humiliation in the Louvre; though we met weekly with his Council, he had not visited me alone since that incident.

'Do you know why he despises me?' he asked.

I regarded him with bleary eyes. 'Yes. He thinks you plotted to kill his brethren and friends. Though we saved his life, he's never forgiven us for that horrible night.'

'No, I mean Guise.' He stepped inside. His shoulder-length hair was tied back from his arresting face; as he neared his thirty-fifth year, his features had grown more defined and angular, like a Valois, though his eyes remained pure Medici: expressive, long-lashed, and exquisitely black. Birago had told me he'd been training daily with his sword and bow and riding for hours every afternoon in the forest; it showed in his taut stance.

'I loved him once.' His face turned supple in the candlelight. 'When we went to fight together against the Huguenots that first time, we ate together, shared the same pavilion; we were more than friends. He was my brother, the brother I'd never had in François, Charles, or Hercule. He watched over me every moment; he claimed he would die before he let anything harm me.'

He gave a soft laugh. 'I fell in love with him. How could I resist? He was beautiful as a god, fierce as a pagan. He was everything I wanted to be.' He paused at my desk, ran his long fingers along the chipped walnut edge as if he were recalling a lover's skin. 'When I finally got up the nerve to tell him, he was horrified. Oh, he hid it well. He said all the right things, that he was honored but unworthy, but I saw the loathing in his eyes. He could scarcely contain it. I could have ordered him to my bed, I could have taken him on his knees like a dog; but I knew that even so, if I wasn't his prince, he would have killed me. Only then did I realize how unworthy he truly was. He took something that was precious to me, sacred, and with one look he made it shameful. I vowed I would never love again, never be vulnerable to another's disdain.'

He lifted his hand to his throat, as though he could still feel the pain. 'And I never did. None of the others, not even my poor Guast, ever equaled the passion I had for him.'

He leaned to me. Still in that low, intimate voice he said, 'I'm finished with it. I want you to find a way for us to be rid of him. Find it soon, before I find it myself.'

He reached into his doublet, took out an unsealed paper. 'From Navarre: he agrees to meet, providing you go to him. He's received all your letters and says he doesn't want war any more than we do. Tell him, if he converts I'll make him my heir and send him Guise's head.'

I started to reach out. Before I could touch him, he drew back and left me.

I reached the citadel of St. Brice in the Huguenot territory of Cognac in mid-December. I had ridden through a frozen landscape of skeletal trees festooned with icicles, the glacial wind barely stirring the drifts of snow at the roadside, but Navarre greeted me in the courtyard dressed in his habitual wool doublet, only he now sported a black cap with a bristling white plume. I was struck by the sight of it, recalling it was the same cap I'd seen him wearing in my vision, so long ago.

He smiled at my scrutiny. 'So my enemies can mark me better in battle,' he quipped, and he leaned to me, his breath warm as he kissed my lips. While the cold had penetrated my bones, he exuded heat like a kiln.

'Tante Catherine,' he said. 'I didn't realize until now how much I've missed you.'

I allowed myself a smile. 'And I see that you, my lord, have not changed.'

'Oh, I'd not say that.' He thrust out his chin. 'Look here: courtesy of Guise and his Catholic League. I didn't have a single white hair in my beard before they challenged me.'

He spoke carelessly, but I heard iron underneath. With a smile I said, 'Then it seems we've much to discuss,' and let him lead me into the house and a private chamber, where he allowed me to warm myself in front of the fire with a goblet of mulled wine.

Then we launched into battle. He had developed his diplomatic skills, I noticed at once; none of my offers moved him to concede an inch. He behaved as though he truly did not care whether he forfeited all.

Finally, I hit my fist on the table. 'Enough. We've been sitting here for over two hours, going around the same immutable point. You know I cannot arrest Guise. He is too powerful; every Catholic in France would turn against us.'

Navarre reclined in his chair with a curious half smile. 'He is only powerful because in allowing him to continue unchecked, you lend him authority. What do I gain by agreeing to your requests, save for a lifelong vendetta with Guise, who is clearly resolved to destroy me?' He rose to refill his goblet. 'Besides, I think if you had true peace, you wouldn't know what to do with yourself. I, on the other hand, am sick of conflict. I wouldn't wage war again if I had the choice.'

As he turned back to me, I thought of the irony that this one man, whose accession could only mean my sons had failed, might be the answer to everything I strived to give France. Had Nostradamus been right? Had I saved him because he was, in fact, my legacy?

The time had come to find out. I now faced my final gambit.

'You do not need to go to war,' I finally said. 'Convert to our faith and you will put an end to it. Guise cannot fight a Catholic heir, which you will be. Your brethren will forgive you. After all, you will inherit France.'

He chuckled. 'Can it be that what they say about you is true after all, and religion really means nothing to you when the Crown is at stake?' His smile faded. 'I said no. I will not convert. Unless you've something else to say, I fear war it must be.'

I put my goblet on the side table and stood, moving deliberately to the window. Outside, winter's early dusk fell like a cloak, draping its black folds over the land. I felt the night in my heart, in my sinews, deep in my bones. Time was running out. I had his answer, and it was the answer I had expected. I could not hesitate anymore.

'What if I give you his death?' I said, without looking around. 'Would that satisfy you?'

I heard sap crackle in the hearth. I waited, my entire body taut. When he finally let out a sigh, I looked over my shoulder at him. Shadows played across his rugged features.

'You know I am capable of it,' I added. 'I have done it before.'

His mouth twitched. He put his goblet on the mantel, stood before the fire with his arms crossed at his chest, staring into the flames. 'Coligny died horribly that night,' he said flatly. 'My brethren died in unimaginable ways. I thought I would die too. I heard the screams and saw my men struggle when Guise's retainers came for us. If it hadn't been for Margot . . .' He shifted his eyes to me. 'He deserves it. He has bathed in Huguenot blood.'

I met his contemplative stare.

'Very well,' he said quietly. 'I agree. If you give me Guise, I will defend your son. And when the time comes, France will find a champion in me, always, one who will seek tolerance and peace, regardless of how my subjects choose to worship.'

I felt my pent-up breath leave my lungs. 'Then for now we must appear to be foes. You will prepare for war behind my back. Guise will learn of it and pounce. But you must not enter Paris nor seek to usurp Henri's throne. Do the deed and return to your kingdom. Leave the rest to me.'

He held my gaze. The quiet between us filled with memories. I saw him as he'd been on the eve of my son François's nuptials, a wary child with prescient eyes; on the day he came to wed Margot and I clasped him to me and felt his strength. I recalled that night of blood, as he lay against Charles with a dagger at his throat; and envisioned him on the day of his escape, riding through our war-torn land for his mountain refuge. I saw him in each incarnation, from child to youth to man; and I knew, without further doubt, that our destiny had been preordained.

We were indeed two halves of a whole.

I sent detailed instructions to Henri and packed my valises for my return to Paris. The day before I was due to leave, a courier arrived with an urgent missive. I tore it open and read; I could not repress a dark surge of satisfaction. Though the event itself was horrific, it couldn't have come at a better moment.

Mary of Scots had been executed at Elizabeth Tudor's command. In her will she bequeathed to Spain her contested Catholic right to Elizabeth's throne; Philip was now free to assume the role of avenger of Mary's death, to rain fire upon England's heretic queen.

And Guise had the perfect excuse to declare war on Navarre.

38

The Louvre rose out of a dense mist. Torches burned on the facade at midday, pockets of light that scarcely illumined my passage through the courtyard. No escort waited to receive me after my absence; only Birago shuffled to me, his cane tapping on the cobblestones.

As he led me into the palace he murmured, 'I brought your letter personally to His Majesty and he has done as you asked. He awaits you in the hall. You should know he has a new companion, one Valette, son of a minor Parisian nobleman. His Majesty made him captain of his new personal guard, which he calls the Forty-five. The king's fear of assassination runs high.'

I nodded in agreement as I moved through the eerily quiet corridors. I could remember a time when laughter and the firefly flittering of courtiers filled every room. I'd been one of them, the foreign duckling in her elaborate gowns, consumed by desire for an unwilling husband and hatred of his mistress. It had been a time when the Huguenots were an unpleasant distraction, when a king of might and wit straddled the throne – a fleeting time of dreams.

Bracketed tapers flared in the hall. A group of dark-clad men stood near the dais; in their center was Guise, also head to toe in black. I resisted the urge to laugh as the men bowed low, all of whom I recognized as Catholic lords I had instructed Henri to invite. Though white was the color of mourning in France, they'd donned Spanish black in a united show of furor over the martyrdom of Mary Stuart. My son had surpassed my instructions with his usual dramatic flair.

I moved to them. They parted. I lifted my gaze to the dais.

Henri sat with one leg dangling over his throne's armrest. He alone wore white damask, a pearl-drop in one ear. Coral bracelets encircled his wrists; in his hand he held a *bilboquet* – a child's toy made of a polished wood stick with a painted ball on a string. He tossed the ball up, caught it in the rounded cup on the top of the stick. Standing beside him was a lean youth of startling beauty, with a mass of dark curls and sapphire-blue eyes; I assumed he must be the new companion, Valette, for he held an identical toy and his stare was fixed on me.

Clip-clop.

Henri smiled. '*Ma mère*, welcome home. I trust you had a pleasant journey, if not a very productive one?' He tossed the ball up.

Clip-clop.

I glanced at Guise. He regarded me as if I were a stranger.

As if he had rehearsed the lines I'd chosen for him, Henri said, 'As you can see, we're in mourning for the unlawful murder of our sister-in-law, Mary of Scots. It is what every Catholic can expect when a heretic takes the throne – persecution and apostasy. God himself, I'm told, is weeping.' He rose and left the dais. I smelled the scent of violets on him as he approached me. 'Come see what we have devised.' The men hemmed me in, oppressive at my back. I regarded a large paper on the table: a map of France with pins stuck in designated areas. Though I'd advised Henri to do this, the physical demonstration of my gambit twisted my stomach into a knot. If we failed, we'd have an enormous Catholic force on our doorstep.

'Three armies,' said Henri. 'One, led by my Valette, will intercept the German mercenaries Navarre has hired to augment his forces. Another, led by my lord Guise, will engage Navarre himself. And the third I will lead personally, to take position here' – he pointed – 'at the Loire, preventing passage into Paris.' He laughed, flipped the ball up. 'Delightful!'

Clip-clop.

'You . . . you speak of war . . .' I feigned shock as I felt Guise step behind me. He was so close his breath stirred my nape. For a paralyzing instant, I thought he could sense I deceived him.

Then he said, 'How could you think Navarre would act honorably? He lies as easily as he breathes. Did he not convert once, only to turn around and revert to his heresy?'

I focused on Henri. He tilted his head. 'So Navarre didn't tell you he prepared for war?'

'Of course not!' I exclaimed. 'I went to discuss terms with him and he –'

'And he made a fool out of you.' Henri rounded the table; Valette stifled a yawn, draping his arm across the throne with the languid grace of a cat.

I stood silent, as though I could not imagine how I'd been played false.

Henri turned to Guise. 'My cousin of Navarre is a sly one. He asked to meet with my mother alone but never mentioned to her that he already recruited mercenaries.' He didn't wait for Guise to reply, turning back to me. 'Unlike you, he knows there can be no compromise between us.'

'I swear to you, I didn't know,' I said, and I almost believed my own fake incredulity.

Henri smiled. Guise said, 'We understand. Your Grace is not who you were. You are weary from carrying these burdens of state. You must rest now and let us assume charge.'

'Yes,' said Henri. 'Rest, Maman. You have done enough.'

He turned from me in marked dismissal. With my head bowed, I slowly left the hall. The deed was done; there was no turning back. For the first time in my long life, I had invited war in. If Navarre kept his promise, he would not invade; he would not take my son's throne by force. He would fight Guise and kill him, and then, God willing, we would finally have peace.

From my apartments, I watched men toiling in the courtyard, grinding swords to a lethal edge, loading carts with munitions. The dragon of war burgeoned before my eyes, and even as I recognized it would be commanded to my purpose, a band of fear circled my throat.

The night after Navarre's troops were sighted marching toward us, Henri came to me. We had deliberately kept our distance and after he shut the door he embraced me. His body was hardened from training; he looked like his old self as he drew back to gaze into my eyes.

'I leave tomorrow,' he said. 'Do you truly believe Navarre will fulfill his bargain?'

I nodded. 'He will. Just remember, you must not enter the fray. Above all else, you must stay safe. Let Navarre have his moment.' I stood on tiptoes and kissed his mouth, tangling my stiff fingers in his long hair and inhaling his scent.

Never had I been as proud of him as I was in that moment.

The army left; Paris was put under curfew. As I waited, my faithful Birago, weakened by years of gout, collapsed at my feet and was taken to his bed.

I immediately called for Paré.

Our elderly doctor hadn't fared much better than the rest of us, health-wise; lame in one leg and losing his eyesight, he peeled back Birago's fur-lined robe, put his ear to my friend's concave chest, and listened. When he righted himself, he shook his head sadly.

Birago chuckled faintly. 'Say a prayer for me, physician. I'm luckier than most to have escaped your potions and leeches all these years.' He turned to me. 'You needn't stay, *madama*. France needs you more than I do.'

'Nonsense.' I fought back the hot rush of tears in my eyes. 'You've served France faithfully; now, let France wait.'

I didn't move from his side. We avoided any mention of the present or future, finding solace instead in shared recollections of the past, of our voyage in stormy seas to France, of my wedding and our years together, shoring up the kingdom, masterminding spies, and tutoring my sons. Of all the men in my life, Birago had been with me the longest. I couldn't imagine my world without him. And yet as the days passed, I watched him ebb. The gout had turned his legs into a morass of inflamed flesh; he began to suffer high fevers and had trouble breathing, so Lucrezia and I took turns sleeping on a truckle bed in his apartments, attentive to his distress.

The day he left me, his breathing was shallow, rattling in his chest. His withered fingers clutched mine. For the briefest moment, his frail smile conquered the pain.

'*Madama,*' he said, 'I will miss you.'

He died as he lived, without complaint. I held his hand as he grew cold and watched the unwavering purpose lift from his face, so that he seemed at peace, youthful again.

I bowed my head. 'Do not stray far, my friend,' I whispered. 'Wait for me.'

I mourned Birago deeply. I felt more alone than I'd ever been, waking every day and half expecting him to limp in with his portfolios. He had been my ally, my counselor; now he was gone. All purpose seemed to vanish from my life, so that I felt lost, bereft of the one person who'd known me better than I knew myself.

Even as I grieved, word came that Guise had clashed with Navarre on a field near the Loire River, with the Huguenot army chanting the Psalm of David as they entered battle behind their king's white-plumed hat. In less than four hours, countless dead lay strewn across the blood-soaked grass. Couriers brought me updates, but everything was garbled, confused. None could say if Guise or Navarre had been injured or killed. I went to my knees and prayed. Toward nightfall I received a letter sent secretly by Navarre. I opened it with quivering hands.

It was brief, devastatingly so.

I have failed. Guise eluded me and has proclaimed victory. I will do as I promised and retreat. I cannot risk my surviving men nor do I wish to endanger you further.

God be with you.

There was no signature, a precaution in case the letter fell into the wrong hands. The paper floated from my grasp. I stood still. I wanted to cry, to wail and curse fate. I made myself envision the worst, seeing myself and Henri beholden to Guise forever, captive pawns in his design to turn France into a Catholic stronghold. The Spanish would overrun us, the Huguenots would be exterminated, and my son's reign would not go out in triumph but in ignominious disgrace. I had been so certain of success, that the prophecy uttered by Nostradamus all those years ago bound Navarre and me to this deed.

But no truth can be certain that concerns the future, I thought, and I pressed a hand to my mouth, stifling an acid burst of laughter. Fate, it seemed, was the cruelest trickster of all.

Then I got up and prepared to welcome my son home. He had done nothing except sit out the short war in his armor, and as he rode into the Louvre I saw the shock on his ashen face.

Louise subjected him to a tearful embrace. 'God save me,' he said as he held her close. 'Everything I have now lies open to Guise.'

I went to him. Trembling, he motioned Louise aside. My voice plunged low. 'Remember, he doesn't know we planned anything. I will invite him to court as if you were still allies.'

'He has an army at his command! He'll ask for my soul.'

'I promise you, he'll not win.' I pulled my son close. 'We have one last chance . . .'

Even from within the hall in the Louvre we could hear the muffled cheers outside in the streets. I could imagine children tossing flowers, women wiping tears from their faces and the men – all the men, the tanners, shopkeepers, merchants, and beggars – brandishing fists as they roared Guise's name, praising the man who had delivered France from the Huguenot menace. I found it grimly ironic that they had no idea who had unwillingly allowed Guise this triumph.

I glanced at Henri, dressed in his crown and gem-encrusted mantle. He was rigid on his throne on the dais beside Louise, whose ringed hands knotted in her lap. I sat below the dais; lining the hall's far wall was the full complement of Henri's personal guard, the Forty-five. Valette, dressed in chain mail with a pistol shoved in his belt, guarded the hall's gilded doors.

Suddenly I heard footsteps tromping toward us. I tensed in my chair, caught up in a vivid recollection of the time when le

Balafré had stormed this palace and I'd confronted him in this very hall, with my son Charles at my side. Then I had been furious, defiant; ready to do battle with the Guises unto the death. My desire for retribution had not waned, but now I waited in apparent tranquillity, like a spider in her carefully woven web.

We had come full circle, yet unlike them I had learned from my mistakes.

I shot another look at Henri; he straightened his shoulders as Guise strode in through the doors, a group of six black-clad lords behind him. He looked enormous in his white doublet and slashed trunk hose, his muscular legs encased in leather boots, his signature red cape girded off one shoulder in the new fashion. His fair beard had been trimmed to a point; his eyes were keen as a bird of prey's in his sun-bronzed face, where only a few lines betrayed the passage of his thirty-seventh year.

He bowed when he came before the dais. 'I've come as Your Majesty requested.'

'My request,' replied Henri, 'was that you attend me alone, without an escort.'

'I cannot help it if the people love me,' Guise replied, with an arrogance that made me clench my teeth. 'If you so command it, I will ask them to disperse.'

Henri rose from his throne in a swift movement. He stabbed his finger at Guise. 'Who is king here, my lord – you or me? You will send your lords away!' As he spoke, his gaze flicked over the Catholic nobles, whose voluminous cloaks might hide a multitude of weapons. As if on cue, the Forty-five unsheathed their swords with a metallic hiss that echoed in the cavernous hall.

The color seeped from Guise's face. It gave me a dark surge of pleasure that we could still rouse his fear. He hadn't forgotten how easily blood could be spilled between these walls. Yet he did not instruct his lords to leave. Instead, he reached into his cloak and removed a scroll.

'The League only wishes to see our agreements honored.' Guise set the scroll on the edge of the dais. 'These are our terms. We request that you establish the Holy Inquisition to rid France of the Huguenots. We ask that Charles of Lorraine, son of your late sister Claude, be titled your heir, and that the heretic Navarre be disbarred from the succession and declared a traitor, forbidden from entering this realm again, on pain of death.'

I felt sudden apprehension as I saw Henri's jawbone clench visibly under his skin. I half expected him to roar out his order for Guise's death, though we had agreed: not here. Not in Paris, where the populace was predominantly Catholic and would wreak vengeance upon us should anything happen to their hero. I realized Louise must fear the same, for her gaze met mine in mute terror. Poor Louise: untrained as a queen, tethered to a sterile marriage with no child to call her own, she was caught up in our maelstrom of hatred and deceit. Henri should never have married her. She had no place here.

My son stared in silence at Guise. To my relief, I marked the subtle lift of his chin, the change of cadence in his tone as he bent down to retrieve the scroll. 'It seems you've thought of everything,' he said, with a brittle laugh. 'You and your lords must dine with us tonight so we can discuss these requests at length.'

Guise frowned. My heartbeat quickened. Had we gone too far in our feigned compliance?

'Once Your Majesty signs the terms,' said Guise, 'there'll be time enough to dine. I'll expect your response in three days.' Without another word he turned and walked out, his red cloak billowing, the lords of his entourage folding in behind him.

As soon as they were gone, Henri flung the scroll aside, abandoning the dais to stride to the casement window. From where I stood, I could hear the people's renewed cries of '*Vive Guise! Vive le duc!*' as Guise and his men emerged from the Louvre.

I went to him. 'Be patient,' I said. 'Your hour will come.'

He did not look at me. 'When?' he asked in a taut whisper.

'Soon,' I said, and I touched his shoulder. 'He has set his own trap. All we need do now is wait and let him step into it.'

Storm clouds converged in the leaden sky, crackling without rain. The air was humid, sulfuric. In my apartments, I missed Birago desperately as I received hourly reports from his informants, who still worked for me. While Guise waited for my son to deliver the signed scroll, symbol of his capitulation, he'd wasted no time in bringing his family to join him in their Parisian house. And as the populace gathered outside his doors in reverential patience, waiting for him to appear, his retainers infiltrated the city.

Paris, seat of the monarchy for centuries, had become his stronghold.

At dawn on the third day, I was awoken by the sound of pulsating drum rolls. I dressed hurriedly. As I reached for my shawl, Lucrezia entered, carrying something wrapped in black cloth. She handed it to me.

'Use this,' she said. 'Plunge it into Guise's black heart. No man has earned it more.'

I unraveled the cloth to reveal a dagger with silver chains interlocked on its hilt: I hadn't seen it since Guast's death, but it was the same one my son Hercule had used to kill Henri's lover.

I rewrapped it and nodded at Lucrezia, making my way through the hushed corridors.

Henri sat in his apartments. I took a seat beside him and we waited, hearing the roar building outside like some savage cry.

Information came to us sporadically; we learned that most of our palace officials had fled when they learned Guise had roused the populace to drag planks across the streets, impeding any escape through our front gates. Except for the gardens of the Tuileries, which were enclosed by gated walls and unpatrolled, every other path to and from the palace was manned by Guise's retainers, as they'd been during the massacre.

All was ready for our defeat. We had not delivered the League's terms, so Guise would bring us down by force and set Henri's nephew, my grandson, on the throne.

At last, Guise had declared himself a traitor. Whatever we did next would be justified.

When word came, it was brought by one of his retainers. Handing the folded note to Henri, the man waited fearfully, glancing repeatedly at the Forty-five stationed at the walls. My son opened the note, scanned it, and let it fall at his feet. He waved the messenger out.

'Guise orders me to submit.' He lifted his eyes to me.

I felt as if I'd lived my entire life in rehearsal for this moment. I went to his table, inked the quill. 'Then you must sign their agreement. Sign it and leave it here. I'll deliver it. Pack what you can carry, take Louise, Valette, and your Forty-five, and make haste for the Château of Blois. You can ride out through the Tuileries, disguised as servants. No one will notice you among the crowd, seeing as they abandon us like vermin.' I reached for the cloth-shrouded dagger. 'When the hour comes, use this in memory of your Guast.'

He gazed for a long moment at the dagger before he leaned over the desk and scrawled his signature on the scroll. 'What about you?' he said, gnawing at his lip. 'How can I leave when I do not know if you'll be safe?'

'Guise will not dare harm me,' I said softly. 'Go. And no matter what, do not turn back.'

Guise didn't assault the Louvre, though he would have encountered little resistance. Our remaining courtiers, servants, most of our hired guards – they had all deserted us, leaving me alone with only my women, to face whatever fate held in store.

As I sat in my rooms, sleepless before my fire, my women around me on pallets in case I had need of them, I thought for the first time of the night when I gave Guise and Henri permission to murder Coligny. Had he waited in that house as I did now, knowing his end was near? Had he prayed to his passionless god in his bed of pain or let himself wander among the scorched recesses of his memories, back to a time in an enchanted palace called Fontainebleau, where he had come upon a young bride, alone and in need of someone to believe in? And if he had thought of me in those final minutes before the door crashed in, did he smile, if only for a moment, knowing that in the end we all meet our reckoning in the same place?

By dawn, bonfires smoked and the barricaders lay sprawled

in heaps, sated on the free wine distributed by Guise. I rose, dressed, and ordered my sedan chair set out in the courtyard. I emerged, blinking, into the cold morning light. Two fishwives lingered outside the palace's front gates. As I moved toward my chair I heard one of them snarl, 'There she is, Queen Jezebel.'

My hand froze on the sedan chair's latch.

'Jezebel,' the other woman shrieked. *'Reine de la mort!'*

I gazed impassively at those twisted faces glaring at me between the wrought-iron gates through which so much of my life had passed, and I was thrust back to that dreadful day in my childhood, when a mob had come for me at my family palazzo.

Down with the Medici! Death to the tyrants!

Then I turned away, tucked my hood about my head. Anna-Maria wrung her hands; she feared I'd be taken captive, though I had Guise's word that once I delivered the scroll he would let me go. I smiled at her as Lucrezia helped work my bloated fingers into my gloves.

We embraced. 'Godspeed,' she whispered. 'We'll see you at Blois.'

'Remember,' I chided, 'my jewel coffer and a decent gown or two will do. The rest can stay here. Let Guise's family melt down the plate to strike commemorative coins.'

A tear dripped down Anna-Maria's cheek. Lucrezia drew her close as I went to my chair.

The rising sun cracked through the white sky. I paused. I was leaving the Louvre, scene of my greatest triumphs and worst blunders, exiled in the end by the family that, for all my wiles, I had not succeeded in vanquishing. In Paris, the people defamed my name, and my son galloped to the Loire with his queen and intimates, leaving behind a swinging postern gate.

And as I took one final look at the old stone palace, transformed to ash rose in dawn's forgiving light, I said good-bye without tears and without regret.

After all, I was a Medici.

39

There is an arabic myth that the day and manner of our death is preordained and nothing we do can change it. I have never placed much belief in infidel credos nor even in my own church's promise of an everlasting life. I've witnessed too much treachery in the name of religion.

Nonetheless, I've had ample opportunity to reflect on this unseen entity who guides our path and to ponder why he has seen fit to test me so. Have I not struggled as much as any other for my blood? Others live fewer years; accomplish a mere fraction of what I have; and yet they sit enthroned with halos about their brows, while I sink like a villain in my own calumny.

As I await the inevitable, I see the dead. The first duc de Guise, the dangerous Balafré; Jeanne de Navarre; Coligny; and Mary Stuart – my sometime enemies and accomplices, each martyrs to their cause. Important as they were in life, through death they have become legend.

And I ask myself, What epitaph will history inscribe for me?

In the great hall of Blois, with its gilded pilasters and violet arches, the assembly of the Catholic League gathered to gloat over my son's capitulation. My embassy to Guise was successful; as I'd anticipated, he did not restrain me. He accepted the treaty and let me come here to join my son, though the journey from Paris, after so many months of anxiety, sapped the last of my strength.

So, I was not in the hall, but I sent Lucrezia and she told me everything. They were all there, all those who'd conspired without cease for our downfall: the Catholic nobles, governors, and officials, the conniving ambassadors and inevitable spies. And on

the dais stood Henri, clad in ermine, his voice calm as he paid
me tribute.

'We cannot forget the trials that the queen my mother has
undergone for this realm. I think it right to render during this
assembly, in the name of France, our gratitude. What labors has
she not undertaken to appease our troubles? When has age or
poor health induced her to spare herself? Has she not sacrificed
her well-being? From her, I learned how to be king.'

I wish I could have beheld the lords' expressions, seen for
myself their discomfort over this praise for the Italian Jezebel.
But I am confined to my bed, the pain like a vise in my chest
every time I draw breath, my body racked by fever and my legs
tumescent with fluid. My ailments have finally shackled me. My
doctors force their foul potions down my throat and wrap bandages soaked in herbal plasters about my swollen calves. They
assure me I'll recover, that this is a temporary setback.

I smile. They dare not say aloud what I already know.

I sleep too much. As snow flutters outside, within my rooms
my women keep the braziers lit. My tapestries and plate, my
favorite portraits and portable desk – everything from the Louvre
is here. Lucrezia is incorrigible. I told her not to overpack and
what did she do? She transported my entire chamber, strapped
to carts and mules.

Sometimes I wake at night and hear my women in the antechamber. Anna-Maria wanted to sleep at the foot of my bed, but
I refused. She is old. She needs her own bed, not a pillow at my
feet. Lucrezia scolded, 'Besides, my lady will never get any rest
with all that snoring you do.'

Anna-Maria snores. I never noticed.

In the deepest night, when I am alone with my thoughts, I light
my candle, set it on the ink-stained blotter of my portable desk,
and pull out my notebooks. I caress the worn pages upon which
have fallen the rains of the Loire, the sun of Bayonne, and sleet
of Navarre. I read them with love, retracing my life. From Florence
to Fontainebleau, from Chenonceau to the Louvre; duchess and
dauphine, queen and queen mother – I have played every role.

I sometimes drift off with the books piled about me and awake to find them gone, hidden again in their niche. Lucrezia always rises before me. She has borne witness to my secret and never said a word. I know that when the time comes, I can trust her to fulfill my bequest.

What day is it? I can't recall. It must be nearing Christmas. Once, time had seemed so precious, so inconstant, evanescent, and ever elusive. Now the hours weave like the threads of Penelope's loom, turning back on each other to stave off finality.

Henri comes to me, trailing musk. He is too thin again, dressed in mulberry velvet with his dark hair loose about his shoulders, and so agitated, pausing to finger the vials on my dressing table, my brushes and hand mirror. I can see he admires the hand mirror; he eyes it covetously, the way he did when he was a boy.

'Why is he still alive?' I ask.

He shrugs, his supple fingers fondling the embossed mirror. 'I'm waiting.'

'Waiting? For what?'

He sets the mirror down and comes to my bed, his face flushed but not with anger. It is pleasure. Something has happened. 'Shall I tell you a secret?' He leans to my ear. 'Philip of Spain sent an armada to invade England. The Tudor smashed it to pieces. All Paris now laughs at Guise, who took Philip's coin to fund his League. They've posted placards in the city: "Lost, an invincible armada! If found, please inform my lord the duke."'

He draws back, laughter pealing. 'Isn't it delightful? The heretic Tudor triumphs and Philip II is ruined. Guise has lost his Spanish alliance.'

I long to rise from the bed, to call for Birago to dissect the dispatches for information we might wield. But Birago is dead and I cannot move.

I can only stare as my son leaves the room, chanting under his breath, 'Lost, lost: an armada at sea . . .'

And I know soon he will reap his vengeance.

★   ★   ★

The fever returned last night. Shadows came and went; whispers: 'Fluid in her lungs . . . she should be bled.' I can feel their fear. They are afraid for me. They think I will die. I want to die. I long to sink into blessed oblivion forever. But not yet.

France clutches at me: she will not let me rest.

The sign is here. It has come.

Early this morning sudden shouting and a loud thump over-head wakes me, as if an argument had broken out in the room above. My son's apartments are above mine; as my ladies stumble in, sandy-eyed from sleep, I see a crimson bead seep through the rafters. It lingers, clinging to the emerald and gold-painted eaves, before it falls to spatter my sheets, next to my right hand.

I gasp. Lucrezia quickly moves to me; I see by her worried expression, in the quiver of the hand she reaches out to my brow, that she and Anna-Maria don't see it. They don't see the drops as they fall one by one, striking my bed with hollow plops. But I do. I see blood. Blood dripping from my ceiling, just as I once saw it in a dream, before Hercule's death.

Only this time, I am awake.

Lucrezia reaches for the vial of poppy at my bedside. As she moves to prepare a draft, thinking I am in pain, I resist. 'No. Go. Find out what is happening.'

But even as she gazes at Anna-Maria in bewilderment, Henri walks in. In his hand, he brandishes the dagger, its blade stained red. He tosses it on my bed. My women recoil at the smear of blood it leaves on the sheet.

'It is done,' he says. 'He fought like a caged beast, but I carved him out of my heart.'

I gaze at him in silence. I see blood in his goatee, a splash down the side of his throat.

'I invited him to share breakfast with me,' he adds, and his voice turns quiet, almost melancholic, as though he is thinking of something long in the past. 'He came with his brother but no others; he actually thought I'd serve him with my own hands.

And so I did. I stabbed him first before I let my Forty-five finish him off. Alas, his brother had to die too.'

I lower my eyes. Guise is dead. My son has finally earned back his throne.

Lucrezia lifts the stiletto by its hilt, and with her skirts she wipes it clean.

I had the dream last night. In it, I saw people crying on their knees. And I saw the room, the black-draped bed – waiting for me. I awake gasping, tangled in my sheets. Anna-Maria and Lucrezia rush in. Not even the braziers can disperse the cold. Their breath issues in tiny puffs as they stand shivering at my bedside, staring at me when I say, 'You must help me get up.'

They try to dissuade me, citing the terrible chill, the fever and congestion in my lungs. They threaten to summon my doctors. I will have none of it. I start to rise on my own, fueled by a resolve as unexpected to me as it is to them.

'I must,' I say. 'I must.'

They dress me in my black skirts and bodice, drape me in a cloak and hand me my gloves. I shake my head. 'No, no gloves. My fingers were bare.'

They look at me as if I've gone mad. Perhaps I have. But I must see it for myself. I must know that what I saw so many years ago, while still a child in Florence, has come to pass.

Through frozen passageways we go, our slippers clacking on stone floors. The entire château is still, an icy labyrinth. I focus on putting one foot in front of the other. My legs feel like granite posts. My lungs wheeze. I can taste blood. Under any other circumstance I would collapse.

I round a corner. There it is – the open door. I hear lamentations coming from inside. Lucrezia grips my arm, whispers that this is the servant quarters and we have no business here.

I shake my head and move to the door with sluggish reluctance, as if I've drifted from the spirit world into an uncertain mortality. I pause, grip the door frame.

Strangers turn to me, tears on their faces. I can't hear them as I confront the hulking bed, its tester draped in black. I find myself moving soundlessly toward it, my nerveless feet treading on crushed winter flowers, inhaling but not smelling the acrid scent of rushes and incense, reaching out my hand to part the curtains and reveal –

I sigh, in long-awaited recognition.

Guise's eyes are closed, his handsome face wiped clean of the blood that spattered him as he fought for his life. His muscled legs seem sculpted of ivory, monumental in their perfection. Dark wounds puncture his broad chest – the stigmata of forty-six daggers, plunged into his flesh. A silver crucifix rests in his veined hands. It seems impossible that this man, whose life has been interlinked with mine, from the time he first played with my children to the night I watched him lose his father, to the violence he unleashed on the Eve of St. Bartholomew, can be so still. He was the last of his kind; as powerful as they are, the Guise family will never recover.

In the end, despite all odds, France has won.

I step back. I turn away. The fever flares. My soul leaps in anticipation.

There is only one task left to do.

BLOIS, 1589

It is over. As the old maestro foretold so many years ago, I have fulfilled my destiny. Already the fever rises and I can feel my heart falter. Soon my household will come to bid me farewell; my son will sit at my side and hold my hand as my ladies weep. The vigil will begin.

I have sealed my last letter to Henri. In it I remind him that the path to peace is now clear. If he seeks accord with his Bourbon cousin, Navarre will safeguard him and France's future. He will let Henri rule, until the time comes for him to ascend the throne.

Now I must close my books. Lucrezia knows what to do; it is my duty, my final sacrifice. I must carry my secrets to the grave. Yet how reluctantly I leave these leather volumes, bleached by the seasons of my life: to bid them farewell is to surrender all I have loved and lost.

This is the final page of my confessions.

I mix the remaining vestiges of the Maestro's gift into my draft of poppy. The vial is clouded, fragile yet deceptively hard; as I scrape powder from its sides into my goblet, I think how odd it is that so tiny an object can hold such power. There is only a little left; it cannot kill me outright, weakened as it is by years of hibernation, but it might quicken my passage.

As darkness draws in, I close my eyes, and for the last time I summon my vision of Navarre, seated on his black destrier, the white plume in his cap. His beard is thick, coppery, his weathered face full of purpose. I watch the page rush to him, declaring, 'Paris will not surrender,' and the flash of impatience in Navarre's eyes as he hears these words. This time, I do not need to strain to hear his response: I do not lose the future's promise in the evanescence of the present.

I see him toss back his head and he laughs, countering, 'Refuse, do they? Well then, I must give them what they want, eh? After all, Paris is worth a mass!'

I sigh. So it is.

Author's Afterword

On January 5, 1589, at sixty-nine years of age, Catherine de Medici died in the Château of Blois, in the Loire Valley. In her will, she left provision for her household and bequeathed the bulk of her estate to her grandchildren. Chenonceau went to Louise, Henri's queen; Catherine's other daughter-in-law, Charles's widow, Isabel (known as Elisabeth) of Austria, resided there with Louise until her own death in 1592.

Henri inherited the remainder of his mother's possessions. Catherine made no mention of her daughter Margot, who remained imprisoned in Usson until 1599.

Foreign ambassadors perfunctorily dispatched the news of Catherine 's death and continued with the business at hand. She had been alternately feared or despised and the City of Paris informed Henri that if he dared entomb her in the Basilica of St. Denis, they'd dig her up with 'tenterhooks' and throw her into the Seine. She therefore lay in state in Blois for forty days before being buried nearby in the Church of Saint-Sauver. Years later, her remains were transferred to St. Denis. During the Revolution, mobs desecrated the Basilica and tossed the royal skeletons into a common pit. However, the magnificent marble tomb that Catherine built for her husband and herself can still be viewed today.

A Capuchin monk allegedly hired by Guise's vengeful sister stabbed Henri III to death in 1589. Before he died, Henri had concluded a truce with his Bourbon cousin, Henri of Navarre; whether his actions were prompted by a final exhortation by Catherine is speculative, but Navarre did ascend the throne as Henri IV and he became one of France's most beloved, tolerant kings. It took him ten years, however, to take Paris. He eventually converted to Catholicism to win over the city, a decision that prompted his famous quip: 'Paris is worth a mass.'

Leadership of the Catholic League, established by the murdered duc de Guise, was taken over by another of Guise's brothers; the League continued to exert significant influence over Catholic France until January of 1596, when Henri IV signed a treaty that put an end to it.

The senior line of the Guise family became extinct in 1688.

Margot was released from house arrest only after she agreed to an annulment. She returned to Paris, where she resided in increasingly corpulent splendor, a legend in her lifetime and author of her own rather fanciful memoirs. She died in 1615 at the age of sixty-one, outliving her former husband by five years.

Henri IV took as his second wife Marie de Medici, descendant of a lesser family branch. In 1601, Marie bore the future Louis XIII. Like Catherine, she endured years of infidelity before rising to power as widowed queen regent for her underage son.

Henri IV ruled France for twenty-one years. Despite his conversion, he still declared circumscribed toleration of the Huguenots and did everything he could to retain religious stability. At the age of fifty-six he was assassinated by a fanatical Catholic in the rue St. Honoré, while riding in his carriage. He bled to death. With his passing, France again plunged into religious tumult. His descendants continued the Bourbon dynasty until its overthrow in 1793. Persecution of the Huguenots ended when the Revolution of 1789 gave them equal rights under the law.

To this day, Catherine de Medici remains shrouded in lurid myth. She's been accused of some of the sixteenth century's most heinous crimes, including the murders of Jeanne of Navarre and Gaspard de Coligny. Some allege she poisoned her husband's elder brother and her two eldest sons, as well as a host of secondary figures at court who resisted or defied her.

Is the myth true? Did Catherine ruthlessly eliminate anyone who stood in her way? Did she harbor 'a passion for power'? Those who knew her personally expressed contradictory opinions; those who didn't likewise disagreed. Elizabeth I once said that of all the rulers in Europe, Catherine was the one she most feared; had he been asked, Philip II of Spain certainly had cause to echo this sentiment. Oddly enough, when overhearing criticism of his late mother-in-law, it was Henri IV who retorted, 'I ask you, what could the woman do, left by the death of her husband with five little children and two families who thought only of grasping the Crown – our own [the Bourbons] and the Guises? I am surprised she didn't do worse.'

To portray Catherine, I had to delve beyond the historical archetype of the black-clad widow, conspiring to wreak evil. Her surviving letters fill volumes, as do those of her contemporaries. I also consulted numerous modern and period sources to augment my understanding of her and of the times in which she lived.

To my surprise, I discovered a brave young girl who survived a dangerous childhood and difficult marriage to become a humane woman with an astounding capacity for compromise. Catherine detested war and fought for peace; she was a queen and mother whose foremost goal was to ensure her dynasty's survival. While she made grievous errors, I do not believe she planned the Massacre of St. Bartholomew; rather, she sought to eliminate Coligny, who can only be judged as a traitor by the standards of his era. In her haste and panic after her first anonymous attempt failed, Catherine failed to anticipate that sending Guise to kill Coligny and the other Huguenot leaders in his house would precipitate the slaughter of six thousand people in Paris and its environs and blacken her name for centuries to come. While not entirely a pacifist in matters of religion, her position was antithetical to that of the Guises, who advocated systematic persecution of heretics. Throughout her life Catherine abhorred the fiery fanaticism that prevailed in Spain and did everything she could to curb it in France. It was her misfortune that few of the men around her shared her commitment to conciliation.

Catherine 's interest in the occult is well documented; like most Renaissance people she had a profound belief in hidden forces. Her instances of visions or 'second sight' were recorded by her family and friends; several of the episodes I describe are drawn directly from their accounts. She patronized Nostradamus until his death; Cosimo Ruggieri was her personal astrologer and did in fact betray her. However, her reputed penchant for the dark arts and poison seems apocryphal; certainly, the legend that she kept a cabinet of poisons at Blois is an invention, the secret compartments still visible there today intended for personal documents, not potions. I found no concrete evidence that Catherine poisoned anyone or resorted to black magic, but many of the objects found at Chambord after his arrest indicate Cosimo Ruggieri may have. Catherine's generosity toward her intimates, her lifelong friendships with her ladies and Birago, and her compassion for animals, unusual for her time, are corroborated by several contemporary sources.

Catherine's barrenness following her marriage to Henri is a subject of endless speculation. Some sources believe the fault was Henri's, who had to submit to a delicate penile operation in order to correct a defect in his ability to ejaculate; others say Catherine herself had a thick hymen that required surgical piercing. Of course, such medical anomalies are impossible to verify, and I believe the obvious explanation is the most likely: Diane de Poitiers curtailed Henri's conjugal visits until she could force Catherine into a situation of utter compliance and establish her own power over the royal marriage. The fact that Catherine suddenly became pregnant at a time in her life when bearing a child had become a matter of survival seems too coincidental. Catherine of course went on to bear seven surviving children; I do not include in this novel the death of a months-old son and her miscarriage of twin daughters in 1556.

Catherine de Medici lived a complex life in a very complex age, and in the interest of sparing the reader a veritable labyrinth of events, names, and titles, I made some minor alterations. For example, I cite only three of her daughter Claude's nine children; of these, the eldest son was named Henri and the second Charles. I switched their names to avoid confusion, given the plethora of Henrys populating the narrative. I also do not mention Charles IX's illegitimate son by his mistress or François I's second son, also named Charles, who died before François himself. And while Philip II of Spain loomed large in Catherine's life, his meeting with her in Bayonne is fictional, though its context is not.

Catherine had almost the same conversation with Philip's exigent representative, the Duke of Alba.

The sheer size of the Guise family poses particular challenges for a novelist; again, in the interest of clarity I kept family members to a minimum. A significant title alteration is that of le Balafré's brother, Monsignor, who in reality was cardinal of Lorraine, not of Guise.

I also reduced the role of the Bourbon princes. Antoine, king consort of Navarre and father of Henri IV, caused significant disruption during François II's reign; he and his brother Condé died in battle within a few years of each other. To facilitate the story line, Antoine is briefly mentioned, but Condé is not.

All other errors, alterations, and omissions, both deliberate and accidental, are my own.

To learn more about Catherine and her times, I suggest the following selected bibliography:

Castries, Duc de. *The Lives of the Kings and Queens of France*. New York: Alfred A. Knopf, 1979.

Chamberlain, E. R. *Marguerite of Navarre*. New York: Dial Press, 1974.

Frieda, Leonie. *Catherine de Medici*. London: Weidenfeld & Nicolson, 2003.

Heritier, Jean. *Catherine de' Medici*. New York: St. Martin's Press, 1963.

Knecht, R. J. *The Rise and Fall of Renaissance France*. London: Fontana Press, 1996.

Mahoney, Irene. *Madame Catherine*. New York: Coward, McCann and Geoghegan, 1975.

Roeder, Ralph. *Catherine de Medici and the Lost Revolution*. New York: Garden City Publishing, 1939.

Sedgwick, Dwight Henry. *The House of Guise*. New York: Bobbs Merrill, 1938.

Seward, Desmond. *François I: Renaissance Prince*. New York: Macmillan, 1973.

Strange, Mark. *Women of Power*. New York: Harcort Brace Jovanovich, 1976.

Acknowledgements

I wish to extend my heartfelt thanks to my partner, who has stood by my side throughout the many years it has taken me to find a publisher and never once told me to stop writing. My agent, Jennifer Weltz, of the Jean V. Naggar Literary Agency, remains my champion and friend. I'm very fortunate in my editor, Susanna Porter, who has guided me through two books and always compels me to look beyond my original vision with her insightful revisions. My assistant editor, Jillian Quint, copy editor Jude Grant, proofreader Karen Ninnis, publicist Lisa Barnes, and the creative team at Ballantine Books have shown me singular passion and commitment. In the United Kingdom, I am also lucky to have my editor, Suzie Dooré, and the team at Hodder & Stoughton on my side.

I must thank all the marvelous bloggers who've featured my books on their sites and shown me such generosity and enthusiasm. Without you, promotion wouldn't be half as fun.

Last, I thank you, my reader. You inspire and challenge me every day and I hope I can continue to entertain you for many years to come. I'm always available for reader group chats.

Please visit www.cwgortner.com for more information.

C.W. GORTNER

The Last Queen

Juana – daughter of Ferdinand and Isabella and sister to Catherine of Aragon – is a woman ruled by her heart, and her arranged marriage to Philip the Fair is unexpectedly passionate and turbulent. When tragedy decimates her family and she suddenly finds herself heiress to the throne, she is plunged into a ruthless battle of ambition and treachery. The future of Spain and her own freedom are at stake . . .

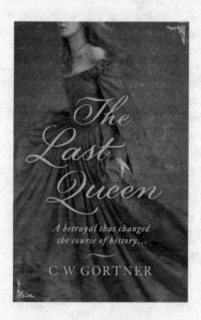

HODDER